CW00644427

Avril Cavell is the pen name of a psychologist whose main interest is child development. She began writing in 1983 and published three non-fiction books, with Anne Woollett, about twins and their families. Born in Essex in 1943, she was educated at grammar school, London University and the Polytechnic of East London. A varied career, haphazardly arranged around four children, has included being a social worker, running a PhD research project for several years and, in default of any other employment at the time, an invaluable spell in a Sainsbury's megastore, which taught her a lot of things about life that don't appear in text books. She enjoys writing about people and many of her characters spring from her experiences as a psychologist and supermarket assistant. Her most recent novel, TWO FOR JOY, is also available from Headline Review.

Also by Avril Cavell from Headline

Two for Joy

The Yellow Silk Robe

Avril Cavell

HEADLINE
REVIEW

First published in Great Britain in 1994
by HEADLINE BOOK PUBLISHING

First published in paperback in 1995
by HEADLINE BOOK PUBLISHING

A HEADLINE REVIEW paperback

10 9 8 7 6 5 4 3 2 1

ISBN 0 7472 4878 8

Typeset by CBS, Felixstowe, Suffolk

Printed and bound in Great Britain by
Cox & Wyman Ltd, Reading, Berks

HEADLINE BOOK PUBLISHING
A division of Hodder Headline PLC
338 Euston Road, London NW1 3BH

For Janet

Chapter One

God rest ye merry gentlemen, let nothing you dismay . . .

In the week before Christmas, 1992, in Trafalgar Square, the words of the carol rose cheerfully above the sound of traffic, wind and rain. Nelson looked down on scurrying crowds, the lions at his feet slicked with rain and pigeon droppings. It had got dark very early that afternoon. Lights winked in the branches of the great Christmas tree from Norway, lashed by freezing sleet. A small and determined group of carol singers huddled beneath black umbrellas burrowed further inside striped London University scarves, shook tins for the homeless and bellowed enthusiastically, with stoical disregard for the miserably unfestive weather. Shoppers scuttled and hurried past, heads down and shoulders hunched, weighed down by carrier bags, disinclined to stop in the downpour. A young woman with a double buggy and two identical little fair-haired boys did stop, rummaged in the pockets of a mock fur coat that had seen better days, and dropped a fifty-pence bit into a tin.

'Why is it the ones who can't really afford it who bother?' remarked one of the singers, admiring her ankles as she walked away. Then he folded his carol sheet against the wind. No one answered him.

Not so far away, underneath the railway arches at Waterloo, the homeless themselves crept out into the gloom from the deeper gloom within their cardboard shacks and stirred the embers of a dozen smoky fires.

'Bloody horrible weather, isn't it?' remarked an educated

voice, anonymous underneath a grey army blanket. A pair of tired grey eyes peered out of its folds, squinting through the smoke and darkness at the dripping rain running down blackened brickwork. 'Fancy. And I was going to hang up my paper chains and put the fairy on my Christmas tree. Oh well. *Tant pis*.' He withdrew into his blanket, pulled it over his head and sat in the fire's dull red glow, unmoving as Rip Van Winkle, listening to commuters streaming past on their way home from office parties and Christmas lunches. His travelling partner, an old man with matted hair, no teeth, an accent that had long ago risen above the mess at Sandhurst, and a startling pair of pillarbox-red breeches on his skinny legs, grinned and poked their fire.

'There's Crisis at Christmas,' he pointed out, through the smoke, with more than a lingering trace of the Hooray Henry he had once been, before cocaine, booze and a dishonourable discharge possessed him. 'They do us a super dinner, old chap.'

'*You* look like a dog's dinner,' observed the first man, looking round the edge of his blanket at the scarlet trousers. 'Where on earth did you get *them*?'

'Costume warehouse at the BBC. I saw in *The Times* they were having a clear-out. They were giving them away. I thought them suitably seasonal.' He spread his legs out stiffly, the better to admire them. 'What do you think?'

'What I think is that I *hate* charity,' snarled the blanket, drawing its feet in in an effort to keep warm. 'When I can stand to think at all, I think that I was earning a hundred grand a year. Now it's bloody turkey hand-outs and fancy dress.' The bankrupt former City dealer, jobless, wifeless, his small children gone with her and his house repossessed, glared out of his shelter. '*Christmas*. What are we supposed to be celebrating? Piss off. Don't expect *me* to be grateful for anything.' He sounded as if he could cry.

'What you never had, you never miss. Our trouble is, we once had. It's always tricky at Christmas.' The old man shrugged indifferently and stirred their embers. The rain ran down the walls into a black and greasy puddle on the concrete, splashing and staining the hems of coats as home-going office workers hurried to catch their trains. He watched with sharp and vicious eyes, reached for the meths bottle in his breeches pocket and tipped it with ironic courtesy towards them. 'God bless you merry bastards,' he said sardonically. 'And you, old fruit,' he added in the direction of the despondent figure under the blanket. It hunched its shoulders angrily. The former army officer wiped the neck of his bottle on his bright red breeches and toasted it anyway, unmoved. He'd seen and heard it all before.

'It's always tricky at Christmas,' admitted Melanie Tilford, vicar's wife and mother of two teenagers, unconsciously echoing the down-and-outs she'd never seen because she was too frightened of them to walk through the arches. She sat in a worn armchair in Relate's offices in Great Cavendish Street, listening to rain beating on the window behind her. The counsellor sitting opposite was listening to *her*, which was a novel and delightful experience. No one else did. Melanie was baring her soul, and enjoying it.

'Our waiting lists go through the roof at New Year,' agreed Ruth Allison, one of Relate's most experienced counsellors. 'People *will* play happy families and it leads to grief. Every year. It's the same with the Samaritans.'

'Quite. So you know what I mean,' Melanie said grimly, adding, in a sudden burst of confidence, 'I never told anyone this before, but because we are in the Church, we have to make out we really *mean* it. And to tell you the truth, I don't. All that happy families and goodwill to all men. What about women? I sometimes feel like yelling *oh stuff it, like the turkey.*' She was pink and trembly and giggled nervously. 'I know I shouldn't say that, but it's a nightmare, keeping up all that Christian love and joy. *You* should try it.'

She sat back and folded her arms, as if to say so there, like a little girl.

'What do you really want?'

'Aaaah. Two weeks in Tunisia and not a turkey in sight?'
'Some people do.'
'We couldn't, because of Giles's job,' Melanie answered wistfully. 'He can't go AWOL at that kind of critical moment. But I'd love to have Christmas on our own.' She leaned forward to make her point. 'And *no church*.'
The rain rattled outside on the window, turning to sleet.
'Giles would think I'd gone mad,' Melanie added reflectively. 'If he could hear what I was saying.'
'You aren't mad,' Ruth said firmly.
'Are you sure? Of course, everyone comes to us, because Giles obviously can't be away at Christmas. We're stuck together for a week pretending we all get on. There's never enough hot water and everyone bickers over the bathroom. Christmas morning we traipse off to church with Giles fretting about what he's done with his potato peelers and how many he'll have to peel after the service. He's got a *thing* about kitchen gadgets, you know. Especially potato peelers. Do you think that means something? It's quite strange, now I come to mention it.'
She sat lost in thought about peelers for a moment.
'Then the kids sulk because they think church is naff and they want to open their presents. Giles only makes them go because Rose – that's his mother – tells him he's a weak father if he doesn't. He tells her if they want to be atheists, that's their business, but he can't really stand up to her. He does try to be liberal, though if I wanted to be a Buddhist it might be a different story. Embarrassing.'
She giggled again nervously.
'Go on,' encouraged the counsellor.
'Yes, well. Anyway. By the time we get home, the kids are fighting and my father-in-law goes all tense and starts rubbing his hands. He rubs them and rubs them. It drives me mad. My mother-in-law goes all quiet and gets heavily into the sherry or gin. She prefers vodka, only she's too ashamed to say so, and I don't buy it. My father is dying to smoke, but Giles won't let him unless he goes outside, and

Dad's so insulted, he won't budge and sits there getting nicotine withdrawal and *terribly* ratty. I think he's practically written us off this year; he was so offended. My mother-in-law oozes into my kitchen, when she's had one too many, and gets in my way, and starts picking at the food with her mouth all pursed up, letting me know without saying *one word* that she knows before she gets it that I haven't got her present right.' Noting that her counsellor had a sympathetic gleam in her eye, Melanie rushed on with a heady sense of liberation.

'Giles, of course, being a *priest*, is her beloved son who can do no wrong. Not even when he starts telling the same awful seminary jokes, because he's finished up several lots of communion wine and too much Sainsbury's sherry. By the time we're into pudding he and Dad are into the bottom of a couple of bottles of claret and maudlin. Dad starts on about the economy and bring back Thatcher and Major's a weed. Giles starts on about the meaning of Christmas and by the Queen's Speech they are all either shouting or barely speaking. Giles starts trying to pour oil on troubled waters, which is a joke, because he starts it all. No one ever tells him anything, though, because he's a priest.'

'Ah,' said Ruth Allison, nodding at her, keeping the floodgates open.

'So I separate them,' Melanie said defiantly. 'I tell Dad to go and have a fag in the downstairs loo and open the window. I let Tom go and play Nintendo. I let Alice spend the rest of the day on the telephone complaining to her friends. I put the gin and tonic where my mother-in-law can get at it without moving, because in the end she'll get absolutely plastered and go to sleep. The rest of us watch *The African Queen* for the hundredth time and eat Dairy Box.'

Ruth Allison visualized Dairy Box contents and swallowed longingly. A grateful client had made a donation in kind to the office, which was in the drawer of one of the filing cabinets, with the coffee cream in the bottom layer still there.

Not noticing Ruth's brief distraction, Melanie hurtled on.

'I wash up for about two hours and just when I've finished they perk up and are the best of friends and want turkey and pickle sandwiches. With plenty of salt. Giles sits there oblivious. I could *scream*.'

Ruth dragged her thoughts away from temptation and thought she had never quite seen someone gnashing their teeth before. Grinding, yes. Gnashing, which was a nice old-fashioned way of putting it, was rare.

'Why don't you?' she suggested. 'Scream, I mean.'

Ruth was keen on screaming and punching pillows to let out tension. She was keen on feminism and equal opportunities, went to assertiveness classes and believed that women should let it all hang out.

'The neighbours would hear,' said Melanie. 'It's obvious.'

'Ah. That would matter, coming from the vicarage.'

Melanie nodded, looked thoughtful and perked up.

'Last year we were still in Norfolk for Christmas. We had a solid-fuel Aga and I went to get some coke and fell down the cellar steps and cut my head open. I know it was stress. I had just found seven empty loo rolls on the floor of the downstairs cloakroom. They couldn't be bothered to pick them up and I felt like a slave. I think I fell down the steps out of sheer rage, so that they *had* to sober up and take me to casualty to have stitches. On Christmas Day. Giles wouldn't come with me. He was too mortified.'

The memory made her laugh, and when she laughed, she was really very pretty, Ruth Allison thought. Without that downtrodden look she became quite girlish.

Melanie had two small frown lines in an otherwise open, innocent, only very slightly horsy face with no trace of make-up. Clear, direct grey eyes, heavily fringed with pale lashes, the healthy, bright-cheeked complexion of a countrywoman who used to spend a lot of time in the fresh air and short, curly, glossy fair hair not yet touched with grey should have made her very pretty in a rather forties, schoolgirlish kind of way. She looked like one of those

Englishwomen from the counties, with haughty noses, the better for looking down. They never quite grew out of horses, could cope with anything, were wonderful with Agas, bad plumbing, children and everyone's elderly relatives, were marvellous in a crisis and made splendid nurses. But, Ruth thought, the air of anxious tension was what one really noticed, which was a shame. Melanie's full and mobile mouth turned slightly down at the corners, giving her a wistful, even melancholy air. She clearly spent too much time coping with life and Agas, and didn't laugh enough.

'So,' she finished, stopping laughing. 'Falling down the cellar was quieter than screaming, but got me just as much attention, which I suppose was what I wanted. I don't know why I've told you all that. I don't really know why I'm here at all. I should be wrapping presents, making mince pies, and listening to our deaconess's false teeth clacking. She came to see me, to worry about her mother's being in an old people's home in Barking for Christmas. She could always invite her. I don't know what she expects us to do about it.'

She looked distracted and nervous, as though the deaconess's problems reminded her of something more about her own.

'The problems people come and talk about at first are not always the ones that are troubling them. It sounds as though Christmas is just the last straw,' Ruth suggested. 'On top of something you aren't ready to tell me about.'

'I don't know about that. *Her* problem is probably that she's fallen for my husband,' Melanie said distractedly. 'They seem to, in droves. I did myself. I don't know why, though I suppose he's tall and quite good-looking. Maybe it's the mystery and the candlelight and the frocks – women like men in uniform, don't they? Even frocks. I suppose you could call it uniform, don't you think?'

Ruth decided to stop beating about the bush. 'What I think is that you are being evasive. Why don't you tell me what really is the matter?'

Her client fidgeted in her low armchair, gazing around the sparsely furnished and nondescript room. Beige and orange curtains covered in enormous sunflowers smelled of the previous couple's cigarettes. Rain still beat on the windowpanes and cars changed gear and squealed wet brakes at the traffic lights on the corner below. She sighed.

'Nothing. No more than usual.'

'*Something* made you want to come and see me,' Ruth persisted.

Melanie ducked her head and plucked at her skirt and admitted, 'The truth is, I'm afraid you'll laugh.'

Ruth put on her blandest expression and shook her head. 'Never.'

'You will,' she said resignedly. 'It was Giles dropping Mrs Tutti Frutti's baby on its head. Last month. In the font. He was christening it,' Melanie explained hurriedly. 'It was bawling its head off and thrashing around in a kind of frilly nylon baby ballgown and he dropped it in headfirst and nearly drowned it. Since then he's gone a bit to pieces and to tell you the truth, I don't think either of us can cope.'

'Tutti Frutti?' Ruth demanded.

Melanie ignored the tremor in her voice and lips, and plunged on. 'I told you you'd laugh. The Tutti Fruttis sell sweeties in the market. It's not that I'm racist, or prejudiced,' she added defensively, in case Mrs Allison thought she was. 'They're Northern Irish, but everyone calls them that. They sell Tooti Frooti gum, or something, I suppose. Can you still get that stuff? It used to stink, didn't it?'

'I don't know. But it's funny you should mention that. I got some fizzy lemonade with a dash of blackcurrant, in Sainsbury's, that tastes revolting, and I knew it reminded me of something. Tooti Frooti gum. What about the baby?'

'It didn't drown. Just dripped all over Giles. It would be a bit like drowning a kitten,' Melanie remarked defiantly. 'They've got five enormous children and the baby is from the last time someone let her husband out of prison. They all have thick, very crinkly black hair, and she irons it. It doesn't work. They look like human Brillo pads. Why do you think ironing doesn't work?'

'I should think it ruins it,' Ruth said, caught off guard and easily distracted.

'So should I.'

Melanie stared at the ceiling and nodded to herself slowly, as if to say *I told you so.* Ruth began to feel that the interview was not, therapeutically speaking, going anywhere. And speaking of going places, Mrs Tilford had a pleasant East Anglian accent and was clearly not from the East End. Ruth Allison tried to remember her details. Melanie watched her trying, suppressed a sudden longing to cry and helped her out, instead.

'We haven't lived here all that long. We moved from Norfolk,' she said. 'Nothing's really gone right since.'

She watched the Relate woman cock her head to one side and look especially intent, to show how carefully she was listening. Priests did that, too, resting their jowls on their dog collars. Melanie knew all the little counselling tricks.

'It took a lot of courage to ring up and make this appointment,' she said defensively. 'As a clergy wife, I'm more used to being asked for guidance by other people. Well, they did at home, because we'd been there fifteen years, ever since shortly after we got married, and Giles got taken on as priest-in-charge. We knew everyone in all the villages. If they wanted a shoulder to cry on, they'd quite often come to see me, instead of Giles.'

Ruth said nothing and Melanie stared at her, unaware of the unhappiness writing itself large across her face. No one ever asked her for guidance in London, except for the wretched deaconess in her ill-fitting dentures, because they didn't need to. They all knew what was what in London very much better than she did. In fact, they could run rings round both her and Giles, and very often did.

'I suppose it's just homesickness as much as anything,' she muttered.

'You were telling me about the baby,' Ruth said firmly.

The gas fire on the wall sputtered and hissed, burning their legs. Outside, traffic roared away from the lights and splashed down Great Cavendish Street towards the West End, windscreen wipers thumping in unison in the unending downpour. Christmas trees dripped and sagged along the façades of half-empty department stores in Oxford Street. Melanie had been window-shopping before her appointment, to take her mind off having second thoughts about going to Relate. She had run from entrance to entrance, her feet soaked, her umbrella catching and tangling other people's, to get out of the rain, unable to browse through windows plastered with sales posters offering fifty per cent of practically everything. Never mind waiting for January, the shops pleaded, bribing the thin crowds to buy, their takings gnawed to the bone by recession.

'Depressing, isn't it?' Melanie answered her at last.

Ruth wondered if she meant Norfolk or having a husband who was a priest and evidently very attractive to his female parishioners. She obligingly guessed, trying to keep up with Melanie's train of thought.

'Is it? I always thought it a beautiful county.'

She saw from the baffled expression on her client's face that she had guessed wrong.

'Neither of you are coping with your move?'

There was a pause while Melanie worked it out.

'I meant the recession is depressing. I think Giles might be going to have a nervous breakdown. Mind you, he's so clumsy, he often drops things, but not usually babies. He's making all our lives a misery since that christening and I don't know what to do.'

Ruth Allison pushed a box of tissues closer to Melanie's chair with one Hush Puppied foot and sat back with an air that suggested it was her client's turn to make an effort.

'Why don't you just start at the beginning, and put all these events into some sort of context?' she suggested.

'The very beginning was the Bishop ringing up, to tell Giles he was going to lose his job.'

'Can you recall it?'

The memory of that morning brought tears to Melanie's eyes. She trumpeted into one of Ruth's tissues and recalled it all too well.

Chapter Two

She had listened to the Bishop's telephone call on the kitchen extension. She always listened in to anything interesting, if it wasn't completely confidential, even though Giles had repeatedly pointed out that eventually she would hear no good about something or other, possibly herself, and would have only herself to blame. At first he bleated on about this and that, no obvious point to the call. When he came to the point, the conversation she overheard left her ashen with shock and anger.

'The Church has to rationalize, Tilford,' Bishop Rupert had shouted pompously down the telephone. He had the long ears, the long, mindlessly stubborn face of an *ass*, she thought, reflected in the braying, penetrating quality of his voice, designed to reach the backs of churches without sound systems. The effect on dozy congregations in churches *with* sound systems was electrifying. 'Tough decisions in tough times. I've prayed for guidance, but it doesn't make this easier.'

She could hear Giles breathing down the line, as mystified as she was.

'I'm having to move people around. Redundancies. I've put your lot on the peripatetic rota, so they'll have to make do with one Sunday a month or drive next door. They weren't a very enthusiastic flock, were they? Black sheep, ha ha.'

'You are putting me out of a job,' Giles had said jokily, too naive to believe a word of it.

'A shake-out,' brayed Rupert. 'Not out of a job. Moving

on, Tilford. Time to find a bit of ambition. Ha ha.'

Ha ha. What about one lost sheep being more precious in the eyes of God than a flock of bloody bishops? His parishioners *need* him, Melanie longed to shout, hitching her bottom on to the rail of the Aga, which had gone out. She had been raking out the ashes when the telephone went, and they got up her nose. She held the receiver at arm's length and a tea towel over it, to muffle a series of explosive sneezes.

'Funny line,' chortled the Bishop. 'I want you to know there's an inner-city job waiting for you, Tilford, should you want it. A challenge. No question of being out of work, just a question of flexibility. You there?' he suddenly shouted, getting no reply.

You *coward,* Melanie thought, listening down the hissing line to her husband's stunned silence in the face of his marching orders. The Bishop's well-fed voice dropped a hundred decibels and oozed on, trying to seduce a reaction out of Giles that would make him, Rupert, feel better.

'We saw no other way, though we tried. It's save money here, and save money there, and no let-up from the powers that be.'

It's save money *there* because you're safely tucked up *here*. You can't lose, you lying rat, Melanie thought, throwing Christian forgiveness to the winds. You are giving my husband orders backed up by *God* and you don't have to take any responsibility at all. He's only priest-in-charge, with no right of tenure. You can move him around just exactly as you like and never mind the consequences.'

Rupert of the big paunch, big asinine ears, big mouth and small, devious eyes was divine authority made all too substantial flesh. Melanie breathed carefully through her mouth, so that she didn't sneeze any more and silently blamed Giles for this sudden and devastating misfortune.

'Chap dropped dead in Stepney. London. I've recommended you. Heart attack at fifty-five. Lifestyle. Ha ha,' Rupert trumpeted nervously.

Rumour had it, Melanie thought furiously, that *his* lifestyle included an inordinate fondness for food and whisky and many a good pair of legs . . . some in short trousers and grey knee socks from the boarding school for small boys on the outskirts of the next village. She felt a sneeze coming on and held her nose desperately.

'It's an area crying out for good clergy,' Rupert enthused, in a headlong rush to get the conversation over. 'I wouldn't have minded this myself, Tilford, in my younger days. Multiculture and all that. An evangelical opportunity *sans pareil*, eh, in a Decade of Evangelism? I gather they're quite a jolly lot in the East End. Music and dancing and what have you. All that stuff old Carey likes so much. It's a change. You'll enjoy it.'

You *prat*, she thought angrily.

Giles came out of his paralysis and made a gargling sound. Melanie willed him not to hang up.

'*Fight* it,' she mouthed, kicking the Aga in frustration. 'Stand up for yourself – for us – for once.'

Giles fought it. Feebly.

'The children are at school here, Rupert. We can't move them. And Melanie won't want to move. She won't want to live in the middle of London. I don't know that she'd cope.'

Irrationally, Melanie bridled. She waited for the Bishop to say of course Mels would cope, but that Giles was misunderstanding; they could stay until the children left school. She calculated hastily. Tom was sixteen and had two years to go. Alice was fourteen and planning to take nine GCSEs. They'd both do A levels and go to university. Three years of grace and the recession would be over. Norman Lamont's green shoots of recovery would no longer be Tory hallucinations, but would be real, thriving bushes. The Church Commissioners would no longer be strapped for cash, could leave Giles's little church in business all year round. The nightmare need never come true.

'You could try putting yourself on the open market,' Rupert agreed in tones that suggested Giles needed his head examining, to contemplate any such thing. 'Personally, I'd think twice before turning a London living down.'

'But . . .'

'Think it over. But remember there's a lot of competition and I'm not sure how much good it will do if it gets about that you turned this offer down.'

Melanie looked into the receiver disbelievingly, shook it and put it back to her ear.

'I shall pray for you both, Tilford,' the Bishop promised, shouting down the line cheerfully. 'I shall pray that you come to the right decision. I have no doubt at all that you'll do splendidly.'

Giles heard his wife shout his name, the sound of an explosive sneeze, then the telephone just buzzed in his hand.

'That hypocritical *wretch.*'

She had been crouched on the cool Aga with the receiver still in her hand when he came into the kitchen, looking at it as if it were alive.

'I've told you not to do that,' he said, fingering his dog collar in the way he did when he was intensely nervous. 'Anyway, you heard. So did Rupert. Heard you hearing, I mean. I do wish you wouldn't do it, Mels.'

'Well, I did.'

She stared past his tall, gawky figure, out of her kitchen window, at the grey stone walls of the little village church, dappled with July sunshine. It was a glorious day outside, blue and gold, the North Sea silvery in the distance. A heron had nested precariously in an exposed bit of the church roof and was sitting nonchalantly on its untidy pile of twigs, unaware that its earthly landlord was about to be evicted.

'What are we going to do?' she said at last.

'You heard what he said. We are going to go to London and start again,' said her husband.

She rounded on him.

'You're giving in to that ass? Just like that?'

'What do you expect me to do?'

'Pray?' she demanded sarcastically.

'No amount of reflection and prayer,' said Giles heavily, 'will change the fact that no one is going to give us any choice, and that, as far as I am concerned, is that.'

'Look, I'm really sorry,' she began, hearing how choked he sounded. But as she slid off the Aga rail to try to comfort him, he stomped off to shut himself up in his church, alone with the heron, leaving her to cry by herself, sneezing helplessly into the ashes as she finished cleaning out the cooker.

'And here we are and here I am,' Melanie said.

'He wasn't made redundant, then,' said Ruth. 'Just moved on. It could be worse.'

Melanie sat bolt upright in her armchair.

'How could it be worse? They sent us to the *East End*. The paperwork from the Bishop's office all made it sound as though he had a choice, but it was cut and dried from the day Rupert telephoned. Lying toads.'

Ruth Allison settled back comfortably. Once clients let their inhibitions go and got angry about whatever was bugging them, they generally started to feel better. She could see Melanie punching cushions yet. She wondered vaguely whether to suggest group therapy for both of them.

'Probably not,' she murmured.

'I beg your pardon?'

'Thinking aloud,' said Ruth.

'Giles is a good country priest,' Melanie went on heatedly. 'He's good at fêtes and visiting old people. He'll never make an exorcist or an archbishop, or anything that makes you stand out and be decisive. He hates standing out. He hates taking decisions even more. Then they go and send him here. Half his parish here are Holy Rollers and dancing in the aisles and half of them are streetwalkers and small-time criminals. Well, some not even that small-time. They go all over the place, to prison. He's out of his depth, Mrs Allison. We all are.'

Ruth glanced at her watch.

'And I'm afraid we're out of time, Mrs Tilford. My next client will be along in a moment.'

'I was just getting into it,' cried Melanie, looking for a moment like a child who has had its candy snatched away.

'Same time, after the Christmas break?' Ruth asked. 'Book yourself in downstairs. They'll ask you for a contribution as well – whatever you can afford.'

'What do people usually afford?' Melanie asked the ample tweed bottom sticking out of the filing cabinet in the office downstairs.

'Ten pounds,' said a flushed face, looking round. 'I *know* I had those notes a moment ago, and I just can't put my hand on them.'

Melanie stood for a moment, contemplating the indignity of having *notes* about herself being lost by tweedy, well-intentioned women. She fumbled in her bag and planted a five-pound note on the counter. The tweedy woman banged the filing drawer closed and came and looked at it. Their eyes met.

'You get out what you put in, dear.'

Melanie opened her purse again and slowly drew out the one remaining five-pound note and put it beside the first. Then the funny side of it struck her.

'Mrs Allison said would you please make me an appointment for the same time after the Christmas break. I can't afford therapy or a breakdown, so what difference does it make?' she demanded.

The tweedy woman snatched the notes before she could change her mind and Melanie pushed her way through the heavy front door, out into the dark and still driving rain.

Chapter Three

'Christmas was a nightmare,' Melanie announced, coming back after the Christmas break. 'Do you know, I don't think I'd have got through it if it hadn't been that I knew I was coming back to see you, and I'd be able to tell you about it.'

Client dependency often developed after only one session. Ruth frowned, decided against a blow-by-blow account of Christmas-with-in-laws and suggested that they might just take up where they had left off.

'The baby,' she prompted. 'You were telling me about your husband and the baby, and how he can't let his mistake be simply that – a mistake. Surely you can all regard it as water under the bridge – especially now Christmas is behind us.'

'It's *Giles,*' cried Melanie. 'No one else could care less. Mrs Tutti Frutti brought him a bottle of Irish whiskey from Ian Paisley, a card from all her other kids, and kissed him on Christmas Eve after midnight mass. She was wrapped round him like sticky tape with her tongue practically down his ear, chewing it off. Probably missing Mr Tutti Frutti, who's on remand in custody. *She's* not the problem, over Ian Paisley. Giles's conscience is.'

'Ian Paisley?' Ruth said, astounded.

'It's a Unionist baby,' Melanie explained resentfully. 'I told you, they're Irish. '

'Ah. And *kissing*? Don't you mind about him being kissed by sticky tape?' demanded Ruth.

'It's always the same. No point minding,' snapped Melanie.

'I told you. I gave up minding long ago.'

She's suppressing her real feelings about this, thought Ruth, her professional nose twitching like a bloodhound's at the delicious scent of a real problem to do with sex.

Melanie's eyes were glazed. Angelina Tutti Frutti was one of the mainstays of the congregation and regarded Giles's church as a cross between a personal social-security office and an outpost of Butlin's. Of medium height, she was wide of beam, blowsy and happy. Angelina sported hips like a hippo's, bad legs, like knotted tree trunks, from too many pregnancies, a startling shock of loose and glorious jet-black curls, orange freckles over her snub nose and over the rest of her a flawless pale skin the texture of thick cream. She had six sisters, all of them living within spitting distance of each other. Their husbands too lived within spitting distance of each other, generally in the Scrubs or Pentonville, depending on who had space at the time.

'She'll be a grandmother before she's thirty-five,' Melanie said crossly. 'She ought to be downtrodden and crabby, with all those children, and living on income support, but she's not. She's so cheerful it's unnatural. The only time I've seen her upset was when she was looking at pictures of children from Romania and Bosnia when she was eating chips out of the newspaper. That made her cry. Though I suppose the vinegar might have got up her nose. A lot of women in the East End are unnaturally cheerful. Why, do you think?'

'The christening,' suggested Ruth, getting bored with demographic information about the East End.

'I'm coming to that,' Melanie snapped.

It was hard to describe. Most of Angelina's sisters, friends and cronies were either Irish, pale-skinned, black-haired and very large, Irish, pale-skinned, orange-haired and very large, or West Indian, black and very large. They had deep, loud voices like men's, with a tendency to shout.

'At first they scared me,' admitted Melanie. 'I come from rural Norfolk, and you don't get a lot of coloured people. I didn't know how to talk to them. We didn't have a lot in common.'

The older black women had vast and rolling buttocks, huge breasts like cushions, sleepy, knowing eyes and thick West Indian accents. Their beautiful long-legged, long-necked, doe-eyed daughters had small, high breasts, ankles like the heron's legs, fine and thin and fragile, and thick Cockney accents.

Melanie sometimes admired the girls and wondered what mystery transformed them into being like their mothers. School and the East End accounted for the Cockney accents. Having children, no doubt, did the rest. Their men were tall and broad-shouldered, with smooth, pink-palmed hands. The smoothness came from doing not a lot and spending a good deal of time banged up twenty-three hours a day in overcrowded prisons. Quite a few of the congregation came to the back door of the rectory to ask for hand-outs, only to disappear again. Giles said they were discriminated against. Whether that was true or not, Melanie thought, it seemed impossible to say.

'The Tutti Fruttis come to worship. Regularly,' said Melanie, following her own train of thought.

In the dancing light that shone through the old stained windows of the old stained church, their upturned faces watched Giles in the pulpit. He looked down on them, marvelling at the way their skin shaded from white through coffee and mahogany into a black so black it shone blue, like a bird's wing. Angelina's black hair stood out, glowing blue in the bright light. It was *really* that colour, and surprised him anew, made him want to put out his hand, guiltily, to touch the soft, springing curls, every time he saw her.

'They all come to church for just one thing,' Melanie added. 'To enjoy themselves. The first time Giles really realized that was at the christening and he was horrified. The place was littered with drums and gourds and when we got to the bit where Giles invites everyone to come and gather round the font to watch him baptize the baby, they all stood up and started jigging about in the aisles, yelling Hallelujahs fit to bring the roof down. We might have got rid of the sparrows, though, which is one way of looking at it.'

'What sparrows?' asked Ruth.

'We've got them nesting in the roof, it's in such poor condition. The Church won't spend and the parish hasn't got any money,' Melanie added gloomily. 'Oh, well.'

The sparrows had squawked loudly in indignation. The roof, thought Giles, distractedly trying to get a grasp on the screaming, thrashing Tutti Frutti infant in his arms and waiting for the uproarious party in his church to die down, needed a fortune spent on it. He looked up uneasily for bird droppings. Damaged in the war, the ancient beams and whitewashed plaster, patched and mended over many years, desperately needed a complete overhaul. His new bishop had other priorities, however, and the old building would continue to leak and lean. Beneath it, a forest of multicoloured heads swayed ecstatically, a host of large feet thumped and jigged as his flock, bright as cockatoos, processed in a spiritual and enthusiastic conga around the church and fetched up, panting happily, in a semicircle around the font.

'Ian Paisley Trevor O'Riordan,' Angelina hissed breathlessly in his ear. 'For Trevor McDonald on the News,' she added, squeezing his arm, giggling. 'I wrote to ask him to come, but he never answered.'

Giles, distracted, nodded.

It had a suitably carrying voice, to justify its first two names, he thought, as Ian Paisley Trevor's screams stabbed his head painfully. A steel band stood ready but unattended by the door of the church. He could see the scarred little door of the mend-the-roof appeal box hanging on its hinges just behind the row of drums.

'Stupid buggers. Fancy thinking there was anything to steal in *there*,' the churchwarden had scoffed, bending down painfully, testing the twisted hinges with fingers fantastically twisted themselves, by arthritis. He straightened up and beamed. 'One thing we can say, Father Tilford, is that it can't be our local lads that done it. They know better than to look for money in *that*.'

Melanie, standing in her usual Sunday place in church, in the front row of chairs, her view of the font blocked by a dense wall of heaving, sweating backs, saw her husband, towering over them, wipe something from his head. She looked up helplessly. An indignant sparrow peered down triumphantly, its head cocked to one side, its little black eye malevolent. It fluffed its tail and flounced; it had scored a direct hit.

'He can't cope, you know,' she repeated, coming out of the depressing memory. 'He's used to people being quietly and respectfully and politely deceitful. He can handle that. Not people dancing and shouting and waving their arms around.' She leaned forward confidingly. 'I don't know what you think, but I feel the Archbishop has let him down. He *encourages* it, you see. Decade of Evangelism and Interfaith Worship and let's all do our own thing. That christening would have been right up Dr Carey's street,' she said bitterly.

'I'm not a churchgoer, I'm afraid,' said Ruth.

'Don't have to be, to have a point of view,' Melanie snapped. 'Giles talked about resigning when the Synod voted for women. I knew the arguments, though. I showed him the bits in his books where it said there were women priests in the primitive Church, until the men threw them all out and pretended it had never happened. We had no more talk of leaving the Church or going into Roman Catholicism after that. What are they going to do with all the wives, while they're busy trying to be Roman Catholic priests and celibate? Do you know what a misogynist is? Hah.'

She snorted and sat back.

'We get a few in here,' murmured Ruth.

'I bet you do. Anyway, at the christening he was in such a state he dropped Ian Paisley Trevor O'Riordan in the font before he even *was* Ian Paisley. That baby was half drowned by the time Giles got his nerve together enough to fish it out, and all the Tutti Fruttis were wailing and shouting, and he just stood there, holding it upside down by its ankles with its nappy *sopping* and all its frills over its head.'

She paused, bit her thumb, put her head in her hands and stopped. Ruth gazed at the top of her curly head and waited while Melanie's shoulders shook with muffled sobs. Then she realised that Melanie was sobbing with hysterical laughter.

'Then he really did it,' she gasped, looking up again. 'He said, would someone please tell him – and he went and said this at the top of his voice, so that none of us could pretend it was a mistake and he hadn't meant it – why someone hadn't drowned it at birth. Like a kitten. And all the time he was standing there, holding this wretched baby upside down and sort of looking at it as though it was something he'd found under a brick, and was about to put back.'

'Oh dear,' said Ruth, beginning to grasp the extent of the crisis.

'The congregation sounded like a pack of hyenas,' Melanie went on mournfully. 'Angelina behaved as though Giles was Mad Max. I found him shaking and sobbing in the vestry after they'd gone. I can't say I altogether blame him.'

'I know he shouldn't have said what he did, but surely the church members will take into account that he's been under a lot of strain? There's no real harm done.'

'No real harm,' Melanie squeaked. 'What do you mean? I don't mean no harm to Ian Paisley. What I'm trying to tell you is that my husband is not the man I married.'

She began to gabble in the manner of a woman released.

'He is out of his depth and wallowing in guilt. He is usually a kind and ineffectual person who never did much harm. In Norfolk we had farmers, poachers, tourists and gentry. They were always shooting birds and animals. Occasionally they shot each other but that was usually by mistake. The girls got pregnant, of course, and half the time it was in the family. But he could *cope* with all that. Give him things he knows about, and he can cope. He can't cope with cons and Holy Rollers. It goes against everything he believes in, and it's too much for him.'

Ruth Allison let out a hissing breath, impressed.

'Incest?'

'What else? Out in those fens they never see anyone. Isolated. You have to drag them out of bed. They are too close-knit.' Melanie looked scornful and hurried on. 'Now he's got this lot in Stepney and he can't handle it.'

'It *is* a rough area,' Ruth murmured, wondering what kind of interesting caseloads they had in Relate Offices in Norwich. Or Ely, in the back of beyond, in the fens. Next time they had a national training session in headquarters, she'd find someone from round there, and ask.

She came out of her thoughts to hear Melanie laughing.

'There is a funny side. He's supposed to give pastoral care to anyone who needs it, not just the ones who come to his church. He goes round the council flats, all full of good intentions, and they mostly send him away with a flea in his ear. You can't blame him for thinking they're all full of burglars, prostitutes, pimps, drug-dealers, teenage freaks and joyriders, can you? He does get the seamy side of things.'

'Some perfectly decent people live in council flats,' retorted Ruth.

'No doubt. But that's not the issue,' Melanie said shortly. 'The problem is that Giles has convinced himself he's no better than the *worst* of them. To listen to him, he's got homicidal tendencies and is about to turn into a cross between Saddam Hussein and Hannibal Lecter.'

Ruth looked up sharply.

'And is he?'

'It's ridiculous,' Melanie snapped.

'Delusions of grandeur?' Ruth asked, excited by the prospect of uncovering a *really* interesting case.

'I said Saddam Hussein and Hannibal Lecter.'

'*They've* got delusions all right.'

'Well, yes,' Melanie agreed. 'But hardly grand. More disgusting.'

They considered that for a moment or two.

'So what are you going to do?' Ruth asked finally.

Melanie shrugged unhappily.

'He won't speak to me any more. I hardly know him. The wrath of God is upon him, and all on account of dropping that Tutti Frutti child, who is as slippery as the rest of them, anyway, and saying what he did. You see, Mrs Allison, he meant it. He wished evil upon a child at the moment he was christening it and it is torturing him. He wants to confess to the Bishop and be defrocked.'

Melanie's voice rose, shrill with outrage.

'He wants spiritual guidance. He can't have it. It's a nonsense. I have two teenage children and he's talking about our livelihood. Never mind his conscience, I want to know what to do to get him out of it.'

She half started out of her chair, subsided and looked the counsellor anxiously in the eye. 'Tell me what I have to do. One of us has to cope, Mrs Allison, and I don't think it's going to be him.'

Ruth ruminated.

'Do you think your husband wants to leave the Church? Do you think he's got a hidden agenda and is using the move to make staying in it impossible?'

Melanie's grey eyes opened wide in astonishment.

'Good heavens, Mrs Allison, that's complicated. I think my husband wants a bit of peace and quiet and to go back where he came from. Well, they won't let him. They won't let either of us do what we want to do, so somehow we just have to take it from there.'

Ruth Allison had been a Relate counsellor for years. In her late forties, she was thin and wiry and neat in green corduroy trousers and a washed-out brown hand-knitted jumper that matched her hair and eyes. Shrewd brown eyes studied her client. She crossed her corduroy legs, from which thin ankles poked out, ending in the sensible Hush Puppies, and cleared her throat as if to come to some conclusion. Melanie stared at her, waiting for enlightenment and Ruth Allison stared straight back.

Mrs Tilford was also slim and neat, and much taller. Beneath a heavy disguise of good, shabby tweeds and a cotton blouse with a frayed collar were delicate shoulders, heavy, rounded breasts and the narrow waist of a much younger woman.

She's hiding like a mouse under all that clumpy fabric and knee-length, practical woolly boots, Ruth thought. The boots were stained with rain. Melanie picked nervously at the worn beige arm of her chair with thin, elegant fingers that had ragged and bitten nails. She had more the air of poor county gentry than of a distressed vicar's wife from the fens.

'Well?' Melanie demanded, tired of waiting. 'I don't want psychoanalysis. I can't afford it. I just want you to tell me what I can do.'

'We aren't here to offer solutions,' said Ruth, busily casting around for one, despite her words. 'Against the rules.'

'Just give me one, and never mind the rules,' her client begged.

'What about making love?' Ruth began cosily. 'Can you get him to relax? Get him in the mood to talk? Find out what's on his mind?'

She hooked the tissues across the scratchy, colourless carpet, towards her own chair, and blew her nose discreetly, to give Melanie time to think about her suggestion. When she looked up, she realised that Melanie was laughing.

'Giles is too busy worrying about his soul to worry about *that*. He comes to bed in his dog collar and socks and reads the Bible. You try getting a man in his state to relax. He isn't coping and sooner or later someone who matters is going to notice and then the fat will be in the fire.'

The room was suddenly overheated, the gas fire a fiery furnace casting flickering orange flames like the fires of hell that Giles Tilford dreaded.

'Literally in his dog collar and socks?' demanded Ruth, taken aback.

'Oh, not literally, but he might as well be. Forget about . . . it. He has.'

'And you?'

'I was never that bothered,' Melanie said stiffly. 'I went right off it after Alice was born. One does what one has to. I haven't come to see you about that.'

One of the things that had put her off coming to see someone was that counsellors insisted on talking about sex. Giles talked about it to couples who came for pre-wedding counselling. Melanie had once asked him for an appointment, to find out what he thought about it. He'd never said anything to her.

'You don't think that might be part of the trouble? Your not being bothered?'

'A friend of mine once asked me that,' her client admitted, appearing to grind her teeth again. 'It was Daffodil Haines. We fell out about it and we haven't spoken properly since.'

Daffodil was the wife of George Haines, a florid gentleman farmer and master of the local hunt, who lent horses to Giles because Giles was a natural, gifted and graceful rider of other people's mounts.

'Giles,' Melanie explained reluctantly, 'is very tall and very clumsy, like a daddy-long-legs who has lost a leg. The poor things lurch all over the place, getting nowhere. The only time he isn't clumsy is when he's on the back of a horse.'

'What happened with Daffodil?' demanded Ruth, dying for Melanie to get to the point.

'He fell into her,' Melanie said simply. 'Off the back of George Haines's best hunter.'

'Right into Daffodil?'

'In a manner of speaking. It was very wet. Boggy. They were trying to avoid anti-blood-sports people making a fuss on Boxing Day, and Giles took a detour. The horse had more sense than Giles and it balked at a gate. It was Giles's fault, for setting it at it in the first place. I gather he went flying and Daffodil got in the way and they ended up in the remains of a haystack in a ploughed field.'

'Not a lot can happen in a ploughed field in December,' Ruth remarked.

'You wouldn't think so, would you?' answered Melanie kindly. 'But then, you live in London. Daffodil lives in Norfolk. She has fat thighs and lives in jodhpurs. She strides around whacking her bottom with a riding crop and falling out of her saddle underneath other people's husbands.'

Melanie studied her hands.

'I don't wish to be uncharitable, but her bottom *quakes* like water does when you blow on it and I *cannot* see the attraction. But there you are. Giles likes to imagine that The Cloth protects him, but of course it doesn't, except when it's me he's avoiding. There's nothing you can't do in a field at any time of the year, if you are so inclined.'

'Well, I suppose not,' said Ruth, moistening her lips.

'That was one reason why Giles didn't argue a lot about leaving. It suited him to get away from Daffodil's thighs,' snarled Melanie. 'Before he wanted them too much and got disgraced. I thought we were over all that, until the Tutti Frutti episode, and now all the old nonsense has come back. He's brooding and miserable and giving up and praying in bed when he should be asleep. He was the same over Daffodil until he got her out of his system.'

'He had an affair?'

'Of course he had an affair,' Melanie snapped. Her eyes filled with tears. 'I could have ruined his career, but what would be the point? Anyway, I know him. He's got a much more passionate relationship with his conscience than he's ever had with me or her. Or anyone else, come to that.'

'Ah,' breathed Ruth. 'Spiritual conflict with matters of the flesh. *Very* difficult.'

Melanie tried to smile.

'Giles has got a thing about big thighs and bottoms in tight jodhpurs. It could be worse. At least it leaves the choirboys out.'

They both contemplated Melanie's sensible tweed skirt

wordlessly. Her thighs were long and slender and she wasn't in jodhpurs. She shrugged, as if to say *oh well.*

The gas fire popped.

'All right, then,' Ruth announced, leaning forward suddenly and turning it off. 'It sounds as though whatever happened with Daffodil is over. You seem very level-headed and sensible and I would say that, as much as anything, what you've got is culture shock.'

'I beg your pardon,' snapped Melanie, offended.

'From village life to the East End is enough to make anyone unstable. You're like babes in the wood. You need a crash course in your parishioners' human failings.'

Melanie glared.

'You've got to get their measure and toughen up.'

'What do I *do*?' Melanie muttered, chewing her thumbnail.

'Get some street cred. What can you do? Apart from being a wife, what can you actually *do*?'

'Not a great deal, when you put it like that.' Melanie picked sulkily at her gnawed fingernails. 'Jam. Jumble. I can organize things. I can clear a blocked pipe and drains. Church houses seem to have terrible drains. Funny, that.'

For the first time since she married Giles and became proud to be a good wife she saw herself through another woman's eyes. The other woman saw a dodo. A dinosaur. A failure.

'I trained as a teacher. But I got married and had Tom nine months later. I only worked for two years. I've no experience.'

'Two years and two teenage children are experience,' Ruth retorted. 'So is organizing things and jumble and putting up with the Mothers' Union or whatever else you did. Go back to work. Get a job in an Inner London school with social problems. Where do you think this lot you're in such a panic about learned about life?'

'Tower blocks? The Scrubs?' Melanie ventured. 'Borstal? Rampton? Broadmoor. Community service?'

Ruth Allison, Relate counsellor two evenings a week,

teacher the rest of her working life, grinned.

'School and parents. The prison service counts as higher education. Start with parents and school, and go back to teaching, Mrs Tilford.' She looked at her watch. 'Same time next week?'

When Melanie had gone, Ruth Allison lay back in her armchair and cackled delightedly. 'In his dog collar and socks, reading the Bible, ploughing Daffodil's fat thighs in ploughed fields. Poor woman.'

Her next clients tramped up the stairs and came in to find her still laughing to herself. The young girl sat down in the armchair where Melanie had been, rubbed her arms through a thin coat and said, 'It's dead cold out there. Can we have the fire on?'

Ruth found some matches and lit the gas again. Orange flames flickered on the orange curtains and Ruth brought her mind back to the present, and the young couple's sexual dysfunction problem.

'Did you do your touching and exploring exercises?' she demanded.

The girl blushed and looked shyly at her very young husband.

'Yes,' he said. 'We did.'

Ruth forgot about Giles and concentrated. Downstairs, pulling the heavy front door closed behind her, Melanie passed two clients, a middle-aged couple, going in hand in hand. Looking at the clasped hands, she put her own hands into her pockets, to keep them warm, turned in the direction of the tube station and began to hurry home.

Chapter Four

The Tilfords moved to All Hallows in the late autumn of 1992. The church Giles inherited from his overworked predecessor dated back to pre-Saxon times. The most ancient fragments mostly took the form of part of the east-facing wall and chunks of wall poking just above ground level at odd spots in its large, overgrown graveyard, where an earlier pre-Saxon building had stood in the very distant past. In early spring of 1993 the graveyard was a profusion of long grasses, wild flowers and stained gravestones covered with moss, their inscriptions worn down by pollution and time. No one had been buried there for years. The present church was small and squat, with thick grey stone walls that had withstood the Blitz. Neglect had done more than the war to damage it, leaving it with leaking windows, crumbling mortar, and an ancient heating system that wheezed and grumbled, leaving it alternately overheated and freezing cold and damp.

'Call me Arfur,' ordered his rickety churchwarden, showing Giles around the first time he went to see it, shuffling along crabwise on legs bent like bows. He had the face of a beaming cherub, belying the impression that the rest of him was crumbling as badly as the walls.

'Father Rod spent a lot of time with the kids,' Arfur pointed out unnecessarily.

'So I see,' Giles answered, gazing at grubby whitewashed stone walls covered in children's drawings, paintings and collages, stuck up with Sellotape and Blu-Tack.

'Are these all from local schools?'

The churchwarden pushed a bit of Blu-Tack back into place, fixed a flapping piece of paper and gave him a pitying look.

'I was told to take them down before you fetched up, but I hadn't got the heart.'

He stood and peered up, his back so bowed he resembled an inquisitive tortoise.

'They're from all over. We tried it all. Schools. Sunday school. Brownies. Mothers and toddlers. Drop-in and crèche. Mothers' Union. Young Wives. Choir. Drop-in for drop-outs. They was mostly junkies. Come summer, he'd go down King's Cross and try to get the girls from round here off the game. Didn't work. Never does. He did the odd retreat, or what have you. It was a day out in the country, really.'

Giles wondered what more they might have, and didn't dare ask.

'Do we get many weddings?' he asked instead, batting gently at several limp helium balloons patterned with hearts in shocking pink and purple. They bobbed half-heartedly, tied with string to the back of a stack of orange plastic chairs.

'What's this?'

He parted the balloons and peered at a piece of paper stuck to the wall behind them, and began to laugh. The Reverend Rod had put up a fragment from the *Reader's Digest*.

> Dr Carey said that the World Council of Churches has 'flirted with the Delilah of paganism and danced with the Salome of communist ideology'. At the Council's most recent assembly in Canberra in 1991 delegates passed the smoke of burning leaves before opening worship service – a pagan cleansing rite – then listened to recorded insect noises and watched a male dancer impersonate a kangaroo. The Revd George Austin, Archdeacon of York, said, 'To me, the WCC seems sick at heart.'

'He had a pretty dark sense of humour,' Giles remarked, letting the balloons bob back.

Confetti lay in little drifts in corners, blown from outside. With the chairs stacked away down the sides, a chipped piano in one corner at the back of the church by the font, and its scuffed floor, the building looked more as if used for religious aerobics than for quiet, contemplative kneeling. The windows were part coloured, part plain glass, their sills stained with seeping rain.

'He used to say hell was not having a sense of humour at all,' retorted Arfur. 'We get some weddings. Mostly they go down the registry office, if they bother at all. They like their funerals round here. The balloons was for Mrs Burrows's birthday, not a wedding,' corrected Arfur, wheezing ahead to open the door into the vestry with an enormous bunch of keys. 'She's ninety-nine and hopin' for a telegram from the Queen next time – not that she'll be able to read it, being blind and can't hear much, neither. But he made sure she was in church every Sunday, even if he had to fetch her himself. Here you are. I started clearing out, but I didn't get too far.'

Embarrassed to see tears in the old man's rheumy eyes, Giles inspected the contents of a cardboard box to hide his own awkwardness. He found some gourds, a mouth organ, a copy of the Koran, a copy of *Malleus Maleficarum*, a packet of broken digestive biscuits, a pile of leaflets on AIDS held together with a rubber band, and several dozen loose packets of Mates extra-strong condoms. In a crate, he found a dozen empty cider bottles, a couple of full ones and a crumpled note to the DHSS on behalf of someone looking for a bed for the night.

'You must miss him,' he said, reading the Taunton Cider labels, his back tactfully turned to Arfur.

The explosive bout of noseblowing that followed warned him that he was right, and that the Reverend Rodborough was going to be a hard act to follow.

* * *

'Good grief, whatever did the old guy *do*?' Giles demanded when he got home, intrigued. 'No wonder he had a heart attack. It's more like a community centre crossed with a Muslim coven than a place of Christian worship. Children, sex, alcoholism and witchcraft all jumbled together in a cardboard box full of spiders. Do you think he might have keeled over because some disaffected parishioner stuck pins in his effigy?'

'It sounds like a popular spot, which will make a nice change, won't it? It sounds as though you've got a lot you can build on.'

Melanie tried to sound noncommittal. Sticking pins in effigies was the nearest Giles had come to making a joke since he had left Norfolk. She didn't want to make him notice he was feeling better about life, in case he relapsed again.

'You were more right than you knew when you called it a popular spot,' Giles gasped a couple of weeks later, having discovered his graveyard – quiet, a little out of the way, very overgrown and roomy, full of hidey-holes – to be a very popular local spot indeed.

He had come across Arfur, after saying evensong to an empty church one pleasantly warm evening, down on his creaking and arthritic knees and a kneeling pad, wielding a pair of shears among the long grass and buttercups bordering the path to the church door.

'You shouldn't be doing that. What we ought to do is take a motor mower to the whole lot and flatten it. Then we could see what's what and start looking after it properly. We'd get enough hay to keep half a dozen school guinea pigs in clover. We could stack the headstones around the wall and make a proper lawn.'

Arfur mumbled and hacked at a patch of dock leaves.

'What did you say?' demanded Giles.

'I said, leave well alone,' repeated the old man, sitting back painfully on his haunches and peering up long-sightedly into the evening sun, half blotted out by his tall employer's untidy shock of hair. 'What you don't know about won't hurt you,' he added enigmatically. He snapped his shears at the grass, leaving Giles staring down, puzzled.

'But it's a mess,' he said, recovering. He marched off to look it over thoroughly, cheered up no end by the notion of doing something as positive and rural as making hay in an inner-city churchyard.

'They make hay over there all right,' he said grimly to Melanie later. 'I nearly fell over a character who looked like Attila the Hun dressed in leather and studs, with a bone through his nose, shooting up – isn't that what they call it? – behind a gravestone with his girlfriend. He *offered* me some,' he added, his voice shaking with shock. 'They were lolling behind the yew trees with their backs to a grave, cooking stuff in a spoon.'

They had sat there gazing up at him, their eyes wary and mean. The girl, in slashed jeans and leather jacket, was shaved as bald as an egg, and was holding the candle flame steady underneath the spoon.

'What do you suppose you are doing?' Giles asked, hearing even as he said it how pompous he was.

They narrowed their eyes against the sun, scrutinized him, dismissed him.

'Piss off,' said Attila, bending back to his needles, tightening the rubber thong around his skinny, sinewy arm with his teeth. It bit into his flesh between two tattoos of writhing snakes, *Mum* entwined in their coils.

'This is *my* graveyard,' announced Giles helplessly.

The bald girl pushed up her sleeves and began to examine her arms dispassionately, looking for somewhere in their ruined veins that would still take a needle.

'I don't think you should do that,' said Giles.

Absorbed, they ignored him, towering over them, tall and broad and muscular, like a Michelangelo painting of the wrath of God. He had a great shock of untidy, wavy brown hair in need of a cut. Luminous brown eyes, a lopsided mouth and a square chin were marred and weakened by deep anxiety lines carving furrows over a long Roman nose.

The girl gave up on her arms, found a bit of vein in her leg and pushed the needle in. She fell asleep with her mouth open as Attila borrowed the same needle, loosened his tourniquet and pumped himself full of heroin. Giles felt sick, tried to make himself look away, and couldn't, until the man had finished.

'I didn't dare interfere,' he groaned to Melanie, running his hands through his hair in despair. 'I wish I'd taken their spoon away, or grabbed their needles. I wish I'd done anything rather than what I did do, which was stand there. I was fascinated and embarrassed, when I should have *done* something.'

'And get AIDS from scratching yourself?' she said calmly. 'Who would that do any good? Ruth said there was a lot of drugs around here. Perhaps that's what the condoms were for.'

'Shooting drugs?' Giles demanded. 'For God's sake, Melanie, don't be stupid.'

'Safe sex for people who share needles in graveyards. They probably do it in all that long grass. I bet that's what old Rodborough had them in the vestry for.'

At the thought, Giles looked momentarily wistful at the memory of doing it in long grass and haystacks with Daffodil. Then his gaze sharpened.

'Ruth?'

I know what you were just thinking, and I'm going to lie straight back at you. We have come to that.

Melanie met his eye guilelessly.

'A woman I was chatting to in the butcher's,' she said.

'Really?' he said, losing interest.

He went off to look in Yellow Pages, to find out the cost of hiring a motor mower to clear the graveyard.

Melanie took a deep breath and spoke to his departing back.

'Giles, I've got an interview for a job.'

He halted and didn't turn round.

'East Stepney School is looking for an English teacher. I didn't tell you I applied, because I didn't think I'd get it. But I think I might.'

He seemed to take no notice and vanished into the hall, where she heard him shuffling through the telephone book.

'*Giles*,' she called, frustrated. 'Did you hear what I just said?'

He came back, holding the directory open at Plant Hire.

'I heard,' he said. 'I'm delighted, because this is going to cost us an absolute fortune.'

Chapter Five

'What a pleasingly peaceful sight,' remarked Hugo Benedict, recently appointed headmaster of East Stepney School, looking across from his study window, which was high up enough to see into the south side of Hugo's church grounds, five hundred yards away.

'What?' asked his head of sixth form.

'Half the fifth year are over the way, stoned out of their empty little skulls on the first day of term. Jolly good. At least they're not beating the hell out of each other or my staff. Perhaps they are celebrating Mr Patten's putting us at the bottom of his league tables, do you think? Just fancy, what a distinction, being officially London's very worst school. Not many can aspire to that.'

'Our exam results are terminally sick, our truancy rate is blossoming, and our Local Education Authority want to close us down,' recited his head of sixth form.

'Can't blame them, really, when you look at that lot, can you?' Hugo agreed reflectively, talking to himself.

All Hallows' church porch and graveyard were favourite roosting spots for more than local tramps and drug addicts. Facing the church, across the flat, tree-lined park set just back from the Mile End Road, stood the grimy walls of East Stepney School. They shared facilities.

The church porch in bad weather was generally busy with kids hopped out of school and across the way to have a fag. At the beginning of the autumn term, the porch was empty, the graveyard grass uncut. Melanie refused to pay for the motor-mower project out of wages yet to come, annoying Giles and making a staunch ally out of Arfur.

On the first day of term half a dozen green-uniformed fifth-formers sat with their backs against gravestones, passing a joint in morning break. Hugo stood watching them until his attention shifted. Melanie Tilford was crossing the playground. He had seen her arrive earlier, looking younger than he had remembered from her interview, in a green linen suit.

'Good legs,' he remarked. 'Wonder if she'll last.'

He had his doubts, but he needed staff and there had been no other applicants for the post. East Stepney's reputation went before it. He returned to his previous train of thought.

'The question is,' he rumbled, craning to see as Melanie disappeared from sight below him, 'have we got the bottle to make this school a going concern again? Do we let them close us down, or do we opt out, go it alone and see if we can turn this dump around?'

Hugo stood ruminating, a dark figure against the glare, filling most of the window, his hands in the pockets of a dark suit that had never been very good, though it had seen better days. He was an amiable, shambling giant whose knees bagged, elbows went out, jumpers sprouted holes and who was in constant need of a haircut. In a ruddy, open face engraved with as many lines as British Rail, bushy eyebrows beetled over a pair of shrewd brown eyes and a nose broken so often on the rugger field it angled well to the left and whistled when he was angry and breathing hard. His mouth had both a ready smile and a sardonic quirk to one side. His voice rumbled in his chest like a volcano, rising to a roar that penetrated the furthest corners of his deplorable school.

Like Giles across the way, he was over six feet tall and both a newcomer and an outsider in Stepney. Leaving a prestigious deputy headship in west London, he had only taken over the headship at East Stepney six months earlier, after the previous head retired from his impossible task, pleading chronic, irreversible ill health. It was a ridiculous career move, but Hugo was undismayed to be the new headmaster of the worst school in the East End. He relished challenges.

There was one brewing in the playground. He watched, amused, as two of his few sixth formers groped each other enthusiastically behind the playground bicycle shed, unaware that they were overlooked.

'Again? A going concern *again*? Were we ever a going concern?'

Behind him, Alastair Croke, head of sixth form and theoretically responsible for the moral welfare of bike-shed gropers, had perked up when Hugo mentioned legs. He hitched one of his own lanky legs over the arm of his chair and shook his head. 'Uh huh, I don't think so.'

They enjoyed the mutual respect of opposites who worked well together. Hugo was mountainous, shambling and brown as a bear. Alastair was long, thin, wiry and strong as a steel spring is strong, giving the impression of being pale grey all over, distinguished even, with a sallow, oval face, light, sardonic grey eyes framed by John Lennon glasses and a long, thin, immaculately groomed black ponytail held back with an elastic band. He was curiously loose-jointed, moving as though hanging from strings; a puppet who might jerk at any moment into a Mick Jagger pelvic frenzy, which gave him a dissipated air at odds with his pastoral duties.

While Alastair lounged in his chair, Hugo went on gazing out of his window and tried to give some concrete form to his dream of transforming this horrible heap into something local people could be proud of.

'We want them to fight to send their kids here, instead of sending them here to learn to fight,' he growled, calculating that the pair in the bike shed would be at it within the next five minutes unless someone stopped them.

'It's always been a sink into which the dregs sank perfectly happily. Why spoil it for them?'

Hugo grunted and cracked his knuckles. It wasn't what he wanted to hear, but Alastair said what everyone thought. The dream was in truth a nightmare. Everyone thought

Hugo was in cloud-cuckoo-land, including himself. He turned on his next-in-command irritably.

'Two of your lot are practically copulating in the bike shed,' he snapped. 'Tracey Papadopoulos and Weasel Watkins. Go and throw cold water over them.'

'That always seems singularly mean to me,' Alastair said, grinning.

Tracey had her hands embedded in Weasel's buttocks and was welded to him like a second skin.

'*Now*,' yelped the headmaster. 'Go and stop them *now*.'

Alastair unwound his lanky body from his armchair and came and squinted into the sunlight over Hugo's shoulder.

'So they are. They say you can let a gun off right by their ears at times like that and they don't even hear it,' he observed.

Hugo banged his vast and hairy fist on the windowsill and looked apoplectic.

'Don't make me lean out and *shout* at them,' he roared.

'All right. All *right*. I'm going.'

Alastair sauntered off.

Some moments later Hugo saw him emerge into the bright September sunshine, cross the playground to the bike shed and shout. The pair behind it jumped guiltily. He said something and pointed up at Hugo standing at the window. Weasel snarled and clutched his crotch. Tracey flounced and pulled her knickers straight. Hugo grinned and returned to surveying his territory. He planned to save it. The odds were heavily stacked against him, as everyone, including his wife, kept pointing out.

'For God's sake, *why*?' Bunny Benedict had demanded when he announced as he was getting into bed one evening that the headship had come up at East Stepney School, and he was going to apply.

'It's a dump and is going to close,' she cried, when he didn't answer. 'Why are you suicidal all of a sudden?'

Bunny, who had been married to Hugo for twenty years,

taught home economics and cooked incessantly, like other women took tranquillizers, to keep herself sane, shot upright, clutched the duvet to her, and stared at him over its edge with narrowed, suspicious brown eyes.

'Have you gone mad?' she demanded.

Behind the duvet, she had nothing on. The head of art in a moment of kindness had once called her Rubenesque. Bunny had eyed her derisively and retorted, 'You mean I'm stout. What makes you think I care?'

She didn't, thought Hugo, grinning at the memory, care about being stout, because she wasn't. She was full-bodied, warm and sensual, the most exciting woman he knew. After twenty years, her radiant smile could still make his heart go bump in his chest. Bunny's smile was something; it was slow and sexy and glowed in her hazel eyes, lit her whole face. She wasn't smiling now.

'Tell me it's a wind-up and a joke,' she ordered hopefully, lying back and looking up at him.

'It's not. I mean it. I want a challenge,' he said. 'I know it doesn't make a lot of sense.'

'Then you'd better start making sense, because I would have thought that keeping a job, paying the mortgage and staying out of negative equity, when everyone else is out of a job and in negative equity, would be quite enough challenge for anyone.'

She was right.

'Something happened that I never told you about, a couple of years ago.'

He sat down on the side of the bed and tried to explain. The memory had come rushing back as soon as he saw the advertisement for the East Stepney headship in *The Times Educational Supplement*. He had sent off for the application forms immediately.

Recruited as part of a team of consultants for the Inner London Education Authority, Hugo had first gone to East Stepney on ILEA business. Three of them had been sitting in the headmaster's room, boring each other with a futile discussion about the shortage of teaching resources. The discussion had been going where they expected – nowhere – when there had been a terrible blundering crash on the door. It flew open as if in a storm.

A youth, his thin, undernourished cheeks defaced with acne, came tumbling through, a knife in one hand, both arms twisted viciously behind his back, kicking randomly at the PE teacher, a smooth and wiry Pakistani with an exquisitely beautiful face who played vicious cricket and spent his spare time making videos with the Grateful Dead and television ads for Calvin Klein underwear. An old friend of Julian Clary, with similar tastes, he spent much of his life going out of his way to avoid having his beautiful face carved up.

'*Bastard,*' squealed the kid, lashing back with his heels.

'*Drop it,*' Mohammed snarled, dodging the kicks with the grace of a dancer, hitching the arm in the arm lock savagely enough to break it.

'Get out of my fucking *face,*' his victim screamed back.

With one last vicious wrench, the knife flew out of the boy's grasp and landed in the side of Hugo's chair with a thud. He leaned over, picked it out and looked at the six-inch razor blade thoughtfully.

'Found him bunking off PE, gobbling speed in the boys' changing rooms. When I told him to move his backside and get outside, he went for me with that. He's high as a kite, so I brought him up here,' Mohammed explained.

The boy stood rubbing his skinny, bruised arms, the fight gone out of him. In cheap denim from a shop that took Local Authority clothing vouchers, jeans rumpled and too long, catching on his heels, bagged at the knees, he looked heartbreakingly young. And this lost already, Hugo thought, holding the blade gingerly. The headmaster came and took it away.

'Well?' he demanded, holding it well out of reach by the handle, between his finger and thumb. The boy shrugged and refused to look at him. The headmaster swung the blade gently.

'Last time I had you in here, Ben, I warned you that if I saw you once more in my office, I'd remove you from my school. As from this moment you are expelled, and I am about to call the police.'

The telephone in the other hand, he shook the knife to emphasize each crime.

'Possession of a dangerous weapon. Assault on a member of staff. Possession of an illegal substance. Smoking an illegal substance. Pushing the illegal substance, too, no doubt.'

'I ain't,' the boy said sullenly, vulnerable, childish anger disfiguring the mean little face.

When Mohammed had gone, the headmaster turned to Hugo. 'Sorry to interrupt you like this. The police will want to take statements.'

Ben Graves started to snivel, wiped his nose on the back of his hand and mumbled.

'What?' snapped the headmaster, punching buttons.

'Me gran just died.'

'You think you can go around threatening my staff with knives because your gran died?' demanded the headmaster incredulously. 'You think that's an *excuse*? If you were not that much too young,' he held up four fingers, 'they'd put you in prison.'

He listened to ringing at the other end.

'She come home from 'ospital to die,' Ben went on stubbornly, as if the headmaster hadn't spoken. 'And me foster mum said, go an' see her, but I never, an' she went an' died last night. I went out last night and I should've gone an' seen her. It's gutted me.'

Ben's mum had run away with her boyfriend and his dad hadn't been seen for years. He couldn't be bothered to go and see his dying gran. He was fourteen with his life already a mess and tears running uncontrollably down his face. Hugo turned away to hide his own as they waited for the police to come.

The sound of Ben Graves sobbing his heart out stayed with him.

'I know the headmaster was *right*,' he told Bunny. 'And I also know that sometimes that's not everything.'

'That is an awful story,' she said from behind the duvet, nearly in tears herself.

'So, I concluded there were no answers to the questions that Ben made me ask myself, but that one day I would go, maybe not to that particular school, but to one like it, and try to sort out a thing or two. Put in my ha'p'orth, for better or worse.'

'I see,' she said, and she did.

It wasn't rational, it wasn't sensible. Careerwise it was stupid. But she understood that it was what he wanted to do.

'You're throwing away an Oxford degree. *And* the deputy headship of a good school. *And* at least our mortgage is in a nice part of London,' she pointed out.

'I know my credentials,' he said patiently. 'To get anywhere with East Stepney, we'll have to live over the shop. Will you mind very much? There are some nice Victorian houses in that part of London.'

She was silent for a long time.

'One condition,' she said. 'I come and work with you. You can't rescue a school that can't cook. The troops have to march on their stomachs.'

'You'll back me?'

'Against my better judgement.'

'You are *wonderful*,' he said.

'I know.' Bunny smiled her glorious smile, emerged from behind the duvet and reached into her bedside table.

'Look what I've got in here. Fresh cream,' she said, undoing the wrapping on a little Thornton's carton, 'flavoured with Grand Marnier. We haven't tried them before.'

She moistened her lips and licked a trace of Belgian chocolate off her finger, holding out the carton. 'Wicked. Want to try?'

'I absolutely adore you,' said Hugo through a mouthful

of chocolate, getting into bed. 'And these.'

He put out one hairy paw, delicately helped himself to another truffle, bit it in half and put one piece tenderly into her mouth.

'It is a definition of perfect compatibility,' Bunny said with her mouth full. 'Two insomniacs truffling in the same bag of Thornton's.'

'If you can't sleep, what else?' Hugo asked.

'Come closer,' Bunny said, 'and let me show you.'

They had been married nearly twenty years, and it never palled.

They met at Oxford. He was a postgraduate, she a first-year student at teacher training college. They met at a party, couldn't take their eyes or hands off each other, were crazily drunk at two in the morning, went down to the river, found a punt and fetched up zigzagging across the Thames in the light of a full and glorious moon, straight into a willow tree hanging right out from the bank.

'Yooohoooo. Ooops,' Hugo yodelled, slid down the pole and disappeared, coming up with a great deal of splashing and swearing. Sobered by the shock of icy water, he thrashed around, tried to climb back into the punt and tipped her in beside him. Further down the river, shouts from Parson's Pleasure told them they weren't the only ones to be dipping in the moonlight.

Bunny, her short skirt up round her waist, T-shirt ballooning in the water, lost her shoes to the bottom of the Thames. She swam away from him, turned on her back and looked up at the luminous deep blue of the midsummer night sky, her long hair floating darkly on the surface of the cold black water like some miraculous weed.

'Ophelia,' he cried, climbing out on to the river bank, standing in a patch of dandelions and nettles. '*Ouch*.'

'Wurzel Gummidge,' she called back.

The moon broke on the water in a thousand silver reflections, an owl drifted over the trees, a white shadow, the spires of Oxford rose up to the brilliant stars and in the fragrant, magical night Hugo fell in love for the first and only time in his life.

He leaned out over the water on an overhanging branch of the willow tree. 'I love you, Ophelia.'

'Ophelia committed suicide,' she called back hoarsely, her teeth beginning to chatter. 'You into death or something? I will be in a minute. Hypothermia.'

She turned on her front and began to swim to the river bank. He shook his head in the darkness and watched her come up out of the water.

'"Blonde Aphrodite rose up excited, moved to delight by the melody",' he quoted, moved to delight himself. 'My God, you are lovely.'

'I thought you said Ophelia,' she said, shivering, her long hair, black with river water, plastered to her body. She scrambled up the bank. 'And I'm not blonde. So make your mind up, you ass, and take me home. I'm *frozen*.'

He put his arms around her to warm her. By the time they got back to his flat, neither of them wanted to let the other go, ever again.

Still leaning on his window, memories of the pleasures of Grand Marnier truffles made Hugo smile to himself as he watched Weasel slink away and disappear into the boys' lavatories, leaving Tracey to sulk on one of the empty metal bars meant to prop up bikes.

'I've been here not quite a couple of terms and all I've achieved is the removal of the stolen bike industry from my patch,' he remarked to a pigeon that flapped to an untidy landing on the windowsill.

Playground trade in stolen mountain bikes had been brisk until last month, when he had forbidden bikes of any kind to be brought on to school property.

Alastair nodded at him from down below and stalked back inside. Hugo opened his window wide, now that the warm and sunny playground was deserted except for Tracey.

The smell of hot asphalt rose in a wave and reminded him of childhood, when the summers were always long and hot and he had once spent an absorbing afternoon making footprints in the softened surface all over his father's drive, semi-liquefied by the scorching sun. Maybe he was mad. His father certainly had been, about his drive. But the day he heard he had got the job at this wretched school, he had punched the air and let out a great shout of delight.

'What about *that*!' he cried.

'What I think is that you had better be careful, or you could find yourself tilting at windmills,' Bunny told him, when he'd calmed down. 'You get too excited about things.'

'I'm an Arien. I can't help it,' he said. 'I like getting excited.'

'Just remember that you can't generally change people's lives,' she warned. 'Sometimes it's better not to try, because they might just end up changing yours instead.'

Chapter Six

East Stepney School was not a place to make anyone except Hugo or an arsonist excited. Depressingly housed in grim and dingy Victorian buildings, it was shielded from a busy road by high, curving brick walls that resembled pictures of Broadmoor. Its well-proportioned, once-elegant windows were grubby and covered by grilles, its red bricks defaced by graffiti, pockmarked by age and holes where old netball nets had hung. The playground, in front of the building, was an empty expanse of asphalt, painted with a yellow and white netball court. To one side the original lavatories, set back to back, had had their entrances blocked up by the caretaker to keep the vandals out. Near the gate the wooden bike shed with its empty slots rotted gently away.

Boys stood in carved relief above the entrance. *Girls* had long since been bricked up to provide extra teaching space in what had once been an entrance hall. Some predictable vandal, more educated than most, had printed *Abandon hope all ye who enter here* on the lintel and the top half of the main entrance door with meticulous care and a can of black spray paint. The caretaker, touchy and self-righteous as his profession demanded, tried to scrub it off. He succeeded only in making it look faded, as though the words had leached their way out of the wood and bricks of their own accord.

On days when the weather was bad and it was nicer indoors, or the Education Welfare Officer had been busy visiting parents and threatening them with fines, more pupils attended than played truant. At those times, the school held around eight hundred, mostly indifferent to education, mostly socially alienated and coming in a wide assortment of colours.

At the beginning of March Alastair Croke sat in the staff room enjoying his lunch break at the long refectory table running right down the middle of the room. He had the *Mail* and a couple of local papers propped in front of his sandwiches.

'Prince Charles is still making speeches about how we should all behave, and after telling us last year that he wants to be a tampon,' he announced, turning the page. 'How astonishing. And by some coincidence, I recall the Archbishop of York telling us that he wasn't saying that people aren't bad, but that often badness is brought out of them by circumstances, by upbringing, by boredom and a sense of hopelessness. It was a dig at the government, but I wonder what the Queen thought of that analysis of the heir to the throne's aims in life.'

He folded the paper carefully, then cackled and reached for a file.

'Here's another one from my records,' he said. 'This is our local celebrities, the Kray twins, speaking. "In our days, no one would dream of mugging and battering old ladies, stealing from their next-door neighbours or molesting and killing innocent women and children."'

'They were talking about what happened to little James Bulger,' said Melanie sadly, waiting for the kettle to boil at the other end of the room.

'Hypocrites,' Alastair retorted, turning over his page at random. He finished his sandwiches and sat industriously pasting bits of newspaper and handwritten notes into his scrapbook. The room, next to Hugo's study, was long, high-ceilinged and full of desks, books, piles of papers, battered armchairs and general untidy clutter. In the middle of it all, Alastair had long since made territorial claims to a windowsill of his own, in the quiet corner at the far end of the room, overlooking the green expanse of the park, looking towards All Hallows on the other side.

'You're head of sixth form, with a room of your own,' little Amadeus Garlick complained bitterly, arriving from the biology lab with a collection of fat and comatose frogs in a glass trough. 'These need a safe corner, and Stan's cat gets into the lab. Why can't you put all your junk in your office?'

'Junk,' Alastair repeated indignantly, looking at the small, bulbous-shaped man over the tops of his John Lennon glasses. He surveyed the freckles on the top of Garlick's prematurely balding red head and wondered, not for the first time, how life came to match a man to his name and pedantic profession with such wondrous perfection. *'Junk?* Those are my archives and league tables. I shall write a book, one day. *A Social History of the Sin Bin.*'

The windowsill was the object of constant friction. Little Amadeus Garlick, head of biology, wanted it for himself, to grow things on. He persisted in producing things growing in jam jars and saucers, and claimed they needed the light. They bickered, not always good-naturedly, neither prepared to give way.

Alastair, tidy and meticulous, liked to organize his surroundings as methodically as he set out historical theories and facts. Lined up neatly on the sill, along with a lovingly tended busy Lizzie and several mugs, containing other people's prehistoric mould, that he refused to wash, was his unique collection of scrapbooks. Every time Garlick complained, Alastair made a point of reviewing the scrapbook contents, to upset him. 'Listen, old prune,' he began with relish, looking at what he had pasted in before being reminded of Prince Charles's longing to be swirled around a lavatory. 'Here's some statistics for you to put in your test tubes and study.'

Garlick flinched and the top of his head went red.

'Leave off,' he muttered, left holding the glass trough helplessly. Alastair eyed one of the frogs. It was very fat.

'Yum, yum. Frog legs. You'd be better off barbecuing

them,' he said maliciously and started to read from his own records.

'This is from the Easter break last year to last July. That's four months. The news is seriously dreadful. Listen. This is what our fine student body collected in the way of public honours. Fist fights – eight that took someone to casualty. Knife fights – two that had the police in and caused indefinite exclusion from school. Actual bodily harm – staff, one: pupils, three. Possessing and pushing cannabis and LSD – thirteen. Glue-sniffing in carrier bags from Tesco's or elsewhere—' He paused, puzzled. 'Why do you think anyone notices which brand of supermarket bag they sniff glue from? And I bet we've got more sniffers than that.'

'I don't want to know,' said Garlick, trying to clear a space on his own desk for the frogs.

Alastair turned his scrapbook pages ruminatively. 'We're quite colourful, really. We had several attempts at arson in the hot summer months when the exams were on and people got either scared or bored and fancied lighting fires in the old loos. Luckily they're as useless at fire-setting as everything else.' He pounced gleefully on a fresh page. 'Wrong. They're good at something. Year on year we have a higher than Inner London average of teenage pregnancies.'

'I wish you'd shut up. I'm trying to get a bit of peace and quiet,' complained the Stud McTavish, head of English. 'It's ghoulish, wallowing like that.'

'It's not. I'm a social historian,' Alastair protested indignantly. 'I collect little stories and press cuttings that vilify our beloved school. You sneak off at weekends and make bets on horses and keep dubious company. Each to his own vice, sweetheart.' He looked round at the crowded staff room and his face lit up. 'I wonder what the rest of us do in our spare time by way of *divertissement*.'

The new woman in the English department looked up from her sandwiches and caught his speculative gaze with a look so instantly and unnecessarily full of guilt he felt a sharp pang of interest. His sharp, sardonic eye held hers, said *you're hiding secrets, lady* until she looked away, confused and frightened.

'*The Gazette* says the police and fire brigade are complaining about us,' he added, speaking directly to her, trimming the edges off a fresh article with fingers like a tarantula's legs and lining it up on his page, unperturbed by her confusion. 'They say we waste their time.'

'Find someone who isn't complaining about us,' agreed the Stud, leaning over his shoulder to look. He irritated Alastair to death. He came to work in darned cardies, egg-stained shirts and old tweed jackets without elbows or buttons, long since pulled out of shape by bundles of bits of paper, scribbled all over with notes on form. His desk was piled with old copies of *Sporting Life* and computer print-outs of long and complex racehorse pedigrees.

The Stud lived downstairs in the same converted house as Alastair, by chance, and they knew each other well.

'Find someone else to fondle. Why don't you give up what you're not good at, which is teaching, and make a living off the blasted horses?' Alastair snapped, wriggling angrily. 'Which you are good at. Get off me, do.'

The Stud had got his unkind nickname on account of his knowing more about horse pedigrees than almost anyone else in the western world.

'If I'd done what I ought to have done, while I had the chance, and gone to Hong Kong years ago, I'd be well out of this nonsense now,' he said agreeably, reading the article still leaning on Alastair's shoulder, pedantically running his finger down the sentences so that Alastair couldn't turn over his page. 'They were sending all the clapped-out horses from Europe there, to race under other names. If you could trace them back to who they originally were, you could find their form, bet with the information, which no one else had, and make a packet.'

'Get *off*,' Alastair snarled. 'I'm not that way inclined.'

'Too late now,' the Stud went on, shaking his head. 'Hong Kong's going. Macao only has a couple of years and computers work my system for anyone. Twenty years ago,' he added wistfully, 'I'd be a millionaire.'

'If you don't get off my neck I'll hit you. And talking of betting,' Alastair remarked, removing Stud's finger forcibly from his scrapbook, 'what odds are you giving against the parents voting to opt out?'

'Odds?' asked Stud innocently, straightening up.

'Don't try and tell me you haven't got a book on it,' snarled Alastair.

'Three to one on.'

'Three to one *on*? You're out of your tree,' Alastair told him, astounded, putting the top on his Pritt Stick. 'The only reason that lot want to learn to read and write is so they can fill in their social-security forms and sign their names with a cross.'

'I don't believe that. They do care but they think we let them down. Perhaps we should open a debate and get them thinking differently,' Melanie said from the far end of the table, closing her sandwich box. They both turned and stared at her incredulously.

'What?'

Alastair guffawed and banged the table delightedly. All round the staff room heads turned curiously.

'Our new teacher thinks we should open a *debate*,' he cried mockingly. 'The only kind of debate you get around here, sweetheart, is the head-butting sort. This isn't the Oxford Union. Even Hugo would give you that.'

'My husband has just moved to the church over the other side of the park, and we have two children in this school, so we care about it. We can't be the only ones. I bet a lot of other parents feel the same, only they need us to start a dialogue,' Melanie began, feeling a dozen pairs of eyes looking her up and down. There was a stunned silence.

'Dialogue!' Alastair burst out joyously, having a natural victim in his sights. 'Hear that, everyone? We need *dialogue*.'

'It's what the headmaster feels,' she said stubbornly.

'It's what the headmaster feels,' he mimicked unkindly.

'That's unkind,' she said, flushing scarlet.

He drew breath to answer, when the bell rescued her. In the corridor outside the staff-room door, pandemonium broke out as the school clattered in from the playground and a dozen fifth-formers straggled in from the graveyard over the way. Alastair stacked his scrapbooks back on his windowsill and winked at her on his way out to his office.

'Upper Sixth history. Double period. Henry the Eighth and the Papacy. Such fun,' he said. 'Do I teach your kids?'

She shook her head.

'Hugo's in cloud-cuckoo-land, you know,' he said earnestly. 'And poor old Stud's quite gaga. They are both romantics, poor souls. Among the many facts they don't like facing up to is that our pupils' tiny minds are concentrated on things that really matter, like scoring drugs, and someone to have sex with, and a house with its window undone so that they can nick its video. You won't get any of that lot interested in coming to meetings and making resolutions about running a school. It's beyond them.' The thin, clever, bitter face was close to hers, his pale eyes sharp and sad.

'Where are your children at school, then?' she asked, retaliating.

He gave a short laugh.

'Once upon a time they were here, too. Then my wife took herself and them off to live with my best friend. Glasgow, Scotland, sweetheart, is the answer to your question.'

'You don't think that's got something to do with it?'

'To do with what?' he asked coldly.

'The way you mock everything,' she said shyly.

'You're *observant*, too?'

'That cheap shot is exactly what I mean. Anyway, we'll see what all the tiny minds think about your ideas this evening,' she said angrily. 'I bet you get a surprise, and that more parents turn up to hear what Hugo has to say than you think.'

'Sure.'

She glared, then infuriated him and surprised herself by giving him a sweet, bright, beaming, wholly sarcastic smile.

Chapter Seven

'I've been remembering another gem from the mouth of our leader,' Hugo announced, coming into the staff room to tell Garlick he'd drawn the short straw, and was to set out the hall for the meeting that evening.

'Must I?' Garlick asked plaintively, looking at himself in the side of the kettle and wondering if rearranging his hair over his bald spot would look any better.

'Yes. Someone's got to,' Hugo said heartlessly. 'I was thinking about Patten's announcement in the Commons that truancy from school leads to a life of crime, and their debate about shady goings-on in those town halls that are stopping schools from opting out. We could tell them a thing or two nowadays.'

'Been round our town hall recently?' enquired Garlick acidly. 'Shady hardly fits the bill. It's so bloody murky down there it's more a case of you can't see your hand in front of your face.'

The opting-out meeting was set to start at eight o'clock. Hugo upset Garlick by implying that his last biology period of the day was dispensable. He had planned to play with the frogs, but spent the time instead supervising his fourth-formers setting the hall with chairs for the parents. They banged and scraped cheerfully, delighted to miss a lesson.

'Put them *straight,*' shouted Garlick, small, harassed and dishevelled, his short legs pumping up and down the rows, straightening chairs fussily, resentful at having his time wasted doing a pointless job.

'Your parents are being asked to vote to keep this school

open, so do for heaven's sake make it look as if you do something useful here. Though even they,' he added under his breath, but loudly enough for several of the kids to hear him, 'are not as stupid as the headmaster gives them credit for. Who does he think he's fooling? They know what's what around here.

'Go on, carry on,' he yelled, as two boys began shoving at each other with a couple of chairs.

The hall needed painting, and new curtains. Its dingy cream walls flaked and the curtains that hung half off their tracks had been fashionable in schools in the seventies. It smelled of chips and burgers from lunch, and sweat and dust from indoor PE and Angelina Tutti Frutti's sister's lazy cleaning. He climbed up on to the stage and sat down to watch the mêlée below, relishing the thought that the parents would have to sit on school furniture for hours, and for once would endure the same discomfort as the teaching staff. Hugo *would* go on and on and on. So was this last period going on and on. Garlick cocked his head, listening for the bell as Alastair appeared at the far end of the hall, spotted him on the stage and drifted down to stand at the bottom of the steps with his hands in his pockets.

'Nearly done,' he remarked. 'Jolly good show.'

Garlick, patronized, glared down and met Alastair's amused gaze.

'By the time the old man's finished enjoying the sound of his own voice for several hours, all our bums will be so numb from sitting on those damn things we'll promise anything just to be allowed to go, anyway. Maybe that's the grand master plan after all. Torture the parents into submission, and sow dissent so that they rat on each other. How to get round the PTA and the likes of the Tutti Fruttis. Make them miserable and insecure and then bully them. The Gestapo did it, and look where it got them. Divide and rule. *Hugely* successful.'

The silly idea entertained him, and he chuckled, looking for all the world, thought Garlick savagely, like a cackling flamingo in a grey suit that needed pressing.

'And what's eating *you*?' Alastair demanded, catching Garlick's venomous glare just as the bell went.

'Wait,' Garlick yelled, leaping up as his class headed for the door like a football mob streaming on to the pitch after a home win. *'Wait right where you are until I tell you you can go.'*

The front of the mob pushed mindlessly out through the swing doors, bashing each other with bags, unheeding. As the doors banged shut on the rest, Alastair grinned.

'Crowd control, our glorious profession, isn't it? Or not crowd control in some instances,' he remarked.

Garlick stuck his hands in his pockets and refused to rise to the taunt. Disappointed, Alastair decided he had better things to do and ambled off. His victim, unmindful of the restive mob waiting to be dismissed, watched him bitterly.

That's right, take liberties. Don't mind me. Just get inside my head. Trample around. Don't bother asking. Feel free.

He sometimes had the creepy feeling that Alastair Croke's tall and mocking presence on earth had been arranged solely to make life intolerable for little Amadeus Garlick, whose favourite Nazi fantasy he had just invaded without so much as a by-your-leave.

Irrational and terrifying, the idea that Alastair could read his mind occurred to him, not for the first time. The thought of Alastair coiled up like a snake in the staff room, waiting to pounce, gave him goose bumps all down his spine. It was no use looking to the others for help: they all either didn't care, or thought the way he and Alastair carried on was *funny*.

'All right, you can go. *Quietly,*' he shouted, as the rest of his class hurled themselves out of the double doors, leaving the front few rows of chairs all over the place.

'Back,' he bawled, stopping the last four or five in their tracks. 'Straighten that lot up. *Then* you can go.'

'Bell's gone,' one of them said sullenly.

Five hostile black faces were calculating whether or not to ignore him and walk out. It was a look he knew well. He narrowed his eyes and looked right back, calmly.

'I'd advise you to just do it,' he said, with very quiet menace.

His pupils knew that Garlick was deceptive. Small, eccentric and shaped like a clove of the bulb he was named after, it was easy to imagine that he was weak. That was a mistake. When he stopped shouting and started to whisper, he meant business, like making them empty their bags and pockets on to the biology benches and confiscating all the things in them that were illegal. Because there were a lot of the latter he could be a real nuisance.

'OK,' the ringleader muttered.

They dumped their bags on the floor and sullenly straightened the chairs. He stood on the very front of the stage until they had finished, leaning on the lectern that he was about to drag down on to the hall floor to hold Hugo's notes during the meeting. Hugo and Alastair would be up at the front, with David Absalom, chairman of governors. Garlick grinned. They saw themselves as the triumvirate, the cavalry riding to save the school at the last moment and never mind the odds.

Then he sighed. They were power-players in life's unfair games, he a mere pawn, and as VIPs they'd expect a jug of water and glasses. He climbed off the stage and headed for the staff room, where such things were kept in the bottom drawer of a filing cabinet, along with a communal bottle of whisky that by common consent was replaced every time it was empty. Noting that his desk was piled high with someone else's books and his frogs back on the top of the filing cabinet, wilting miserably in their tepid puddle of water, well out of the light, he banged open the bottom drawer angrily and fished out the water flask.

'Scotch is about finished,' he announced, picking it up and eyeing the dregs in the bottom critically. 'That one's only a few days old. Wonder what the parents would say this evening if they knew some of us drink like fishes. Cirrhosis is an *exceptionally* painful way to go, I'm told,' he snarled, planting the bottle in front of Alastair, who was sorting through a pile of test papers with Mohammed. His files were carefully stacked in small piles, side by side, so that there was no room to put anything more on the windowsill.

'And my specimens won't be much good if you keep putting them in the dark. How am I supposed to teach biology?'

'Badly, probably,' Alastair answered with casual cruelty. 'Like these asses have organized the National Curriculum tests. What do they think we're running? A twenty-four-hours-a-day factory?'

He pushed the bottle out of his way and went on stacking bits of paper, unmoved. Garlick gave up.

On the way back to put the carafe in the hall, his habitual resentment burned unusually and painfully brightly because, with his amused remark about the Gestapo, Alastair had stumbled unwittingly into Garlick's best, most personal and most cherished daydream.

Playing Nazis; it was his way of passing time. It whiled away endless hours of assemblies and parents' evenings. Six feet tall, aquiline features sharp and incisive below jet-black hair (blond and baby-faced would have been a *complete* cliché) he dreamed that he was irresistible. In black leather riding boots, long leather greatcoat, gold death's-heads upon its shoulders, he goose-stepped down long hours of boredom and frustration. The details didn't vary very much.

The torture chamber was a favourite for parents' evenings. He trained his spotlights on the sparse and cringing little groups of stubborn parents who came to sit before him. Except for the rare bright spark, who would pass like a shooting star through Garlick's little firmament and fizzle off to university, his pupils were mostly what Hugo delicately described as *non-academic material.*

'Thick as two short planks,' he snorted, hurrying down towards the hall.

But *non-academic material* was a phrase that came in handy at parents' evenings, which came round with terrible regularity. He detested sitting, on display, in the hall, with its scuffed floor and torn curtains, almost colourless after nearly twenty years of dirt, neglect and sun. Smeary windows looked out over the car park at the back.

They sat in lines, attendance registers and mark books in front of them. The attendance registers were records of truanting, the mark books full of gaps. Hugo was trying to seduce parents into school, didn't want to confront and alienate them with their children's bad behaviour, and had forbidden the use of the word *truant*.

'All criticism is to be constructive,' he bellowed at a staff meeting, confronted by a row of mutinous faces. 'And you can take that look off your faces.'

'What are we supposed to say?' Garlick had demanded. 'Did you hear about the woman who has been ordered to get her daughter into school, or it's off to prison or a thousand-pound fine? *That's* more like it.'

'I don't agree. Ask them what they think would improve their son's or daughter's erratic attendance,' Hugo told him. 'Ask them what we could do better.'

'You don't mean that,' Mohammed cried, scandalized and incredulous. 'Can you imagine some of the suggestions they'll make. What is this? Torment-a-teacher year? This your idea of a joke?'

'No. I want the parents to think we are on *their* side. Then they'll do the pressurizing, not us. Psychology.'

'Would that were true,' muttered Mohammed, shocked.

Hugo's face had been perfectly straight. He meant it. The result was, everyone's style was cramped. As the Stud remarked later, one could no longer call a spade a shovel, and what on earth was the bloody point.

'We are trying to *understand* them,' Garlick told him sarcastically. 'Forget about teaching.'

The drill at parents' evenings was invariably the same.

And how is little Johnny doing in biology, Mr Garlick?

Little Johnny is doing splendidly.

Garlick shuffled his mark book, lied his head off and went

mentally AWOL. They came to school for good news and generally didn't take agreeably to bad. Fathers who had been known to break other people's legs for less sat breathing beer and fags all over him, flanked by large, demanding wives with tree-trunk thighs. If the news was bad, it was Garlick's fault. If the news was good, it was their fault. Parents frightened Garlick, who was a very fine scientist with very short legs, thinning hair and a first-class degree from London University in the days when only real universities gave degrees.

Garlick slid into teaching because there was nothing else to do. He meant to do pure research and spend his life in a laboratory. Research money was nonexistent, jobs of any kind hard to come by, living on the dole humiliating and nasty, the world an unfair, unfriendly place.

'Be *positive* when you are dealing with parents,' Hugo demanded.

'Whatever happened to truth?' Garlick snarled, but he was scared of Hugo, too, so he snarled under his breath and kept the truth to himself.

Little Johnny is a lout with zits and a personal odour problem. When he chooses to grace my classroom with his presence, which is not often, he openly enjoys cutting up dead frogs in a way that suggests he is psychopathic and ought to see a psychiatrist. He spent my two-hour video lesson on human reproduction and AIDS (that I spent ages preparing) sniggering and upsetting the girls with offensive comments.

Mustn't whine, Garlick told himself sternly, rounding the last corner on his way to the hall, but his imagination raced on.

You try facing a mixed-sex class of fourteen-year-olds and showing them how to put a condom on an oversized courgette. Little Johnny entertained us all by putting a condom over his head and blowing it up.

He mentally added the *coup de grâce.*

Everyone knows his mother's been on the game for years. He probably knows more about condoms than is legal at not quite fourteen. He ended up looking like Mr Spock in a space helmet. Little Johnny is a loser and ain't goin' nowhere except maybe down the Scrubs, or Brixton.

Hah. Non-academic material indeed. A peculiar smile passed across Garlick's lips. A good session with the Nazi fantasy did wonders. Water torture was fun, spraying water cannon of the sort they used on the students in Paris when they rioted in sixty-eight. Or the leaking tap treatment. Drip, drip, drip, so soft and insistent, so *very* soft, until the victim screamed and screamed and screamed for it to stop. The Gestapo liked drowning prisoners in iced-water tubs, until the last moment, when they forced them up, gasping, blue, struggling for air, to live to have their kneecaps broken and their nails pulled out.

At the very long meetings boredom would force him to imagine more arcane practices. Electrodes, pincers and mincers, turning up the current on parental testicles that had produced the little monsters who inhabited his biology lab, year in, year out. After a while, the excitement wore off and in the end it wearied him.

'I am in fact kind to dogs and mice and little old ladies, and I give up my seat in the Tube to pregnant women,' he mumbled, after one particularly trying parents' evening. The hall was nearly empty, the clock over the swing doors said a quarter to eleven. Parents' evenings were supposed to finish at ten, and for once he sympathized with Stuttering Stan, glowering from behind them, waiting to lock up, while Hugo jawed endlessly with the last stragglers. 'It's just that I am *extremely* fed up with all of this.'

Chapter Eight

Angelina Tutti Frutti didn't like Garlick. She thought him peculiar and superior, didn't appreciate his manner.

'That one's a bit funny in the head, if you ask me,' she told Hugo bluntly, in the course of a chat in the playground.

'Do I employ you?' he asked cautiously, surprised to find her there, carting a bucket around, about to empty it down an outside drain.

'It's a job share,' she said with her most winsome smile.

Hugo waited patiently. The winsome smile faded, replaced by a shifty grin.

'You employ my sister, Mr Benedict.'

'That's what I thought.'

'They stopped my social by mistake. While they're sorting their mess out, what do they think I live on? We go halves.'

'I imagine they think you might be living on your income from your market stall?' he suggested mildly.

She leaned on her mop, sopping in her bucket after finishing spreading dirt more evenly over the main corridor. It stank of disinfectant.

'Recession's hit the sweets trade,' she said blandly. Her big Irish eyes widened, innocent as an angel. 'Parents out of work, kids got no pocket money. I only keep the stall to keep my licence. I trade at a loss, Mr Benedict. I got the books to prove it.'

'Is that a fact?' he said drily. 'But if you want to go on cleaning in my school, you will kindly consult me about it another time. And would you go easy on the chemicals. I can hardly breathe in the entrance hall.'

'Well, now. Talking of chemicals,' Angelina retorted, unmoved, 'I asked Mr Garlick to leave his room tidy, so that I could clean. He doesn't listen, Mr Benedict, so I can't get in there. I found locusts in there the other day, all left out on the bench. You can't expect me to clean up around a pile of dead insects.'

'I wasn't aware I was expecting you to do anything,' Hugo snapped. 'You don't work here. That's what I'm objecting to.'

'And what's that stuff that pongs that he keeps things in?' she went on, disregarding him. 'He'd spilled it and it didn't half smell horrible. It could get very nasty if someone hurts themselves with bugs and chemicals, couldn't it, Mr Benedict? I'm only thinking about your insurance and what they'd say about negligence.'

'Formaldehyde, probably,' Hugo said irritably. 'All right. You win. I'll have a word with Mr Garlick.'

Out of the corner of his eye, he watched Melanie Tilford come round the corner with one of the first years and turn into the main entrance, pulling faces at the cloud of bleach that billowed out to meet them. They were chatting animatedly.

'She's doing a lot better than I expected. There's been no riots in her classroom,' he had remarked to Alastair that morning. 'She seems able to control the kids.'

'With that lot? It's a matter of time. Her moment will come,' Alastair said spitefully, with a small grin.

Cynicism depressed Hugo. With half an ear, he waited for Angelina to stop carrying on.

'It's not just that he's untidy. He's excitable,' she was saying. 'I'm standing there, trying to reason with him, and he looks like he isn't exactly with me. He gets a very strange look in his eye, Mr Benedict, like he was watching a film inside his own head.'

'Uh huh?'

Impressed by her turn of phrase, and the fact that he had thought much the same thing himself on occasion, Hugo put on a noncommittal, headmasterly expression and escaped without answering, not to be drawn on the peculiarities of his teaching staff, least of all by Angelina. Disappointed at his lack of response, the epicentre of the local gossip network dragged her bucket back towards the front corridor, and maliciously decided to give his study a good going over with disinfectant.

In the hall, Garlick planted the full carafe of water on the table by Hugo's lectern, where the chairman of governors could reach it.

'I've popped a spot of strychnine in it,' he told the empty chair. 'Cheers.'

Garlick disliked David Absalom intensely. The chairman of governors was Jewish, had lived all his life in the East End. He ran a tat and shiny rubbish wholesale shop down the Commercial Road, and called it costume jewellery. He knew about money, local politics, and graft. Having barely been to school himself, he believed in education with the fervent passion of a convert, and was a committed and devoted governor of the worst school in London.

'Wily, devious, streetwise and a crook,' Garlick muttered.

He hated Absalom because he was jealous. The businessman was all these things, and successful. He had a big house in Islington, a flashy boat in the South of France, and a *pile* of money.

'And looks like a cockroach,' Garlick added, visualizing the spare little man with his round pot belly. 'It's the whiskers and the shiny brown head and the shiny brown suits. I wonder if he knows that the biggest cockroaches in the world live in Bermuda. Roaches like damp, hot climates and wooden floors to scuttle around and breed in. Bermuda's perfect. You should go there,' he told the chair viciously. 'It would suit you.'

As well as being whiskery, brown and shiny, Absalom was short, had small, very shiny black eyes and a monstrous nose that dwarfed the face it grew on, like a carbuncle.

'Or Tel Aviv. Saddam Hussein might start up again and

chuck a Scud at you. Not that the old guy's aim was ever very good.'

Garlick sighed. If they opted out, Hugo and Absalom would be the Saddam Husseins of East Hackney.

'The world is run by dictators,' he muttered sadly.

Once they opted out, Absalom, Hugo and Alastair would be responsible to no one except each other and the other governors. It gave them mind-boggling power over everything and everyone to do with the school, including him. It was not a thought he relished.

Chapter Nine

'Sieg heil, mein Führer,' he mumbled half-heartedly, turning to go.

For once, the game failed to amuse him. Saddam and the Gulf War had not been in the least bit funny, what he had done to the Kurds abominable. Annoyed that the thought of Absalom could even spoil his sense of humour, Garlick snapped rigidly to attention, punched a sarcastic salute and stood like a small, portly ramrod, his clenched fist in the air.

'Heil Hitler.'

'What *are* you doing, Mr Garlick?'

'What? Who said that?' Garlick yelped, spinning round guiltily, astounded. Motormouth. The hall had been empty. He'd let himself wander, his mouth go off of its own accord. There was a girl he didn't recognize standing at the back of the hall, gazing up at him.

'What do you want?' he snapped, putting his arm down.

'Why were you doing that?' she said, imitating his salute. 'To a chair with no one sitting in it, Mr Garlick?'

Two very direct hazel eyes waited for an answer.

'Nothing,' he bleated, like a sleepwalker just woken up to find himself about to fall off the edge of a cliff. 'Nothing. I wasn't doing anything. Why haven't you gone home?'

'You weren't doing nothing, you were doing a Nazi salute. Mr Benedict is going to sit in that chair this evening.'

'Aaaah,' Garlick gurgled, trying to think of something to say that would make her go away.

'My dad says most headmasters are little Hitlers,' she went on comfortingly. 'He says that's why they do the job.

They like power. I don't suppose Mr Benedict's like that.'

'Don't you?'

She shook her head.

'Oh.'

Her catching him out in his secret, stupid, embarrassing game, standing there with those big knowing eyes, laughing *with* him, made his knees wobble.

'Uh,' he spluttered, sitting down abruptly on Absalom's chair.

She knew *exactly* what he was up to, and it amused her. He couldn't look at her, it was such an intimate feeling.

'I . . .' he began diffidently, wanting to talk to her.

Stan banged in through the swing doors behind the girl, and broke the magic. He was oozing self-importance.

'I t-t-t-t-t-t,' he announced. 'I t-t-t-t-t-t . . .'

'Damn,' said Garlick.

Stan worked his false teeth frenziedly, producing a small shower of saliva.

'Spit it out, old son,' Garlick said savagely, his dream shattered.

Stan twisted his fleshy, round face into a scarlet gargoyle of effort, clasped his hands fervently, as if in prayer, closed his eyes in concentration, and spat.

'I t-t-t-t-t-told the headm-m-m-m-m-master I have to l-l-l-l-l-l . . .'

'Lock up?'

'Yes,' said Stan with his eyes still shut.

'By ten?'

It was always ten. Caretaker Mafia rules. Out by ten. Insurance. To negotiate was impossible. Stuttering Stan ruled with a rod of iron, his authority unchallengeable and unshakeable, for in his fifteen years caretaking East Stepney, he had always been completely incoherent.

'Yes.'

'Then why do you bloody well have to announce it every time, as though there's something to discuss?' Garlick demanded.

Stan scowled, squeezed his eyes tighter than ever, took a mighty breath and bawled.

'AndnowI'mt-t-t-t-tellin'youtheyalltobeoutbythen.'

'I doubt it'll go on that long,' Garlick snapped. 'And if it does, you can go and argue the toss with Mr Benedict, not me.'

Stan scowled, wiped his mouth with the back of his hand, walked backwards into the swing doors and banged out again.

The girl was still there.

'Why does he always do that?' he asked plaintively. 'Always bangs and clatters and spits, making the same old points. Who does he think cares?'

'He knows no one cares, that's why,' she said. 'He's sad.'

'Well, now, I know just how he feels,' he said waspishly.

'Poor Mr Garlick,' she said. 'Do you really?'

Riveted helplessly to Absalom's chair, his knees trembled.

Oh, oh. Here we go again, the back of his mind warned. Don't do this. Sixteen. Girl. Pupil. Taboo. Don't be a jerk, Amadeus.

He opened his mouth to tell her to go away, and shut it again. It happened every year. Crushes. Agony. Unrequited, ludicrous, guilty crushes. Pupils were out of bounds, a hanging offence. Every time he got over it, he swore *never again*.

'Oh, *lord*,' he groaned. 'I can't believe it.'

'Mr Garlick?'

In the fusty school hall, across rows of chairs waiting for a meeting he considered doomed before it started, the ticking of the clock above the swing doors audible in the sudden silence, the school nearly empty, against all his better judgement, Garlick fell helplessly in love.

Pure St Trinian's, he thought. That's her. Pure ass. That's me. Self-assurance, self-possession, pert self-confidence of the teenage sort devastated him. A lot of the girls were prettier than her. A narrow face, small, full mouth and big, curved nose gave her a haughty, horsy air, with something familiar about her that he couldn't quite place.

Like everyone else, she had the St Trinian look. Long, gawky legs, skinny ankles and sharp knees in black stockings, scuffed black platform lace-ups, with a navy blue lycra microskirt from Marks and Spencer moulded to her bottom under a man's extra-large green pullover. It was a travesty of school uniform that made Hugo rant and rave and send notes home to parents who couldn't care less.

'Your hair is vintage Gerald Scarfe,' he blurted.

It was the hair that made her stand out. Thick, glossy, uncontrollable ringlets waved around her head like a sunburst, almost to her waist, shining reddish gold.

She shrugged.

'It's hell to comb,' she said coolly.

'Do I teach you?' he asked, getting off his chair and advancing to the front of the stage.

She grinned. He knew, she knew. He knew he didn't. She was *extremely* noticeable, and if he hadn't noticed her, she wasn't one of his pupils.

'I don't do biology,' she said.

'What's your name?'

'Alice Tilford.'

Melanie Tilford's daughter. It was the English county lady look that was familiar. Garlick liked Melanie, not least because Alastair teased her, too. It was nice to have a fellow victim.

'Your mother teaches here. She sends you here, too? Good grief.'

He came down the steps. She was taller than him, like her mother. No doubt her father was tall, too. Garlick, having a sister of five foot ten, and a brother over six feet, had stopped growing at just over five foot six. Six inches more leg would have changed his life. He considered the whole business of genes and inheritance *bitterly* unfair.

'My *dad* sends me here,' she said scornfully, understanding exactly that he thought her mother crazy. 'My dad thinks it's cool we're at the school my mother teaches at. He's a priest, and he's got principles. This is a dump, but *he* wouldn't know. My brother wants to walk back to Norfolk, like a cat, only he's too lazy.'

'Teenagers can be the kindest of creatures, except when it comes to parents. If your parents had wings, I bet you'd pull them off with horribly detached clinical interest, to see if it hurt. Like flies.'

'You say very peculiar things,' she answered. 'Dad's coming to this meeting, so he'll see for himself.'

'I was putting the finishing touches to that,' he said nonchalantly. 'We can't have Mr Benedict and Mr Absalom and Mr Croke with dry throats. They enjoy the sound of their own voices *much* too much.'

'Sure.'

He put on his most forbidding expression, as though the moment they shared had never happened, walked past her, and marched off.

Chapter Ten

'I just bumped into your daughter.'

He found Melanie in the near-empty staff room, sitting at the end of the refectory table, racing through a pile of marking. Alastair was bent over his windowsill, with his back to the room, absorbed in his files.

'I hope she wasn't doing anything she shouldn't. Kettle just boiled,' she said, glancing up.

'There's one tea bag left,' he said, looking in the Earl Grey box. The last person to empty the tea bags was supposed to buy the next one, out of the kitty. Garlick put the bag back. He couldn't be bothered going round, trying to get money out of them.

'There's some disgusting first-year cookery disasters as well,' she added, throwing an essay half obliterated with red pen on to a pile. 'With *eat me* on them. Very appropriate. Eat those and you'll start shrinking. The Queen of Hearts left them.'

Bunny had whirled through the staff room earlier and left a tray of rock cakes by the kettle, with a scribbled note, saying *Ex first-year cookery – please eat*. They were greyish, full of little burned black lumps.

'Dead fly cemetery. Blue Circle cement,' remarked Garlick, helping himself. He took a big mouthful, spat it straight out into his hand. 'Good grief.'

'I warned you.'

He put the cake back on the tray.

'No wonder she hasn't let them take them home. I didn't realize you had a child in school.'

'Alice is doing GCSEs. Tom's got A levels this year. Lots of fun. Hysteria and nervous breakdowns twice over. Aren't we lucky?'

'What on earth made you bring them here?' he demanded inquisitively.

She planted her elbows either side of her pile of papers, fed up with criticism.

'What makes you think I had a choice? My husband works for the church, who closed him down. They offered him the job across the way at All Hallows. It was come here, or be out of work. I can't teach in one school and send my children somewhere else. So we just have to make the best of it.'

'You practise what you preach,' he remarked.

'I leave preaching to my husband,' she snapped. 'It's what he's good at.'

'What are you grinning at?' Alastair demanded five minutes later, turning round from his windowsill, catching sight of the Stud's smirking face coming round the staff room door, closely followed by Mohammed. The lithe and elegant Asian minced in with his nose in the air, above an armful of dirty kit.

'Me? Won on the four o'clock at Newbury,' the Stud said obligingly, throwing Garlick's rejected tea bag into an unwashed mug and chucking the box into the bin. 'Eight to one. Not a bad afternoon's work.'

The Stud was a slob, didn't care about staff-room protocol, and wouldn't bother buying tea bags. Garlick sighed. He'd end up doing it, when he'd forgone his cup of tea so that he *wouldn't* have to do it, and when for the life of him he could not imagine that *his* afternoon's work had been to any purpose, or that his carefully arranged chairs would be filled that evening at eight o'clock. The Führer could plot and plan as much as he liked but it wouldn't work.

'And *we* won seven–two against St Joseph's.'

Mohammed chucked his pile of kit carelessly on the floor where it would get in everyone's way.

'Put your knickers away, for God's sake,' snapped Garlick.

Mohammed grinned and left a Calvin Klein jockstrap straddling the top of the heap. The whole pile stank of Calvin Klein aftershave. He opened the top drawer of the filing cabinet, took out a mirror, leaned it against one of Garlick's bean jars, long since dead, threw back a fringe of blue-black hair and began examining his eyebrows minutely with a pair of tweezers.

'*Must* you?' complained Alastair, kicking the heap under the table where no one would trip over it.

'Yes,' said Mohammed.

'Be thankful for small mercies. He doesn't do his bikini line in public,' muttered Garlick, leaning towards Melanie. 'You know something, he shaves all over. Last Christmas we gave him a thigh and chest wax. He was delirious with pleasure. If you ask him nicely, he'll show you his G-string and thigh leather boots. Four-inch heels. And he's got a dinky line in handcuffs. Suede-lined, luvvie. He'll probably show you whether you ask or not, come to that.'

'Doesn't he *itch*?' asked Melanie, practical.

'*Do* you itch?' Garlick demanded.

'I shave because I model,' Mohammed said, wielding the tweezers expertly. His coffee-coloured face was smooth and finely boned as a girl's, doe-eyed, lashes so long and dark he could have been wearing kohl, but wasn't.

'He ain't saying,' said Garlick darkly. 'Read into that what you will.'

'You look a bit like Michael Jackson, only more beautiful,' Melanie said. 'Since he had his face rearranged.'

'Any objections to that?' enquired Mohammed, unruffled.

'I read he can't go out in the sun, or his face starts to fall off,' Melanie answered.

Mohammed worked his gorgeous face into a grimace by way of answer.

'The parents would string you up,' threatened Alastair, 'if ever they recognized the berk on the telly in a choker and high heels and not a lot else. It only takes one dad around here to put two and two together, and you're for it. They may thieve and fight, but about that kind of thing they're puritanical as hell. You're asking for trouble.'

'What do you mean? Of course he's asking for trouble. He'd *adore* being strung up,' retorted Garlick.

'I did a video,' Mohammed said proudly, turning round and waving the tweezers at them. 'With The Grateful Dead. And Jules once asked me how I did my make-up. We're thinking of doing something in dog collars, based on Peter Ball.'

He wiggled his hips, flicked his hair, executed several dance steps and stood rock still, lost in self-admiration.

'Julian Clary,' murmured Garlick. 'Yeeeeeuck. Who is Peter Ball?'

'The Bishop of Gloucester,' Melanie explained. 'He resigned.'

'Why?' asked Alastair.

'Don't you read the papers?' demanded Garlick. 'He admitted to gross indecency with a seventeen-year-old monk. Just think.'

'Something in habits?' suggested Mohammed, flicking his hips sideways and clattering his heels on the floor. 'A tap dance, d'you think?'

'You should know about habits. Narcissism and bondage,' snorted Alastair. He turned to Melanie.

'There's a pervert in every staff room. In ours, it's our fine team-sport teacher, would you believe. Cricket is a chance to pad himself out, and rugger a nice big feelie grope. God help him if County Hall ever finds out what kind of team sports he's really into.'

She started to laugh, bit her lip, went bright pink and concentrated hard on her own pile of National Curriculum work.

Alastair stared at her downcast face. At that angle, and with that flush in her cheeks, she was more than just pretty. Mohammed put his mirror back in the filing cabinet and grinned.

'I don't play rugger, sweetie. It would spoil me. You're right about the *delicious* gropes, but some things one has to sacrifice. And as for County Hall, we're opting out, so it can go put its hand up its own backside,' he said cheerfully, grubbed underneath the table for his kit and sauntered out, trailing fumes of Calvin Klein's Obsession.

'I wouldn't be so sure about that,' said Alastair, to his departing, exaggeratedly mincing back. 'And you'll catch a fly.'

Melanie, who had her mouth open in sheer amazement, shut it hastily and went brighter red than ever.

'What *do* you reckon is going to happen this evening?' Garlick asked.

'Not a lot. To run a successful opt-out, you need nice, middle-class families who believe in education, or people Hugo can bully,' Alastair answered. 'Just look at what we've got.'

'Half the get-the-Kray-twins-out-of-prison-and-Broadmoor brigade,' Garlick said bitterly. 'What a load of nerds. Half the rest are black or brown and don't speak English and won't know what opting out even means. To think that all I ever asked for was a nice quiet life and a job in a decent lab.'

He sounded so wistful, Melanie looked up, sorry for him.

'What's that? Putting fags in beagles' mouths,' suggested Alastair cruelly. 'And calling it research.'

'Cellular biology,' yelled Garlick, slamming his fist down, making Melanie's papers jump, slide and scatter. 'I'm a cellular biologist, a *scientist*, not a fucking beauty therapist. And sometimes animals are necessary, whether you like it or not.'

'Now look what you've done,' she shouted, grabbing her marking back. 'Those are very racist remarks, and what do you mean, beagles? You've never made animals smoke in a lab, have you?'

'Until Animal Rights got going,' Alastair murmured, just loud enough for her to overhear. 'Then he got scared.'

'Did you?' she asked.

'I once applied for a job,' Garlick said defensively. 'I didn't get it and I didn't really want it. It was a way of trying to get into research.'

Alastair snorted.

'Stop it. He's nearly crying,' Melanie hissed. 'We used to hunt in Norfolk and the anti-blood-sports people used to follow and be a nuisance. People are entitled to their opinions, and you shouldn't try and impose yours.'

'You *approve* of vivisection?' Alastair demanded, rounding on her, changing the subject to suit himself, only nobody noticed.

'*No.*'

Stud McTavish wandered over to the window, which looked out over the graveyard opposite. The sky was overcast and dull, and the light was on in the church porch. Figures seemed to move in it, but he couldn't be sure; it could have been illusions from the wind in the old yews. He blew on his tea, slopped Earl Grey down his cardigan, calculated his winnings again, thought once more about the fortune he could have made in Hong Kong's Sha Tin and Happy Valley, if only he'd gone before it was too late. The others were shouting at each other about animal rights and the pros and cons of bombing scientists and their laboratories. Stud sighed, mentally started to plan the next week's lessons on Jane Austen and stayed well out of the ensuing row.

Chapter Eleven

'What's the matter with you lot?'

Bunny hurtled through the staff-room door and came upon Garlick and Alastair shouting abuse at each other, waving their fists in excitement.

'They're about to hit each other,' cried Melanie. 'Make them stop.'

'Please, I am trying to work,' added the Stud, his fingers pointedly in his ears. He looked up, raised his voice. 'Lend Bunny a hand, you prats.'

Bunny filled the staff room with a faint cloud of subtle, expensive perfume. Alastair sniffed, dropped his fists and turned round. She carried several Sainsbury's carrier bags in her hands and a large paper bag in her teeth. Alastair abandoned the enjoyment of tormenting Garlick about the rights of foxes and took it from her mouth gently.

'I didn't realize they paid Hugo so badly,' he said kindly. 'They ate cardboard during the war, but there's surely no need to eat this kind of thing now.'

'What's in there are soggy tissues,' Bunny answered. 'Very soggy, very disgusting. I couldn't leave them for the cleaner. Put them in the bin, will you, Alastair, there's a dear.'

'Amy,' he called, tossing the paper bag to Garlick. 'You're by the bin.'

Garlick caught it by reflex and threw it into the bin underneath the kettle.

'My name is *Amadeus*,' he snarled.

Melanie's eyes widened. Seeing her put her hand to her

mouth, to pretend she wasn't laughing, Garlick kicked the bin and tipped it over, writhing inwardly. This was Alice's mother. He made a great effort.

'My parents enjoyed Mozart,' he said stiffly. 'I can't help it if they gave me a ridiculous name.'

Melanie spluttered.

'Amadeus. *Amy*. Are you musical?'

'Now look what you've done,' Garlick snarled at Bunny. 'If it weren't for Hugo's ridiculous meetings, I could go home, and I wouldn't have to put up with this.'

'You have nothing to put up with,' Bunny snapped. 'You should see what I have to put up with. I just had a whole classroom crying.'

'What's so bad that they've been crying?' Alastair asked, sounding anxious.

'We've *all* been crying,' Bunny told him, dumping her carrier bags in a corner where dust eddied in little drifts, untouched by Angelina's sister. 'That's for a microwave demonstration to parents tomorrow. I know down to the last tin of tuna and grain of rice what's in those bags, and heaven help anyone who steals anything. I will report them to my husband the headmaster.'

'Ooooh, *my husband the headmaster*. Go on, terrify us,' Alastair mocked, but he looked at her closely. 'And what have you all been crying about?'

'Life and death,' Bunny said abruptly, and was suddenly very busy looking through the contents of one of her bags. 'We just had a lesson on bereavement. It was meant to be fairy cakes. Third years. Bereavement overtook the fairy cakes, and it wasn't exactly easy.'

'Let us not be sexist about this,' Hugo had argued, when he decided that home economics up to the third year should be compulsory for boys and girls alike. 'Why shouldn't boys learn to make apple crumble and tuna bake? Or whatever?'

'Can *you* make apple crumble?' Bunny demanded.

'I had a sexist education,' he argued ingenuously.

'Hah. *Fairy cakes?*' she persisted. 'You want me to teach

that lot how to make fairy cakes?'

'Sponge.'

'Fairy. They are a standard part of the syllabus. Can you imagine the jokes? Are you hellbent on making my life a misery?'

'Fairy cakes are on the syllabus, and a syllabus is a syllabus. Argue with the National Curriculum if you must,' said Hugo, and refused to discuss the issue any further.

'Fairy cakes in period four got the usual tedious sniggering,' Bunny started to explain, when the Stud interrupted.

'I was reading an article about teaching English as a foreign language the other day, and the difficulties translators have with different cultures. You've reminded me of a choice bit about fairies.'

'You're a choice fairy yourself,' muttered Alastair. 'But go on.'

'It quoted the *Asian Times*. The Australian prime minister has been talking to the Japanese prime minister. The Nip was being obtuse, and the Aussie ran out of patience. He told him to stop playing silly buggers and get on with negotiating. The translator told the Japanese prime minister that the Australians were telling him to stop being a humorous homosexual, and to get on with his job. The paper suggested that it did not exactly enhance Aussie-Japanese relationships.'

The Stud was shaking his head and grinning, enjoying the joke.

'*Anyway,*' Bunny said. 'As I was saying. Period four. It was awful.'

Chapter Twelve

'Today we are going to make fairy cakes,' she announced in a freezing voice that suggested that dirty jokes about fairies, gays, poofs, queers and safety pins would lead to instant and prolonged detentions.

She glared at her class. Thirty thirteen-year-olds of assorted colours and sizes jostled and shoved around the scarred and beaten-up tables in the home-economics room, wrapped to their necks in pinafores. They scuffled and clattered, pulled up stools, ran out of steam and settled down. No one answered back and no one tittered.

'Good,' said Bunny. 'Now, watch me.'

It rained incessantly, running down the long half-open windows, making runnels in the dirt. It seemed to have rained forever, turning the ground to a quagmire, depressing all their spirits. But through the spatter of raindrops, as she weighed and mixed fat and sugar, measured flour and cracked eggs, writing quantities on the blackboard behind her as she went, she could hear nesting birds singing and squabbling in the bushes outside the windows. Spring was here, and Easter round the corner. The class relaxed and watched with interest, for once, looking forward to eating cake. Vanilla smelled strong and sweet, like talcum powder, as she added it to her mixture. It was an afternoon, she thought happily, spooning batter into cake cases, to make the daily struggle of teaching all worthwhile.

'You've all got your own ingredients measured out?' she asked, when she had finished and a rich smell of baking cakes began coming from the oven. 'Mine will be ready by the time you put yours in the oven, and we can eat them while we're waiting for yours to cook.'

Two hands went up.

'We forgot,' said Dora and Dorcas Murgatroyd in unison, from their place at the very back of the class.

The illusion of peace and harmony was shattered. She had not noticed that they were painting their nails and taking no notice. At least, for once, they had been doing it quietly.

'Was there ever a week when you remembered?' Bunny demanded, exasperated. 'And you can put that nail varnish away and pay attention. *Now*.'

She kept stores for when they forgot to bring their ingredients. The Murgatroyd twins forgot every week.

'Yes, miss.'

'Go and get your stuff out of the cupboard, and if you forget again, I'm going to give you a bill for your mother.'

Dora and Dorcas leaned nonchalantly against one of the ovens and regarded with satisfaction the fingernails they had been painting throughout Bunny's demonstration. They looked at Bunny with identical blue eyes, worked at chewing gum with identical pouting mouths and blew on deep orange nails with intense concentration.

'*Now*,' Bunny said through her teeth, hanging on to her temper. 'Flour and sugar in the larder, margarine and eggs in the fridge.'

'They'll chip,' Dorcas pointed out reasonably, holding her fingers out and admiring her handiwork. 'You have to leave twenty minutes for them to dry.'

Bunny took a deep breath and pointed her wooden spoon at them.

'Cut out the nonsense and get on with the lesson like everyone else.'

The twins looked bored and blew on their talons some more. The burnished varnish matched the rest of them, went with their pale skin with orange freckles and hair the colour of rust. They wore identically stained crumpled school blouses that had been in the wash with something orange that had run. They needed, Bunny thought, to start wearing bras. Someone ought to speak to the mother. Again.

'You have some of the worst manners I have ever seen,' she added, going round the back of a couple of ageing, wheezing refrigerators to snatch their nail varnish away. 'And I'm confiscating that.'

'Why?' asked Dorcas sullenly.

'Because you are insolent and stupid and you are too old to think it doesn't matter that you are being rude and throwing your education away. You are too old not to care,' Bunny said furiously. '*I* care.'

The twins rolled their blue eyes, checked that their polish was dry, then began sucking their thumbs indifferently. The class put down its wooden spoons, left its cake mixture curdling in its bowls and waited for the explosion. As Bunny drew breath to shout, the home-economics room door inched open. A lanky, shambling black boy with soaking hair, clutching a stained pinafore, slunk into the room and tried to hide at the back.

'Sorry, miss,' he mumbled, looking at the empty table in front of Dorcas and Dora, trying to find something to do, to look busy, anything that would help him fade into the woodwork and avoid being noticed. He began tying his apron around his waist.

'Nathan Smith, what *do* you think you're doing?'

Bunny let out the breath she had been holding in frustration, and pounced.

'*And* you've spoiled the cakes,' she yelped, stopping to draw breath on the subject of manners and lateness in class. Smoke trickled from her oven, filling the classroom with a choking smell of burning.

'*Miss,*' Dora and Dorcas chorused urgently.

Bunny banged open her oven door, took out trays of blackened cakes and threw the whole lot on the draining board, where it hissed and steamed and sizzled.

'Give me one good reason not to shout about *that*, Nathan

Smith,' she called, pointing at her ruined cooking. 'Sit down and keep quiet. It's too late to start now, and you missed the demo. Dora and Dorcas, get your ingredients *now* and the rest of you get on, or the bell will go and we'll have a roomful of uncooked cake mixture.'

She turned her back on the class and began scraping burned sponge out of the tins. Nathan crumpled into a chair and stared at the floor.

'*Miss*,' called the twins desperately.

Bunny turned round with a cake tray in her hands.

'*Now* what? I told you to get your ingredients out.'

'His brother,' said Dora.

'Died,' said Dorcas.

'Of Aids,' said Dora.

'He's late,' said Dorcas.

'Because his mum made him look after his sister,' said Dora.

'While she went down the hospital and fixed,' said Dorcas.

'His funeral,' said Dora, starting to cry. 'And you *shouted* at him.'

A gleaming teardrop of snot gathered on the end of Nathan's blunt nose. He wiped it with the back of his hand and went on staring at the floor.

'Oh, my God,' cried Bunny, aghast. She ran down the room and took him in her arms, cuddled him like a baby and ended up in tears herself.

'We all ended up crying,' she told the staff room later. 'The whole class. They were sweet, and they really cared. We spent an hour talking about dying and death and grieving and they all went and cuddled Nathan and told him they were sorry. I need a strong G and T,' Bunny cried.

'Tea and scotch?' offered Alastair.

'Yes. No. Scotch. Screw the tea,' she answered, drying her eyes.

Alastair fished the bottle out of the filing cabinet and rinsed a mug.

'Dora and Dorcas are in my tutor group,' said Melanie.

'They may be sweet to Nathan and good in a crisis, but the rest of the time they are impossible.'

'The two Ds are *another* awful story,' Bunny snuffled, coughing over her whisky. 'Have you heard it?'

'I know their mother comes in and shouts at me whenever she has an off day, which seems to be most of the time,' Melanie answered.

'Egyptian mummies,' said Alastair mysteriously, glad to have the atmosphere lightened. He went over to the far side of the room, opened the window by his files, and leaned on the sill. The roof of the bicycle sheds was covered in moss, and rain on it all day had brought out a rich, peaty smell. Puddles in the playground reflected a shiny grey evening sky, still full of rain. 'Oh, well. That's the problem with the two Ds,' he said enigmatically, his back to the room. 'They are the product of mummies of a very peculiar kind.'

'*What?*' Melanie demanded.

'Their mother is that big, blowsy-looking woman with big breasts, no bra and a lot of red hair in a plait,' explained Bunny. 'She flops from the waist up. Always shouting.'

'I know her. The twins don't wear bras either,' Melanie said. 'They chew gum, paint their nails, smoke and walk out of class when they feel like it. Last time she came in, I suggested the father should come in and have a chat.'

'No father,' Alastair guessed bitterly, talking to himself into the warm evening air. *My children have no father, because their mother wants me out of her life.*

'What happened to him?' asked Melanie.

'She told me the story one day,' Bunny went on. 'She decided at thirty-five years old that her biological clock was ticking away, and it was time to have a baby. So she went to the British Museum and looked at the mummies.'

'Looking at mummies gets you pregnant? Someone ought to tell Robert Winston and he could put it into his infertility programme,' remarked Garlick.

'She's got an anthropology degree, a flexitime job in a feminist bookshop in Islington, and a flat in the block just across from you, Melanie,' Bunny went on. 'She thought she was ready.'

'Ready for Tutankhamun,' muttered Alastair. 'Wow. I knew there was something funny about those girls. They were a perverted lot, those Egyptians. Into incest. Have you noticed the two Ds have very straight noses?'

'She said,' Bunny went on loudly, drowning him out, 'she wanted the right kind of father, and any man on his own looking at mummies on a Saturday afternoon in the British Museum was either a weirdo, or gay, or the right kind of chap. Educated. She wanted brains and good bone structure, so that she'd produce decent-looking, intelligent children. She picked one such up, and took him home. Bingo.'

'I must go to the British Museum,' Alastair said to himself. 'Women will take me home and ask me to go to bed with them. Thanks, Bunny.'

'If it's a question of bone structure,' said Garlick, '*you* can forget it. Judging by the two Ds, she picked the weirdo.'

'She never saw him again,' Bunny finished.

'So their father is a complete stranger,' said Melanie. 'That explains a lot.'

'I asked her if she thought the twins are happy about having a father from the Egyptian Room,' Bunny said. 'She gave me a very tired look and said she hadn't got the faintest idea what they were or weren't happy about. She said I should ask them myself.'

'And women say men use women,' Alastair remarked. 'Imagine.'

There was a reflective silence.

'I know those twins,' said Garlick, more kindly. 'They are not stupid, just beyond any reasonable person's control. The old girl went off to Greenham Common and lived in a tree and left them to fend for themselves when they were practically still babies. Social services shoved them into a foster home and she nearly never got them back. I don't think she would have, only who else would want them?'

'I could wring their necks,' Bunny said.

'Someone should,' Melanie said acidly. 'I have to give them social responsibility tutorials instead.'

They all laughed. Hugo made them take their tutor groups for an hour each week for meaningful discussions about life.

'We're supposed to teach them to be nice to little old ladies, only beat up people your own size, and have safe sex in the context of loving relationships,' Alastair jeered, waving a long finger in the air. 'What a joke. Our lot wouldn't recognize socially responsible behaviour if it jumped up and bit them. I have the answer, though.'

He waited.

'What?' Melanie asked obediently.

'Pindown,' he announced happily. 'Pindown strikes me as a bloody good idea. Nail the buggers' feet to the floor, lock the door and throw away the key. Very occasionally social workers do something sensible. It's funny, though – I can't make Hugo listen.'

'In my classroom those twins are about as constructive as a couple of Cruise missiles on the loose, with their guidance systems up the creek. Mum should have stayed at home,' Melanie said crossly. 'Home is what counts.'

'Are you a sociologist or something?' the Stud asked with interest, slurping lukewarm tea with the remains of the Scotch in it, setting Alastair's teeth horribly on edge. 'I admired the Greenham Common women.'

'If you were less of an old woman yourself,' Alastair muttered balefully, 'you'd be more tolerable.'

'I am not a sociologist. I just know that kids can't help the world they live in,' Melanie answered heatedly. 'They didn't make it. They didn't go to the British Museum and pick up a father.'

Alastair glanced over his shoulder at her with interest. She was learning to stick up for herself quite well.

'I've got a worse story than that,' Garlick began, stopping her from going on. 'We were doing worms a while back, talking about hermaphroditic reproduction. One way or another, we drifted on to homosexuality and someone started on about how his mum only fancied other women.'

'Her *son* did?' Melanie demanded, starting to pack up her work. 'How, then, did she . . . ?'

He crooked a finger at her.

'Precisely. Artificial insemination. She'd read that the sperm in the sperm bank gets donated by medical students. She, I recall from parents' evenings, is small and blonde and pretty. So she reckoned the result would be a small, blonde, pretty, *brainy* female offspring.' He chuckled, lay back in his armchair and perched his short legs on the end of the table. 'Look what she ended up with. Our lovely Lesley. She had him in frocks and long hair until he was five and had to go to school. Even the poor kid's name is ambiguous.'

'Big Les is a large disappointment all round,' said Alastair, who had tried and failed to teach him and had heard the story before, from Hugo.

'A brainless giant,' Garlick cackled, thumping the table with his feet in mirth. 'Can you imagine it? Looking at our Les, the odds are his dad was a black American footballer. Just think, knowing that possibly the only reason you exist is because someone ran out of money in London and sold the only thing he had, which wasn't between his ears. It could drive you mad.'

'That isn't nice,' Melanie snapped, then tried and failed to suppress a grin. 'We ought to get him and the two Ds together. Think how much they've got in common.'

'Who said people are nice?' Garlick agreed gloomily. 'She felt short-changed. Never stopped complaining he wasn't a girl. Then she wonders why he's got a chip on his shoulder bigger than his dad's shoulder pads, and an arsenal in his back pocket.'

'He hasn't been in school since half term,' Bunny said sadly, finishing her drink. 'From what I hear – and this is strictly unconfirmed rumour – we have ourselves our first crack addict.'

'We *are* moving with the times,' said Garlick savagely. 'Our local social historian here can put that horrible fact in his files, and my beans back where they belong.'

'I hope that story isn't true,' Alastair said. 'I do not want to start putting crack stories in my archives, nor your fucking beans anywhere at all. When are you going to understand that I don't give a toss about your greenery?'

'Why,' Garlick asked plaintively, 'when I am a pleasant and reasonable man, do I always come off worst?'

Melanie sat with her chin in her fists, gazing out of the staff-room window at her husband's church opposite. She tried to imagine what made people do things like that, tried to put herself in the angry red-haired woman's place, wondered why she was so angry, with her two children, her anthropology degree, her flexitime job and her well-barricaded council flat.

'Fancy having children with a complete stranger,' she said, coming over to lean on the windowsill next to Alastair.

'Lots of people have children with complete strangers. It's called marriage,' he answered sourly.

'That is the most cynical thing I ever heard,' she snapped.

'True, though,' he said softly. 'Isn't it?'

Melanie stared at All Hallows, its tower casting a deep shadow over the grass in the park, and couldn't say a word.

'You know something,' Alastair remarked to the Stud in an undertone, when she'd gone home. 'When she forgets she's a vicar's wife and acts natural, Mrs T. is one hell of an attractive woman.'

Chapter Thirteen

'You are *going* to let us do them, so give over, you old bag.'

The words came, carried on the wind as drizzle turned to rain. Melanie hurried across the park under streetlamps beginning to flicker on. Inside Giles's church porch, away to her right, the light she had seen earlier from the staff room window was burning more brightly as early evening turned to darkness. Stained-glass windows glowed very dimly, lights left on inside somewhere, the red lamp by the sacristy gleaming dully. There were shadows on the porch wall, dancing to the sounds of a struggle within.

She stepped into the shadow of the yews, out of reach of the streetlamps. As she drew nearer, the dancing shapes on the walls became part of a whispered, muted commotion. Dorcas Murgatroyd's voice came clearly.

'You're *goin'* to get them done, so give over a minute and help me, instead of making all your fuss.'

'An' you can fuck orf,' a gravelly voice snarled back.

Brief heavy breathing and the sound of silent tussle ended in a thump, a sharp bark of protest and a yelp of fury. Melanie crept up the grassy edge of the path, and peered inside.

A Tesco trolley, piled high with all her worldly possessions in an assortment of carrier bags and bin bags, and a small yellow dog in the baby seat, was pushed into the far corner of the porch, while its owner kicked and yelled and swore like a docker. The mangy little yellow dog barked shrilly and tried to hide under a bedroll tied up with a bit of string.

'You are *goin'* to let us do it,' Dorcas repeated, bending

over the elderly bag lady and recoiling. 'Fuck, Angie, you don't half *stink.*'

'Fuck *off,*' panted the bag lady furiously, upended on the porch floor like a beetle on its back, the spitting image of Grandma, out of a Giles cartoon. Round as a barrel, hair like a chimney sweep's brush, small black eyes screwed up with rage, she was wriggling helplessly inside a dozen layers of unwashed garments, colourful as Joseph's dreamcoat and ripe as a well-hung grouse.

'One each,' Dora said, grabbing one of the waving feet. 'Heave.'

The twins yanked one foot each into the air and dragged off Angie's once stout, broken Oxfam Reeboks. Two feet pounded the air in outrage, their toes bent and gnarled and crooked as roots. They were bound and bandaged, padded out with corn plasters, bloody in places.

'*Pooh,*' chorused the twins.

Angie lay on her back with her legs in the air, glaring.

'They bin givin' me 'ell,' she snapped.

'That's your fault,' snapped Dorcas.

'Stuff from the doctor's in the trolley. Go on, get on with it,' she growled, wheezing. 'I 'aven't got all night. The 'ostel's open and the best beds'll be gorn.'

'If you'd wait in casualty, you could get it done properly,' said Dora, rooting among the carrier bags, setting a plastic bottle of extra-strong cider to one side while she hunted for the package from the chemist.

'An' wait all night for them to be rude to you?' Grandma retorted. 'They know me. I just get a prescription out of the pharmacy and run. They know I'll discharge meself.'

Dora found the medication as her sister began peeling off old bandages.

'It's getting a bit better,' she said, tugging the last layers off.

Angie yelped and squawked and swore in pain.

'What on *earth* do you think you're doing?'

Melanie interrupted the cabalistic scene, marching into

her husband's church for the first time in weeks.

"Oo's she?' Grandma demanded, freezing, all fours in the air, peering venomously out of her wrappings.

Rain dripped down the porch doorway in the sudden silence. A witches' coven, Melanie thought. They could be something out of the Middle Ages, including the awful smell.

'Well?' she said, when no one spoke.

'That's Miss Tilford from school,' Dorcas told Grandma, her rust-coloured hair darkened to copper by the dim light. 'Hold *still*.'

'We do her corns and her bunions and her horrible old toenails for her, because she won't stay and see the doctor or the chiropodist. They give her the stuff down the hospital, and we do it for her. The nurse showed us how. Said it was better than nothing. She *hates* doctors,' Dora explained.

Grandma, resentful at the interruption and not being the centre of attention, mumbled, sucked her teeth and jerked her legs, threatening to roll over and get up. The twins grabbed a foot each and waited politely for Melanie to go away. Outside the rain poured down, the wind picked up, and Hugo's meeting was less than two hours away. The twins stared pointedly, still waiting, buxom, gingery, braless, flat-footed, plain as their mother and full of what Garlick called unnatural teenage kindness.

Melanie found herself quivering with laughter. All that trouble spent in the British Museum picking out bone structure and genes had done no more than produce clones of Ms Murgatroyd. The results of her eugenics were one–nil to natural selection. Exasperated by the delay, Grandma growled and cussed.

'All right,' Melanie said, and ducked out into the weather.

Inside, all alone, Giles knelt at his altar rail in the dim light of his church, head bowed, eyes closed.

'I'm losing my faith,' he said, raising his head and looking up into the darkness of the roof. Looking for the faith that had been the bedrock of his life was like coming home to a house that had always been full of family and warmth, to find it cold, empty, dead.

'Or my mind,' he said. 'Dear God, take my mind, but not my soul.'

Either way, it terrified him. He closed his eyes once more, and strove with all his power to pray.

As he lay prostate before a pitiless God, Grandma hobbled to her feet, freshly cleaned with a bottle of sterile water and cotton wool, her sores anointed and bound in a manner befitting some Old Testament story. She swore at the twins, just to be friendly, and disappeared into the rain, pushing her trolley and little yellow dog in the direction of the Salvation Army, a long walk away, towards Bethnal Green and Hackney.

'He's still in there,' whispered Dorcas, opening the door a crack and seeing the motionless vicar crouched at the front of the building. He was talking to himself in a very low voice, very passionately, his hands clasped over his face.

'Look at him,' Dorcas muttered. 'He's in a really bad way.'

'Yeah,' murmured Dora. 'Leave him be.'

Steel drums from last Sunday's service gleamed in the shadows, reflecting the red lights of the sacristy. Battered orange chairs were pushed back in stacks against the walls to allow for dancing. And chanting. And screaming. And wailing. And hugging and kissing and clutching. The previous Sunday service had been a watershed of despair.

Giles was muttering into his clasped hands, but neither of the twins could hear a word he said.

'That wasn't an Anglican service of worship. That was a Bacchanalian orgy. I might as well have turned up as a druid or wearing nothing but a pair of horns. What in Your own name do You expect me to do?'

They had skipped and swayed, gyrated and clapped, feet pounding, heads thrown back, singing and hollering at the tops of their voices. The women, especially, worked themselves into a state of excitement, got frenzied, enjoyed it so much they fainted, came round, praised the Lord and started all over again. Little Ian Paisley Tutti Frutti had been very sick in the middle of it all, jolted and whirled and shaken dizzy in his mother's arms. There was still the very faintest trace of sal volatile mixed with baby vomit, sweat and cheap perfume floating on the air. Perfume brought it all back.

'*No*,' he begged.

It did no good. Behind closed eyes, Giles could see her clearly, dancing before him as she had that Sunday, skirt straining across her wiggling, bouncing buttocks, stretched over thighs that leaped and pumped and . . . while she yelled to the glory of God, and he lusted shamefully after her.

Giles groaned.

'My wife will divorce me,' he pleaded, gazing up at the crucifix on the altar before him. 'I will be cast out into the wilderness. The Archbishop is adamant. You get divorced, you quit. No more job.'

The last temptation: Christ confronted with Mary Magdalen, sexuality stirring in his loins, resisting its lifelong denial. Surely He would understand and come to the rescue. He crouched lower, humble and terrified; the profanity of it was awesome.

'No more job,' Giles argued passionately. 'I have children to keep. I am *sorry*. I am truly *sorry*, but I can't help it. Oh, God, who am I kidding?'

He lived for Angelina's radiant smiles across the sanctuary, her full, red, painted lips yelling praise to the Lord, eyes squeezed shut in ecstasy, hair damp with perspiration, curls standing on end, frizzy with abandon.

Abandoned. The word went round and round in his head like a mantra. Some of the things that went on in his graveyard . . . abandoned things . . . he could see from the damp little staircase with peeling distempered walls that led up to the clock tower, to a window slit. *Voyeur. Peeping Tom*. If anyone caught him looking, it would mean disgrace.

He could see the sniggering headlines in the tabloids. *Porno Priest Peeps Again.*

Giles shuddered. They'd unfrock him. Couldn't get away from frocks. Daffodil didn't wear frocks. She wore jodhpurs and neighed with excitement, on her back in her husband's haystacks. She had curly hair, a lot like Angelina's. Angelina's was more like Alice's. All the women he fancied seemed to have glorious hair, so like his daughter's.

'Oh my *God*,' Giles cried aloud, opening his eyes and staring speechlessly at the altar in front of him.

He sank his head in his hands and contemplated the appalling thought that maybe the root of his trouble was that, really, he fancied his daughter.

'Should we have told Miss Tilford?' Dorcas asked doubtfully, eyeing the figure crouched in the shadows at the front of the church with its shoulders hunched, shaking with misery. 'He's been crying and he keeps talking to himself like he's off his head.'

'Nah. Don't be stupid,' whispered the other Good Samaritan. 'She's a *teacher*.'

They stuffed Grandma's discarded dressings into a paper bag, threw it in a bin by the church gate, pulled their blazers over their heads against the rain, and scarpered.

Chapter Fourteen

'What on earth!'

Melanie hurried round the gate into the rectory's untidy front garden and froze. Her front door hung open, banging in the wind and rain, its coloured glass panel smashed, shards of glass scattered as far as the laurel bushes lining her path. The hall light was on. A trail of wet and muddy footprints led across to the bottom of the stairs. There were too many footprints for Tom and Alice to have made them all, and they shouldn't have been there at all.

A very dense, very prickly, very dark green holly hedge sheltered the front of the big, run-down, double-fronted Victorian house from the road. It could easily shield a lot of burglars, give them plenty of time to break in.

'I *told* Giles so,' Melanie muttered.

'Gloom, gloom, gloom,' she had said when she first saw the old rectory, on the day they moved in. 'No wonder you didn't want me to come and see it before. I hate it. And I hate that hideous holly hedge. Let's dig it up. Get rid of it. Get some light in those dismal downstairs rooms.'

'And have half the flats on the other side of the road looking straight in?'

'I'll get blinds. Or net curtains,' she wheedled. 'It's like a dungeon and that hedge makes it worse. We could cut it down and get a tree surgeon to take the roots out.'

'Do you know what that would cost?' he said, in the way that meant he didn't want to know. 'I don't want the whole world looking in.'

That was his final word.

'This is the good shepherd talking?' she said, when he was out of earshot. 'Love thy neighbour, and all that. You were never unfriendly like this at home.'

Now she muttered, 'Getting rid of that hedge wouldn't have cost as much as this is going to.' She was terrified of what she was going to find if she went inside, not knowing if the intruders were still there. If Alice had got home first, she could be . . .

'Alice,' she yelled, throwing her briefcase and the bag of frozen pizzas she'd got for supper on the sodden grass. Alice raped. Alice hurt. Alice dead. Crunching glass, she stormed through the broken front door into her hall, shaking with fear and rage, ready to kill.

'Come out *now*, wherever you are,' she shouted.

The house loomed around her, dingy, dark and brooding. It was still and silent except for the drumming of rain, the regular squeaking of the front door behind her and the frantic banging of her own heart.

'Alice.'

Silence.

'I am going crazy,' she said conversationally to herself after several moments that seemed like hours. 'I can hear someone giggling.'

She listened hard. Someone *was* giggling.

'Alice,' she screamed at the top of her voice. Only serial killers and psychopaths giggled over their victims.

There was the definite sound of muffled laughter from upstairs, then a thump, a high yelp, and someone saying *shut up.*

Melanie moaned.

'You've gone a bit white, Mum. Are you all right?'

Grinning like an ass, Alice peered down from the top of the banisters, standing unharmed on the landing above.

'Alice.'

'Mum.'

'I'm so glad you find this amusing,' snarled her mother, clutching at the foot of the banisters in shock. 'I had you raped and dead. Who have you got up there with you?'

'Bertie and Baby Jane. We've called the police,' Alice said helpfully. 'You don't have to look like that. We're waiting for a jam sandwich. Bertie says they take absolutely ages to come, so I've been helping her sit on Weasel until they get here. It was a bit of a struggle, I can tell you.'

'You're waiting for a takeaway?' Melanie asked stupidly.

'Don't be silly, Mum. Jam sandwich. Police car with red and orange stripes. *You* know.'

'Weasel?'

Behind her, a gust blew the front door shut, bringing in with it a drift of last year's dead holly leaves. They rustled drily across the stone hall floor, like rats' feet. Melanie shivered.

'Weasel Watkins, from school, is in your bedroom, trying to steal things, only now he's got Bertie sitting on his head. He can't run away. He's been crying. I don't blame him. I wouldn't like to have her sitting on *my* head, I can tell you. When she gets fed up, she's not very nice.'

'Bertie?'

Melanie felt eerily that she was beginning to sound like the British Telecom woman. *The number you require is . . . I repeat. The number you require is . . . I repeat.* She was probably a synthesizer, anyway, a robotic yellow pages, or they'd have had to take her away, gibbering telephone numbers into infinity, gone completely mad.

'From the flats,' chirped Alice.

'Baby Jane?'

Alice hesitated and looked guilty.

'I asked you, who is Baby Jane?' Melanie yelled up the stairs, wondering whether someone ought not to come and take *her* away in a strait-jacket.

Alice beckoned.

'Come up and see. The place is a mess, I warn you. Baby Jane went round swinging on things and pulled one of your curtains down. Then Bertie had to chase Weasel all over until she caught him, and that made a bit of a mess. She thumped him until he lay down quietly and then she made him tell us he's done this lots of times before.'

'Here?' said Melanie helplessly.

'He knows where to look for things worth stealing. Bertie says he used to break in when the old man lived here, and he ought to know by now that anyone who lives in this house won't have anything worth stealing. I suppose he wasn't to know we're the same. She says you have to feel sorry for him, really, he's such a dickhead.'

'If that's what Bertie says, I don't like her language,' Melanie snapped, starting up the stairs. 'Where are your father and Tom?'

'How would I know?' Alice answered rudely. 'Not here when needed. Are they ever?'

There were sounds of a rumpus from overhead.

'Bertie and Weasel are at it again,' said Alice, grinning.

'How *dare* people start fights in my bedroom,' yelled her mother, storming up the stairs.

'Hi,' said Bertie affably, as Melanie came into her bedroom.

About to shout a piece of her mind at them, Melanie found herself speechless. A very tall girl, of twenty-two or three, was sitting on Weasel, one leg either side of his prostrate body. His legs poked out of torn jeans, stretched out underneath her dressing table, their blood supply cut off. Weasel whimpered wretchedly and wiggled, trying to ease his pain.

'Are there any more of you in here?' Melanie asked at last, suppressing an urge to go looking in cupboards and under the bed.

'Just us, and her,' said Bertie, jabbing a knee into Weasel, who promptly lay still.

Melanie followed her pointing finger and her eyes widened. A very small dark monkey, a red leather collar around its neck, sat on the top of the wardrobe, swinging its tail happily, one of Melanie's bras on its head, playing peekaboo with two 36B cups.

'That's Baby Jane up there,' said Alice. 'Isn't she *cute*?'

She went over and started clicking her tongue, holding out her hands, trying to persuade the tiny creature to come down.

'Wizened and wicked, like Bette Davis,' explained Bertie. '*Whatever Happened to Baby Jane?* Yes?'

'Gerroff of me,' Weasel begged.

'You are hurting him,' Melanie protested, staring up at the little monkey playing with her underwear, mesmerized.

'Him? Nah. Don't upset yourself, honey. The little runt ain't worth it.'

Baby Jane had been having fun with things Weasel had pulled out of drawers and cupboards. Several of Giles's dog collars were scattered around, mixed up with old stockings, knickers and overwashed grey Y-fronts. She looked back at the top of the wardrobe and wanted to rub her eyes in disbelief. Baby Jane grinned and chattered back.

'It is a peculiar thing, but a monkey capering around my house seems to sum up my life at present. Now, if that's your pet monkey, who are you? And if he was in my house to steal,' Melanie demanded, clutching her brow with one hand and pointing at Weasel with the other, incensed, 'how come you were here to stop him? Are you a burglar too?'

'That's Boglabol,' said Alice, starting to laugh.

Melanie glared.

'You used to read it to me when I was little,' Alice protested. 'Burglar Bill. Boglabol. He met his wife through his work. Two of them at it in the same house one night, and they fell in love and took back all the things they had stolen. It was sweet. Remember?'

'This isn't sweet,' snarled her mother, dodging out of the way as Weasel thrashed about and tried to get up.

'Why don't you shurrup,' suggested Bertie, in a not particularly unfriendly way. 'It only hurts more if you make me hit you.'

He collapsed again.

'I'm not a burglar. I'm Neighbourhood Watch,' Bertie announced, holding out a handful of blood-red nails that would have made Dora and Dorcas sick with envy. When Melanie didn't shake them, Bertie dug them into Weasel's shoulder instead, and watched him flinch.

'You're Neighbourhood Watch?' Melanie repeated. 'You'll excuse me if I find that a bit hard to believe.'

Bertie looked more like a model, or a dancer. A less likely candidate for the nosy-neighbour brigade would be hard to find.

'Convince me,' Melanie said.

'Ask the police,' Bertie answered, finding something funny. 'They know me. Bertha Barnard. Barnard because I was found on a doorstep and fetched up in Barnardo's. Sometimes I say I'm related to Christiaan Barnard, which gets people going. God knows why Bertha. No one ever said. AKA Bertie. Me and Baby Jane live in the flats and twitch our nets. We like to keep an eye, don't we, Baby? Huh? You up there, answer me.'

'I thought Barnardo's only took boys,' said Melanie.

Baby Jane picked determinedly at the fastenings on Melanie's bra with tiny white teeth and watched Bertie with tiny, bright black eyes.

'She ain't got no discipline, that monkey,' Bertie remarked, nudging Weasel casually in the back. 'None at all.'

Melanie stood staring from one to the other, scared and suspicious. Bertie looked like a fashion model, sounded like a lunatic and could just as well be a serial killer who had started on Weasel and lulled Alice into a false state of security, merely interrupted by her own arrival. Appearances meant nothing. Jame Gumb made suits for himself out of women in *Silence of the Lambs*, and he looked perfectly normal when *he* first opened the door to Clarice Starling. He loved his dog and probably gave donations to the ASPCA. Bertie had a monkey and didn't even *sound* halfway normal. Melanie backed off, caught her knees on the side of her bed and collapsed, terrified. Tom had got the video out and persuaded her to watch it. It gave her nightmares for weeks.

'We are not serial killers, are we, Baby Jane? We're just

nosy as hell. We know everyone's business. That way, you stay safe in the block and you can blackmail the neighbours when they get to be a nuisance. I was peering out to see what everyone was doing this miserable afternoon, having nothing better to do, myself, at the time, when I saw this little shit breaking into your house,' Bertie said winningly, reading her expression exactly and guessing her thoughts. 'I followed him in and here we are. That's all. Cross my heart and hope to die in a cellarful of rats if that isn't the honest truth.'

'All right,' Melanie said grudgingly. 'I suppose I ought to be saying thank you. What are you going to do with him?'

Alice collected knickers, worn and discoloured from overwashing, and folded them up. She put them in a pile on the end of the bed, directly in Weasel's line of sight when he lifted his head.

'Let me do that.'

Melanie snatched the clothes, stuffed them in their drawer, embarrassed.

'We're waiting for the constabulary. Those aren't exactly Madame Lucie,' Bertie grinned, snapping her fingers at Baby Jane, who clicked her small teeth back and stayed on top of the wardrobe.

'What's Madame Lucie?' asked Melanie, resigned.

'Friend of mine. The *grande dame* of underwear. You'd never go into Marks and Sparks again. She's got a shop in Sloane Street. She'll charge you a hundred pounds for a bra, and that's at the cheap end. Shopping in there is *absolutely* delicious.'

'*A hundred pounds for a bra,*' Melanie squeaked. 'Whatever do you do that you live in the flats and can afford that kind of money?'

'*Mum,* don't be so rude,' Alice cried.

'Oh, I don't know.' Bertie ignored the question, thrust her chest out and looked down. 'Look at that. I'd say a hundred quid or so was a really good investment.'

Melanie looked her over carefully. Bertie was folded up on top of Weasel with all the softness of a packet of razor blades. In contrast to her cleavage, the rest of her was lean, elegant and sexless. She had the body of an anorexic ballet dancer, all finely tuned muscle, not an ounce of flesh. As she squatted astride Weasel, a black suede mini skirt rode up, showing black fishnet stay-up stockings, six inches of lace clamped around firm, well-muscled thighs. A chin-length bob, bleached almost white, fell forwards and obscured her face, which was high-cheekboned and hollow, jet-black eyes making a startling contrast beneath thin, dark, well-plucked brows. She wore a thong with a slender steel chain on it around one thin wrist, a lead for Baby Jane, who danced along the top of the wardrobe and took a flying leap on to the curtains. She clung, swinging and squeaking excitedly, as the ancient curtain track sagged.

'Babeeee,' Bertie screeched. 'Geddown.'

Weasel, thinking her distracted, tried to leap up.

'Oi.'

She kicked him casually with three-inch high heels, like spurs. Weasel began to cry.

'Those are like Vivian's boots in *Pretty Woman,*' Alice remarked enviously. 'Only hers weren't suede.'

'She stored condoms in them,' said Bertie, grinning.

Melanie opened her mouth to ask if she kept condoms in hers, and shut it again. She often wondered what it was like to be bold and shameless, fanning condoms out right under Richard Gere's nose. *Cosmopolitan* said women should keep condoms in their handbags, just in case.

Just in case of what? Did women snatch them off the shelf in Sainsbury's and rush out with the breakfast cereal and chops, for urgent, red-hot sex in the car park or the bushes behind the recycling skips at the side of the store? *Cosmopolitan* seemed to think so, but although she'd kept her eyes open, so far she'd never seen condoms in anyone's trolley. Nor on the checkout belt. Melanie had studied them on the shelf and wondered wistfully what it would feel like to have a lover, and to need them. She'd waited once to see if anyone picked them up, but no one had. *I got green ones, I got red ones, I got gold ones . . .* Melanie sighed. In the film, Julia Roberts was a prostitute, and if the contents of Giles's vestry was anything to go by, the church was the local supplier, not Sainsbury's.

'I'm going crazy,' Melanie muttered. 'I keep thinking of films we could be in. Perhaps we are in a film. Perhaps I *am* crazy and don't know it.'

Weasel snuffled wretchedly.

'And in any case, the police could easily count those heels as offensive weapons, and book the both of you,' she added.

'Talking of which, they're here,' said Alice, peering out of the front window.

'About time,' Bertie grumbled, picking at false eyelashes dislodged by the struggle with Weasel. She pulled them off and licked them, tried unsuccessfully to fix them on again. 'We could all be dead by the time they've put batteries in their Noddy car and wound themselves up. The luvvies do their best. *Stop that,*' she snarled suddenly, jolting Weasel's head sideways. Baby Jane leapt without warning from a perch on the top of the open door, landed on the bed, climbed down and sidled over on to Bertie's shoulder, where she picked lovingly at her hair, parting and searching, grooming.

'I really don't think you should do that,' said Melanie anxiously. 'You could hurt him.'

'He was trying to bite,' Bertie said casually, cocking her head to make things easier for the monkey. 'Panicking because the force is with us at last. Don't start feeling sorry for the little toad. He'll do you over again next week, if he can. The old man used to say the neighbours knew what he owned *far* better than he did, they did him over so often. I tried to keep an eye out, but in the end, he kept open house. Never bothered locking a door. Once they'd sniffed around a few times, everyone knew he stopped replacing his videos and stuff and there was nothing worth taking any more. Then they left him alone.'

'You knew him, then.'

Bertie held out her thin young face, all sharply aggressive planes and angles, for the little monkey to stroke, with a tiny, gentle paw.

'Yes,' was all she replied, in a way that said she didn't want to take the topic any further.

Chapter Fifteen

The police were hallooing in the hall downstairs, opening doors, searching. They brought normality, sanity, security, big muddy boots and crackling radios.

'Up here,' Alice called from the bedroom doorway.

'Anyone would think you'd been catching burglars all your life,' said Melanie, watching her daughter's cool performance with amazement. 'You'd never know the only time you had anything to do with the police was when next door's tricycle went missing and we had door-to-door enquiries, right through the village!'

'It's you, is it? You took long enough,' Bertie complained as the first officer arrived in the room.

Weasel lifted his head from the floor.

'Gerreroffme,' he begged.

The officer had his hat under his arm, showing receding sandy hair, horn-rimmed spectacles, and a serious air more suited to a university lecturer than a police officer in the toughest area of London. When he opened his mouth, his accent was pure Welsh Valleys, the Metropolitan Police a straight escape route from some closed and rotting coal pit.

'Oh, well I never,' he sang. 'Who have we here, then? A nice little party of regulars.'

'Regulars?' sighed Melanie, wobbling at the knees again. Regulars, plural? Jame Gumb after all? The second officer arrived and stood grinning in the doorway.

'You, is it?' he remarked in a flat North London voice. 'It's getting so every time I turn round you're behind me.

We can't bloody wipe our noses round here without you fetching up under our feet.'

'Just doing my civic duty.'

Bertie held her loose eyelashes carefully in one hand and started to climb off Weasel.

'I saw him breaking in. I wouldn't have bothered, only I saw Alice, here, come home, and I thought, oh-oh, and came on over to make sure she didn't come to no harm. Get him out of here now you *have* turned up.'

Turning her back, she began inspecting her fishnets minutely for damage. Weasel got painfully to his feet, a wary eye on his tormentor, and began hopping up and down, getting his circulation back. Right over their heads, the clatter of a helicopter flying very low made them all look up. Melanie went to the window and looked out at it, hovering just above the rooftops. The noise was deafening.

'What's it doing?' she called.

'Police,' shouted the Welshman above the rotor blades, his radio crackling urgently into life and jabbering. 'When you've finished dancing around, Weasel. We haven't got all day.'

'We had a lot of military helicopters in Norfolk,' she said, inaudible over the noise. She felt rather than heard the front door bang.

'Giles,' she cried in relief, and went to tell him what had happened as the helicopter swung away over the common and the noise of rotors retreated.

'It's me,' said Tom, appearing at the top of the stairs, soaked with rain. His long hair, growing into a ponytail like Alastair Croke's, dripped down his blazer. 'Why is there a police car outside our house with Weasel Watkins being put inside it?'

'We've had a break-in,' his mother said. 'It was Weasel. Do you know where Dad is?'

'No. Did he take anything?'

'We caught him.'

'I told you and Dad you shouldn't come and live here,' he

remarked patronizingly, dropping his school bag in the doorway so that everyone would trip over it. 'You know it's the highest crime rate in Britain. We'll probably get done over every week and Dad will moan like mad about insurance.'

'Don't you *dare* get smug,' his mother yelled. 'Where were you when you should have been at home? Alice could have been murdered or raped and taken to Epping Forest and dumped by now, and you walk in and *preach.*'

'Anything missing?' asked the Welshman, looking out of the bedroom to where they stood on the landing.

'He didn't have a chance, thanks to me,' growled Bertie, hitching up her stay-ups, yanking them into place. 'I better thank myself, since no one else seems inclined . . .'

The helicopter swung back towards them, its blades sounding close enough to slice up all the chimneypots.

'What's it doing?' shouted Alice, frightened.

The Welshman tucked his notebook into his breast pocket, spoke dispassionately.

'We found a little girl over the way, in the bushes. They're up there looking for the animal that raped and strangled her.'

The helicopter swung away, sweeping bushes and paths with its spotlight, clattered towards All Hallows. It circled clear of the church tower, then came round in a tight turn, back over the graveyard, to the open space where a path wandered through bushes and a little copse of stunted trees. Police tape was tied around their trunks, cordoning off the spot where the bloody little body had been found earlier by a railway worker on his way to the late shift. The helicopter swung its searchlight and steadied. It seemed to hover there forever.

Giles, walking home across the churned and sodden grass, watched it come and go, saw the tape around the trees and bushes. Against the glare of the spotlight, he ducked his head and hurried on, wondering what was happening. When the helicopter came down very low, hovered right overhead, its bright white light engulfed him, tracked him, held him. Confused, he covered his eyes, began to hurry. The light followed, the blades roaring, whipping Giles's long skirts, beating the bushes flat. From somewhere within the terrifying noise, a man was shouting.

Giles began to run and dodge, slipped on the greasy, water-logged grass, stumbled to his knees and looked up. Dazzled, his eyes blinded, he could see nothing but all-encompassing, brilliant light.

St Paul on the road to Damascus. *Let thy light so shine upon the world . . . he was blinded by a great light*. Giles struggled to his feet, began to run, arms over his head, blotting out the noise. To the men watching above, he looked like a man fleeing, as guilty as a man can be.

They came from all directions, running towards *him*. 'Forgive me,' he shouted, reaching his hands to the rain and the sky in supplication, his long black skirts blowing in the fierce downdraught from the helicopter overhead. 'Dear God, forgive me, I never meant to hurt her.' The helicopter rose, clattering, drowned his cries. They went on coming, running and running, beyond its circle of light, running fast and low, to get him.

Chapter Sixteen

'He was kneeling in the grass, soaked to the skin, crying and saying *forgive me* over and over again,' reported the arresting officer. 'He was babbling on and on about he never meant to hurt her. He was admitting to it before we even reached him.'

'He'll sign a confession, then,' said the detective superintendent in charge of the murder hunt.

'We cautioned him. He said he understood, but he went on and on about forgiveness. He dug a nice big pit and jumped straight into it. It'll be a formality,' agreed the arresting officer.

'Right. Let's go and see him, and strike while the iron is hot,' said the superintendent, getting up.

'My wife,' he cried, when they put it to him that he knew what he had done, had raped and strangled a six-year-old, had admitted it to the arresting officer. 'I meant my wife. I meant, I never meant to hurt my wife.'

He stared at them, haggard and bewildered, covered in mud and grass.

'You done your wife in as well?' demanded the superintendent incredulously.

Giles clutched his brow. '*No.* I don't know anything about a child. I saw the stuff round the trees, and I didn't know what it was there for. I was in church all afternoon. Praying. Contemplating. I have a lot on my mind, you see.'

'You're going to have a hell of a lot more on your mind unless you had someone with you,' observed the superintendent. 'You got any witnesses? Can anyone corroborate that story?'

Giles shook his head wretchedly.

'It's not a story. It's the truth. If you let me ring my wife, I can prove she's all right and I haven't hurt her. You have to let me make a telephone call.'

'I advise you to use that to call a solicitor,' said the superintendent.

'I don't *need* a solicitor. I'm innocent,' Giles yelped. 'This is a misunderstanding.'

'Innocent people don't generally go around publicly saying they're guilty,' remarked the superintendent, unimpressed. 'Everyone feels misunderstood. You'd be surprised how many misunderstood criminals we have in here. We practically weep, don't we?'

The officer taking notes nodded.

'We do,' he agreed.

'I couldn't conceivably kill a child. I'm a *priest*,' Giles said heavily.

All he got in return were a couple of fishy stares.

Why didn't you drown it in a bucket at birth? All little Ian Paisley did was cry.

Giles's eyes glazed with horror as the superintendent watched his thoughts play across his face, and believed him less and less.

'Rasputin was a monk. Didn't stop him doing nasty things,' the superintendent answered. 'Look at the Inquisition. The Crusades. Knights Templar and all that. Rosicrucians. You've been killing each other for centuries. *Someone* raped a little girl this afternoon. You were on the spot, you were alone, you ran away when we approached you, and you started begging for mercy before we even cautioned you. All that circumstantial evidence, and you expect us to believe you couldn't have done it because of your calling?'

'Yes,' Giles said eagerly.

'Sex crimes and clergy,' ruminated the superintendent

gloomily. 'They go together like a horse and carriage. Half the Catholic lot are paedophiles. Or gay. Celibate? Don't make me laugh.'

'I never felt less amusing in my life,' Giles told him earnestly.

'I don't find it funny,' the superintendent assured him. 'I don't find *you* funny.'

'Nor do I,' Giles cried, relieved that they saw eye to eye about something.

'It's gradually coming out, these days. There's what's-his-face, the Bishop Irish Annie is suing for child support. He's Catholic. Then there's the Bishop of Gloucester and his poor little monk. The tip of a very big iceberg, but you try doing anything about it. They all cover for one another. So, tell me, Reverend. Since when was being a clergyman an argument for being innocent?'

Giles sat with his mouth open, thunderstruck. The superintendent's thin face was shoved right up against his, narrow and yellow as a ferret's, intense and sharp as a carving blade, his horrible words spraying out smelling of cigarettes, wounding as bullets.

'When you put it like that, it isn't,' Giles whispered. 'But . . .'

'That's what I think,' interrupted the superintendent. 'There are some very fine clergy, men to respect, but it's not *automatic*, is the point I'm making. It isn't an *argument* of any kind. You only have to look around you. Read the news.'

Giles buried his head in his hands. The only way out was to tell them everything, to explain what *forgive me, I never meant to hurt her* meant. The consequences of that were so awful they didn't bear thinking about. It would be gossip, would get out. He had been thinking about those consequences all afternoon. They were *still* unthinkable. The consequences of *not* telling were unthinkable. Prison. A worse disgrace. His was the very kind of corruption the superintendent was busy castigating. Giles clutched at his rumpled hair and groaned.

'Happily married, are you?' asked the superintendent cannily.

He received a look of such desperation, the ferret scented blood.

'I thought not. Is that why you chase little girls?'

'I don't chase little girls,' Giles shrieked, appalled. 'I only chase big ones. *No*. That's not it, either. No, no, *no*.'

He clapped his hand over his mouth, frightened brown eyes starting from his head, round as golf balls, struck dumb by his own words. The superintendent beamed with all the warmth of a piranha spotting fingers trailing in the water above its head.

'I knew we'd make progress,' he said, opening a packet of Silk Cut low tar. 'Smoke?'

Numb with horror, Giles shook his head.

'I didn't mean to say that,' he blurted, as the officer lit up and blew smoke out of the side of his mouth.

'I don't suppose you did. But you have. My colleague over there has written it down, so you don't forget. Haven't you?'

Giles gazed at the young man at the other corner of the table, writing slowly, busily, his face screwed up in concentration. He lifted his head.

'Yes, sir,' he said woodenly and waited, pen poised.

'Now then. Shall we go back and start again?' the superintendent suggested kindly. 'And shall we tell the truth this time?'

'I *am* telling the truth.'

'This is not a good attitude for an intelligent man like yourself,' said the superintendent reproachfully, blowing smoke at Giles deliberately. 'Do you know what they think of child molesters in prison? They have to be kept apart for their own safety. They are beaten, pissed upon, buggered over a barrel to within an inch of their lives, and after a few weeks they are prone to being found somewhere, discreetly tucked away and very, *very* dead. It's terrible, but people feel strongly. Tsk, tsk.'

He clucked his tongue and the ferrety face moved towards Giles and murmured confidentially.

'My officers don't like them, either, and I might have trouble preventing them acting a little . . . ah . . . sullen, when I send you back to your cell. Now, if you were to be a bit more helpful . . .'

He leaned back in his chair, blew a smoke ring and watched it float away.

'I am not a child molester and I don't suppose your colleague here records the fact that you have refused me a telephone call to my wife, and that now you are threatening me,' Giles said bitterly.

The ferret smiled and turned into a Cheshire cat.

Giles expected no answer, and there was none. Sweating, he unzipped the velcro on his dog collar and pulled it off, threw it on the table and gazed at it silently.

It was his life. He was lost without it, and they would take it away, now, no matter what he did, because he had betrayed everything. Sitting with his head in his hands, confronted with the end of life as he had known it, he tried to pray. The prayer became an argument, sterile and hopeless.

One sinner who repents is more precious in Your sight than all the righteous.

I am *sorry,* he cried passionately, pleading silently.

Of course you are, said a cold little voice inside his head. *You got caught.*

No, no, no. I'm truly sorry, I'm really and truly sorry. One sinner who repents? The prodigal son?

He meant it with all his heart, but *sorry* was an empty word. *Judas,* whispered the icy little voice. *Betrayer. What about Melanie?*

'I'm sorry,' he wept, his head on the table, under the indifferent gaze of the police.

'Then tell us the truth,' said the ferret patiently, lighting another Silk Cut.

'I didn't do it, and I'm sorry for what I have done, but that's nothing to do with you.'

'Carry on digging a nice big pit for yourself to fall into,' suggested the superintendent. 'If that's the way you want to play it.'

'I'm sorry for something *else*,' Giles yelped desperately.

It did no good. *Sorry* brought no comfort at all.

Chapter Seventeen

Only the muddle of clothes still on the floor and a tear in the ancient curtains made by Baby Jane were left to show that anything out of the ordinary had happened. It was not yet quite six o'clock.

Bertie was rummaging in Melanie's dressing table, looking for something to stick her eyelash back on with. Tom stared at her, his mouth open.

'No,' said Melanie, asked for glue.

Bertie put a bit of spit on her finger and dabbed at her loose eyelash, tried to fix it, her face tipped up in front of the mirror. Tall as Giles, at eighteen Tom was six foot two, and towered over tall Bertie by several inches. He had Giles's unruly dark hair, Melanie's grey eyes, and at the end of the afternoon, adult five o'clock shadow covering the last traces of adolescent acne.

Bertie got the lash on, grinned, blinked two coal-black eyes, tucked bleached white hair behind her ears and gave him the come-on over one angular shoulder.

'Don't you dare,' Melanie said under her breath. 'Don't you *dare*. Either of you.'

'That was so *cool*, the way you handled Weasel,' said Tom admiringly. 'Most girls would have been scared stiff.'

'I'm not most girls,' Bertie breathed, asthmatic with invitation, straightening the fishnets again, bending down so that Tom was staring straight down one of Madame Lucie's hundred-pound bras at two full and pretty breasts.

'Tom,' yelped his mother.

'No,' her son breathed back, wide-eyed.

'Thomas.'

'Weasel's a wally. Don't get so stressed up, Mum.'

'I'm not talking about Weasel,' Melanie hissed.

Baby Jane leaped on to Bertie's shoulder and wound herself around her neck.

'Be nice and make friends,' Bertie ordered the monkey. 'Say hello to Tom.'

Invited to come close, Tom stroked her, his hand brushing Bertie's hair.

'She's sweet,' he breathed.

Alice snickered, made sick noises and announced she was hungry.

'What's for supper, Mum?' she demanded.

Tom's shy, enchanted grin as he held Bertie's little monkey was too much. Melanie turned and took her feelings out on Alice.

'You could have just said there were pizzas defrosting in the hall,' Alice shouted back, when her mother ran out of breath. 'Don't get in a mood with me. *I* didn't burgle your room, *I* just happened to catch the burglar.'

'*I* caught the burglar,' said Bertie, nudging up against Tom's arm.

'She did *not*,' Alice cried furiously.

Bertie stroked Baby Jane, who was cradled in Tom's arms, and smiled.

Who caught Weasel is not what Tom's noticing, Melanie thought, gritting her teeth. She's twenty if she's a day, and he's eighteen. *Too young*. And she's too old.

Too old for what? demanded a small voice in her head.

To have my son, she thought furiously. Tart.

She stamped crossly downstairs to a hall full of wet leaves and boot marks, rescued the pizzas from their defrosting where she had dropped them on the floor, and threw them angrily into the oven. Then she leaned on the sink, contemplated the remains of breakfast floating on the water, a mass of soggy cornflakes, and looked out of the window at the darkening garden. The common was dark, its lamps flickering on above the place where a little girl had died, and no one had seen it happen.

'Six years old,' she said to the cornflakes in the sink. 'Six years old. How do you imagine a thing like that?'

There was nobody there to answer as tears spilled down her face.

In less than an hour the meeting would start. The news would have got round about a child's death on the school's doorstep. Bunny would know what to do.

'Bunny would get out the G and T,' Melanie said to herself. '*That's* what Bunny would do.'

She peered at her pizzas in the old eye-level oven, its door black with burned-on grease, its controls unreliable. They were overdone. Melanie wiped her face on a kitchen towel, blew her nose, threw the singed pizzas on to plates, and headed for the pantry.

Because they were looted regularly from the vestry, in among the brooms, dusters, a couple of old-fashioned mousetraps and a large collection of old cans of paint and floor polish, Giles kept his communion supplies hidden in her pantry, in a cardboard box. He had fifteen bottles squirrelled away. She helped herself to two, found a corkscrew, laid the table with four water glasses, went to the bottom of the stairs and shouted at them all to come down and have their supper.

'OK,' she said, handing a bottle to Tom. 'Open it. We need a drink.'

'Here,' Bertie said, holding the glass out to Baby Jane, perched on her shoulder. 'Château Stepney. You try it.'

Baby Jane dipped a paw in the wine and licked it, came back for more.

'What a lush,' sighed Bertie. 'Yum, yum.'

'It is *disgusting*,' Alice corrected her. 'This is Dad's wine. You're only meant to have one sip, in church, not drink it by the bottle.'

'I don't care if it's meths,' her mother said grimly. 'The world can only improve through the bottom of a bottle.'

Bertie took her wine away from Baby Jane, drank half the glass and gasped.

'Told you so,' said Alice.

'Help yourself,' Bertie ordered, giving it back to Baby Jane. 'You should see this one when she gets drunk. She leaps at all the men and starts nibbling their ears. Then she offers them her bottom. What a tart.'

Melanie looked up sharply, but Bertie was grinning innocently, offering a spoonful of communion wine to the tiny animal.

'My mother is going to turn up at school drunk,' Tom remarked.

'Drunk as a monkey,' giggled Bertie.

'*Good*,' his mother snapped back, and poured the second bottle.

'She's not exactly drunk, just a mite unsteady,' Bertie said kindly, as twenty minutes later Melanie went to school, to the meeting, and the front door slammed on the sound of the wind getting up, the rain coming down harder than ever.

She went the long way round, staying close to people and lights, avoiding the dark, and the cordoned-off place in the park. Her umbrella blew inside out and tore itself when she was halfway there, leaving her to get soaked. Cutting across the grass, near the road, almost at the school gates, she slipped and slithered, noticed the lights gone out in her husband's church porch, and how dense the darkness was, under the yews.

'Where *is* he?' she muttered crossly, stepping straight into a puddle up to her ankles. Ahead, East Stepney School blazed with light. Behind her, the wind howled across the sodden empty park where a child had died. A sudden surge of fear made her run, shoes squelching, hair plastered to her face, into the safety of the school playground.

'You look an absolute sight, and you're only just in time,' said a familiar, sarcastic voice. 'I kept you a front-row seat next to mine. Hugo's chatting and doing his warm-up act before starting properly. Putting parents into a proper frame of mind.'

'You wouldn't know what a time I've had,' she cried. 'Have you heard what happened?'

'I hear they caught someone. Have you been crying, by any chance?'

'No,' she lied.

He looked intently into her face.

'You have, and you smell of cheap wine, Mrs T.'

'Communion wine. Sweet Spanish. *Awful,*' she admitted.

'We will have to go to the off licence one day, and I will give you a lesson in how to drink decent plonk on a teacher's salary. Do you like Chardonnay, Mrs T.?'

'I don't know. The Communion wine is Giles's. We were burgled as well,' Melanie went on. 'I went home and found Weasel Watkins in my bedroom.'

'No one should have a murder and a burglary in one day, but since you have, shall we go and have a good laugh at Hugo trying to reform the unreformable?'

'The unspeakable in pursuit of the uneatable, as it were?'

'Something like that,' agreed Alastair.

The hall was filling up fast, a wedge of chairs to one side reserved for staff. He had kept two seats right at the front.

'There you go, Mrs T.,' he said.

Looking round, she could see no sign of Giles.

'Thanks. It looks as though my husband isn't coming,' she said.

'Cheer up.'

He reached over and squeezed her hand. Without thinking, she squeezed his hand right back.

Chapter Eighteen

'What have you got in there, then? Thermos flasks and sandwiches?'

Angelina shoved a couple of carrier bags and an enormous broken handbag under her chair and ignored Alastair's jibe. Along the row, the All Hallows brigade, in colourful turbans pocked and stained with rain, parked dripping umbrellas, planted their substantial buttocks on the unfriendly chairs, and waited with an expectant air, immovable as the siege of Leningrad. Five hundred parents filled the seats from the back, flowing forward like a reluctant tide, refusing to sit at the front underneath Hugo's nose.

'There's a *hell* of a lot more parents here than I thought would come,' Alastair remarked. 'It looks like Hugo has a point after all.'

'You haven't by any chance, any of you, seen my husband?' Melanie leaned past Alastair to ask. He smelled of whisky from the fresh bottle in the filing cabinet, and faintly spicy aftershave, and was watching Bunny settle herself down, a few chairs away, his expression inscrutable. Angelina and the brigade shook their heads. Melanie craned round, busy keeping an eye on the door, in case Giles should come at the last moment.

Proceedings were due to start at eight. At two minutes to, the local Labour Party stormed through the doors and settled itself fussily, filling up the back of the hall, some staying standing as if for a fast getaway. Others climbed over everyone else to find seats in the middle, treading on toes and being a nuisance. Winanda, Dora and Dorcas's cross, red-haired mother, sat by herself to one side, glowered, counted heads and announced to her nearest neighbours that they had a quorum.

'Got a what?' demanded Ernie Woolf, of Woolf's Family Butchers, who put contracts out to have people done over if asked in the right way, and was president of the local branch of the get-the-Kray-twins-out-of-prison movement. Ernie had the square build of a Chieftain tank, weighed eighteen stone, was thin on top and had small, twinkling eyes in a round and jolly face that ended in half a dozen chins. He liked to compare himself to Robbie Coltrane, whom he reckoned to be the sexiest man on television. He edged nearer and took the chair next to Winanda's.

'What's a quorum when it's at home?'

'Having the right numbers. You can't take decisions without a quorum,' she snapped. 'It's the rules.'

She was big, blowsy, loud and confident. Interested, Ernie looked her over curiously, examined her hand-knitted bobbled cardigan out of the corner of his eye and guessed 40D cup. Looking more closely, he decided two of the bobbles were nipples, very possibly unprotected by underwear. He cleared his throat, about to chat her up by asking her to explain more about quorums, when Hugo appeared at the back of the stage with outstretched arms, beaming all over his big hairy face, as if about to give them all a papal blessing, or launch into some comic vaudeville act. Absalom scuttled in behind him, gleaming in his best brown suit, false teeth glowing brightly under the neon lights, accompanied by a woman in an anorak, knitted suit and sensible boots.

'Why do they have to do that and make an entrance from the back of the stage?' complained Alastair aloud. 'Who do they think they are?'

'Shhh,' Melanie answered.

'Our dearly beloved representative from the Local Education Authority is the spitting image of Ted Heath when he was prime minister, don't you think?' Alastair mumbled in her ear, breathing whisky into it, which tickled. 'Put her and Hugo together, and you've got a real pair of bruisers.'

'Right,' Hugo called, by way of telling everyone to be quiet, that business had started. He came down the steps at the side of the stage and stood at his lectern, shuffling bits of paper while the other two arranged themselves on their chairs. Absalom dusted his with a white handkerchief, pulled up shiny brown trousers and sat down, displaying neat white socks. Ted Heath sat with sturdy legs apart, knitted skirt stretched tight across spreading thighs, revealing maximum-support stockings and a hint of sensible pink knickers. Garlick took one look at the triumvirate and promptly retired into the comfort of the inside of his own head.

His new fantasy was a corker which he had been looking forward to all evening. It had come to him after reading an article in the *Daily Mail*. Doctors were using eggs from aborted foetuses to make infertile women pregnant, and the *Daily Mail* was agitated about the moral consequences. On the opposite page it reminded its readers that only the previous year a fifty-nine-year-old businesswoman had just had twins.

'Now OAPs will be wanting child benefit along with their pension. And Major says he wants to cut back. Where is this going to end?' Alastair had said acidly when shown the paper. He gazed at a photograph of Robert Winston, the infertility specialist, looking boyishly serious, posing outside the big brick gates at the Hammersmith Hospital, next door to Wormwood Scrubs.

'Worms have no trouble doing it to themselves,' said Garlick. 'Being hermaphroditic seems such a sensible arrangement. If humans were like worms, the world would be a much safer place. No love affairs, no jealousy, no sexually transmitted diseases. Just think.'

'Bully for worms. Perhaps after a holocaust it will be worms who inherit the earth, then,' Alastair suggested, not very interested. 'If I were a worm, though, I don't think I'd fancy myself very much, which might defeat the purpose,' he added by way of an afterthought.

'In Russia, in the fifties, they gave people radiation just to see what happened,' Garlick persisted.

'Cancer happened, I should think,' said Alastair, bored.

'These things go on all the time, and they come out in the end. People think only crooks, communists and Nazis do experiments, and they are wrong. You might say Dr Mengele was simply ahead of his time.'

'You might say it, but I don't think I would.' Alastair shook his head in wonder.

'We'll be rehabilitating him next,' Garlick said. 'What with transplants and foetal eggs and the like.'

'He cut up living children and experimented on twins. You talk such bollocks,' snapped Alastair.

Garlick didn't mind, already lost in thought. It was a moment of pure inspiration.

Dr Mengele. The Angel of Death, he thought happily, fixing his sights on Absalom's scrawny neck. Delicately, mentally balancing it in his palm, he picked up a scalpel and gazed at Absalom thoughtfully. Interesting question; on a human cockroach, where to make the incisions without killing the patient. Absalom had a bloodless look; it shouldn't be messy. Unfortunately, retirement to Brazil had not produced the definitive textbook on human experimentation that one would generally have expected from a distinguished research scientist like Mengele. He'd have to experiment for himself. Garlick sighed, and settled down happily, as removed from opting-out proceedings as if he had gone to the moon. On the other side of the hall, as Hugo began to speak, Ernie scratched his crotch with enjoyment, watched the bobbles rise and fall, out of the corner of his eye, as she breathed. He was *certain* they were nipples.

'We are delighted that so many of you have ventured out in this foul weather,' Hugo began. 'I am sorry you have to sit on our horrible chairs. Your children complain about them.

We all complain, but to deaf ears. New chairs for the hall are one of the many things our Local Education Authority will not fund. I will tell you more about how our school has been starved of money later in the evening. Meanwhile, I would like to introduce you to the representative from that very Local Education Authority, Mrs Jemima Habgood.'

Unmoved by her introduction, Jemima Habgood nodded her bulldog chin and stayed in her chair, watching the arrival of the last remaining official British Trotskyites since the fall of the Berlin Wall, who shared their income support and a seedy flat down towards the river at Poplar. They came marching in to stand with their backs to the Labour Party, pointedly defiant in shaved heads and genuine grunge from down the seediest end of the indescribably seedy Brick Lane market.

'Oh, lord, what a shower. Probably all got sociology degrees from polytechnics,' Alastair muttered, tickling Melanie's ear pleasantly. She shivered and drew away.

Two men followed the Trotskyites in, sporting yellow stickers on their chests saying something unreadable in Welsh.

'Bloody social workers and a couple of miners hustled in for good measure. That's ridiculous. *Way* over the top for an opt-out. Wonder how they got them to come. Remember Arthur Scargill and his *dis*putes?'

Melanie touched her ear involuntarily, where his lips had been, and smiled.

'We are faced with choices,' trumpeted Hugo, getting into his stride. 'Mrs Habgood and her colleagues want to close our school down, arguing that as we are at the bottom of Mr Patten's league table, we should go. What that table does not show is that our children are some of the most diverse and disadvantaged in Britain. Their parents often speak no English, are frequently out of work, live in conditions that Mrs Habgood would not tolerate herself for one moment and does nothing about. That we *do* achieve a level of GCSE passes, and that some of our children stay on in the sixth form and *do* go on to university is a great deal more to their credit than any league table would have you believe.'

A solitary pair of hands clapped slowly. Ernie's two fat sons had started truanting when his wife left him for one of Angelina's cousins. Hugo personally chased and tormented them until they found it easier to give in and come back into school. Now they had five GCSEs between them.

'I agree with that,' called Winanda, joining in.

There was a flutter at the side of the audience as six rows of Bangladeshi parents translated Hugo's words rapidly among themselves, and clapped timidly. Scattered clapping rippled over the parents for several moments. Absalom mopped his brow and looked relieved. Mrs Habgood stared straight ahead grimly.

'I'm glad to see we have *some* satisfied customers,' Hugo beamed.

'What do you reckon on the troop deployment?' Alastair whispered under his breath ten minutes later, bored, looking along their row.

'What?' she whispered back.

'How'll they vote? History and English are rightish. The Stud will vote in favour. Mohammed will do whatever keeps his job. Garlick's fascist, of course. Science sits on the fence. Sociology is lunatic fringe. I don't know about mathematics and the rest. Hugo thinks one-third of us will vote against him.'

'I'll vote in favour,' she whispered back.

Bunny, relaxed, a smudge of self-raising flour on her forehead, seated in the very middle of the row of teachers, was smiling up at Hugo, wholly absorbed in him.

'I wish a woman would look at me like that,' Alastair murmured wistfully.

'What?'

He pressed his arm against hers in a jokey kind of way. *Take no notice of me,* it said.

The Trotskyites were good at disruption. As Hugo began

to carry his audience with him, they began to shuffle, stamp their feet and look for the best moment to heckle. Jemima Habgood looked up sharply, frowning. Coalitions of convenience with unstable groups were dodgy, a necessary evil. No matter what one tried to teach them about strategy and discipline, this lot *would* jump the gun.

Hugo soldiered on.

'An independent company will ballot parents and teachers if we decide to go ahead with a vote on opting out. If we vote *no*, then so long as the school remains open, we must repeat the vote each year until we vote *yes*. Once we begin it, we cannot abandon the process. I hope we will all consider the arguments patiently and remember that the question is what is best for our children, not what is convenient for certain people's political beliefs or self-interest.'

'Wouldn't be about your own self-interest, would it? Nothing to do with keeping yourselves in a job, and power-broking?' jeered one of the Trotskyites from the back, kicking off the political ball. Mrs Habgood watched impassively. It wasn't a bad start. There was perfunctory and reluctant stamping from the Labour Party. Hugo spoke slowly and intently.

'For East Stepney to opt out is a highly political move. A lot of people forget that it is an *educational* move. I can see a lot of people here, who have nothing whatsoever to do with this school, or with education, who have simply come along to peddle their political leanings and make trouble.'

He grabbed the sides of his lectern with hairy paws and leaned on it, glaring at the motley gang at the back, facing them down. *No, no, no,* Bunny begged silently, biting her nails to suppress an urge to stand up and shout at him.

No, no, no, Alastair echoed. *Drop it, Hugo. Whatever you do, don't start winding them up. There are dangerous people here.*

'How are you going to turn things around if you think our children are so deprived they can't be expected to do any better?' called Winanda. 'You are contradicting yourself, Mr Benedict.'

A faint smile touched Mrs Habgood's full lips. Every head turned towards the speaker, swivelled back to hear what Hugo had to say.

'Yeah, contradicting yourself.'

The murmur swept over them as the Labour Party stamped its feet in agreement. Looking apprehensively round the audience for signs of support, Absalom stiffened. Discreetly embedded among the parents, well away from the left wing, the National Front lurked. Not bovver boys, but neatly dressed in denim and jumpers, unobtrusive.

What a line-up. Everyone sitting there waiting for an excuse to cut each other's throats. David Absalom tried to catch Hugo's eye.

National Front are here. He willed Hugo to look his way, but he was out of Hugo's line of vision. Mrs Habgood smiled, noting that Absalom's forehead was finely beaded with sweat.

'They are disadvantaged most by other people expecting them to fail. I want to have the kind of school that *demands* results,' said Hugo evenly.

'What are you actually going to do?' Winanda demanded.

Ernie sat open-mouthed with admiration for a woman who not only flaunted 40D tits, but had the nerve to make a cracking little speech in public as well.

'Turn morale around. Give each child an education to the limit that they are capable of. You would be *amazed* at what a difference a teacher can make if allowed to give children the quality of education they deserve.'

Garlick emerged from a search for Absalom's heart, which was proving hard to find, supporting Garlick's hypothesis that he hadn't got one. Mentally he put down the scalpel and took a rest, to hear the hall resounding with enthusiastic clapping, half drowned by booing and hissing from the gallery. Hugo waited for the row to die down.

Yah Boo. Absalom leered from the operating table. *We're going to win,* he taunted. Caught out, Garlick waved his scalpel menacingly. *I underestimated Hugo. You lie down and shut up.*

You could cut this atmosphere with a slice of toast, Hugo thought.

'I'll buy it,' a plumber sitting towards the back called. 'You just got my vote, Mr Benedict.'

'And mine.'

'Mine, too,' shouted Angelina, causing the entire row of turbans to droop and rise like wind passing over a field of outsize chrysanthemums. All over the hall there was a ripple of interest, a murmur of agreement. Parents who had come to the meeting because their friends and next-door neighbours had said *shall we go and see the old dump shut down?* and because it was a chance to gossip about the murder on the common sat up and took an interest.

Mrs Habgood gave an almost imperceptible nod to the back of the hall. She had hoped this wouldn't be necessary, but it was starting to go too well.

'We could see you get what you deserve, Mr Benedict,' someone said softly and clearly from near the back of the chairs. Alastair craned to look back over his shoulder, recognized an older, heavier, more vicious Ben.

'Serious trouble,' he muttered to Melanie. 'The neo-Nazi bunch are here. We expelled one of them for attacking Mohammed several years back.'

A beer-bellied, wart-faced Nazi from Bethnal Green, in neat jeans and a Marks and Spencer jacket, fidgeted a couple of rows behind the mild little Pakistani chemistry teacher, curled in her bright sari like a small bird. He stared at the glossy black plait down the back of the sari, cracked his knuckles and longed for action. The clothes irked him. The bossy old bitch at the front had been adamant – Marks and Spencer, and a clean shirt, because he'd never get inside the door in leather.

Garlick came back to the present and studied the rows near him anxiously. Now he was looking, he could see several of them, National Front heavies, especially Raymond

Warburg. They'd expelled him for beating up a black kid, at around the same time as they threw Ben out. Ben was stupid and pathetic. Warburg wasn't stupid, had been going to take GCSEs, lost his future in one vicious punch-up over some imaginary insult.

Oh my, Garlick thought, worried. Old grudges are surfacing tonight. Old wounds reopened by an invitation to debate the future of the school they hated, that let them down.

He leaned his fists on his short legs and discreetly tried to study as many faces as he could see without turning right round. It couldn't be a coincidence that they were all there, carefully dispersed among the crowd. The police were all tied up trying to find a rapist. Someone said they'd got a man, but it wasn't official.

Out of the corner of his eye, Garlick could see Warburg's knuckles clenched, bone white. Ray Warburg was eaten up with rage at the bitter memory of one black kid who'd picked a fight and won. Unemployed all his life, Raymond didn't forget and didn't forgive, hated the government with vitriolic loathing. He massaged his knuckles and cracked them loudly. More and more anxious, Garlick waited.

Chapter Nineteen

Oblivious to the nasty atmosphere building around him, the Stud punched the button on his stopwatch and looked at it. Hugo's speech had been *much* shorter than anyone had expected. Seventeen minutes, fifty-three seconds. He frowned. He was nowhere near, at thirty-five minutes. So far as he could recall, the nearest guess had been half an hour, which meant the French department's syndicate of three had won about fifty quid between them. The squat and disagreeable-looking woman from the LEA was waddling up to the lectern, looking as though at any moment her tremendous jowls would swell into a vast blister of indignation, like one of those frogs who puff out their necks when threatened.

Or was it when a filly frog cantered past and got them all excited? Garlick would know, since he knew so much about animal courtship and nothing at all about the human. Stud picked dried tomato ketchup off his tie, irritated. He hated losing bets.

'Don't be deceived. This is a Conservative plot,' Jemima Habgood shouted. 'They want to bring back selective education. Before you know it, you won't have a community school, you'll have a grammar school, creaming off the best.'

She banged the papers in front of her energetically, dropped half of them, and ranted on. Hugo watched apprehensively as she worked herself up.

'This school is bottom of the league table. You've got the poorest record in the whole of Inner London. Do you think,' she yelled, smacking the side of the lectern with gusto, 'depriving it of Local Authority resources will *help*? Without our support, and our expertise, you'll sink to the point where it's no longer viable to keep you open. Is that in anyone's interest? Except,' she hissed scornfully, 'the Conservative Party's and yours, Mr Benedict? *And* yours,' she panted, rounding on Absalom, who jumped nervously and mopped his brow.

'You intend to close us down, and sell the site,' Hugo said. 'If we opt out, you say we'll end up closing down anyway. What have we to lose?'

'Hidden agenda,' she shot back. 'Selective education. You'll change the nature of the school. This is a Labour borough. We'll never stand for it.'

'Never,' yelped one of the Labour Party, setting off a storm of foot-stomping and rowdy jeering.

She pointed a fat, accusing finger at Hugo.

'Hypocrite. You came here from a selective school, in West London. That's what you want to bring here. We have no plans to close this school, but you've got plans to change it, and drive out local children, who will have to go elsewhere.'

'Aaaah,' sighed the fickle hall, seeing Hugo on the ropes.

He appeared lost in thought.

'There you are, you got an undertaking. She won't close you down, so you don't need to do no optin' out,' Ernie called.

Hugo roused himself.

'And I tell you this lady is a liar,' he returned pleasantly. 'As quite a few of you in this hall who are not our parents, particularly you from the National Front and the local Labour Party at the back there, know perfectly well, being of the same persuasion yourselves.'

The hall, for one long moment, froze.

'Hugo, *no*,' Bunny groaned aloud and buried her head in her hands. Melanie clutched Alastair's arm. Garlick closed his eyes. All that was left was to hope no one got killed.

'You calling me a liar?'

Hugo recognized Ben as he uncoiled like a cobra, the blade in his palm flashing as the front rows erupted and fought to get out of his way.

'You gonna get what's comin' to you,' Raymond hissed softly, lumbering out of his seat.

Ben, lithe and supple, slithered through the uproar, overturning chairs, waving the gleaming knife at terrified people scrambling to get out of the way. The rest of the National Front leaped at Hugo and Absalom, pulling knives from their sleeves. Hugo turned, found Raymond crouched behind him, grinning from ear to ear, waving a four-inch blade in his face.

'Put it down,' Hugo snapped.

'She's orchestrated this,' Alastair muttered, pushing Melanie to one side of the hall, out of immediate harm's way. Mrs Habgood stormed about like a loose cannon, yelling at them to stop.

Absalom reached into his belt, his hand hidden by his jacket.

'Behind you,' he shouted at Hugo.

Ben darted on to the stage, swift and sudden as a lizard. Hugo spun round, his baggy corduroy jacket as neatly slashed as an advertisement for Silk Cut.

'Good God,' he said, standing stock still and staring at the damage. Raymond moved in, dancing on the balls of his feet, weaving the knife in the air.

'*Hugo*,' Bunny screamed.

'Jesus save us,' Angelina shrieked, diving for the door at the back of the hall.

'*Hallelujah*,' the turban brigade yodelled frantically, a Pavlovian response to *Jesus*, eyes rolling in fright.

Raymond snickered, licked his lips, lunged, then choked on his own front teeth as Hugo's fist connected viciously.

'And you,' Absalom snarled, drawing a knife on Mrs Habgood. 'You set this up.'

'No,' roared Ernie, hurtling forward. Ben howled briefly,

then gasped silently and desperately for air, as eighteen stone headbutted him in the solar plexus. The knife shot from his grip with such force it embedded itself in the discordant old grand piano on the far side of the hall with a *plink* of a single key.

'We can't 'ave governors using knives,' said Ernie reproachfully, getting between Absalom and Jemima Habgood, and watching the winded Ben clutch his stomach and go dark blue in the face.

'Stop panickin',' he yelled. 'It's over.'

The audience stopped fighting to get out all at once, and stood still. Absalom nodded, put the knife back in his belt and wiped his brow. Hugo marched over, pulled it out again and threw it into the back of the stage in disgust.

'You ass, you've sunk us,' he snarled. '*Everyone* saw that.'

'I didn't see nothin', did you?' Ernie addressed the silent crowd. 'Except a man who knows how to handle trouble. And he's got enough of it comin' when we have Mr Benedict's vote and give him all this responsibility he wants for settin' a good example to our kids.'

'*Oh,* what a *man,*' breathed Winanda, pushing and shoving like a bulldozer, hurrying to her hero's side before anyone else could snap him up.

'After that it was all over quite quickly, wasn't it?' Hugo said smugly, dishing out coffee in the staff room, while Stuttering Stan cowered just out of sight, scared to pursue the urgent question of locking up. With a temper like that on him, a lethal left hook, and a chairman of governors who carried a knife and knew how to use it, Hugo and co. were not to be messed with. Stuttering Stan was lost in admiration.

'Burglary, murder and a riot in one night,' said Melanie faintly to Alastair, who was trying to find his umbrella. 'Giles never turned up.'

'Not one of life's better days,' he agreed with his back to her, his voice muffled because he was hunting behind the filing cabinet for his umbrella. It was hidden in the whisky drawer. 'I bet the Stud put that in here deliberately. Is it still raining?'

'Pouring,' Melanie said, her nose to the window. Outside looked horrible.

He waved the umbrella at her.

'Yours is wrecked and I don't want you getting pneumonia. So come along, Mrs T., I am going to walk you home.'

Chapter Twenty

The rain had eased off when they came out of the school, the wind risen higher, leaving the night sky streaked with ragged black clouds, scudding across the brilliant face of a full moon riding high. Streetlamps killed the moonlight, cast dense shadows under the holly bushes in Melanie's front garden, their dark leaves shining black and wet in the yellow sodium light. Across the road, lights were on all up the flats and on the third floor Bertie's curtain twitched as she watched Melanie, in the glow of the streetlamp, hunt for her front-door key. A long, thin, dark figure, whom Bertie didn't recognize, stood over her.

'Come and meet Giles,' Melanie told Alastair. 'We can tell him what a drama he missed.'

'Dad's out,' said Alice, in her dressing gown, coming downstairs and finding them standing in the kitchen. She eyed Alastair dubiously.

'Mr Croke kindly walked me home,' her mother snapped, intercepting the look.

'*Mum*, he's a teacher,' Alice hissed. 'You can't start bringing them home.'

'So am I a teacher,' her mother answered repressively. 'Go to bed.'

Alastair smiled.

'She thinks I'm a kid,' she complained, half smiling back.

'*Bed*. Didn't Dad come back, or ring?' Melanie called after Alice, who flounced indignantly and shook her head.

'He generally rings if he's going to be this late,' Melanie said, filling the kettle.

Even if half the time he was lying, she thought, having long since worked out that his occasional disappearances, on some ecumenical excuse or other, generally coincided with George Haines's equally occasional business trips away from King's Lynn. The thought that he might have started that up again made her so angry she slammed the kettle on to the stove, making Alastair jump.

'Are you all right?' he demanded.

'No,' she snapped, meaning to lie and say *yes*, and was saved from explaining by a knock on the back door.

'That'll be him, forgotten his key. Where *have* you been?' she cried, opening the door, to find Bertie leaning on the wall outside. The wind blew her long coat open, showing a very short black leather dress, the same thigh-length boots, black velvet tights in place of the fishnets. She had her head right back, was surveying the moon. Dressed in a tiny red jacket and scarf against the wind, Baby Jane was wrapped round her neck like a little stole.

'You can see the man in the moon clearly tonight. When the clouds get out of the way.'

Melanie eyed her in the light from the kitchen window.

'I thought you were Giles, Bertie. I have had an *extremely* trying day and I'm not going to ask you in, if that is what you wanted.'

Bertie turned, her eyes glittering, enormously ringed with kohl, shrewd and hard as nails.

'I'm on my way to work, and I don't want to disturb you with your gentleman friend. I haven't got time,' Bertie said coldly. 'I've been waiting for you because I have something to tell you that's urgent.'

Melanie held the door open.

'Now I'm invited in,' Bertie remarked to herself. 'This is confidential,' she added.

She brought a cloud of Chanel No. 5 into the kitchen, where the kettle was boiling itself dry while Alastair looked for mugs. Baby Jane's big eyes blinked warily and she sniffed the air.

'In the bottom cupboard. Bertie, this is Alastair Croke. We teach at the same school. Bertie caught Weasel. *Alice*, go to *bed*.'

Caught, Alice made a show of stamping upstairs again, crept back down, put her ear to the keyhole and stood trying to listen while her feet froze. It was all for nothing. The old rectory's thick Victorian walls and solid doors let nothing through. Frustrated, she couldn't hear a thing.

'I told the kids to clear up,' Melanie was saying.

The kitchen table was a litter of dirty plates, discarded crusts of pizza, cold coffee cups and apple cores. The washing-up from breakfast was still in the sink, their cornflake-encrusted glasses from supper thrown in on top.

Alastair found three clean mugs, cleared the table, slid coffee in front of them.

'If it's anything to do with burglars or Neighbourhood Watch, Bertie, couldn't it wait until tomorrow?'

Bertie crossed her legs. The leather skirt rode up until she met Alastair's amused gaze. She uncrossed them hastily.

'Do you or don't you want me to tell you?' she snapped petulantly. 'Your old man's in the police station and they're trying to charge him with murder and rape.'

'Is this your idea of a joke?' asked Melanie furiously.

Bertie scowled and appealed to Alastair.

'Make her listen, will you?'

'He hasn't been home,' he said. 'And Alice said he hasn't called. I think this is not a joke, Mrs T.'

'They won't *let* him call,' Bertie cried crossly. 'And the idiot hadn't got a lawyer down there when he started confessing. The Law's just laughing their heads off.'

Melanie was white as a sheet.

'I don't believe you,' she cried. 'You're lying.'

'How do you know all this?' demanded Alastair.

'I'm a host*ess* in a drinking club,' hissed Bertie, baring her even white teeth at him in a smile. 'We get the Law in there and I hear all sorts of things.'

'You mean the child in the park?' said Melanie,

bewildered. 'They think he killed the child in the park? Did you say he's *confessing*?'

'That's what I hear,' said Bertie. 'It's red-hot gossip, I can tell you.'

'*Gossip*,' muttered Alastair, shocked.

The tap dripped in the silence.

'What should I do?' Melanie asked at last.

'Ring them up in the morning and ask nicely to go and see him. Look, I'm going to work.'

'Shouldn't I go to the police station now?'

She sounded dazed.

'It's midnight,' Bertie pointed out impatiently. 'You get an appointment in the morning and tell them you want to see the custody officer, and ask him if you can see your old man. He might say no.'

'Why might he say no?' asked Melanie numbly.

'Depends,' Bertie answered shortly, getting up and clicking her fingers for Baby Jane.

'What on?' cried Melanie. 'He's *innocent*.'

Bertie drew a finger across her throat.

'*No*,' Melanie cried violently.

Eventually, Bertie shrugged.

'Depends whether the custody officer got out of bed the right side, whether he feels like being nice to a murder suspect. And if your old man *is* innocent, it means whoever *did* do it is still out there,' she hissed, buttoning her long black coat. 'So keep your doors and windows locked.'

Then she was out of the kitchen, out of the house, disappeared into the cold and dark, Baby Jane wrapped close around her neck.

Chapter Twenty-One

Red-eyed and exhausted, Melanie watched dawn break, bringing a dull, grey, overcast morning, the north wind still rattling in the holly bushes. From her bedroom window she could see the ancient cherub in the distance, scurrying like a beetle on his rickety legs in and out of the gravestones. At six o'clock she couldn't wait any longer and telephoned the police station.

'Yes,' said a surly voice. 'We're holding Mr Tilford here.'

She did as Bertie told her. After a long wait, the surly voice came back and told her she had an appointment to see the custody officer at eleven.

Time dragged, the sky darkened, and the cherub disappeared inside the church. Then the rain came down again, so heavy she could no longer see the bushes where the girl had died, at the far end of the park. At seven o'clock, she filled the bath with very hot water, lay in it mentally reviewing the contents of her sparse wardrobe. She shivered. Even boiling hot water couldn't warm her up. She got out and went downstairs, wrapped in Giles's old felt dressing gown, and went into his study. Alastair was fast asleep on the couch. He was snuffling rhythmically, buried in a duvet, his feet hanging over the end of the scratchy old sofa. She sat down on the end and looked at him crossly.

'I'm awake really,' he said with his eyes shut.

'You are now. I couldn't sleep and I'm cold. I've been watching our churchwarden. He's been out there since daybreak. I wonder what he's doing,' she said listlessly. 'What does one wear to go and bail out one's husband? I thought I'd leave my tiara at home.'

She tried to smile at her own feeble joke.

He opened one eye.

'You look awful,' he said.

'No murderers or rapists came in the night,' she said shortly. 'I should know.'

'I'm sorry,' he said humbly. 'But I'm afraid I slept like a log.'

'I don't want the kids to know you are here. They'll start asking questions and I haven't got the answers.'

'I'm not here,' he agreed happily, closing his eyes again. 'Wake me up when the coast is clear.'

She banged the door enviously as she went out, and left him until they had gone to school.

Showered, shaved with Giles's razor, and in one of his clean shirts, Alastair looked dapper, his hair in a neat ponytail held in a red rubber band. Down at the police station, at eleven o'clock precisely, the custody officer regarded them both with undisguised suspicion.

'You a relative?' he demanded.

'Mr Croke is a friend,' she said defensively.

His lip curled. She flushed and fought a longing to turn around and run right away again.

'In here.'

He took them into a windowless, claustrophobic interview room that smelled of stale fish and chips and cigarettes, pulled out a scarred wooden chair for Melanie.

'Yes?' he said unhelpfully.

'I'd like to see my husband,' she said, smiling nervously.

He stared back, not smiling at all, black as ebony, the whites of his hard brown eyes very bloodshot.

'Why?' he asked, folding his arms, muscles bulging under the dark blue jacket.

Melanie met his scrutiny blankly. She couldn't think of one good reason.

'I just want to see him. I didn't come with an excuse,' she said lamely. 'I want to know what's going on.'

His bloodshot eyes looked right through her, made her uneasy. He had an educated accent, no trace of the West Indies left after three generations of his family born in London. He pulled at his lower lip and considered. Melanie waited.

'Mr Tilford says he was in church all yesterday afternoon. He says he was saying his prayers and contemplating his sins. He also says he was full of remorse and asking God to forgive him.' The bloodshot eyes weighed her up. 'Did you see him at his prayers? Did you go into the church? Did he come home and just happens to have forgotten about it? Have you come to give your husband an alibi, Mrs Tilford?'

'What? No,' she said, frightened by the sarcasm in his voice.

He said nothing.

'I was at work yesterday, until very late. I'm a teacher at East Stepney. We had a meeting that went on until nearly ten, and I expected my husband to come to it. We were burgled, and if you ask, you'll find I was expecting him to come home while the police were there.'

'He is being questioned about a very serious offence,' he said abruptly.

Melanie leaned over the table towards him. He had a strong, hard face, very coarse, pitted skin, his beard already showing in mid-morning.

'Why are you questioning him? What's he done to make you think he's done anything?' she blurted.

'He's been acting very guiltily,' he said simply.

Melanie looked away and tried to think clearly.

'What does that mean?' demanded Alastair.

'He ignored his caution, kept telling the arresting officer that he didn't mean to hurt her. He has made a statement that is only just short of a confession. If a suspect says he's guilty, he generally is, in my experience.'

'He can't be,' Melanie said flatly, stunned. 'He must have got confused.'

'He doesn't seem confused. He seems remorseful,' the

black officer said. 'His behaviour is really rather damning, all in all.'

She tried to match his ghost of a smile.

'Giles is always feeling remorseful. He goes blundering around. Then he dwells on things and they get on top of him, but he couldn't kill anyone.'

'I don't suppose Sonia Sutcliffe thought Peter had it in him, either,' he said coldly. 'People are surprising. Look at Fred West. Nice bloke who was good for a pint down the pub. Quiet, family man with a garden full of bodies. You can't *tell*.' He leaned forward until their noses almost met over the table. 'Just how well do you really know your husband, Mrs Tilford?'

'We've been married twenty years,' she said after a long pause.

'You can be married twenty years to a stranger,' he said bluntly. 'Or he might have flipped, due to a lot of pressure and strain since you moved here from the country. He isn't happy, Mrs Tilford, he's a very tormented man.'

The bloodshot eyes held hers unwinkingly.

'Giles seems to have told you a lot more than he tells me,' she said reluctantly.

'This is the point I am making,' the custody officer said.

'I feel sick,' she said.

The two men sat and looked at her.

'Dora and Dorcas. Their mother picked their father up in the Mummy Room. I find that disturbing.'

'I don't think she's very well,' said Alastair. 'Will someone bring her some water?'

'I don't want water.'

Melanie turned back to the officer.

'I remember, now. I did look in at the church on my way home from school last night. Dora and Dorcas Murgatroyd were in the porch, changing dressings on an old woman's feet.'

'You said you didn't see Giles,' Alastair prompted.

'I didn't. What he just said about strangers reminded me

of the two Ds and their mother having them with a stranger. I always thought that was an absolutely shocking thing to do.' She laughed harshly. 'I should criticize. You are saying I've been married all this time to a homicidal rapist. I never suspected a thing. How about that for going with a stranger?'

Alastair started out of his chair.

'Look,' he began angrily.

'I'm all right,' she said tonelessly.

Maybe she didn't know Giles at all. Eyes fixed on nothing, she shook her head wordlessly.

'Since he's being so helpful, why should I let you see him?'

Melanie looked dazed and shook her head again.

'OK. Half an hour. Before you see him, WPC Jackie Smith will search you,' he said, getting up.

'*Search me?* What for?'

'We are now among the criminal classes,' muttered Alastair. 'And will be treated with contempt. I warned you.'

He had stayed with her, had warned her about all sorts of things, made cups of tea, waited up with her until she was exhausted enough, he thought, to sleep. She had gone over and over the terrible things that could happen, until two o'clock in the morning.

'They do get it wrong. They make mistakes. Look at the Guildford Four,' she argued.

'That's the IRA.'

She pushed a mug away from her fretfully.

'I can't drink another drop of tea. I don't want to spend the rest of my life campaigning to get Giles out of prison. Does that make me terribly selfish? And what am I going to tell the children? Daddy's going to get life for murder?'

'Tell them nothing. He hasn't even been charged. Go,' he said firmly. 'Try to get some sleep.'

'You know,' she announced, getting up, 'I'll kill him for this.'

She picked a plate out of the cold greasy water in the sink

and dropped it back again. 'This is growing things and I don't care.'

She faced him.

'Daffodil was bad enough, but getting accused of murder is criminal.'

'Daffodil?' asked Alastair, yawning.

'Giles's mistress,' Melanie said brightly. 'She was fat and horsy and a cheat. Thinking about her makes me feel better, because I get angry.'

'I don't think I take to your husband,' he said quietly.

'The church turns a blind eye so long as I do, too, and don't do something unforgivable, like wanting a divorce.'

'The wife wanted a divorce,' he answered bleakly. 'So I gave it to her and then she took my kids away.'

His thin face was sad and vulnerable, the acid-tongued tease all gone.

'You are too nice a man for her to do that,' she said sadly. 'There's a couch in the study, if you want it. It's not very comfortable. Or perhaps you'd rather go home.'

'No. Since you ask, I'd rather stay, keep an eye on you and be on the safe side.'

'And I would like you to,' she said.

Chapter Twenty-Two

'You've only been in here one night and you look like something out of London Zoo. Who do you think you are, Brian Keenan or John McCarthy, or something? Giles, *what* is going on?'

Melanie peered from behind the shoulder of the odious Jackie Smith as she opened the door of Giles's cell, and was brought up short by the sight of him hunched on a mattress, almost curled into a foetal ball of misery.

'I warned you we were very sorry for ourself,' said WPC Jackie Smith smugly.

Melanie regarded her with her nose in the air and faced her down. Just because WPC Jackie Smith was tall and willowy, with a bust like Raquel Welch, a face like Brooke Shields, and had just examined her down to her knickers and more didn't mean she had the right to make personal comments. Melanie wished furiously that Bertie had warned her about the searching.

'Can't really imagine him murdering someone, can you?' Jackie murmured. 'Not enough backbone. He's all yours for half an hour, Mrs Tilford. Make the most of it.'

She grinned wickedly and held the door open.

Melanie swallowed an impulse to explain how *extremely* much she disliked her, and marched into the cell.

'I'm just outside,' Jackie said sweetly.

'I bet you are,' muttered Melanie, pushing the door shut savagely with one foot, hearing the key turn on the other side. As the door clanged shut, she folded her arms in a gesture of pure rage, all sympathy evaporated by the sight that met her.

Giles lay hunched awkwardly on his mattress, all jutting bones and knees, like a cornered giraffe, his eyes alarmed, bloodshot and staring on the end of a neck long and naked without its dog collar. Long legs covered in mud from where he had knelt on the sodden ground folded up beneath his chin, his arms wrapped tightly round them. His lopsided, untidy face, dark with stubble, had cocooned itself in misery.

'You could get up and say hello to me,' Melanie hissed, shaking with shock and fury. 'Giles, *look at me*.'

'Hello. I didn't expect you to come,' he said, unwinding his arms. 'They haven't let me ring you. They won't let me ring anyone.'

'I just realized something,' she announced ominously into a prolonged silence. 'In all the time I've been married to you, I've never really lost my temper. I'm about to do that now if you don't get up and start behaving like a normal human being.'

'I wouldn't do that here,' he said in a hollow voice. 'They'll have both of us inside for assault.'

Any response was a sign of life. Melanie waded in.

'*What* is going on?'

'They're accusing me of murder.'

'I've been talking to the custody officer. They haven't accused you of anything. They suspect you.'

'It means the same thing.'

'It does not. Have you?'

'Have I what?'

'*Killed someone*,' she shrieked, her nerves giving way.

He pointed at the door and shook his head.

'I don't care if *God* is listening, I need to know,' she hissed.

'He is,' said Giles resignedly.

Melanie clenched her fists.

'Really? Then you'd better start praying He won't let me hit you,' she threatened. 'Because I'm at the end of my tether.'

Giles cowered. On the other side of the door, Jackie Smith

cracked up with laughter, then stood shaking her head, listening to them shouting at each other for all they were worth.

'They've questioned me,' Melanie yelled. 'Then they imply that I'm lying. Then they *body-searched* me.'

Giles stared at the wall, counted the ticks on a calendar that someone had etched into the plaster, blotting out a wife who shouted and swore, whom he had never met before.

'Don't you *dare* shut your eyes and ignore me,' she shrieked. 'They are treating me like a criminal. What do you expect me to tell the kids?'

'I don't know what you can tell the kids, except they are treating me like a criminal too,' he answered.

'If you go confessing to things you haven't done, what else do you expect, you ass? Even that silly bitch next door thinks you're too spineless to murder anyone, so what on earth are you doing, making them think you have?'

Jackie Smith bridled, folding her arms vengefully, her face drawn in on itself like a prune. Wait till Mrs Tilford wanted a favour, once they'd charged her husband. She'd want visits, to bring the kids in . . . phone calls . . . Until they remanded him in custody, Mrs Tilford could have quite a frustrating time.

'Well?' yelled Melanie.

'It smells in here. You don't have to stay,' Giles said. 'If you can't calm down a bit, Melanie, I'd rather you went away.'

A stained toilet in the corner smelled of urine. Melanie came over and sat down on the end of his mattress.

'I will stay,' she said mulishly, 'until I know what is happening.'

'They won't let you,' he answered.

'I have half an hour, and it's going to be the longest half-hour of our lives, unless you start making sense.'

Arms folded, she looked immovable as the Sphinx.

He was up one of life's cul-de-sacs, and his wife was waiting at the end of it, with a metaphorical rolling pin in her hand, to dish out a monstrous headache.

'Remember you insisted on knowing.'

Giles turned towards her, resigned.

'You look shifty,' Melanie exclaimed, surprised. 'You don't look like someone who is being accused of something they didn't do. You look like someone who has got something to hide.'

Giles made one last evasive effort.

'You could be wrong.'

'After twenty years of marriage,' she said evenly, 'I've just discovered I don't really know you, but I know when you're lying, because I've had such a lot of practice.'

His shoulders stiffened.

'For once in your life, Giles,' Melanie said, her voice sinking to a whisper, 'why don't you just tell me the truth?'

They kept her waiting in the claustrophobic, shabby little interview room for ages and ages, before the black officer came back to see her, at her request.

'Yes?' he said, pulling out a chair and sitting down.

Melanie swallowed, her mouth dry as dust, fiddled with her wedding ring.

'This is *extremely* embarrassing, but I have some things to tell you, so that you can let my husband go.'

'Yes?'

'If you say *yes?* like that once more, I'll scream,' she said matter-of-factly.

'Yes.'

She looked at him hard.

'I mean, uh huh, go on,' he said.

'He's been having an affair with one of his parishioners, when we were in Norfolk. I've just told him I knew all along.'

'Yes?'

She glared.

'Now he says he's very attracted to someone in his present congregation, and although it hasn't led to anything yet, he's afraid it will. He has a weakness for women. He even imagined he was attracted to our daughter and that has been preying on his mind. He hadn't touched her; it's all in his mind,' she added hastily.

The big black man stared, his eyes more bloodshot than ever.

'You believe that?'

'Yes,' Melanie said firmly. 'Alice is perfectly all right.'

'You'd never think it, would you, to see him? He doesn't look like a Casanova,' he said finally, screwing his face up as if trying to visualize the impossible. 'Do women go for the frock?'

He was black, and she wasn't racist, and if she was, this was not the place to show it. Melanie struggled not to hate him for mocking her, hated him all the more, and ploughed on.

'He knows there's been drug-taking and . . . other things in his graveyard, which he should have stopped.'

'Been snorting and rolling in the hay, have they?' said the officer expressionlessly. 'Rolling in the hay isn't a criminal offence. Enough to give them rheumatism, with all the rain we've been having. Top of a gravestone isn't my idea of comfort. The old man used to hand out condoms. And ran a needle exchange. But he'd never have anything to do with hard drugs or crack.'

'What the old man did and didn't do has been half the problem,' she said dismally. 'Giles can't live up to him.'

'Few could,' the officer said shortly.

'Don't *you* start,' she snapped. 'And there've been desecrations and swastikas daubed. He found a cross burned upside down in one of the mausoleums. He's done nothing about it, because it scares him stiff.'

'It's their idea of fun,' he said calmly, sounding more friendly. 'Oddballs, Hell's Angels, kids from your school, National Front. It passes the time, and we know where to find them. They take ouija boards and tarot and all sorts in there. The old man made them show him the ouija board, so he could stop them getting hysterical when it went bad.'

'Giles found books on witchcraft.'

'The old man liked to keep up with the kids' interests,' he answered, grinning.

'I think if my husband hears one more thing the old man did, he'll move away,' she answered grimly.

'Then he'd better go back to the country,' said the black officer stolidly, without a trace of a smile. 'Because around here, that is how it is.

'So,' he said. 'We got adultery, with someone in his church. Intended adultery. Abuse of trust. Abuse of consecrated land and lack of pastoral care.'

She gazed at him, the stark light above them reflected in his shiny black eyes. Her dislike faded into respect. He was merely telling her the truth.

'That's why he ran away from your helicopter. He was confused. He thought he was having a vision, like St Paul. He'd been on his knees all afternoon, praying for help, and when he comes out of church, the next thing he knows is there's a great light shining and people calling to him to give himself up. All his confessing that you thought was about the murder was about what I've just told you.'

He glanced at the clock.

'We'll let him go. Sounds like he could use some help.'

'They'll offer him spiritual counselling,' she said drily. 'And sweep it all under the carpet.'

She was pale and calm, sat with her fingers laced in her lap, marble-faced with exhaustion.

I don't chase little girls. I only chase big ones.

The officer sighed. It had seemed too good to be true, and it was. They still had a killer on the loose.

'OK. We've still got a murder investigation on our hands,' he said briskly. 'You can take him home, Mrs Tilford.'

He went out of the room, then poked his head back in again.

'The gentleman is still waiting outside,' he said, expressionless.

Her pallor changed to a thin flush. He evidently thought that Alastair and she . . . He grinned at her acute discomfort and went off to talk to CID.

Chapter Twenty-Three

They set Giles free immediately.

'He went,' said the WPC on the reception desk when Melanie came looking for Alastair. 'Said to tell you he's gone to school.'

The woman watched her face fall and thought *poor old vicar. His wife's in love with the ponytail man.* Alastair was only being tactful, but Melanie was taken aback – shocked – at her own disappointment not to find him waiting there.

Giles embarrassed them both by crying on the way home. Like one of the tramps dozing away the damp and drizzly afternoon on benches, he shambled beside her on the short walk, blew his nose and tried to talk about the future.

'I haven't got one. I have to tell you that I can't stay here. I can't face it,' he announced.

'You haven't got any more than you had coming to you,' she snapped, hanging on to her patience. 'You could brighten up a bit. You're not going to prison, you're going home to nothing more terrible than a hot bath and a change of clothes. You could at least be grateful and remember that your future could easily have been in Wormwood Scrubs. Ever since we moved here, you've been so sorry for yourself, I could strangle you.'

'I'm the one who is supposed to be strangling people,' he said, with a macabre grin, looking for a tissue in his pocket and pulling out a crushed dog collar. 'Look at this. Ruined.'

'Uuuurgh,' snarled his wife, between her teeth.

Giles stumped morosely forward, hoist with his own petard, emotionally speaking, not grateful in the least that she had helped him stay out of worse trouble.

They squelched over a corner of the park; at the other end the police bunting hung limp around the bushes where the child had died.

'That foxy little Welsh policeman suggested you should go and see the parents,' she said. 'I don't suppose you'll be able to now. It wouldn't be exactly tactful, seeing as you've just stopped being the prime suspect.'

The black joke amused her and she laughed for the first time that day.

'When I have had a bath and got into clean clothes,' he said, unamused, 'then we will decide what to do.'

His words brought back a sudden, vivid memory of her grandmother, long thick grey hair in a bun, warm and comfortable, ample-lapped and cosy, scented with eau-de-Cologne, fanatical about clean underwear, in case you had an accident.

'Clean every morning,' she said to little Melanie, stirring fizzing Andrews liver salts into a glass of water, which Melanie thought were lemonade and begged each morning to share. 'If you have an accident, darling, you don't want them seeing dirty underwear.'

Melanie had been in her teens before she realized that changing underwear was not merely for the benefit of doctors and nurses. In her grandmother's house, she was taught, emergencies and cleanliness went together. This was an emergency.

'No,' she corrected him. '*I'm* going to have a hot bath. *I'm* the one who had that woman's hands all over me. The only time I felt naked like that in front of another person was when I had the children, and then you're so doolally on pethidine you couldn't care less. What's the matter *now*?'

Giles was holding his hands in front of his face, coughing like a patient with terminal tuberculosis.

'Ange . . . Mrs Tutti Frutti,' he spluttered.

'Oh, *really*. Babies think if they can't see you, you can't see them,' she snapped back. 'That's one of your congregation coming towards us, and she's seen you, all right.'

She smiled charmingly and waved at Angelina in the distance, picking her way round puddles, on her way to school, to her flexitime cleaning job. Angelina changed tack, veered towards them, beaming from ear to ear, and yelled at the top of her voice.

'*No,*' groaned Giles. 'Not her.'

'Oh. She's the one. She's the one whose baby you dropped as well, isn't she?' Melanie muttered, picking up his panic and the reason for it with the accuracy of twenty years of marriage. 'She cleans at school.'

She stared briefly at Angelina, trying to imagine Giles and the cleaner . . . though he'd sworn, in his cell, that nothing had gone on, and refused to name the woman.

'Mels,' he hissed, speeding up. 'Come *on.*'

Melanie began to walk fast, trying to keep up with him.

Angelina's voice carried sweetly and clearly down the clear, rain-washed air. On benches, sleepy heads raised, damp newspapers fluttered, children looked, and several people walking dogs turned to stare.

'Vicaaaar. So glad you're out of jail, Vicaaar,' Angelina shouted. 'We were goin' to visit. *We* never reckoned you done nothing, don't you worry about that.'

Giles groaned. She was catching up with him, out of breath.

'Just wanted to tell you, Young Wives want to keep the crèche on. They know the kids are safe with you,' she carolled. 'See you Sunday, Vicaaaar, if you can't stop just now.'

'Sunday,' gasped Giles, half saluting, half swatting her away.

Others weren't so sure, said her tone of voice. Young Wives had already gossiped themselves silly over it, and he'd only been in the police station overnight.

He began to race for home, stopped short. Guilty men run. In an agony of self-consciousness, he slowed down, walked the rest of the way to the gate by the holly tree at a dignified pace, followed to the corner of his road by a dozen attentive, speculative, judgemental pairs of eyes.

'That's done it. The whole world knows now,' he cried.

'This is the East End,' Melanie yelled, exasperated. 'Half of them probably knew before I did that you were inside. We'll have to face it, Giles, you can't keep secrets here like you did before.'

When they got home, they found every bit of crockery they owned was overflowing from the sink.

'Hasn't anyone done anything while I've been rotting in that place?' he complained, picking at the algae of grease and food growing busily on top of cold washing-up water.

'Yes,' she said icily. 'I've been doing something. I've been burgled, we've had a violent riot at school, I've got you out of jail and on top of all that, I've been *thinking*. One of the things I've been thinking is that you can do the washing-up yourself.'

'Mels,' he protested, but she stamped upstairs, locked the door, was busy emptying the hot-water tank into the bath.

'Soothe and relax,' she muttered, reading the side of an ancient pack of bath salts in a damp and swollen box. 'That's me.'

She tipped the whole boxful into the boiling water, threw her clothes in a corner and got in.

Downstairs the front door went, and she heard Tom, home early from school. Free periods for study were indicated by the music from the last video-taped episodes of *Neighbours* drifting up. Giles's voice interrupted and there was silence again. She wondered what Giles would say to the kids about what had happened, how Tom would react, whether she should tell her father. Rose and Andrew would have heart attacks, were best left in ignorance about their beloved son's double life. She swirled the water, dissolving the overdose of bath salts, and considered.

Alice and Tom would sit in judgement on everyone concerned; teenagers always did. Everyone else would have a glorious gossip – the Vicar, Daffodil, the Holy Roller and the Wife. It sounded like a film.

'They should make one,' she told the soap dish, fishing soap out with her foot. 'Then *Time Out* and *The Sunday Times* could be rude and look down their noses and say *this couldn't happen*. People always think things can't happen, just because they're improbable.' She dropped the soap and fished for it. 'Look at Woody Allen and Mia Farrow and *their* carryings-on, with a dozen or so adopted children. Put *that* in a book, and who'd believe it!'

It was a comforting thought; other people had *much* bigger scandals than theirs. She lay back in the scalding water, the bathroom shrouded in steam. Pine-scented Radox brought memories of pine trees in copses at the top of the dunes, breaking the winds sweeping the great, empty North Norfolk beaches, blowing from Siberia across the grey-green sea, endless and empty, a long, curving horizon with a ship, ghostly in the sea mist, sliding over it under the vast, dull white bowl of the sky. I do miss it, sometimes, she thought.

There had been good times, moments to cherish. One blustery Sunday afternoon, years ago, after lunch and before evensong, she had walked hand in hand with Giles, Alice in a baby carrier on his back, Tom toddling on ahead. Their feet crunched fallen cones in the fine sand, under the pines at Holkham Nature Reserve. The pines smelled strong, heavy with resin, the sea smelled of salt and weed and faraway places. The beach was deserted but for them, a flock of gulls and two distant figures down near the water's edge, walking briskly, heads down into the April wind. One small figure wore a headscarf, long coat and wellingtons. The other, tall and dressed in a navy raincoat, walked just behind. Giles had put his arm around her shoulders to stop her, called to Tom to come back.

'Sssh. That's the Queen,' he said. 'Down there.'

Melanie had looked hard. Except for the familiar headscarf, the tiny figure could have been anyone.

'How do you know?' she asked, not quite believing him.

'She's at Sandringham. With Princess Margaret and her mother. That's her detective, behind her.'

She stared. As if feeling her gaze, the Queen turned and looked towards the pines, saw them standing there.

'What do we do?' Melanie whispered.

'We pretend we never saw her, leave her to walk in peace.'

The small woman half raised her hand, the gesture automatic. The navy-coated man was between them and her in a moment, the half-wave lost from view, and the Queen began her pacing along the water's edge again, her detective dropping back, no danger here on the wild, deserted coast.

'She looks as if she's all alone in the world,' Melanie whispered, feeling sorry for her.

'Can't be much fun,' he said.

Alice had started to cry, her cheeks chapped by the wind, and they walked back, out of the cold, leaving the small woman to her solitude. Some months later, Giles took a service at Sandringham when the minister there went away. Melanie took Alice and sat in the front of the church, but the Queen was on a state visit to somewhere or other, and none of the royal family was there.

'Poor old Queen.' Melanie sniffed Radox sadly, sneezed, and tried to turn the leaky chrome tap at the end of the bath off with her toes. 'But at least she doesn't have to worry about money,' she added savagely.

The tap refused to turn.

'I'm lonely *and* I'm going to have to worry about money,' she muttered. 'What does a divorced minister's ex-wife have to live on? I am going to be a divorced minister's ex-wife who is about to find out.'

She sat examining the tops of her knees, poking up through the cloudy water, as though she had never seen them before, trying to grasp that the end of her marriage was staring her in the face.

You'll live on not a lot, said a small voice in her head, making an inventory of its own accord. She'd have to move out of the rectory; would have not much furniture; a junior teacher's pay; two teenagers who were bottomless pits of expense. All the parents would have fits; her father would say *I told you so*. Rose and Andrew would be mortified, blame her, might never speak to her again.

'I should be so lucky,' she said, sliding under the water and holding her breath, wondering whether one could drown in a bath. Not without slitting one's wrists. That was no good; she was too much of a coward about blood.

'At least I've got a job,' she said, spitting water as she came up again. 'And Hugo looks as though he's going to keep the school open.'

She felt a great rush of affection for Hugo, Bunny, all of them. She was going to need them.

'And Alastair,' she said, admitting the truth to herself.

Exhausted, she put her head on her wet knees and had a good, long cry.

Chapter Twenty-Four

The story made all the local papers and several of the tabloids carried it as a small item in their inside pages. Giles pored over them gloomily the day after his release.

'Alastair will put those in his files,' Melanie said, reading them, embarrassed to death.

'What files?'

'One of the other teachers collects press cuttings as a hobby.'

Talking about Alastair to Giles made her feel irrationally guilty, as though she were betraying both of them. She decided not to mention him again.

'I've been summoned,' Giles said the following day, after a telephone call in his study. He wandered into the kitchen as Melanie ate cornflakes on the run and tried to collect what she needed for the day's lessons and enough courage to go into school and face the stares. It was pouring with rain again, the ground too wet to soak it up. Easter holidays were only a couple of weeks away, and might bring some hope of spring. She glanced out at the garden, shrouded in the downpour, and thought *two weeks feels like eternity*.

'Again?' she asked. 'What do they want now?'

'Not the police. The Bishop.'

She put her cornflake bowl into the empty, freshly scrubbed sink.

'Is he going to sack you, do you think?' she asked lightly.

'Only if I do two things.'

Melanie turned.

'Which are?'

'Tell him the truth, as I told it to you, and get divorced,' he said abruptly.

They faced each other across the cluttered table, hearing Tom go out of the front door on his way to school. She folded down the liner of the cornflake packet carefully and closed the box.

'Tom has A levels in May, and Alice has GCSEs,' she said. 'Those are more important than the Bishop, so you will have to lie to him, and we will have to wait.'

'You mean, wait to start a divorce?'

She put the packet on its shelf and picked up her briefcase.

'Lying to the Bishop is digging a bigger hole for myself to fall into,' Giles pleaded. 'Mels?'

'Not now. I have to go,' was all she said.

'I have made it public that I am critical of the police,' said the dapper and worldly Bishop late that afternoon. 'What I do not understand, Tilford, is how they came to make such a mistake in the first place. Extraordinary. Scotch?'

Giles shook his head, afraid to speak.

'I have a very good single malt. Excellent. Sure you won't?'

'No, thanks.'

Richard 'Dickie' Dickinson got up from behind his desk and wandered over to a tray full of decanters and fine cut glass on a sideboard. He lived in a large, recently built Barratt home, on an estate of large and exclusive Barratt homes, while the Church Commissioners tried in vain to sell the draughty, thirty-roomed palace not far away that former bishops had lived in for the past eight hundred years. He stood holding his glass and fiddled with the central heating thermostat on the wall above the tray.

'Wonderful,' he enthused. 'I am warm, the bathwater is hot, the kitchen works itself and there isn't a ceiling more than ten feet high. And it's cheap to run. I told them, you can't have me living all by myself in a place that costs three times a clerical salary every year just to keep from falling down, when I am having to put my clergy out of work. And since I don't want to have to put *you* out of work, suppose you tell me what's wrong.'

Startled, Giles looked so guilty the other man nearly laughed.

He fumbled for words under Dickie's shrewd gaze. Dickie had never married any of the women with whom his name had been linked, had stayed a bachelor and indulged expensive tastes. Exquisitely tailored, he liked good entertainment, good food, good Scotch, central heating and beautiful women. It was hard, Giles thought, to imagine him coming horribly unstuck in his personal affairs, or having much sympathy for one who had. Dickie wasn't one to comfort muddlers.

'I think I'm losing my faith,' Giles mumbled, taking up his fall-back position, deflecting any discussion of the real issues. And that he was losing his faith was true.

'Really?' Dickie asked, looking at him keenly. 'That made you run around in the rain giving the police cause to claim you were confessing to murder? You sure it's faith you're losing? Nothing else? Your marbles? Your liver? Your wife?'

Giles looked away.

'Very well, Tilford, old chap,' Dickie advised, pouring single malt from a cut-glass decanter, 'I'd suggest you let me arrange some counselling, some pastoral guidance, but I suspect you will turn me down.'

'I don't even know I'm a Christian any more. I pray and pray, but I am empty,' Giles said desperately.

'Oh, for goodness' sake, so was Jesus in the wilderness. One soldiers on,' answered Dickie sharply. 'Expecting faith to come and stay like a kind of monogamous marriage where neither side is attractive enough ever to get tempted to stray is a medieval kind of notion. Even Canterbury gives the nod to that, what with ordaining women and all those pompous asses rushing off to join Rome because they don't approve, and all the rest of it. You don't have to make a song and dance out of a bit of spiritual turbulence, Tilford.'

'Don't I?' Giles bleated. 'Actually, I thought of joining Rome myself, until my wife made me see the error of my ways.'

Dickie chuckled, downed his malt in one and raised the twinkling glass.

'Here's to a wise wife. Sure you won't join me in another?'

Giles held four fingers of superb whisky and gazed at it mutely. He had heard this conversation before. Something bothered him, something he had read. It came to him; Blake Morrison's *And When Did You Last See Your Father?*

The Yorkshire vicar called round when Blake Morrison's father died, florid of face, purple of prose, rabbiting about Christian burial for a lifelong, ardent atheist, asking his mother what kind of funeral Morrison senior had wanted.

'Short,' said the widow of only a day.

Blake Morrison had listened to the discussion that followed, had listened between the lines. 'I know you don't believe in any of this God nonsense, but never mind, it shouldn't stop you going to church – after all it hasn't stopped me running one. I know your spouse never went to church in his life, but that doesn't matter, indeed in some ways it's better: it makes the funeral all the more of a challenge.'

The modern way, Giles thought. The road to hell used to be paved with good intentions. No longer the road to hell they once were, good intentions these days are enough to see you through the pearly gates.

'Cheers,' he said, raising his glass to St Peter, or whoever changed the rules, moved the goal posts while he wasn't looking.

'Cheers,' echoed Dickie comfortably. 'So you'll put all this nonsense behind you and get on with the job. And let me know if you want to have a chat with someone – you're far from being the only one to raise doubts, I can assure you. Any other business while you're here?'

Giles downed four fingers of excellent Scotch in one desperate swallow.

* * *

'Look at this,' Alastair said several days later, shaking the local paper open and spreading it on the staff-room table in morning break, as the kettle whistled and Bunny tipped the empty biscuit tin upside down with an exasperated cry. 'They got the right one this time. The wife took the cat to the RSPCA with something stuck in its throat, and the vet pulled out a bit of human finger bone. Good *heavens*, Mels, just imagine that.'

'I'd rather not,' she said stiffly.

Glancing at her expressionless face with sympathy, the whole staff room crowded round to see.

'The police have found two more children's bodies, decomposing in acid in a oil drum in a council-house garage. Near Epping,' Alastair read out for Melanie's benefit. 'There was a long and bloody scuffle, it says here, before they arrested a martial-arts fanatic who put three of the arresting posse in hospital with broken bones.'

'That is supposed to make me feel better?' she said.

'Apparently he screamed *I don't know nothing about it!* when they came to arrest him and showed him what was in his garage,' Alastair went on regardless. 'He proceeded to lay about him with a lawn strimmer. The journalist says he danced on the balls of his feet, light as thistledown, and that the strimmer whistled, its nylon line uncurling like a party popper as he whirled it around his head. Good, eh?'

'I wish some of my English language class could write fiction as good as that,' remarked the Stud, glancing at the smudged photographs in the paper. 'That journalist should go a very long way.'

'He liked watching videos,' observed a neighbour darkly to the television cameras.

'What sort of videos?' asked the interviewer, rain dripping from her hair in the arc lights.

'Oh, you know. Video nasties,' the neighbour said vaguely.

The camera panned back to a police van coming round to bring reinforcements.

'With Frederick West's back garden still being dug up in Gloucester,' cried the interviewer, 'police are under pressure to ensure that there is no similar garden of death here in the small town of Epping.'

As the van drew up, the crowd of journalists and television crews jostled and fought for the best view of police removing bodies, the murderer's four small children, his wife, wife's relatives, anything that moved, right down to the famous tabby cat, sitting on the front path of the council house washing its sparse fur, seemingly impervious to the hysterical attention it was attracting.

'I wouldn't be surprised if that cat hasn't eaten a good few very nasty meals,' the neighbour went on, pulling a meaningful face. 'They never fed it. I always thought it looked very poorly, but I thought it was just undernourished.'

Essex Man Caught By Cannibal Cat shrieked the tabloids ghoulishly next morning.

'You can never tell about people, can you?' said Bunny, shocked, rereading the paper when Alastair had finished. 'Can you imagine living with someone and not knowing they are doing something like that?'

'You can't tell about people,' said Alastair from within the filing cabinet, checking on the liquor supply because, after that, he felt like a pick-me-up in his tea. 'We're running low again.' He raised his head accusingly. '*Garlick.*'

Melanie got up unnoticed, and left.

He followed her.

'Why are you taking this personally?'

'It sickens me,' she said in a low voice. 'That story *sickens* me, and we've been a part of it.'

'That is nonsense, and you can't keep running away,' Alastair said, stopping her from disappearing down the corridor, blocking her escape. Children streamed and screamed around them, milling in after break for periods three and four, pushing and shoving, peeling off the main corridor into classrooms.

'Don't run,' he yelled and lowered his voice. 'Mels, no one thinks anything of Giles's arrest now and everyone knows it was a mistake. It's history.'

'And will go in your archives, no doubt,' she said drily, dodging half a dozen of the school basketball team and their sports bags, flashing past in a gaggle of black faces, white teeth and size thirteen feet in trainers.

'Those boys scare me, they're so *huge*,' she said, ducking as they raced past. 'What everyone knows is what Giles didn't do. They don't know what he *did*. Except you. Are you going to put *that* in your files, Alastair?'

'I am putting in my files that our kids have got to the finals of the London Schools Competition, and winning has made them stop bunking off and start coming to school because they want to win some more. Hugo is right about high expectations. Talking of which, I have noticed a good half-dozen kids who should be reading *Romeo and Juliet* in your English group acting like Romeo and Juliet over in your husband's back yard,' he told her severely. 'I have passed by and heard a certain lack of discipline in your classes, and I tell you as head of sixth form that I am not happy.'

She was frozen-faced. He could see more grey in the fine blonde hair than there had been before, more lines around her eyes. She was thinner than the day she had arrived in her good green suit, sharper, harder, no longer a naïve doormat who looked like a county lady.

'I need the holiday. It's been a long term, and I'm still finding my feet.'

He lost patience.

'You can't live a complete lie forever, Mels. It's getting you down, this nonsense with Giles, only you don't see it.'

He was rewarded with a tight-lipped stare.

'Not anyone's business,' she snapped back. 'Professionally, I won't let it affect me any more.'

'You are wrong,' he said gently.

'They won't go over there any more. If Giles won't chase

them off, I will personally go and haul them back.'

'I didn't mean . . .'

'I said, it won't happen any more.'

She turned and walked away. A piano thumped from the far end of the school, as in the gym thirty-six pairs of feet pounded in time to the music. A door opened and Garlick's voice thundered about anaerobic respiration until it banged shut again behind a girl who scuttled off towards the lavatories. Unseen in the deserted corridor, Alastair spread his hands in angry defeat.

'When are we going to get some decent expectations into *your* head?' he muttered, and wandered off to teach.

Chapter Twenty-Five

'Are you speaking to me again?' he asked at the beginning of the last week of term, by himself in the staff room. 'I detect a slight thawing in the air.'

'Don't be childish,' she snapped, racing in to find *The Whitsun Weddings* for her next lesson. 'Have you seen Philip Larkin lying around anywhere?'

'Good, you are talking to me. So how's your singing voice?'

He was stabbing at a pile of paper with a chewed pen, which evidently amused him, since he was chortling like an idiot.

'Deep, husky and gorgeous,' Melanie answered sarcastically. '*Have* you seen Larkin? I left him here, and someone's moved him.'

She rummaged in the piles of books and papers lying on desks, frustrated.

'If I had, I'd give him a wide berth. Philip Larkin was gloomy, lived alone, wrote obscene letters to his friends and masturbated an unnatural amount. He wrote inflammatory things like *they fuck you up, your mum and dad,* and he shouldn't be read to impressionable minds. Why give teenagers ammunition?' Alastair said slyly.

'Tell that to the exam board,' she snapped. 'What about singing?'

'We have such treats to come,' he explained happily. 'Until Hugo and Absalom's plots hatch, and the Secretary of State coughs up the millions they're demanding, we have no money, so Bunny's been having inspirations about fund-raising. Hugo's excited as a pig in muck, claiming they're all his own ideas. Here's the list.'

He waved his bit of paper and chuckled.

'What kind of singing?' she demanded suspiciously.

'Karaoke,' he shouted delightedly. 'We're having karaoke evenings. Hugo has broken Stuttering Stan's kneecaps, and persuaded him to let us stay open, so everyone can come and get drunk at a licensed bar. The basketball team are queuing up to be bouncers. Bunny says let's cater for the gamblers, so she's got a video racing game you bet real money on. Then she wants pop concerts, barn dances and car boot sales on the sports field. That'll give the PE department something to holler about. Mohammed offered to get some of his mates to come and help him do a strip to the karaoke, but Hugo had a fit and vetoed it. Shame.'

He gnawed the end of his pen.

'Good, eh?' he asked, when she didn't answer.

'Before we came, everyone used to come over the way to have a good time. Giles has stopped all that. He says churches are for worship, not whooping it up.'

'There's a name for that. Blight,' he said cruelly. 'Your husband is like the Channel Tunnel – blight, with a missing link or two.'

He snickered at his own humour. Melanie narrowed her eyes and glared.

Furious, she stalked to the far end of the room and began searching among Garlick's dead, dried bean shoots and untidy heaps of books and papers on top of the filing cabinets, to see if someone had put sad, acid, searingly insightful Philip Larkin, who would have agreed with Alastair about Giles, up with the dead beans in their jam jars, the empty fish tank whose goldfish had long since floated belly up, and several dusty spider plants. Larkin wasn't there.

'How good's your imagination?' he asked brightly into the freezing silence. 'We have to find something positive to say, here. Records of Achievement. You got a moment?'

'You know perfectly well I haven't,' she snapped. 'And if you think you can say what you please . . .'

Interrupting the scene about to brew, Bunny hurtled in backwards through the door with a vast ghetto blaster clutched to her substantial breast, encased in white-floured pinny.

'You got a free?' she demanded, looking from one to the other.

'No,' Melanie shouted, dropping books in her rage. 'I have *not*. I have lost Larkin.'

'I'm not *teaching*,' Alastair said pointedly, shuffling his big pile of reports, hiding the fund-raising list underneath them. 'I could always go to my own room if there are going to be a lot of interruptions, Bunny.'

'Keep an eye on this until I finish, so no one nicks it before I can lock it up. It's got mikes and everything you need for karaoke,' she cried, dumping it on top of his work. 'One of the first years said he'd lend it to us, and his mum just brought it round.'

She flew out again, floury finger marks on the monster's matt-black plastic casing.

'Sulking in a woman is very offputting, and I really *could* use a bit of inspiration,' Alastair said, shoving the mammoth ghetto blaster to one side.

'That's a sexist remark, and I bet *you* would sulk with my kind of provocation.'

'It's your Christian appetite for provocation that I love, Mrs T.,' he observed casually. 'I find it a challenge, and *hugely* entertaining.'

Melanie looked startled, flushed, climbed down from searching the filing cabinets and came over, despite herself, to look at what he was doing. He shuffled the top of the pile and laid down two papers.

'Look at this. It's quite moving, really, seeing what the kids think of themselves, all put down with unbelievable effort and ingenuity. I'm checking them for the more implausible lies. I started with the two Ds and I'd value your opinion on whether I should let it go through? What do you think?'

Melanie leaned over his shoulder and laughed out loud.

'I thought it'd amuse you.'

It was the first time in ages he'd heard her laugh properly, since Giles had come out of the police station. Leaning on his shoulder, she giggled, reading the joint 'Record' that Dora and Dorcas had written.

> We want to be beauty therpists and manicure nails. We practice a lot and work hard in scool. We are good at helping peple. We are helpful and polit and we will go to tec and lern how to get a certificit. We might do hairdresing as well. We get on well with peple and we will work hard.

'They'll make jolly good manicurists,' she said, stopping laughing. 'And we can say, hand on heart, that they take every opportunity to get practical experience at school. If you correct the spelling, whoever reads that won't know they paint their nails in class and not a lot else. And they're right, they can be kind, and occasionally quite sensible.'

Alastair leaned back and found himself leaning against her.

'OK. I pass it, then. Did you know their mother is teaming up with our Ernie, the Kray twins fan? They came and saw Hugo and offered to put the frighteners on any parents who won't take part in a repainting party to smarten up the school. They have got a warehouse full of paint that can fall off the back of a lorry if Hugo just says the word. They are extremely earnest about it. Hugo is beside himself.'

He shook with laughter and she let him go so suddenly he nearly fell off his chair backwards.

'Good,' she said with clumsy sarcasm. 'Wielding a stolen paintbrush is exactly what I need. We know, don't we, how understanding the police will be. I *meant* well, Officer . . .'

'It is not a good idea to bottle things up,' he said quietly.

'Why won't you let anyone help?'

She stared at the back of his ponytail.

'I was there,' he reminded her. 'You could talk about it.'

'And start more gossip?' she cried bitterly. 'Bertie has kept her mouth shut, which is something. Home is like that party game – whisper, whisper, whisper, just too faint for you to hear.'

'Does avoiding me make it any better?'

'*There* it is. *You* had it all the time.'

She snatched *The Whitsun Weddings* from underneath his pile of papers.

Her class was in uproar, she was so late. She remembered Alastair's critical words and hated him. Discipline, she thought furiously. This time, at any rate, it's all his fault.

'Right,' she shouted. 'Page eighteen, *when* you're ready.'

She bent open the book fit to break its narrow spine and gave English set three half an hour of hell.

Chapter Twenty-Six

It rained and blew gales all Easter, filling the newspapers with stories of rivers bursting their banks, floods, bringing ever more disastrous times for seedy and run-down British holiday resorts struggling with recession.

'Holiday? What holiday?' Melanie asked, looking out at endless rain, keeping everyone indoors. 'The kids are moping upstairs with exam blues, threatening to stay in bed when the time comes, and your parents are coming to stay at this time, of all times. Why couldn't we give up pretending to be a family for Lent? Then we could have given up having your parents to stay, instead of the few things left that we enjoy.'

'Giving up my parents if we get divorced will be one of the pluses for you,' said Giles. 'You can think about that when they get impossible.'

They smiled conspiratorially, enjoying a rare moment of understanding. A ghost of a smile crossed his face, which since his confession was generally set in a permanent, anxious frown.

'I knew this wasn't a good idea,' she said later, as togetherness at Easter went from bad to worse. Tom and Alice bickered, Giles hid in his study and pretended to write sermons. They all resented the prospect of having the house full of grandparents, at being expected to be helpful, at being expected to go to church.

'I've got things to do,' Tom announced at breakfast on Good Friday.

'An omnibus edition of *Neighbours*?' asked Giles mildly.

Tom wore a martyred expression and went on eating half a box of Coco Pops.

'So have I,' announced Alice.

'Revision?' said Melanie hopefully.

'You don't have to go to church,' Giles said stoically, chewing toast. 'Your mother hasn't been to church for months. But Gran and Grandpa will ask questions, and everyone will look at the front pew and *notice*. You will have to put up with a row with my parents, who get an enormous amount of pleasure from the family receiving the Eucharist together at Easter. This will be the first year we have not, but there's no pressure. No pressure at all.'

'That's the kind of no pressure parents do all the time,' Alice mumbled. 'On top of no pressure from GCSEs and teachers. We get both, and every time I look up, Mum's standing there. Brilliant.'

Giles started to tell her not to be rude to her mother, but on looking at her thought the better of it and opened his newspaper instead.

Alice could barely speak and was sitting wrapped in an old kimono dressing gown, drinking milky coffee through a straw. Her face was bright and patchy blue, cracking round the edges, eyes like poached eggs on a Wedgwood china plate. The sunburst hair was held back in an orange spotted bandanna, larded with a film of henna, parcelled into clingfilm wrap.

'You look like something out of an anthropology magazine,' Giles muttered from the safety of *The Times*.

'She's too young to need that stuff,' her mother snapped. 'What have you got on?'

'Mud,' the Alice mask whispered. 'Can you get me some day-glo eyeshadow, Mum?'

'Day-glo *eyeshadow*? Whatever happened to socks? And when are you getting down to your revision?'

It was hard to argue with a stiff-lipped blue freak busily drying out at the breakfast table. Alice slurped her straw, meaning she wanted more coffee. Melanie snatched at her mug, fed up. Giles sneaked off, leaving the last half-slice of toast on his plate, chickening out of a mutiny waiting to happen.

'*Giles*,' she shouted.

The telephone rang in his study at the critical moment. He gave a look-how-busy-I-am grin and vanished. Melanie's lips tightened.

'Gran and Grandpa are coming as usual, at tea time,' she said evenly. She executed her boiled egg like Robespierre topping Marie Antoinette, glared at her children. 'And you will both be nice to them.'

'I thought I heard you in there. I bought that to last the weekend,' Melanie cried, finding Tom with his head in the fridge, later that morning. She grabbed the big Sainsbury's plastic orange-juice container, shaking it in disbelief. 'You're a pig. And I want a word with you. Is two days of moderately good behaviour too much to ask?'

'It seems to be too much to ask of you and Dad,' he retorted, muffled by the inside of the fridge. 'You could at least go to church with him and make him feel better. It's you who argues with Dad, and then you blame us.'

She stared at the back of his head for what felt like eternity.

'It's not as one-sided as you think,' she said, holding the orange juice out of his reach as he took his head out.

Gales of audience laughter came from across the hall, followed by the high nasal whine of an American voice.

'I'm watching the best bits of *Roseanne*,' he muttered, shoving past.

Garlick had said it. *If parents were flies, teenagers would pull their wings off, just to see if it hurt.* She hugged the Sainsbury's container like a talisman and stared up at her only son, who stared right back, cool-eyed, unshakeably dug in on dizzyingly high moral ground as he went off to doze in front of the television when he should be up in his room, working for a future. Straight for the jugular, she thought furiously.

They don't even have to *try*; emotional annihilation for mothers, delivered with one casual swipe. She threw the juice into the fridge and marched into the sitting room.

'I'll ignore what you just said,' she yelped, leaning over and pinning him down by his shoulders. 'Do you think I don't know what that funny smell is in your room? I know Bertie and you sit up there smoking. *Ouch.*'

'Sorry.'

'No, you're not,' she yelled furiously.

He had skinny elbows sharp as skewers, knees like bludgeons, the reach of an Olympic fencer.

'Then let me go,' he said, trying to see round her, to keep up with *Roseanne*.

'And four litres of juice *in one day*? What do you think we are, made of money?'

'Ger*off*, Mum.'

She straightened up. Curls and whiffs and drifts of woodsmoke puffed from the fitful fire spitting resin in the grate. Roseanne delivered a one-liner that flattened her sassy children and her fat husband.

'I wish I had a tongue like hers,' Melanie muttered through gritted teeth, as from the television came howls of studio laughter.

'Turning the Other Cheek.' One of Giles's more successful sermons, always delivered with passion, went down less well these days, she thought grimly, storming back to the kitchen. Depends which cheek . . . Daffodil's bottom or Angelina's, for a start. Her hands itched to wipe the expression off that smug, know-it-all teenage face, passing judgement when he knew nothing at all.

'Why doesn't violence work? It jolly well *should*,' she spat, wrenched open the fridge and threw the container, with its teaspoonful of orange, in the bin.

The Tilfords senior arrived long after tea time, when the crumpets and hot cross buns had long gone cold.

'She'd got the *A to Z* upside down,' explained Giles's

father, rubbing his hands together critically, leaving Melanie to take their case upstairs.

'Your grandfather's got rubbing his hands down to an art form. If I was on a jury, trying your grandmother for murder, I'd acquit once I saw the provocation,' Melanie hissed at Alice, finding her taking next door's cat off the bed in the spare room. It left a neat mat of moulted ginger hair in the middle of the pillow. 'How did that get in here?'

'Through the window. It's got an awful lot of fleas.'

'Then they're going to itch,' said her mother, dumping the case.

Alice's pretty orange mouth pursed, then she giggled, dropped the ginger tomcat back on the bed, threw her arms round Melanie's neck and hugged her tight.

'Cheer up, Mum,' she whispered. 'They'll itch like mad in a couple of days.'

'She who doesn't drink will have a G and T,' Andrew Tilford said, following Melanie into the kitchen with the tray of cold crumpets and tea.

She tipped the teapot down the drain and wished it was over his head.

'How's the job?' he asked, wandering all over and looking out of the window at the sodden garden, a tall, gaunt, much older version of Giles, loose-skinned, dry as a stick. It was hard to imagine he had ever been young. She sometimes wondered if Rose, devout Anglican, had actually, without realizing it, had an immaculate conception.

'Going well.'

'Going well, eh? I can see it doesn't leave you much time.' He looked round the untidy kitchen, scrawny neck twisting this way and that inside its loose collar, managing to convey criticism with every move. The turkey for Sunday lay on top of the fridge, where it had been taking up all the room.

I'm going to enjoy stuffing it, she thought, as he rubbed veined hands cheerfully. *And* I'd vote for a hanging sentence, even though I don't believe in it. Turn the other cheek. She smiled a bright, hard smile.

'There's tonic in the fridge door and you know where the glasses are,' she said.

'Only forty-eight hours to go,' she muttered as he opened the fridge. She found herself crossing off minutes as a prisoner chalks off the days on his wall, and looked at the clock on the cooker. 'Five fifty-two, sun not quite over the yardarm, and she'll be in here any minute . . . *now*.'

Portly little Rose wandered into the kitchen, bundled in woollies and dark grey pleated skirt, her face rosy and shiny as a Cox's Pippin, a picture of good nature and grandmotherliness, faded grey eyes watery with age and an inordinate fondness for gin.

'I bought Sainsbury's own brand. It's cheaper than Gordon's,' Melanie said, planting the gin bottle on the end of the kitchen table nearest the door. 'Andrew's got the tonic and the glasses.'

'You shouldn't bother,' said her mother-in-law.

'That's what I tell myself,' Melanie agreed. 'The budget doesn't really stretch. But if you sit there and don't do anything except keep out of my way, you can stay and drink it.'

Rose glanced at her sharply, took the bottle daintily and looked at it in puzzlement.

'Never mind making out you never saw a gin bottle before, just open it. In fact, you can pour me one,' said Melanie, pulling on a scarlet plastic apron from the back of the door. Orange letters across her chest shouted COOK.

'I didn't think you liked it,' Rose answered, unscrewing the top expertly.

'I'm getting to like a lot of things I didn't,' Melanie retorted, threw a heap of potatoes into the sink and began to scrub. Over the clink of ice in glasses, the front door banged.

'You've got what looks like a trapeze artiste in your hall, Melanie,' Rose said, looking at her gin, puzzled, as though it might be stronger than she thought. Melanie turned to look as Bertie strode in with Tom behind her, hand in hand.

'Does she drink gin?' asked Rose, looking Bertie over, enormously impressed. She reached for the bottle and looked round for another glass.

'Where on earth did you get that outfit, Bertie? You look like a camp stormtrooper out of a Berlin nightclub,' Melanie snarled over her potatoes. 'You are every mother's nightmare and I don't know what I did to deserve you. This is Tom's grandmother.'

Bertie smiled sweetly, encased from head to foot in a powder-blue, soft-as-butter leather catsuit with a silver zip from neck to crotch, black jackboots to her knees. Her white bob had been cropped to a crewcut, making her black eyes and brows more startling than ever. Baby Jane curled around her neck, in a tiny matching bolero.

'Bertie's a very unusual name for a girl,' remarked Rose, putting the gin bottle back on the kitchen table. 'I must say, you're unusual for a girl, yourself. Sure you won't have some?'

'Call her Barbie Doll, then,' Melanie snapped. 'She isn't into gin. Has other habits.'

Bertie grinned, stood back and waved Baby Jane's tiny paw. 'Baby Jane says hi, everyone.'

'Don't you *dare* fall for all this nonsense,' Melanie groaned, but it was too late. Rose's watery eyes were enchanted.

''Lo, Gran,' Tom grunted from the doorway. He came in, brushed his grandmother's wrinkled cheek with his, reached behind her to the fridge, heaved out her bottle of tonic and tucked it under his arm. 'Thanks.'

'What are you doing up there? Don't you *dare* take drugs.'

Running after them with cold wet hands, Melanie watched one bottom in washed-out Levis, one in pale leather, disappear upstairs to Tom's room. She came back into the kitchen.

'Don't you dare say a word,' she yelped defiantly, seeing the look on Rose's face. 'Don't say what you are about to say, because I have thought every one of those thoughts before, and if *you* start going on, I'll scream.'

Coming out of the sitting room, Giles's father stood rooted to the spot, watching them climb the stairs, his mouth open, looking like a beaten spaniel.

'My *word.* Is she one of Giles's?' he demanded nosily, rubbing his hands energetically.

'One of Giles's *what*?' Melanie shrieked, her nerves in shreds.

'Customers, of course,' he answered, looking bewildered. 'What else did you think I meant?'

Not one of Giles's, seeing as he likes them short and stout and blunt in mind and figure. Bertie and I are long and skinny and sharp. Perhaps she's my son's Oedipus complex. I could kill her for it.

Going across to lay the table in the draughty dining room, she sniffed. The unmistakable smell, faint and sweet, of cannabis wafted down the stairs.

Safely in the larder, she swore, kicked a crateful of empty milk bottles that no one had put out, picked up a fresh tonic and an armful of greens. Banging a saucepan on to boil, she shredded cabbage savagely. Boiled cabbage should drown it out, put the drug squad off the scent, keep the Gestapo at bay until another day. She could see it all coming, even worse than before. *Sex-Case Vicar In Drugs Seizure.* She stabbed the greens furiously.

'You haven't touched your drink,' Rose said, wandering in for a refill. 'Can I lend a hand? Are you quite all right, dear?' She eyed the mangled cabbage on the draining board uneasily, saw the chopper in her daughter-in-law's hand, backed away.

'I'll just take this in the other room, dear. For the others.' She darted at the table, snatched the gin, and fled.

Chapter Twenty-Seven

'Everyone ate and nobody fought,' Giles said smugly. 'Shall we ask my parents to stay on?'

Melanie felt her expression shrivel as though a shower of acid had turned her into a prune.

'That was a joke,' he said.

Your daughter is plugged out of it on Sony. Your mother is out of it on gin. Your son is out of it on I hate to think what. Your father is in my sitting room, looking at them all like Dracula watching his next meal walking by. You are as doolally as the Easter Bunny and we are just waiting for the end.

'Sure, joke about your parents any time, why not?' she said, with a smile that hurt her face.

In the sitting room, they were watching *Indiana Jones and the Last Crusade*. Indiana Jones arrived in Venice, began breaking up the marble floor of a church used as a library. He bashed the floor. The librarian, stamping books in unison, heard the crash, gazed at his stamp, astonished.

Rose snored quietly in what had been the old man's favourite wing chair, until he was found dead in it after his heart attack. She had her gin glass balanced on her bosom, both hands around it, and her mouth open just enough to dribble gently. Melanie's mouth twitched. Rose wouldn't snore so peacefully if anyone had thought to tell her that she was sitting right where they'd found his body, unmovable with rigor mortis.

Indiana Jones was shouting about his father and Nazi archaeologists. Tom, hunched up next to *his* father, watched through half-closed, sleepy eyes. I know that look, Melanie thought wearily. I last looked like that when I was floating in a cloud of pethidine in the labour ward.

The labour ward was an eternity away. Now, the chicks are big and recently Mother Sparrow opened her eyes and found herself looking after a cuckoo's nest. What then?

They sat so quietly, watching Good Friday television. Giles and Andrew had voted to watch the story of the crucifixion on BBC2. They had all bickered over the *Radio Times*, taken a vote, settled on BBC1 and Indiana Jones.

'We get enough Jesus,' Tom mumbled.

Alice put her hand up in agreement. Rose nursed her glass and didn't care. The crucifixion minority overruled, they had given way without a struggle.

If you didn't know better, Melanie reflected, watching flames dance in the fire, you'd think they were all perfectly normal. Alice had drawn the curtains, turned on the lamps. The high Victorian ceiling had ornate cornices and splendid roses, laced with cobwebs, well out of reach. Rich cream wallpaper, yellowed by dust and time, was marked all round by heavy mahogany furniture pushed back against it. What had once been an opulent Indian carpet had had its pattern worn almost to nothing. Depressing and dingy in daylight, the room was softened at night by brown parchment shaded lamps, lending it a heavy, old-fashioned splendour. It smelled of woodsmoke, old carpet and damp.

When they first moved in, Giles found sinister-coloured mushrooms growing in wild profusion out of one of the kitchen skirting boards. Rentokil came, tore off bits of rotting wood and clucked his tongue.

'I just want you to get rid of the mushrooms,' Giles ordered.

'No can do without you take the boards up and do the whole floor,' the man said smugly. 'You looked at your damp course and your joists recently, Reverend?'

'It's the church,' Giles explained irritably. 'They won't spend.'

Rentokil poked around, lifted the carpet, dug out bits of

wood, crumbled them in his fingers. 'Dry rot, wet rot, beetle and worm. I reckon you got the lot here, mate.'

'Can you just rid of the mushrooms?' Giles insisted.

The man scowled, sulked, sat in his van for ages, complaining on the car phone to his superiors about professional standards. Eventually, weeks later, someone else turned up to paint the corner with chemicals that for weeks corroded their nostrils and smelled far worse than the damp.

The fire flared into life, glowed and crackled, spat glowing splinters on to the hearth. Melanie threw on another log and pushed Alice's feet off the sofa at the far side of the fire. She knew the film by heart, the kids had watched it so often. Tired, she lay back and listened to the rain coming down again, beating on the French windows, seeping and trickling into little puddles that crept towards the carpet, coming in through wood frames rotted with neglect. No wonder the old man got burgled all the time. With a swift hard kick, the whole door would fall to bits. Rose snored loudly and woke herself up.

'I hope that clears up for Sunday, or we'll be soaked going outside in procession,' she remarked, taking up the conversation she had been having with herself before she went to sleep.

Indiana Jones waded through a pothole full of rats, dragging a glamorous blonde after him. The rats squeaked and milled in best Hollywood rent-a-rat fashion.

'Imagine directing a thousand-and-one rats,' Andrew remarked. He sniggered and made a bullhorn out of his hands. 'Take fifty-six. All rats hiding under the set will come on out *right now* or forfeit their pay.'

'Pay?' asked Alice.

'Dried rat food, probably,' said her grandfather, making his bullhorn again. 'All skivers will run a maze back to the funny farm and medical experiments.'

Alice had her Walkman abandoned round her neck.

'That isn't *funny*,' she said indignantly. 'Rats have rights.

They should have an agent to look after them.'

'Shhh,' said Tom.

Andrew scratched his chin and considered.

'They'd be laboratory rejects,' he decided. 'Too stupid to learn mazes and be respectable at experiments. Probably went into being professional film extras because being kicked and despised was all they were good at.'

'I never thought about it like that,' Alice said. 'Poor old rats.'

'It's a thankless job, being trodden on. You don't even get a mention in the credits.' Melanie heard herself join in the absurd conversation. Indiana Jones kicked several dozen little grey creatures out of the way, went splashing on, trod on them carelessly, didn't even look down.

'Anyone who puts up with being trodden on like that,' Melanie added softly, full of fellow feeling, 'deserves an Oscar.'

Rose's remark drifted into Giles's consciousness.

'My present congregation are not put off by a bit of weather,' he said from the depths of the sofa.

Dr Jones was being nearly burned to death, had taken shelter with the glamorous blonde underneath a prehistoric coffin, sunk in water enthusiastically and professionally infested by the rats. Giles stretched his long legs, hogging the space by the fire.

'They'll hop, skip and jump to the Good Lord's praise until they are giddy, come rain or come shine,' he went on. 'In fact, the giddier they are, the better they like it. I should warn you that Easter isn't going to be what it was in Norfolk.'

His mother woke up properly and looked round for the gin.

'They are long on enthusiasm, a little short on dignity,' he explained, handing it to her, warm from being too close to the fire. 'The Easter Bunny, one might say, comes leaping into church like the Mad March Hare.'

Rose squinted and unscrewed the top.

'Rabbit or hare, I do like us all being together,' she said cosily.

Indiana Jones descended to the bowels of the earth, walked across a snake pit, clawed his way across a column of Nazi tanks, got shot at, betrayed by the glamorous blonde, bickered with his batty father, and pointed out that the mess they were in was all his fault.

You couldn't always find anyone to blame. It was life, and you had to get on with it. Melanie closed her eyes and drew a deep breath.

'Not all of us, I'm afraid, Rose. I'm not coming, this year.' She hoped that, if she mumbled into a particularly loud bit of shooting, her words would fall into some subliminal part of their brains, be registered without them actually noticing what she had said, so they wouldn't react. Indiana Jones retreated behind some rocks, sheltered from the shooting. Momentarily it all went quiet.

'Not coming to church?' Rose demanded, coming to life, peering round the wing of her chair, a desert rat coming up for air. Melanie could have kicked the television. Indiana Jones had let her down completely.

'I'll stay and do lunch,' she offered with her most winning smile. 'If I get the turkey on and have it all ready, I thought that would be rather nice.'

'Melanie's going to make lunch. Let's not make an issue of it, Mother,' Giles said.

'She's got a duty. She's part of the business. Whatever will people think?'

Andrew looked sideways at his son, rubbed his hands uneasily.

'Stop talking about me as if I'm not here. I don't care what people think,' she said calmly.

They all stared at her, aghast, as Indiana Jones stepped off the face of a cliff into the void, found his foot on an invisible bridge, seemed to walk on air.

'*Well*,' her mother-in-law began. 'I must say . . .'

And was instantly quelled by a glare from Giles that

stopped her saying anything more at all.

No one tried to stop Melanie as she got up, picked up Rose's bottle, left them to watch the end of the film. She sat in the kitchen alone, listening to the ceaseless rain drumming on the windows, running and dripping from blocked gutters. The gin was strong and bitter, bringing back the memory of Alastair.

We will have to go to the off licence one day, and I will give you a lesson in how to drink decent plonk on a teacher's salary. Do you like Chardonnay, Mrs T.? She wasn't about to admit she didn't know what Chardonnay was.

'Here's to the rats,' she said, toasting herself, as in the sitting room Indiana Jones passed the tests that only a good man could, crossed the invisible bridge and entered the mountain to seek out the Cup of Life.

Chapter Twenty-Eight

Melanie studied the diagram in *Cosmopolitan* and knew from the sound of Big Ben that Indiana Jones had finished and they were watching the news. From her perch in the kitchen, she could just hear Trevor McDonald's voice, reading headlines. She went back to the article and turned the diagram with how-to-find-your-G-spot instructions upside down. It looked no more probable – or accessible – than the right way up. She wondered about telling Giles she was looking for her G spot. He'd think she was on the spiritual straight and narrow at last – in search of God.

Something disturbed her; a carefully controlled click as the front door closed behind Tom, going out without telling anyone. She got up and went into the cold, dark front room, without switching on the light. From by the window, she tried to see past the holly tree, to the windows in the flats opposite, the picture blurred by rain. She counted three storeys up, on the left hand corner, and waited. After several minutes, the curtains on those windows closed.

I don't *know* they're Bertie's, she told herself sternly. I haven't been there. I don't *know* Tom's over there with her. She rubbed the windowpane and peered through the rivulets running down it. Yes, I do, just like I knew Daffodil was rolling in haystacks with my husband.

She left the tattered curtains open; pulling them closed could make them fall apart in her hands. The flats, filthy and ugly by day, looked less vicious, more inviting by night, many windows softly lit, curtains drawn against the wild weather.

In her bedroom, she opened the bottom drawer of her chest of drawers and took out a tissue-paper package. A loose and voluptuous yellow silk robe tumbled out of its wrapping. It was the colour of daffodils, soft and heavy as moleskin, with a wide silk belt. She laid it out on the bed, stroked it, put it to her face, imagined how lovely it would feel, then tossed it carelessly on to the end of the bed. It was a gesture of longing for luxury, to go to bed each night in pure silk and to wake to sunshine spilling through shuttered windows, and a lover's tender touch.

She laughed and felt foolish.

You should write Mills and Boon, Melanie, she told herself briskly. *And* it cost the earth, but it's cheaper than divorce, and worth a try. She stroked it once more and left it lying there.

In the bathroom, she dropped a silver pearl of perfume into steaming water and propped the magazine on the side, soaked until she relaxed, was just getting down to reconsidering the G-spot question when she heard her parents-in-law come up to bed.

'You in there, Melanie? Aliiiice?'

Rose rattled the door handle and shouted at the top of her voice, as though the bath was half a mile away.

'Me,' Melanie called back, making the sign of the cross in the bubbles, knocking the magazine into the water. She fished it out, pages glued together, shook it with frustration.

'We're just coming up,' Rose yelled.

'You don't need to shout,' Melanie shouted back, resigned to getting out.

'When you're ready, dear.'

'Just coming,' she called, and started to laugh, got out and wrapped a towel around herself. 'Coming,' she shrieked right by the door, making Rose jump and recoil on the other side.

Coming. Orgasm. The big O. *Cosmopolitan* and all the glossies did articles about it nearly every week. She read them with absorption, had become quite the armchair expert.

There were so many ways to do it. On your back, on your front, oral, do-it-yourself, standing up, sitting down, lying down, upside down, five times a night . . . vibrators, dildos, G spots, hot tubs and Czech therapists who said relax in a bath and you could *come* in every cell of your body. She read about an American grandmother who masturbated for a living, taught other women how to do it, either one to one or in groups of eight, thought about ringing her up. One to one. Not seriously. Melanie hummed 'Air on a G String'. The Czech therapists didn't have to listen to their mother-in-law listening to them in the bath, on the other side of the door. She sighed and put the G spot away in the airing cupboard to dry out, to try another time.

Sitting on the side of the bath dragging a comb through her wet hair, she thought *Cosmopolitan* didn't say anything about what to do when you had never even felt the faintest stirrings of orgasm, were as lonely as a woman could be, aching with longing, in a big old double bed, next to a man absorbed in his own guilty conscience, his back turned and a Bible under his pillow. The agony aunts and Ruth said talk, talk, talk. They never seemed to realize that if the other person didn't listen, talking was a sad and lonely waste of time. She heard Rose go across the landing, the guest-room door close.

You'd think journalists would know that, she thought, being in the communications business. The yellow silk robe might communicate something to Giles tonight, if only that she was almost over the limit on her credit card. She tied his old felt dressing gown around her and made a dash for it down the cold landing to her own bedroom, before Rose could come scuttling out of the guest room like a spider crab out of its shell and catch her out again.

Chapter Twenty-Nine

She had bought the silk robe on the last Saturday of term and it had cost almost a month's salary.

The rain stopped, giving way to a clear, bright, sunny day, full of the heady promise of spring. The silk gown was the same colour as the daffodils in Hyde Park, where she walked in several slow circles, enjoying the brief hour of sunshine and summoning up the courage to go into the discreet little shop in Sloane Street, to see Bertie's Madame Lucie.

At first she hurried past. Then she stopped and pressed her nose against the window. There was nothing on display but a vase of silk flowers and a sleeping grey cat, curled up on a blue velvet cushion. Looking right inside the shop was like looking into someone's front room. It had faded blue and gold on the walls, and a huge cream sofa with its back to her, lingerie thrown over it as carelessly as though it were in someone's private bedroom. Anything Madame Lucie sold, Melanie could see, would be absurdly and impossibly expensive.

She walked past a dozen times, waited until she was certain there were no customers inside, dashed at the door, almost fell over her feet in her haste to get inside before she lost all her courage, stood feeling like a great ugly gawk, grotesquely out of place, wishing with all her heart that she had never taken Bertie's advice to buy sexy underwear, never let her persuade her to come here. Melanie wished that she had never even *heard* of Madame Lucie.

'Come in, madame. I am wiz you in one moment, when I get zeeze out of 'ere.'

The warm, throaty French voice came from the far end of the long and narrow shop, from behind a small counter heaped with underwear, scattered with expensive wrapping and opened boxes. Someone was rummaging, throwing up garments into a pile that resembled a molehill of silk about to register 6.6 on the Richter scale. As Melanie dithered, a tiny woman dressed all in brown darted from behind the counter, hands outstretched as if to greet a long-lost friend.

'Soooo, madame. I see you looking in, and at last you come in,' she cried.

Madame Lucie not only threw up molehills on her counter, she *looked* like a mole, not five feet tall, almost blind, spectacles wedged on the bridge of a wide, snub nose. Dressed all in dark brown velvet, she was perched on brown stiletto heels, four inches high.

'You find me,' she beamed, great dark oyster eyes impossibly magnified behind the thick and rimless glasses. 'Good. Bertha tell me you are coming. A tall Englishwoman 'oo is shy. You are Bertha's friend, *non*?'

'Not a bit of it. I am Bertie's sworn enemy,' snapped Melanie. 'She is very peculiar. I *know* she's hiding things; she doesn't belong where she says she does. She's got too much money, no Cockney accent when she should have, and she is after my son. I'm only here because she made me behave extremely badly. *You* tell me what's wrong with her.'

'Ach, *poor* Bertha. She does no 'arm.'

The tiny woman plucked at her with blunt hands, like small and gentle shovels, drew her in. Melanie smelled expensive perfume on Madame Lucie's hair, looked at the pile of silk on the back of the tasselled sofa and admitted to herself she'd *enjoyed* behaving badly.

Bertie had come in through the back door, in the evening, in jeans and sweatshirt, eyes black with kohl, scarlet-mouthed and pouting with boredom, her crew cut razed almost to the skin. Baby Jane fidgeted on the end of her thong, sulking on Bertie's shoulder in a tartan jacket. She found Melanie at the kitchen table, half poring over National Curriculum syllabuses, half wondering how she was going to put up with Andrew and Rose for Easter. Bertie skulked on past, looking for Tom. The smoke from the hand-made cigarette in her mouth was aromatic and familiar.

'Tom is working for his exams, and you are *not* going up,' Melanie snapped, offended by Bertie's taking liberties. 'Beyond that kitchen door is out of bounds, to you, and how dare you come into my house openly smoking that stuff.'

Bertie sat down and shrugged and Baby Jane sat and shrugged on her shoulder.

'What do you want?' Melanie demanded.

'Some company.'

'Go and hostess for company.'

'Night off. What makes you think hostessing has anything to do with company? They are *boring*.'

'Haven't you got any other friends?' Melanie snapped, out of patience. 'Other people who you could smoke that stuff with, and get into trouble?'

Bertie put her elbows on the table, dragged on her fag and held her breath. Baby Jane slid round to the back of her neck and went to sleep.

'One or two,' she answered, smoke trickling out of her nostrils. She looked Melanie full in the face. 'You got any friends, Mrs Tilford?'

'I want you to stop smoking in my house, and to leave my son alone,' said Melanie, after a long pause into which the tap dripped at long, regular intervals.

'Why're you so *friggin'* uptight, Mrs Tilford?'

Melanie opened her mouth to tell her to get out of her kitchen, and nothing came. Bertie held out the half-smoked joint.

'Here.'

Melanie stared at it for what seemed like an age, took it in her fingers, put it in her mouth, puffed and went into a paroxysm of coughing.

'Let me show you,' offered Bertie, grabbing her joint back

before it got completely mangled.

The rest was a floaty dream. She remembered telling Bertie about Giles and Daffodil, Andrew and Rose, and at some point they had had a long and serious discussion about masturbating American grandmothers. They had shrieked with laughter, shushed each other, smoked more joints, locked the kitchen door on the inside in case anyone came down, and giggled themselves sick.

'Look, you got to go and see her,' urged Bertie, scribbling Madame Lucie's address on the back of one of Giles's bank statements. 'She ran away from the Nazis and made a pile of money on the black market in the war. In the rag trade. Then she started making corsets. She'll give you advice about men.'

'How come you know her?' asked Melanie suspiciously.

'Friend of my mother's.'

'You said you were brought up in Dr Barnardo's.'

'My mother abandoned me,' said Bertie. 'On the steps of a church.'

'You tell so many fibs, I give up,' said Melanie, and took another drag.

That night, Melanie slept as if she were dead, woke up relaxed, wondered for a moment what had happened. Downstairs, she found the bank statement getting wet on the draining board, scrawled with Madame Lucie's almost illegible address.

'Oh, my God,' she groaned, trying to read Bertie's erratic scribble. 'We got well and truly stoned.'

The shop was faded, dimly lit, its windows heavily curtained in blue swags and tassels, as if shading the windows of a private parlour.

'I notice, when you look een my window, wiz your nose right up my glass. I sink, Bertha's friend is like a race'orse, elegant and nervous. If she just come in, I make 'er look *stunning*.' She whipped a tape measure from round her neck, reached up and threw it around Melanie's chest and hips.

'*Ah, bon,*' she chirped. 'You see, *you* are not ze English pear. You are ze English beanpole. Zey can look *so* elegant. What can I show you, madam?'

'Do you sell underwear to suit beanpoles?' Melanie gasped. 'And interest uninterested husbands?'

''Usbands are fools,' retorted the tiny *corsetière*. 'It eez better to 'ave someone else's fool as a lover. I 'ave new sings from Italy and Paris. I just unpack, you can see. Delicious. *Ver'* sexy. I show you.'

Madame Lucie darted round the counter and disappeared, rummagings and chucklings coming from behind the heap. White and ivory scraps of lace flew up in the air, scattered like confetti.

'Catch,' she ordered from underneath the counter.

Melanie caught, delicate foreign confections of silk and lace falling around her head.

'*Attendez*, madame. We sink about colour,' she chirruped softly, pulling Melanie towards the window. 'Madame is spring, I sink.'

'I'm spring?' said Melanie. 'I came in for a bra.'

'Spring,' Madame Lucie said firmly. 'For you, coral, orange, camel, yellow, mauve. *Les couleurs du printemps.*'

She pecked at the pile in Melanie's arms, threw several garments back on to the molehill.

'White make you look dead,' she went on. 'You wear ivory, cream, beige. *Nevaire* silver. Eef you wear jewellery, only gold.'

'I don't somehow think that jewellery is one of my more pressing problems,' said Melanie. 'I haven't any.

'I am used to a subtle, well-washed grey,' she explained, pushed towards the back of the shop to try things on. 'I wear a lot of it. I may look like a racehorse, but I'm actually a working shire. Plod, plod. I shouldn't be here at all; it's false pretences.'

She began to edge back down the narrow shop to make a getaway.

'Zis is not funny,' Madame Lucie said sternly. 'You come

back 'ere and you try zem on, madame.'

The cubicle had a triple mirror and a row of hooks for clothes, smelled of Dior and Chanel. She pushed Melanie inside.

'Eh, alors?' she demanded five minutes later, sweeping back the curtain imperiously. 'You like zem?'

Melanie, stark naked in front of the triple mirror, studied herself in dismay.

'You 'ave a good figure,' the *corsetière* announced briskly. 'I 'elp you keep it.'

'Shut the curtain,' muttered Melanie.

'Zere is no one else in ze shop,' Madame Lucie pointed out.

'By my*self*,' Melanie hissed at the myopic little face gazing through the gap in the curtains.

'Ze English are zo *uptight*,' murmured Madame Lucie, and left her customer to it.

'I ask myself, why eez zis beautiful woman's 'usband not buying 'er pretty sings?'

The molelike little face reappeared in the crack in the curtain, unabashed by Melanie's hostile expression, looked her over with a professional eye.

'My husband doesn't earn French lingerie kind of money,' snapped Melanie, doing up a silken bra with a three-figure price tag dangling from it.

'No cleavage,' announced Madame Lucie, whipping another bra from behind her back. 'Try zat.'

Sidling into the cubicle, she reached up helpfully, unhooked the no-cleavage garment.

'You 'ave a lover? You buy for 'im?' She shook her head. 'Eet eez ze wrong way round, *cherie*. You send 'im to me and I sort 'im out.'

'I have *not* got a lover,' said Melanie, feeling ridiculous. 'I have an uninterested husband, like I told you.'

'Zen zat is a *terrible* waste,' the tiny Frenchwoman said quietly. She did up the fresh bra, cupped Melanie's breasts gently in her hands, over creamy French silk embroidered with tiny fleurs-de-lis. 'Zat is perfection. I 'ave ze knickers to match.'

Melanie recoiled, pushed the hands away.

'Don't.'

The two women stood close as lovers.

'You don't like anyone should touch you,' Madame Lucie said softly. 'Eet ees so long, madame?'

Melanie shivered, flushed, brilliant with shame.

'My husband is the one with the lovers. Help me get this off. I am being stupid and it's all Bertie's fault.'

Melanie collapsed, naked as a baby, on to the armchair in the cubicle, wept, ground her teeth, told Madame Lucie all about it, and blew her nose without thinking on a pair of fleurs-de-lis knickers with a hundred-pound price tag.

'I'll wash them,' she said, handing them over for wrapping, much later. 'And the bra to match. Isn't *that* gorgeous?'

Madame Lucie tucked them into a silver box, on top of *that*, a yellow silk robe, delicately folded inside its tissue heart.

'Bertie has an *awful* lot to answer for,' Melanie said guiltily, kissing the little *corsetière* goodbye, after signing a credit card bill for well over five hundred pounds. 'But you have made me feel a million times better.'

She stood in her bedroom, in the felt dressing gown, listening to Giles talking to his mother on the landing. Rose's voice was low; she was probably complaining. Giles moved into the bathroom. She moved to pick up the silk robe from where she had thrown it on the end of her bed, and paused.

The head of their bed was against the wall. On the other side, a few inches away, Rose and Andrew lay. A chill, damp wind blew through the half-open window, threatening more rain. The north-facing room got very cold at night.

It was no good pretending. A yellow gown was for making love in a sunlit room in the morning; in some softly lit chamber with closed shutters at night. It was to wear for seduction, laughter, passion, for *love*.

'*Fool*,' she cried. 'I am being ludicrous.'

Trembling with haste, before Giles came in, she picked up the box, crammed the robe and the fleur-de-lis away. When he got into bed, the other side, turned on his bedside light and began the familiar rustling that meant he was reading the Bible, she was pretending to be fast asleep.

Long after Giles had turned off his light, and Alice had gone to bed, she heard Tom creep in. Then the house was silent. She felt across the bed and touched Giles's warm back. He didn't move. She slid her hand gently down, touched him for the first time in months. He was limp and soft, like a little boy.

Easter. The resurrection and the life, she thought, taking her hand away. He'll celebrate them in church, tomorrow, but on the home front, they just aren't there.

She crept out of bed, went downstairs, knelt on the hearth, warmed by the still burning embers of the fire. Madame Lucie had said *go*. It wasn't so simple. She would lose much if she stayed with him; he would lose everything, wife, children, home, job, career, if she went.

'What kind of responsibility is *that*?' she asked the last flames sputtering in the grate. As the fire died, she began to shiver, crept back upstairs and fell into an exhausting, nightmare-ridden sleep.

Chapter Thirty

The summer term brought GCSEs. Alice plodded stoically through and complained that she was bored when they were over. A levels started, Tom's exams only days away, bringing tensions.

'And every excuse for being impossible,' complained Giles, bad-tempered himself.

A shaven-headed young school leaver with his first job took over their post round from the grumbling old postman whose bunions forced him into early retirement. The bald boy was ambitious; they got their post before breakfast time. Giles came in from early morning communion, caught him at it, shouted that he saw no advantage to starting the day earlier than was absolutely necessary with bills.

'I'll be glad when they leave home,' he scowled, coming in with a fistful of brown envelopes. 'They might get cheaper to run.'

'They don't. They get worse,' said Melanie. 'The government keeps cutting back on grants.'

'It's our own fault for electing Tories. Why do old people need so little sleep?'

He glowered and poured himself a mug of coffee.

Up since six o'clock, he paddled across the park through early morning rain. Mid-week communion at seven thirty brought out a scattered congregation of malcontent and insomniac octogenarians. They needed little sleep and came to early morning service because they were bored and had nothing else to do. Mrs Burrows had been particularly trying, cupping her ear in her hand and shouting *what?*

what? all through the service, not having the faintest idea where she was, or what was going on. Giles did need sleep, had forgotten to shave, was damp, bad-tempered and preoccupied. He made a mental note to complain to the warden of Mrs Burrows's old people's home, and went back to ruminating on his brand-new problem; Angelina was on the rampage, they'd put her husband back inside.

She had come ringing the front door bell the previous morning, when everyone else was out.

'You got a moment, Father Tilford?' she asked, Ian Paisley lolling indolently in her arms, small pudgy hands on her full breast, pink gums grinning. She wore bare legs, stout as tree trunks, a short skirt and baggy green jumper, had the clear eyes of a child in a crafty face. Her beautiful hair curled in tangled profusion. She couldn't, he thought, be more than thirty-five, possibly nearing forty. She must have started having babies before it was legal.

'If we can keep it short,' he said, backing in.

'He got four years. Drunk in charge of a burglary,' she said, following him down the passage to his study.

'I heard he thumped the arresting police officer senseless and obstructed him in the course of duty,' said Giles. 'He was lucky he didn't get ten. The police don't like people who hit them. What brings you round?'

''Tisn't up to the police. It's the judge. He ain't too keen on the police, no more than you are, are you, Father Tilford? He'll be out in two and a half, if he behaves himself.'

Giles winced.

'Do you want to sit down?' He waved at the chair with the lumpy seat, in front of his desk. Instead, she dumped Ian Paisley, without asking, on his lap.

'Ian Paisley looks as though he's had his hair cut at Her Majesty's Pleasure, like his dad,' he joked, shifting the baby to the edge of his knee, where an accident would do least harm. She scowled. Ian Paisley's bullet head was thickly covered with mousy spikes, like an overused tooth-brush.

'Sorry,' Giles muttered. 'It's just my sense of humour.'

'You hang on to him a mo'. Now, look, I can't make these out,' she cried breathlessly, spreading family fund claim forms out on his desk, scattering his notes for the next month's sermons. As she leaned over, he could smell her warm, milky smell and, for a moment, it made him dizzy. She straightened up, struck his desk with the flat of her hand in annoyance, produced a slip of paper from her skirt pocket and thrust it under his nose.

'The electricity sent me this. I want a lump sum for it, and I don't want to have to friggin' pay it back. I went down the DSS and they said I can get a loan. I don't want no *loan*, I want them to pay it. Where do they think I'd get money like that?'

'The DSS have people in their offices who can tell you that,' he suggested hopefully. 'Why don't you go and ask them? You know *much* more about all this than I do.'

She took no notice.

'They're coming to cut me off. I went down the electricity to argue, but they were *rude*. I told them I'll go to the papers. I said, you're goin' to let five little children and their expectant mother freeze to death? They go, pay your bill, then. I go, I fuckin' can't. 'Scuse me, Father Tilford.'

Giles rubbed his forehead and tried reason.

'It's May,' he said soothingly. 'People don't generally die of cold in May. I should have thought that what with the money you're netting in benefits already, and the sweet stall, you were rather too well off to get extras. I can't see the DSS wearing this, or responding well to blackmail. Have you tried Probation? Don't they deal with families in prison?'

'*I'm* not in prison. If I was, I wouldn't have all this hassle. Probation's got their hands up their backsides. Anyhow, I got a letter from the doctor,' she went on stubbornly. 'And I want one from you to say you've seen the damp on my walls, and the mould in the kitchen, and that the baby's got bronchitis and needs the heating.'

Something registered in his mind.

'Did you say expectant mother? Are you expecting again, Angelina?'

'Three months gone. I fall that quick. I don't know how I'm goin' to manage, with him away. Not that he's any use when he's there. He's always goin' straight until he does it again. Arsehole,' she added contemptuously. ''Scuse me, Father Tilford.'

She gazed at him, tears squeezing out, unshed in those wide, cunning eyes, caught like jewels on thick black lashes. She cast her gaze down.

'If it's a boy, he said to call him Giles, after you,' she murmured hopefully. 'If you wouldn't mind, Father. I tell him, when he's away, you're such a help to us.'

'*He* suggested that?' he demanded suspiciously.

Angelina didn't bat an eye. Giles nearly groaned aloud. Husband in Durham Gaol and Giles with her child named after him?

'I'd be very flattered,' he said.

Ian Paisley, thrashing about on his knee, trying to slide off, didn't smell too fragrant. Shifting him more downwind, he pondered the prospect of becoming a surrogate member of the Tutti Frutti Club. It wasn't good. Three years she'd be without a man. Maybe the husband got her pregnant to lessen the chances of her going off with someone else.

He caught the agonized eye of Christ, looking down at him from the crucifix on the wall behind her. *Thou shalt not covet thy neighbour's wife.* He scrubbed at his face with his fingers, pulled himself together, afraid that she would surely read the guilty longings in his face. Ian Paisley threw himself backwards and started to howl.

His mother smiled slyly.

'So. Will you christen him for me, like you did him?' she asked, taking Ian Paisley off his lap. The baby plucked and rooted at her jumper, shrieking.

''Scuse me,' she said, lifting up the jumper, exposing a huge, white, blue-veined milky breast.

Giles had a terrible spasm of coughing, fidgeted

wretchedly and coughed some more. The baby sucked noisily, contented.

'I'll try not to drop the baby next time,' he gasped, when he could speak again.

'The old man used to say the heating in that church is diabolical. He got some nasty coughs as well,' she remarked guilelessly. 'Ian Paisley's got the asthma, as well as the bronchitis. I had to take him down the hospital, you know.'

Giles had a brief vision of Satan tending the flames in the old church boiler, maliciously understoking. It made a change from the usual image of him feeding the hellfires like billy-o.

'Asthma, has he? I didn't know that, no.'

Ian Paisley dropped her breast, wriggled and burped loudly. She smiled bravely, chucked the baby under his milky chin.

'He could die of it. The doctor goes, they can get chesty. You don't always know what sets them off. Do you think it could be not being able to breathe or something? We need the heating money, Father Tilford.'

Or something. Like not being able to breathe because some idiot dropped him into a font full of cold water.

She tucked her jumper down.

'You'll write me a letter now, won't you, Father Tilford?'

Fitful sunlight broke through the rain clouds, played on the threadbare carpet, showed up all the dust on his desk and glossed her tangled hair with bronze. She had freckles across the bridge of her nose, already had the soft look of pregnancy, that look of ripeness. He wrenched his thoughts away.

'I expect you worry most when you leave Ian Paisley down the road with your mum and go to the pub of an evening,' he suggested, pulling a letter pad towards him. 'When you get out to spend the money you make helping your sister clean at school. That's after you shut the stall up, of course, and you've cashed your giro.' He unscrewed his fountain pen, frowning. 'What was it? Flexitime, did I hear someone say? Didn't I hear Mr Benedict say something of the sort?'

Angelina's voice was suddenly steely.

'They depend on me. I'm mother and father to that lot while he's away. It wouldn't do to have anything happen to me, because I'm all they've got.'

'Really?' he said harshly. 'And the rest of you? Ian Paisley has enough aunts and uncles and grandparents to start a tribe, never mind enough brothers and sisters and cousins to make a couple of soccer teams, with Giles junior, here, on the way.'

'They're mostly inside with him,' she said scornfully. 'We scrape so's we can get the fares to visit. Do you know what the coaches cost? The Scrubs, you can go by tube. But when you start talkin' about Winson Green, and Durham, and the Isle of Wight, and Lewes, it's a lot of money. Us, we're just aunts and little children, left to carry on. You know what He said?'

'Who? The judge?'

She jerked a thumb at the crucifix behind her.

''Im. Suffer little children . . . Father?'

Giles knew he was defeated, gave in, and wrote a note for the DSS.

The breakfast table was a litter of Sainsbury's cornflake boxes and dirty mugs.

'Why can't you finish one packet before you open another?' Giles asked crossly, shaking packets with a helping left in each. He looked for a clean bowl, found the crockery cupboard empty.

'You'll have to wash one up,' Melanie called, going to pick up the post from the front door.

He focused his irritation on his children.

'You on study leave?' he growled at Tom. 'Is that why you get up whenever you feel like it, and go to bed at two in the morning? It's not meant to be another word for feckless.'

Tom chewed steadily on cold toast and refused to be drawn.

'You are supposed to *work*.'

He turned on Alice.

'Will you either eat those, or leave them alone?'

Each morning Alice stirred cornflakes round and round in a bowl, until they went soggy enough to justify putting them in the bin.

'Are you thinking of being anorexic?' he snapped. 'Because your mother and I have quite enough to cope with. We haven't got time for eating disorders.'

'I'm actually thinking of being bulimic. Mum makes me have them, and I hate cornflakes.'

She got up and exaggeratedly tipped her cereal down the cluttered sink.

'If he can't be bothered to get into university, what does he think he's going to do?' Giles persisted, frustrated that no one would argue with him. 'Lie in bed all day, on the dole? *I* should be so lucky.'

'How would you like your *whole life* depending on some stupid exams and UCCA?' cried Alice.

'UCAS,' said Tom pedantically.

'I've *done* those stupid exams and UCCA,' snarled Giles. 'Been there, seen it, done it.'

'And I don't want to end up where it got you,' said his son, plastering the last piece of toast with peanut butter.

'*Thomas,*' Giles roared.

'He didn't mean it like that,' cried Alice.

'Just how did he mean it, then?'

The three of them glared at each other, set for a really good fight.

'There's one from the research firm that did the parent ballot, to say we've given Hugo the go-ahead for opting out,' Melanie said excitedly, coming back into the kitchen. She propped a pile of envelopes in front of Giles's coffee mug, turned one of them, picked it up again, tore it open.

'This is from Hugo Benedict. What have you lot been doing that I get a handwritten letter?'

Cheated out of their row, they stared at her.

'He's made you redundant,' guessed Alice, heading out

of the kitchen while the going was good. 'Cool. I won't have to keep listening to *everyone* telling embarrassing stories about things you say in class. I could die.'

'A personal invitation to his karaoke evening?' suggested Giles. 'And when you see him, you might tell him that I've had to rearrange my communion class because they'd all rather go to his do. Even old Mrs Blunt flatly refuses to miss it.'

'Old Mrs Blunt is weighty and deaf and a raging dipso,' retorted Melanie, unfolding the note. 'Hugo's giving out a free glass of wine each. She'll be there with her tongue hanging out. I wouldn't be surprised if that's why she wants to be confirmed. Hair of the dog free first thing in the morning, several times a week. You'd better watch it – she'll knock back the lot and you'll have to keep on consecrating wine by the *gallon*. What a scam. At her age. Just think.' She chuckled, amused, and started to read her letter. Giles's face snapped into disapproval like a hair-trigger mousetrap.

'And why does Hugo want me to go and see him at lunchtime?' she demanded. 'What have you been doing?'

They both vanished smartly, before she finished reading and looked up.

'Maybe he's offering you promotion?' suggested Giles, pouring cornflakes into a pudding basin. 'You shouldn't go assuming the kids are in the wrong.'

'This letter says he wants to see you, as well,' she said shortly. 'This morning. That's why I know that something's wrong.'

There *was* something wrong. It had been at the back of his mind all the time Angelina had been in his study.

Hair like a bottlebrush. Straight. Tufty. Mouse.

Ian Paisley's West Indian dad had tight black Caribbean curls. Angelina had tumbling wild Irish curls, black as her husband's. The children had Brillo-pad curls and huge black eyes, like both their parents. Ian Paisley had grey eyes. Flexitime working down King's Cross, thought Giles. *That's* what she's up to. They're all at it, they stick together. When the money runs out, the Tutti Frutti women are out there, making it up and paying the bills with a spot of whoring down the King's Cross way. He knew her sisters did it, but Angelina came to church and was on East Stepney's PTA. Not reasons for not whoring; it had just never crossed his mind.

That Angelina was available was so appalling, so exciting, he leaped off his chair and rushed out of the room, leaving his cornflakes spilling all over the table. His wife stood holding Hugo's summons, staring after him in amazement.

'Giles.'

She heard the door go.

'What's got into him *now*?' she asked, mopping up the mess, but they had all gone, leaving her late for school, and to wonder on her own.

Chapter Thirty-One

'Do you know why Hugo wants to see us?' Melanie asked in an undertone as they filed into assembly behind the prefects and the rest of the sixth form.

Alastair wondered what to say, decided she would understand professional discretion, that his duty to Hugo was to lie.

'Not a clue,' he murmured back, not looking her in the eye. Halfway through 'Dear Lord and Father of mankind, Forgive our foolish ways' she decided she wasn't such a fool any more. If Alastair had to lie about it, it was very, *very* serious. Redundancy. No job, no money, her escape routes cut off, or social security in bed and breakfast, like half the families in Giles's parish. No good going back to Norfolk; even fewer jobs, there. She would end up leaving him, only to go to him, like the rest, cap in hand. *Help me.* Irony so awful was almost funny, but while the school sang the rest of the hymn with discordant gusto, her throat was too dry to speak.

Giles could sense the wrath of God building into a thunderbolt, aimed straight in his direction.

'I deserve it,' he thundered, raising his hands in furious supplication, losing his temper. 'But *I* can't seem to help myself, and the more I ask, the less You help me.'

'Stay cool, man,' Attila the Hun advised, drifting through church on an opiate cloud, dead cool and pleased with himself. Threatened with eviction from his blanketed corner in the vestry, he had roused himself to do some housekeeping, tidied his sleeping bag into a roll, rearranged his meagre store of food and cleaned his gear, wrapping his syringes and clean needles carefully in a cloth, then rewarded himself with a good, strong fix.

'I am not cool,' Giles roared, pacing up and down. 'I am overwrought and worried. And when are you going to move out of my vestry and leave me in peace?'

'You been doing that shouting and yelling ever since you came rushing in and disturbed me,' Attila answered, sitting down on the altar steps, about to go on the nod. He put his head back, closed his eyes and announced smugly, 'I thought you said church was for prayer and meditation. It looks to me more like a punch-up. It ain't healthy to get that stressed out.'

'Don't you *dare* sleep there,' Giles yelped. 'Get back in your vestry.'

Attila looked at him with sleepy eyes.

'There you go, *my* vestry. I knew you didn't mean it. I could lend you a fix,' he offered contentedly, his head falling forward. He began to snore. Giles clutched his rumpled hair and swore fluently, in full sight of God and all his angels looking down with bright, dispassionate faces from his one and only stained-glass window.

If he had to lie about them, Alastair decided after break, he could at least monitor events. Melanie had hardly spoken to him in the staff room, had sat clutching a cold cup of tea, staring at the clock over the door as though waiting for the electric chair, her worry so palpable it was painful to see.

Giles loped across the playground and came into sight through the main entrance, crumpled, his hair all on end, but on time.

'Good morning,' Alastair said pleasantly, just happening to be standing there, nonchalantly examining fading photographs of last year's sports day and the small array of out-of-date lists of mock A level results. From the depths of the building a series of shrieks echoed.

'What's good about it?' Giles asked gloomily. 'Summonses from headmasters don't usually mean anything good.'

The shrieks continued.

'You torture your pupils these days?' Giles demanded.

'Only when they deserve it.'

At the look on Giles's face, he nearly laughed.

'Martial arts practice,' Alastair explained. 'Mohammed is very good at martial arts. We have a thriving club. The screaming is meant to put your opponent off.'

'It puts me off,' Giles said with feeling. 'So, to tell the truth, does your headmaster.'

Alastair smiled politely.

'Shall I show you where to wait for your wife and Mr Benedict?' he offered.

Giles gave him a hooded, suspicious look, but Alastair's expression was helpfulness itself. They both knew that Giles knew where Hugo's study was. Unknown to Melanie, he had been there shortly after the move, to suggest closer partnership between school and church. Right in front of Alastair, socialist Hugo sent him away with few words and a great big flea in his ear.

'And I'd be very grateful if you'd clean that damn graveyard up, so I can keep my kids out of it,' he growled, seeing him off the premises with just the right amount of chilly courtesy, to deprive Giles of the satisfaction of being able to make any complaint.

'You only want him to tidy up so that you can see more easily who is over there,' Alastair remarked when Giles had gone, while they were waiting in the staff room for Bunny to be ready to go home. 'You'd hate it if he actually stopped them going over there, because they'd only go somewhere else, where you couldn't spy.'

'He's not to know. We're polyglot over here, I told him. A bit of everything and everything in its place, including religion. If they want church, they can go over the way and get it. Assembly is as far as I'm prepared to go,' said Hugo.

'When the old man was there, a lot of the kids *did* go to

church,' Alastair pointed out. 'It's not our job to be prejudiced one way or the other.'

'That was the singer, not the song,' Hugo snapped.

They were just squaring up for an argument when Bunny came whirling in.

'We've been waiting,' complained Hugo.

Bunny beamed.

'My tutorial lingered on,' she said. 'We were going through what it was like to be away from home, and at university. Homesickness, and making friends, and all that. Just when the bell went, we got stuck into what it's like in Freshers' Week. That's supposing UCAS ever lets any of them within spitting distance of a university. I told them, it's not Freshers' Week, nothing to do with freshers, it's Fuck a Fresher Week for everyone else, and they can either get fucked and into trouble, or they can be sensible and go on the pill and have some condoms tucked inside their pockets. Either way, they'll get f—'

There was a crash as Garlick dropped a tray of new beanshoots, destined for the windowsill. Alastair looked at Bunny, brought up short in mid-four-letter-word, at Garlick's earnest, stricken face, at broken pots and compost on the floor.

'That'll teach you to creep about behind my back,' he shouted, and let out a great roar of laughter.

Giles sat in the same low chair as before, and was hating every moment of the interview.

'Not in my school,' Hugo thundered. 'Tom has one more chance. I won't have drugs in school.'

Making parents sit on very low armchairs while he sat on a swivel chair behind his desk was an arrangement that worked entirely in Hugo's favour.

'I don't think Tom has ever brought anything into school,' Melanie said.

'David Absalom and the governors have debated this very closely.'

Hugo waited.
'And?' asked Giles.
'*Suspicion* that a pupil is involved, in or out of school, will lead to instant suspension. We have been having talks with the drug squad, and a Sergeant Philips will be coming to talk to a special parents' evening, as soon as we can arrange it.'
Melanie sat obediently in her low chair and tried to work out what was going wrong. Hugo tolerated cannabis, out of school; it was a fact of life. He could – and did – lean on his windowsill and watch his pupils smoke. Everyone knew they did, mostly in Giles's graveyard. In East Stepney they had the highest truancy rate in London. Telling teenagers they couldn't come to school when they didn't want to in the first place was hardly an effective way of stopping them doing something they did want to. Hugo didn't make sense.
'I thought it was school policy only to take action about other drugs, or crack,' she said. 'So many of them smoke, we'd close ourselves down if we expelled them all.'
Giles gazed at her with surprise.
'It goes with the job,' she muttered, realizing with a shock how far she had moved from the old days, when she didn't know what crack was and hadn't got an opinion on anything much, had tried nothing for herself. 'We have to know about drugs.'
'The governors won't tolerate it any more,' Hugo said repressively.
And you are sitting here as a parent, not a member of staff, she heard him say, between the lines. It *didn't* make sense.
'We don't need Sergeant Philips to tell us about cannabis,' Giles said. 'We've got a resident expert, haven't we, Melanie?'
No one had come in the kitchen when she and Bertie . . . Melanie flushed scarlet, *extremely* embarrassed. Hugo wondered why, glared at Giles, and thought it a poor moment to joke.
'You think I'm joking? You think you're the only ones who know what street life is?' Giles demanded, interpreting

the look correctly. 'You should see what's in my vestry.'

He wasn't joking at all. Attila the Hun had been living in his vestry since he fell out with his girlfriend and lost the squat that went with her. At first it was just in bad weather.

'I keep finding you in here,' he complained, falling over Attila squatting in a corner, shooting up, his belt round his arm, held in his teeth, so he couldn't argue. All his tackle, neatly arranged, was spread out on the floor. He let go his belt, closed his eyes and nodded off, out of reach on cloud nine, and quite at home. It was impossible to argue with someone who was invariably on the way in or out of unconsciousness. Giles worked around him, got used to him. After several weeks of uneasy cohabitation, Attila settled in and Giles learned every little habit, the gruesome A to Z of heroin addiction.

'You know, you're getting a bit like the old man,' Attila said grudgingly one evening, just before evensong, as Giles held his head in the sink and helped him be sick. He shook violently, sweated, looked fit to die.

'Are you going to have a fit?' Giles asked anxiously.

'They cut the stuff with fucking poison,' Attila panted, clawing his way over to the sink again. 'I don't want no fucking ambulance.'

Giles held his head again, worried about whether to call an ambulance, desperate not to let Attila die, because that he was like the old man was the nicest thing anyone had ever said.

The next day he *had* called an ambulance. Early morning communion was enlivened, the elderly congregation woken up, by Attila howling like a dog in the vestry, staggering through into the middle of 'Our Father', overdosed on slimming pills and frothing at the mouth. As the ambulance crew loosened his leather, bits of bondage and a pair of handcuffs fell out. They uncovered a curling whip, tattooed across his neck and back, as the fine bone in his nose vibrated like a violin string.

'That whip appeared shortly after several packets of

communion wafers went missing,' Giles told the paramedic darkly.

'What would anyone want with communion wafers?' the man asked, putting a needle in Attila's arm.

'He probably sold them to Satanists. If so, they were cheated. They weren't consecrated.'

The paramedic looked up.

'Probably just ate them,' he said.

Giles hoped he was right. From time to time there were peculiar smells in the church of an early morning, strange disturbances. Mud and hair where there shouldn't be any, chairs moved, flowers spilled.

'Winos. Foxes get in. Come from all over, right in from Epping. And birds. And there's things escape, in graveyards,' the rickety cherub had said, chuckling, daily more and more twisted up.

'He looks like Charles Laughton in *The Hunchback of Notre Dame*,' Giles told Attila, betraying his churchwarden angrily. 'I half expect to come in and find him swinging from the bells.'

He hoped the cherub just meant methane, or whatever might seep from the ancient burial ground. But sometimes, lying awake at night unable to sleep, he got the heebie-jeebies badly and didn't find the churchwarden's words the least bit funny.

There was a taut silence. It isn't like Hugo, Melanie thought, to be so formal and so heavy, going on pompously about Sergeant Philips from the drug squad, saying that he would be coming round to see them. Hugo saw her frown, saw her face clear, saw the penny drop.

If someone could show we have a drug problem, and are doing nothing about it, they'd close us down, she realized. This was all about the opt-out, the dirty tricks campaign. It wasn't about drugs, or Tom, or East Stepney's pragmatic policies, at all. Someone, somewhere, was putting *Hugo* under pressure.

'I've got no option but to co-operate with the drug squad,' he said, indicating that she had got his message. 'And so, if you are wise, will you. Sergeant Philips is Irish and has kissed the Blarney Stone. As a talker, he outclasses me. No competition. Perhaps we should get the Stud to open a book on how long he'll last around here before someone kicks him out and we have *real* trouble.'

'Send him round to Attila,' suggested Giles.

'There are an awful lot of you,' Hugo went on. 'Don't go thinking you're alone. Free karaoke tickets to the winning family, do you think?'

His voice was light, his eyes were worried.

'I thought you were going to tell me I was redundant,' Melanie said.

Hugo grinned.

'Putting a different sort of frighteners on you, I'm afraid,' he joked. 'Good luck with Sergeant Philips.'

'I have a feeling we don't know what the frighteners are until we've had the sergeant round,' Melanie said, scared.

'Can't be much worse than interviews with the headmaster,' Giles answered.

He went out into the playground in a rare burst of sunshine, to go back across the grass to take confessions.

Confessions.

We've got a resident expert, haven't we, Melanie?

She watched him hurry away, wondered how much he really knew, how much of a dark horse her husband really was.

'All I know is, I don't know,' she murmured, and turned to go to fetch her books from the staff room, to go back to her job, to teach.

Chapter Thirty-Two

Sergeant Philips looked like a travelling salesman and liked to think he had quite a sense of humour. He hadn't wasted time, rang to announce that he was coming, staggered up the front path after school, a heavy case in his hand, the following day.

'We generally come at five in the morning. We don't bother to ring – just come straight on in,' he chuckled, before introducing himself, puffing past the holly tree. 'Makes a bit of a mess of the door, but we don't worry too much about that just yet.'

He was as tall as Giles, wore twill trousers and a blue jacket, walked with the precise and rigid strut of a guardsman. The heavy case was stuffed, like a macabre doctor's bag, with samples. He planted it on the kitchen table, settled himself at the table, took out a stack of pale blue files and arranged them as neatly as Alastair's archives, lined up precisely in front of him.

'Do sit down,' he invited them with a jolly laugh, indicating the chairs. 'A lot of the youngsters I see find that I'm just like one of the family.'

Not here, Tom mouthed silently.

'I've got a lot of homework. I'm in the middle of A levels,' he said mutinously.

'I like you to look on me as a friend. Shall we have a cup of tea, Mother?' he asked chummily, looking at Melanie.

'*Mother*. Not slow to come forward, is he?' hissed Melanie, outraged. 'Who *does* he think he is?'

'Shhhh,' warned Giles, running a finger round his dog

collar, sweating, more rumpled and disorganized than usual in dark green corduroys and black shirt.

'What's the matter with you?' she cried, exasperated.

'I think I've got a phobia,' he mumbled miserably. 'Since, ah *hem*, you know? Every time I see a policeman, I start coming out in hives.'

Sergeant Philips settled himself down as though he lived there, shuffled through his files and pulled one out. He opened it and put it on the table, angled away so that no one else could quite make the contents out.

'This is you,' he said to Tom.

'Is it?' asked Tom unhelpfully.

'It is.' He ran his finger down a page. 'We know a lot about you. Been watching you for months. Been watching *dozens* of you for months. God, you're a nuisance.'

He drummed his fingers on the files stacked on the table in front of him. Very short cropped hair and the guardsman's stance were the only things that would make him stand out in a Sainsbury's queue. He was mousy, colourless, a couple of shaving nicks the only feature that would make anyone notice a slightly receding chin. Flakes of dandruff speckled his shoulders. Sergeant Philips looked a nonentity, *was* a nonentity, doing a job that terrified his clients out of their wits.

'Now, then,' he began, flattening his file carefully. 'I've got three children and a nice house and a very nice wife. I wouldn't want them to come to any harm, and God help anyone who brought that about. So. I know I wouldn't feel pleased if any child of mine brought a raid to my door.'

'Raid?' said Melanie, putting down the empty kettle. 'You are in my house two minutes, and you're talking about raids?'

He didn't look at her.

'I've been counselling families about drugs for twelve years, Mother, and I often find they're very grateful. Teenagers can be a problem. My job is to help them not to be bigger problems.'

'You said five in the morning,' Melanie persisted.

'Oh, almost certainly while you'd still be in bed,' he agreed, as though they were discussing their milk delivery.

All the hairs on the back of her neck stood up.

'Giles,' she appealed.

Giles was gazing at Sergeant Philips like a mongoose at a snake.

'You get no warning, so we can catch you at your lowest. Secret police tactics,' he said chattily, smiling a smile that didn't reach his eyes. 'Ha ha.'

'Are you menacing us?' asked Giles, not enough conviction in his voice to shake a rabbit. 'That's against the law.'

'I am counselling you about what happens in cases of use, possession and pushing of prohibited substances,' Sergeant Philips agreed without hesitation, rubbing at one of his shaving nicks, causing it to bleed. 'Do you wish to interfere with my carrying out my duty?'

'I wish to throw you out of my house and call the police. But since you *are* the police, I expect you would just arrest me for obstructing your right to threaten and intimidate,' said Giles. 'That's what they threatened last time I asked a policeman if he was threatening me. So you had better carry on.'

'Thomas Tilford,' read Sergeant Philips expressionlessly, looking inside the pale blue file. 'Eighteen. East Stepney School. A levels. Wants to go to university. Hasn't found settling in easy after move from the country, and hasn't got a lot of friends. The one or two he has, I can tell him, he'd be better without. Otherwise not a problem lad, other than being a frequent smoker of a prohibited substance, who is about to get into serious trouble.'

Tom looked down at the kitchen table, the faint scars of early acne standing out, livid on his skin, white with resentment.

'That you?'

'No.'

Sergeant Philips paused. They often started out truculent and bloody-minded.

'This is a file on you,' he began again, tapping it with a nicotine-stained finger.

'You smoke,' said Tom.

'I wouldn't go on that way, if I were you,' suggested Sergeant Philips.

Tom stared pointedly at the discoloured finger, and sat in sullen, angry silence.

'Don't be rude to the officer,' Giles said. 'Don't make it worse, Thomas.'

Sergeant Philips smiled again.

Teenagers could be hard to impress, hard to crack. It was much easier to terrify parents. Parents *owned* things, had possessions that could be wrecked, reputations that could be doubly wrecked, especially middle-class ones, like these, or single parents, or parents with lovers, or any other of a galaxy of guilty secrets to hide. Sergeant Philips had something on most people, little odds and ends, little habits, family ways, skeletons kept in cupboards; things no one wanted brought out in court, no one wanted some drug counsellor, lawyer or probation officer to hear. Sergeant Philips mopped at his chin, brought his finger away and eyed a small smear of blood.

'I wasn't paying proper attention with the razor this morning,' he remarked, fishing a handkerchief out of his pocket. 'I knew I'd got you lot to sort out. You were on my mind.'

Melanie was staring fixedly at Tom. She had been to marriage guidance. Giles had had a bad time when they picked him up by mistake on a murder charge, and wasn't doing too well in his parish. He had an inferiority complex and was looking at his son as though he was something the cat had brought in. No one in the Tilford family wanted any more trouble. The officer grinned. No one brought more effective pressure to bear on erring youngsters than frightened, guilty parents.

'In the church, are you?' Sergeant Philips said, apparently reading Tom's file.

'You know very well that I am,' snapped Giles.

'Tsk, tsk.' The officer shook his head as if rebuking a naughty child. 'And Mother is a school teacher.'

'Yes,' Melanie muttered.

'Sister called Alice?'

'Yes.'

'We're not interested in her.'

Then why ask?

He took his time, running his finger down the page, hiding it from them, so they could not overlook.

'We have a very full picture,' he remarked, sounding satisfied. 'Times, places, contacts, amounts spent. Corroboration and names. Enough.'

'Enough for what?' asked Giles.

'A criminal record. Hoping to go to university, is he? Go into a profession? Get a visa to go abroad? Take out insurance? Get himself a Barclaycard? Tsk, tsk, tsk.'

Giles and Melanie paled.

Sergeant Philips seemed to have an afterthought.

'I don't suppose you wanted to follow your dad into the church, Tom?'

'So what if I did?'

'How do you think the church looks on candidates coming in with a history of family drug addiction? Shall we ask your dad to tell us?'

Giles half put up his hand, like a child in school answering teacher's question.

'You are overstating your case. A bit of teenage experimenting isn't family addiction.'

'Try explaining that to the authorities when Sonny Jim here hits the local headlines. It's a good story – *Local Vicar in Drug Ring* or some such gibberish. From the editor's point of view, the angle is that young Thomas here is the son of a local clergyman. They won't spare you, especially as you've already been in the national press. On suspicion of rape and murder?' He made out that he was reading it all afresh, um'd and ah'd. 'My word, you lead quite an interesting life here, Vicar.'

Giles wondered what was in the file that he *wasn't* reading out, and looked sick.

'Would you like me to go through Thomas's record, incident by incident? You want to go through the whole length and breadth of it? Right you are.' He pulled the file towards him. 'We have times when he and others have brought drugs into this house, while you were here, and while you've been out. That involves you and Mrs Tilford. How do we know you don't condone it? What have you been doing about it? One friend in particular features very regularly.'

He leaned forward.

'How much do you think you *know* about his friends, Mr and Mrs Tilford? People you've been inviting to your house. Shall we look?'

Bertie, thought Melanie. I'll kill her.

Sergeant Philips tapped his file, made as if to turn it to show them.

Suddenly she saw it as some court would, the whole distorted story.

'No,' she cried.

'Did you have any idea it was this bad?' Giles demanded.

'No,' said Melanie, looking ten years older.

Giles glared at Tom in horror and shook his head.

Gotcha.

Middle-class pushovers. All you had to do was *suggest* things; they supplied the details for themselves. Parents were easy. Teenagers, as a general rule of thumb, cost a lot more effort. Sergeant Philips always concentrated on the parents.

He sounded bored.

'Please yourselves. Procedure, as it were. We bring sniffer dogs and crowbars, and we go over your house with a fine-tooth comb, and we don't say *please*. By the time we leave, you won't have much left that you recognize.'

Melanie began biting her nails, and watching her, tears crept into Tom's eyes.

'To be specific,' continued Sergeant Philips, apparently taking no notice, 'we rip open your furniture, take a sledgehammer to your walls, tear up your carpets, mash the contents of your fridge, throw out what's in your freezer. We tip out every drawer, every cupboard, tear the lining out of every coat, case, bag, until we are satisfied we have found all the drugs in your home. Then we go away again and put the prosecution case together.'

And you enjoy every moment of it, Melanie thought furiously.

Giles was listening intently, wooden-faced. Tom was crying.

'OK. Now let's talk about what drugs do to you, as opposed to what the drug squad does to you.'

They sat like a row of cuckoos, their mouths open. Tom cleared his throat hoarsely, looking for a handkerchief.

'Most families are very interested in this,' Sergeant Philips said reproachfully. 'I've had parents ring me up in tears to say thank you.'

'I can believe they ring you up in tears,' mumbled Melanie.

'Ah. Now, Tom. Do you know,' the sergeant demanded in a whisper, 'why you put a cardboard filter on your smokes?'

Tom blew his nose. Sergeant Philips turned to Melanie.

'He doesn't seem to know. Do *you*?'

'No.'

'Because smoke from tobacco mixed with cannabis resin gets so hot, you need the filter to stop it blowing the back of your throat out.' He pushed his chair back and balanced on the back legs. 'I've seen kids who've left the filter off. They don't talk so well.'

'Oh,' moaned Melanie.

'Cannabis makes you sleepy, slow to react, uncoordinated and inclined to look for better, bigger kicks.'

'I don't think that's proven,' said Giles.

'Spare me the middle-class liberals. It makes you a sitting target for pushers of other stuff,' snapped the sergeant. 'You think about it. One stoned, stupid kid sitting with his eyes going round like Catherine wheels and his brain parked in a cigarette pack.'

He picked at his chin and looked glumly at the scab of blood.

'Along comes Mr Big. Mr Big is some other kid, probably in the same class at school. The people who make the real money out of kids like yours and mine never stick their noses on the high streets or outside schools. They use children to sell to children, when they have their big promotions going. Think of the first approach as a loss leader, like you're in the supermarket, with cheap child labour stocking the shelves. Kids like you, sunshine. Pushing.'

'I don't push,' Tom said wretchedly.

'Picture the run-up to exams, like now, when the pressure's really on. It's so bloody easy.'

He put on a mock seductive voice, a wheedling expression.

Hey, this is cool, Tilford. Real cool. Try some? Nah, doesn't cost for you, mate. It's a prezzie.'

'And before you know it, one more *asshole,*' he leaned forward and spat the word in Tom's face, 'is hooked.'

Melanie was crying freely, her hands over her face, Tom watching her, his face warped with misery.

'Crack is coming.' The sergeant had his face right up against Tom's. 'You read what crack does, sunshine? You want to be there when they got a crack promotion going, out of your tiny skull on some kinda chemical, ready and waiting? 'Cos one thing I can tell you for sure. It's on its way, and so are you. To prison.'

Tom began to cry like a little child, his chin quivering uncontrollably, nose dripping an elastic teardrop of snot.

'You got something you want to say to your mother?' demanded Sergeant Philips.

Tom got up slowly, put his arms around her shoulders.

'Sorry,' he mumbled. 'I'm sorry, Mum.'

'That's better,' said the sergeant. 'You stay away from drugs and you won't hear any more about it. But you slip, and I'll see you in court. And if I see you in court, I'll see you in prison.'

Through his tears, over his mother's neck, Tom shot him a look of pure hatred.

Chapter Thirty-Three

'He never showed us his samples,' Melanie said sarcastically, as Sergeant Philips hefted his briefcase down the front path again. 'God help Bertie when I get my hands on her.'

'It's not Bertie's fault,' cried Tom, a six-foot coil of gangling misery. He threw himself back into a kitchen chair and knuckled his nose like a little boy. 'She doesn't give it to me.'

'Where *do* you get it, then? What did he mean, *times, places, contacts?*'

'I don't know,' Tom cried. 'He was making up half of it. I get it off people at school. Everyone knows. You can see Mr Benedict watching from his office. It's only a bit of weed, Mum, nothing else. I've been offered other things, and I always say no. They stash it in Dad's graveyard, down the mausoleum.'

'So *you're* responsible,' she yelled, rounding on Giles. 'Since we moved here, you've put me through attempted murder, burglaries—'

About to say *Daffodil, incest and tarts*, she remembered Tom just in time to bite her tongue painfully.

'*Ouch*. You've got addicts crawling out of the woodwork every time you go to work and your children on drugs. You've got your head so buried in the sand, you don't care what wreckage is piling up around you.' She put her finger in her mouth, tasted blood. 'Now look what you've made me do.'

'Wrongful arrest,' he said plaintively. 'Not attempted murder. And only one of my children is taking drugs. Soft drugs. And if he's going to do it, I'd rather he did it where I can see him. I thought Hugo Benedict was of the same view.'

Melanie's hand closed on a knife lying on the table.

'Mum,' Tom yelped.

With a great effort she pushed it away and let go.

'I don't know about wrongful,' she said. 'Sometimes I think they had the right man, wrong crime. Why ever did I come and get you out?'

'You don't understand anything *at all,'* Tom suddenly shouted. 'All I've done is smoke a few times. I've said I'm sorry.'

'It's illegal,' Melanie shouted back. 'Visiting your father in the cells was bad enough. You, I couldn't bear.'

'So is crack illegal, so is cocaine, so is heroin, so is stealing and so is beating old people up for kicks and so is killing little kids like James Bulger, and I don't do *any* of the awful things I could.' He hung over the banisters and screamed, 'If I did, *then* you'd have something to argue about.'

The crash shook the whole house as he slammed his door.

'*We* have just been threatened by the drug squad, and *he* is misunderstood. Garlick is right about teenagers,' said Melanie.

'It is time he left home,' said Giles gloomily.

'For once, no doubt he'd agree with you. For heaven's sake, don't sit there with your hands like that, as if you're *praying,'* she snapped.

'I *am* praying,' Giles protested, running his hands through his hair until it looked like a mop. 'I pray constantly for help and guidance in what used to be my home and has turned into a lunatic asylum.'

'Daffodil, incest and tarts,' she said furiously, getting it off her chest at last. 'You get on and pray about it. I'm going to do something useful and have it out with Bertie.'

'I'm sorry about Daffodil, incest and tarts,' he said sadly.

The tap, more and more in need of a washer, dripped in the sudden silence.

'You're going to get caught one day, Giles. Like that judge did, kerb-crawling, or something.'

He started. She was psychic. It preyed on his mind ceaselessly that Angelina could be found of a Saturday night down the King's Cross Road, *and that any day now, he was going to go and look.*

'Anyway, I'm going to give Bertie a piece of my mind,' she cried.

'Mels . . .'

'I need to shout at someone *who will listen*.'

She grabbed her cardigan from the back of a chair, and ran.

Once on the pavement, she slowed down. It was warm, the false promise of summer made every year in the middle of May showing in soft warm air and the deepening blue of the evening sky. The sun still shone as a translucent moon balanced, huge and delicate, on the edge of the rooftops. A light breeze stirred the smell of new tarmac from a little roadwork across the way from her gate. They had been drilling and banging all afternoon in a hole with white and blue tape around it, tied on half a dozen cones. A *Thames Water: running water for you* van stood empty, next to the hole, no driver inside. If they leave that there until tomorrow, she thought, crossing the road and heading for Bertie's stairs, it'll have no tyres and half its engine out.

Two fourth years from school pedalled past on mountain bikes, Walkmans in their ears, shorts up round their bottoms. They waved, wobbled and disappeared around a bend, heading for the Slug and Lettuce, where the landlord turned a blind eye to the licensing laws.

She reached the tower block, where shrill, excited voices of little boys playing football in the cage at the side of the flats were drowned out as someone turned a ghetto blaster up. Metalica burst forth at full throttle. Raves. Lasers, Ecstasy and chilling out. Ecstasy turned their eyes black. Sergeant Philips was right. She turned in, and climbed Bertie's staircase to the third floor. Unemployment was good news for locksmiths, she realized with amazement, looking down the long concrete walkway. The row of mustard-yellow front doors that gave directly on to it bulged with locks, protecting frightened tenants from their bored and violent neighbours. She walked slowly round, counting. Number thirty-four was round the corner of the building, opposite her own house. She looked over the parapet, could see straight into her bedroom window, could see the chest of drawers in which the yellow robe was hidden like a talisman, no place for it here, among ugliness. She counted more doors, and came to a frightened halt. Number thirty-four's mustard door hung open. Its locks were broken, hung loose in splintered wood. There was no one in sight. Up and down the stairs and walkways, there was not a movement anywhere.

'Bertie? Is anyone in here?'

Melanie knocked and waited, knocked again, cautiously pushed the door wide.

The door opened on a cramped, narrow corridor, the kitchen directly to the right, other doorways straight ahead, all closed.

Go and dial 999 said a sensible voice in her head. About to turn away, a flash of brown behind the kitchen door caught her eye.

'Baby Jane?'

She went in. The little monkey chattered frenziedly from behind a box of cornflakes, leaped into the air and shot inside the half-closed door of a cheap gas oven, pulling it shut behind her.

'Even the animals around here have funny habits,' Melanie gasped, rubbing goose bumps on her arms, her heart pounding.

Unlike her own untidy, neglected house, Bertie's council flat was neat. A small fridge hummed next to the sink, the mouselike scrabblings of the monkey in the oven the only other sound. A row of herbs in a plastic tray leaned towards the light on the windowsill. The mouselike noises stopped, and the oven emitted a series of heartbroken cheepings.

'That thing can't be *on*. You're never cooking!'

She knelt down and opened the door. Cowering at the back, Baby Jane's tiny face was twisted up.

'Baby *Jane*. You're crying.'

The oven was cold. Melanie reached inside.

'You can stay in there and roast, for all I care,' she shouted, cradling her hand, turning on the cold tap, washing blood running from the bite marks on her finger. Winding a sheet of kitchen towel round it, she went into the corridor. The first door led to a minute bathroom, empty as the kitchen. The door to the living room was closed, voices behind it. She knocked.

'Bertie?'

It was the television talking in the mean little sixties room, peach-painted walls, sparsely furnished with a cheap brown suite, plants either side of a small electric fire on the wall. A picture window overlooked a narrow balcony, a washing line drooped across, hung with a couple of pairs of plain white knickers. Bertie's showy glamour was nowhere in evidence. The tidy, impersonal flat could have belonged to a very old woman, or a single man, not at all what she expected.

Puzzled, Melanie looked back at the front door nervously, was about to run away, quick. A sound, halfway between a cough and a groan, came from the room at the end of the little hall, made her hair stand on end. She flung the bedroom door open.

'*Bertie*. Oh, my God, she's dead.'

The bedroom was a fantasy, a suffocating, overheated, ornate, absurd and tented brothel. A gilt four-poster, smothered in looped and swagged red velvet dragged down from its hangings, filled the small room. Cupboards with pleated silk tacked on to their doors hung open, their contents tumbling out, torn and soiled and trampled. In a corner, under the window, a Hollywood dressing table lay ruined, its lights smashed, its make-up spilled, perfume reeking in the stifling space.

'Bertie?'

Melanie went and looked down at her, lying across the four-poster, her clothes torn, blood running from her nose, one eye half closed, a cut above one black eyebrow.

'I'm not dead. Bugger off,' she mumbled through swollen lips. 'Leave me alone.'

'I'll call the police,' said Melanie.

Bertie raised her head and rolled over, hid her beaten face, bruises darkening underneath the bleached fuzz on her near-shaven head.

'*Don't* call the police.'

'Shall I call an ambulance?'

'Don't call fucking anything.' Bertie jerked away, rolled on her back and lay exhausted. 'They've gone. They won't come back.'

'Who? The rest of your flat is untouched,' said Melanie. 'Baby Jane is hiding and biting in the oven.'

Bertie grunted into her pillow.

'Have they taken anything?'

'Only what they wanted.'

It seemed a room that would hold nothing of value – torn curtains, strewn clothes and sad chaos.

'My choker. Then they beat me up to teach me a lesson.'

Melanie looked at Bertie's bruised and discoloured throat.

'It's the one thing you can't change,' said Bertie flatly. 'I wear Baby Jane or a choker.' Her Adam's apple bobbed. 'Gay-bashers. I'm not gay. I wish I was. It would be easier.'

Melanie sat down on the side of the bed.

'I knew there was something about you . . .'

'I am a *girl*,' Bertie said tiredly. 'Trapped in a man's body. Don't you start.'

'Is this why you're living here?'

Bertie closed her swelling eye and nodded.

'My father threw me out. My mother helps, but she daren't let him know. The council gave me a flat when my doctor threatened all hell if they didn't. I was suicidal, and he said he'd see them in court if they pushed me to it. He's kept me going.' She squinted up, followed Melanie's gaze. 'I bind them up, so they don't show.'

Melanie flushed.

'I'm waiting for the operation,' Bertie went on. 'Chop, chop. Before they'll do it, I have to live as a woman for two years. I was at an all-boys boarding school, spent four years wishing I was dead, and running away. The day I was eighteen, Dad said he'd had enough.

'I made a pass at Tom,' she added. 'I thought he knew, but he was practically in the oven like Baby Jane when he saw. You don't have to worry, Mrs Tilford. Your baby's still a virgin and one of the kindest people I ever met. You should be proud.'

She dragged herself up and surveyed the damage.

'I like to come in here and put the lights on, and a silky robe, and perfume, and run my hands over my breasts and feel like I'm a woman. It's my dream. It's me they want to trash, not the flat.'

They sat looking at the chaos until Melanie got up and began folding things into a pile. Underneath the upturned stool from the dressing table, she found a shiny yellow satin shift, from Marks and Spencer.

'That's my favourite,' whispered Bertie hoarsely, her voice almost gone. 'Could you open the door and call Baby Jane?'

Melanie stood feeling the cold, slippery weightlessness of the gown for a long moment.

'I know exactly what you mean,' she said, going to the door. 'And I'm sorry I got mad.'

'Know Jemima Habgood?' whispered Bertie much later, her swollen eye completely closed.

'Local councillor,' said Melanie, dissolving paracetamol in hot lemon juice.

Bertie, bathed and smelling sweet, held a bag of ice cubes to her bruises, watching her stir the liquid.

'Her husband's a property developer. Wants to turn your school site into flats. Recession ending. Demand coming back. Jemima can fix cheap sale if you close down. Lots of money up for grabs. That's why you got the visit from the drug squad. Not me.'

Melanie put the glass to cool on the bedside table, bent down and picked up a dozen and more brown chemist's bottles from the floor, arranged them in a row on the dressing table. Hormones. Breast increasers, hair decreasers, a sad row of sex-change pills.

'So that's what that's all about.'

She put the last of the bottles tidily in the row.

'Now you understand everything,' Bertie croaked.

Melanie gave her the cooling paracetamol and thought *understand*? She certainly did.

Chapter Thirty-Four

'I hear the Tilfords are having problems,' remarked Bunny the following day, fishing a silver-foil package out of her bag at the beginning of the lunch break. She had on an old-fashioned flowered and frilled pinny that gave her a bust like a shelf.

'You look like Hattie Jacques,' Alastair observed.

'How kind of you, Alastair,' she answered, pleased. 'I liked Hattie Jacques. I hadn't noticed that either of the Tilford children was difficult. Have you?'

'Compared to most, perishing little angels,' muttered Alastair *sotto voce*. He was sitting by the window, curled in a grubby chintz armchair like a question mark, trying to concentrate on the pile of essays in his lap on the ravages made by Henry the Eighth on the Church. Garlick sat nearby at the long table, sorting through a box of glass slides of blood cells. He stacked them carefully, making two piles for the afternoon's lab class to look at through a microscope, to draw what they could see.

'Copying these will drive them out of their empty little minds with boredom,' he remarked. 'I wouldn't know about the Tilfords. I don't teach either of them.'

He balanced his piles perfectly, muttering, 'Red cell, white cell.'

He scrabbled in the bottom of the box for the last few.

'Nearly there.'

'For goodness' sake, what are you playing? She loves you, she loves you not? I shouldn't bother. She doesn't,' Alastair snapped, irritated by the pernickety performance.

Garlick stared at the slide in his hand, dumbfounded. He'd done it again. How could Alastair know unless he could read the inside of Garlick's head, that mention of the Tilford children brought Alice to mind like a rush of blood to the head, and she loves me she loves me not was *exactly* the game he had been playing? He looked round guiltily, but the rest of the staff room was absorbed in its own business, absent on dinner duty, or simply absent. No one answered Bunny's question.

'Oh, well. Anyone want a sandwich?' She unwrapped her big silver-foil parcel and spread out sandwiches. 'Homemade bread and homemade chicken pâté with salad. I made too much and couldn't get it in the freezer. Help me out by eating it.'

She brought the parcel over to them.

'What sort of problems?' asked Garlick cautiously, after a pause, picking out a handful of wholegrain brown bread. 'This looks a bit nourishing, Bunny. Chewy till our teeth fall out. Couldn't we have white bread next time?'

She parked the sandwiches in front of them and sat down.

'Melanie says the drug squad called at the vicarage and threatened to do them over, thanks to my husband the headmaster,' she said, lowering her voice to a whisper. The three of them drew together like conspirators.

'Why?' whispered Alastair, scribbling on the margin of one of his papers.

'Because we can't afford a scandal about drugs in school, and being seen to do nothing about it. He's had to go public about the fact that we *do* have drugs in school, and be seen to act. They've threatened several children with expulsion. They included Tom and Alice Tilford. *Do* help yourself.'

Alastair's pen froze in mid-correction.

'I suddenly lost my appetite,' he said in a more normal voice, pushing her away. There had been a time when he wanted her close, dreamed of it, would have chewed those abominable sandwiches until his jaws ached, to please her. His waspish face stared up at her, dark hair more than usually severely scraped into its ponytail. *'Expulsion?* Is he mad? Tom Tilford is one of the very few who will get into university this year and I'm expecting Alice in my sixth form with ten GCSEs. Why on earth has Hugo gone that far?'

'Local politics and vested interest have come crawling out of the woodwork,' she murmured, very low, bending down until she was almost whispering into his ear, the sweet smell of vanilla on her pinafore, from making sponge cakes in morning classes. 'Very nasty. Absalom has been playing his cards very close to his chest. All the governors have been worrying what to do for days. Hugo tried not to involve the police, but in the end they had to. He had to look serious as *anything* about clearing the problem up, or the education secretary would have had to say no to our opting out. You don't keep a bad school in business if it's got a major social problem and the management who are promising to turn it around are turning a blind eye.'

'What you're saying is someone's blackmailing Hugo,' said Alastair, tapping his pen on his teeth. 'Who stands to gain most if he lets us get closed down?'

'Bloody lefties,' snapped Garlick. 'Local authority die-hards. Town hall ideological in-fighting, like Hugo said. They debated it in the House of Commons, remember. Dirty tricks campaigns, to stop schools opting out? Local authorities don't want to lose control.'

'I don't think so. That lot in our town hall couldn't organize a piss-up in a brewery,' said Bunny dismissively. 'I have a feeling it's something else altogether.'

'Who else stands to gain?' persisted Alastair.

No one knew. The three of them drew apart, and sat thinking over what they'd said.

For Garlick, it had Absalom written all over it, sending in the heavies to threaten and frighten whole families, keeping his nose clean in case he lost his precious school, and in case Hugo lost his job. Everyone knew Hugo had given up a comfortable deputy headship to come and save East Stepney. Now he was saving face, would blame the school's closing on a few kids smoking weed, if it came to it. The cockroach was at the bottom of everything devious and nasty. Garlick, sickened, put his sandwich back in Bunny's silver foil, the food in his mouth turned as dry as straw.

Damn, thought Alastair, picking at his essays, all his concentration gone. Things must be worse for Hugo and the school than he had realized, worse than Hugo had let on. No one had meant it to go this far, for *her*, a member of staff, to have the frighteners put on. *That* would account for the fact that she wasn't in the staff room when she wasn't on dinner duty either.

Alice, thought Garlick, as next to him Alastair fumed and fretted, you have been taking drugs and playing straight into the cockroach's hands. They'll expel you and I won't be able to save you, you stupid, *stupid* girl.

He fingered the rest of the glass slides, overwhelmed by the frustration and boredom of the coming afternoon, the general impotence of his whole life.

'Can't I sell these to anyone?' begged Bunny, indicating her uneaten sandwiches.

'Sorry, Bunny. We're not hungry,' they both said.

Pictures of Gouda cheese and clogs cluttered the board in the staff room that held the timetable for the whole school, postcards left over from last Easter's school trip to Amsterdam and the tulip fields. Alastair eyed them with distaste as he looked up Melanie's classes for the afternoon. After hauling half the kids out of the red-light district in Amsterdam in the early hours, steering them away from places devoted to the consumption of drugs, and existing on disgusting rubber cheese for five days, he had sworn never to take a school trip abroad again. *Ever*.

Melanie was on the timetable as taking her fourth year tutor group for the first period of the afternoon.

'Thanks for lunch, Bunny.'

'You didn't eat it.'

He didn't smile, put Henry the Eighth and the dissolution

of the monasteries in his briefcase, and abandoned the staff room for his own office, an untidy room on the top floor of the sixth-form wing, a dilapidated addition to the old building that was supposed to make them feel independent. Its windows were falling out and its roof leaked, but it was their own. The walls were covered with save-the-dolphin posters, pictures of horrific suffering in Bosnia, dying children in Somalia and recruitment appeals from universities and former polytechnics.

A small queue of sixth-formers roosted in a row outside his office, sitting on the corridor floor in jeans and sweatshirts, cans of Coca Cola wedged on the window ledge above their heads. Two girls had brown envelopes from UCAS in their hands and were threatening to burst into tears.

'I suppose you all want to come and talk about interviews and rejections? Anybody got *more* urgent business? No? OK, Melinda. You look as though you're first.'

The stout Asian girl with hair on her upper lip and a long black plait down the back of her scarlet sari nodded; she wanted to be a doctor. Her parents spoke no English.

'They want me to marry Nazir from the corner shop,' she burst out, before he could shut the door. 'My father says he will lock me up. Mr Croke, what shall I do?'

Alastair sat down and pushed his box of tissues across his desk and waited for her to calm down. It had happened before. He'd end up going to see the parents, wage a long, exhausting battle on her behalf, knew all too well she might not win.

Before the bell went for afternoon school, Garlick cruised back to his biology lab, books, briefcase and the slide box in his arms. The corridor was empty. He could see his lab door standing open at the far end. Careful not to shake the box of sorted slides, he walked towards it slowly.

Absalom. The cockroach still crawled. He had never finished the search for its heart, interrupted by the fight at the meeting. Maybe there was just time, while he set up the microscopes for this afternoon, to take up the scalpel again . . .

'Heil Hitler!'

'What?'

Garlick jumped, squawked, whirled round, dropped his box. Glass slides tinkled and slithered down the corridor.

'Sorry,' said Alice, grinning from ear to ear. 'That's the second time you didn't hear me coming, Mr Garlick.'

His eyes shut, his heart pounding, clutching his briefcase like a shield, he leaned on the wall.

'Don't *do* that,' he yelped.

She giggled.

'I could wring your neck,' he gasped, his heart rate coming back to normal. 'But since you are here, I want to have a word with you. First of all, you can pick my slides up, and put them back in here. I spent all lunch hour sorting that lot out.'

'Sorry, Mr Garlick.'

'No, you're not. You think it's funny,' he snapped. 'When you've picked every single one up, you are to come straight in to see me.'

Melanie sat in her empty classroom, gazing at a copy of *New Scientist* without seeing it. First period after lunch, she had her tutor group. They wanted to debate animal rights and cosmetic testing. That was because the two Ds wanted to be beauticians and had brought the subject up. Rabbits having shampoo dripped into their eyes was a depressing topic. So would the second period after lunch be depressing, when they were to study Philip Larkin's 'The Old Fools'. Decaying old men waiting for death. Melanie sighed and tried to concentrate on the animal rights article, to fend off Philip Larkin. His misery on top of rabbits' was the last thing she needed. A few moments later, she gave up the pretence, pulled the *New Scientist* off the pad of writing paper hidden underneath, reread for the dozenth time what she had written.

Dear Anna Raeburn,
I never thought I would write to an agony aunt. But your answers to other people always make a lot of sense. I have tried a lot of things you often recommend, like marriage guidance. In a way, it only made things worse. I want to leave my husband, but he is in the church. So if I do, he will lose his job and we will both lose our home. We have two children . . .

Footsteps came down the corridor towards her room. She snatched the writing paper, tore it into several pieces, and threw them in the bin beside her desk. Stuttering Stan ambled past her open door with a broom over his shoulder, studying page three of the *Mirror*, whistling to himself. He disappeared down the corridor. She picked up the wastepaper basket, picked out the fragments of paper, smoothed them out. Angelina Tutti Frutti and her sister did the cleaning and she wouldn't put it past them to root them out and stick the bits together. She sat smoothing them and smoothing them. Stupid idea. Anna Raeburn couldn't help. She tore them into tiny pieces, numbly waiting for the bell to go.

'I want to talk to you,' said Garlick fiercely.

Alice wandered up and down the lab, looking at things pickled in jars. She picked up a specimen jar with a heart in it and pulled a face.

'I couldn't stand the thought of looking inside dead things, and cutting them up.'

'And I can't stand the idea that you've been taking drugs.'

'Who told you I take drugs?' Alice demanded.

'I hear the drug squad was at your house.'

She weighed the jar thoughtfully in her hand.

'Sergeant Philips is not a nice person. The drug squad are not *at all* nice people,' said Garlick. 'I am extremely shocked that you are getting mixed up with them.'

'I do not take drugs,' Alice said very clearly.

'I know you do. Don't lie,' he snapped.

Her face shrank with fury.

'I don't lie,' she said contemptuously. 'I wouldn't bother.'

Garlick experienced a sharp twinge of uncertainty, began to sense the enormity of his mistake.

'I'm sure Mrs Benedict said they had been to see you,' he said.

'It's Mrs Benedict, is it?' she said furiously. 'Spreading gossip about my family.'

'I'm speaking out of turn,' he said humbly. 'I see that. It's only because I *mind* about you.'

Her lip began to tremble like a small child's.

'I don't see why anyone should tell you, but they came to see my brother and my mother's scared to death.'

The trembling lip was his undoing. His arms were around her shoulders without a second thought.

'I can't bear the thought . . . I love you, you see. I only want to help.'

'Don't *touch* me,' she shrieked.

As he groped to reassure her, she clutched the jar and threw.

The pickled heart hit him in the face with a squelch and a shower of formaldehyde. He fled to a sink, ran cold water over his head, scrubbing at his face.

'You *bitch*,' he gasped.

'Dirty old man,' she yelled back. 'You ever touch me again and *I'll* go to the police.'

Listening to her Doc Martens clumping furiously across the room, heading for the door, he leaned on the cold, chipped edge of the sink, breathed formaldehyde, and was abruptly sick.

'Career blown if she tells anyone,' he gasped, running his head under the cold tap again, dismissal staring him in the face, a lifetime's ban on teaching. 'Well done, Amadeus. *Sieg Heil* to you, old cock, you crashing idiot.'

With his words, as he stood there dripping, the bell for afternoon school went.

Chapter Thirty-Five

The last of the lunchtime dramas over, Alastair took Henry the Eighth out of his briefcase, lined the small stack of essay papers up in the empty spot in the middle of his cluttered desk and fished a red pen out from among the collection in his marmalade jar. He fingered its white crock rim. It was a Dundee marmalade jar, all the way from Dundee itself, sitting on his desk to remind him how much he hurt. Since the night he stayed with Melanie, slept on Giles's couch, the memories had begun to lose their pain, become what he needed them to be. Just memories.

Honor had dragged the children all over the country, running after a lover who was running away from a vengeful wife.

'*She* left me. She had no right,' he raged at his solicitor.

'Who said the law was fair?' the man said. 'Judges think children belong with their mother.'

Alastair could barely sit in his seat in the court.

Visiting rights every other weekend, ruled the judge, giving her custody, taking his children away, even though he had a job, a stable home, all the love in the world to offer them.

'I won't pay her a penny,' he raged afterwards.

'Tell that to the court,' advised his solicitor. 'I don't think you'll find them very sympathetic.'

She broke the order again and again. He took her to court.

'It upsets the children,' she argued. 'I just get them stable, settled down, and he comes to see us, and they are all distressed again. They don't want to see him.'

'They *do,*' Alastair yelled from his place on a hard and narrow bench.

'*Silence,*' thundered the judge.

Alastair subsided.

'Be careful about breaking court Orders, Mrs Croke,' was all the judge said.

Alastair had a tantrum, fired his solicitor on the spot, was threatened with contempt of court, apologized. The judge retired, satisfied by the plaintiff's behaviour that he had made the right decision. Alastair concluded that employing solicitors and fighting cases did solicitors a lot of good, himself no good at all.

When he stopped asking to see them, Honor became contrary, accused him of not wanting to stay in touch, told him he ought to visit.

'Glasgow,' he exclaimed, looking at the address on her letter. 'What the hell's she doing in *Glasgow*?'

'Settling down,' she said on the telephone. 'Nearly as far away as we can get. John got a job at the university. The kids love it, and Scottish schools are brilliant. Why don't you come and see us, if you want?'

She expected him to say *no, it's too far.* Instead, he argued with the previous headmaster, banged the desk and shouted, was given annual leave in the middle of mocks, went all the way north by coach. Twelve hours from Victoria coach station, he turned up exhausted, to find her gone out, the children not there. He hammered and raged at the front door of the flat in a huge converted Victorian house in Bearsden, until the neighbours came. Bitter, he left his children for good, and brought back a pot of Dundee marmalade and a Dundee cake, so as not to come home empty-handed. The black and white marmalade pot had held the pens on his desk ever since.

'Damn,' he said, throwing the red pen into a corner. He took the rest of the pencils out of the jar, tossed it in the wastepaper basket under his desk and went to see that Melanie was all right.

He could hear the noise from down the corridor. Her classroom was in uproar.

'A hundred dumb animals to make it, one dumb animal to wear it, dummy,' shouted Dora, lunging at the skinny little West Indian girl who tried to defend doctors' testing drugs on animals, and who knew a thing or two because her father ran the local chemist's shop.

'*Let go*, Dora,' Melanie cried.

Dora scrabbled for a hold on Afro curls too close to the skull to grab, failed to get a purchase, bared her teeth and bit.

'You're behaving like a dumb animal yourself,' shouted Melanie, yanking her off.

The chemist's daughter screeched and bit back.

'Stick to cosmetics, never mind getting sidetracked into fur coats,' Melanie panted, dragging Dora off by her ear. 'You want to be a beauty therapist, not scar her for life.'

'They should burn down laboratories where they do experiments. And shops. Your dad's a cri-mi-nal,' Dorcas taunted, leaping in in defence of her twin, still thrashing in Melanie's grip. The wiry little West Indian lunged. They went rolling enthusiastically between the desks, scratching and kicking and squealing.

'Pull them apart,' Melanie yelled, appealing to the rest of her class.

Invited to pile in, they did. Within moments, the pandemonium got completely out of hand.

Alastair simply stood in the doorway with his arms folded and let his presence speak.

'Mr *Croke*,' hissed one of the boys.

Gradually they fell silent, slunk to their feet, shuffled back to their places, sat down and looked bored.

'Mrs Tilford, there is an urgent telephone call for you in the office. I'm quite sure your class will get on quietly with their work.'

'You can read the magazine articles on the topic that I photocopied for you, and you can sit quietly and *think*.

Don't you dare talk,' Melanie quavered.

'They won't so much as *breathe*, will you?' Alastair said harshly, looking round at a dozen flushed, evasive faces.

Out in the corridor she marched ahead of him.

'Thank you,' she said stiffly. 'I'm sorry. It won't happen again. We were discussing animal rights and they find the whole thing so emotional, it got out of hand. When you think what people do . . . it's terrible. They got . . . I'm sorry . . .'

'Stop it,' he said.

They turned the corner. Ahead, worn steps led to the cloakrooms and lavatories, deserted during lessons. She went down and leaned on the wall, shaking.

'This can't go on,' he said, standing several steps above her.

'I need the job,' she said. 'It won't happen again, I promise.'

'I'm not talking about your job. There's nothing wrong with what you're doing. This is one of the most difficult schools in London and you're a bloody good teacher.'

'You said . . .'

'You are about to crack up, aren't you?'

She leaned her hot forehead on the cold wall.

'Don't turn your face to the wall like that. Bunny told me what happened with the police.'

'It's not just the police.'

She turned her head away and stared at the entrance to the girls' lavatories, mortally depressed.

'You've got to leave him,' he said.

'I keep telling myself that.'

'Then do it.'

'Giles has suggested that he should convert to Islam, and then he could have several wives under Islamic law and a spiritual relationship with me. I'm not sure what English law would have to say about it. He's been spending a lot of time in the mosque on the Mile End Road. He says. God knows what he's really doing.'

He began to laugh.

'Is that all he wants?'

Melanie sighed, tried to smile.

'I told him to get lost.'

'Good.'

'Do you know, Tom's best friend is a boy waiting to be turned into a girl. She . . . he . . . *she* got beaten up, and by the time I'd finished looking after her, I thought, she's more of a woman than I am. Sometimes, I feel like no one at all.'

'I couldn't fall in love with a no one,' he said abruptly. 'I could only fall in love with a very lovely woman.'

She used shampoo with a light, musky scent. He breathed it in, and hoped like crazy that some kid with a bladder problem wouldn't have to come down and use the loos.

'If I had the same standards of hygiene in my kitchens as you've got down here, we'd all be dead of food poisoning,' Bunny accused, trotting alongside Stuttering Stan, emerging from an inspection tour of the boys' lavatories at the far side of the cloakrooms, out of sight of Alastair and Melanie. 'They stink,' she went on sharply. 'They are disgusting. All that graffiti needs scrubbing off. If it won't scrub, paint over it. It doesn't even show imagination. Why are males so *boring*?'

Stan scowled and dragged his feet. If he wanted to keep his job when they opted out, he'd better stay on the right side of the headmaster's wife.

'How about I g-g-g-g-g-g . . .'

Bunny, impatient, strode ahead, rounded the corner, skidded to a stop, turned and gave Stan a hefty shove in the chest.

'G-g-g-g-g-go back and start cleaning off all the anatomical sketches and *Sharon gives blow jobs*? Good idea, Stan. Excellent.'

'Beg pardon? demanded Stan, looking down at her hand on his substantial breast, outraged.

'I said, what excellent ideas you have,' she shouted, steering him backwards like a tug boat going round a difficult bit of harbour. 'Go on, do it, *now*.'

She raced back round the corner, hooting and chattering in full flood.

'Melanie. I thought I saw you out of the corner of my eye. Look, it's messy, this opt-out thing, and you are due an absolutely *grovelling* apology from Hugo about Sergeant Philips. I've been meaning to invite you for ages. The important things get forgotten, don't they, when the pressure's on? Oh, you're here too, Alastair. I thought you were upstairs. Melinda's been crying about her arranged marriage, and said she'd talked to you. Would you do me an enormous kindness and bring Melanie to supper? Just a staff get-together. To cheer us up.'

Melanie flushed scarlet.

'I just got rid of my marmalade,' Alastair said dreamily.

'Really? You'll be hungry, then. Half past seven?'

She steamed off up the corridor without waiting for an answer, turned and trotted back.

'I'd forget my head, given half a chance. Half past seven, tomorrow. One other couple coming.'

'Couple?' said Melanie. 'She said a staff get-together.'

'There goes the kindest woman in the world. I shall always love her,' Alastair said, watching Bunny trot away.

'Alastair,' Melanie said urgently. 'The Sergeant Philips thing wasn't Hugo's fault. Bertie told me. Jemima Habgood's husband is a property developer who wants to buy us cheaply and turn us into flats. He told Whitehall we have a drug problem and Hugo's complacent about it. Hugo *had* to act.'

'So that's it,' he said. 'Tell him that tomorrow evening.'

As he spoke the bell went and they had to let each other go.

Chapter Thirty-Six

It was easier to lie to Giles than she expected.

'I offered to stand in for someone who called in sick,' she told him. 'We're taking a group of fifth years to see Shakespeare at the Barbican tomorrow. It's their set text. I'll be home late. You can send Tom out for fish and chips and if Bertie should come over, will you count her in? She's been mugged and could do with cheering up.'

She prayed he wouldn't ask which play, then read the paper and find out it wasn't on.

'I'll get Tom to ask her over, if you like,' was all he said.

She went to bed early, tossed and turned all night.

The day dawned misty and chill. The forecast promised it would clear up later, giving a warm and sunny afternoon. Giles was up and out before six for early morning communion. Exhausted, Melanie drew the curtains, watched him walk across the grass to the church, her heart jumping with excitement.

'At your age?' she asked wryly. 'You surely can't go breaking out and behaving like a teenager.' Her heart pounded at the thought and she spent so much time getting ready in the bathroom, Alice came banging on the door.

'Wait,' shouted her mother.

And she *could* wait, Melanie told herself, scrubbing off smudged mascara and starting all over again.

'Garlick looks like a frightened rabbit every time he sets eyes on me,' she told Alastair at lunchtime. 'I keep bumping into him and he jumps and runs as though I've got the plague. What's the matter with him?'

'His mother lay on him when he was born? Probably took one look and felt sorry for him – like animals.' He shrugged. 'Who knows what goes on in that peculiar little mind?'

'He looks guilty.'

'Then he probably is,' said the Stud, drifting past, stopping by where they were sitting to pick dried tomato ketchup off his lapel. 'The odds on being guilty, if you act it, are pretty high.'

'You'd better act innocent, then, Mels old thing,' muttered Alastair when the Stud ambled off.

She blushed to the roots of her hair.

Across the way, the church was silent except for the low murmur of one arguing passionately with himself. Just before the bell signalled the end of afternoon school for his wife, Giles came out of his trance in front of the altar, and got up off his knees. The promised sunlight played on the windows, the birds sang in the rafters, lining the pews with droppings. No thunderbolts disturbed the peace of late afternoon as he gave up arguing, closed his mind to the likely consequences, and went to look for Angelina.

She didn't recognize him for a moment, in green cords and a jacket, without the dog collar. Angelina's mother stood in her doorway and crossed her arms aggressively. He smiled winningly. Angelina used him and used the church, in her own way and for her own ends, but he hoped that just occasionally a little religion rubbed off. He knew very well her mother had no time for either.

'She isn't here,' she snapped.

'She was worried about Ian Paisley's chest,' Giles explained in his best pastoral manner. 'I was passing, so I thought I'd call in for a moment and see if he's all right. Do you know if she got her DSS grant? I gave her a letter about the electricity bill.'

He *loomed*, she thought. He gave her the creeps. She'd told her daughter that new vicar brought her out in goose bumps. Angelina laughed and wouldn't listen.

'Do you know where she is?' Giles asked desperately.

'Out,' she said shortly, starting to close the door. Behind her, he heard a baby cry.

'You've got Ian Paisley there, haven't you?' he cried.

She slammed the door in his face.

Deduction, he thought, walking rapidly away. Angelina is out. She is not in the pub, because I've looked, and she is not away visiting prison, because she went last week. She could be with one of the sisters, but she'd have Ian Paisley with her. And Ian Paisley is with Grandma. There is one likely reason for that. His mother is working and it *has* to be King's Cross, because the rest of them work that patch and they always stick together.

Feeling in his pocket, to make sure he had his wallet on him, he marched, head down and eyes on the pavement, his mind empty of what he planned to do, down White Horse Lane to the Stepney Green Tube.

In the house he shared on Cable Street with two male, non-smoking teachers from other schools, Garlick sat in his small room, in a sweat of hopelessness. It could only be a matter of time before Alice Tilford let on to her mother what had happened, and Hugo gave him the sack. Their cat rubbed round his ankles, mewing to be fed.

'You're out of luck and out of Whiskas,' he told her, rummaging without success in their untidy kitchen cupboards. 'Go and catch your own supper while I go the launderette so I have a clean shirt in which to shoot myself.'

He picked her up and put her out on the windowsill, where she sat down and started to wash. The launderette beckoned in the shape of a sack of dirty linen on the kitchen floor and an open packet of Daz. He had not a single shirt left.

'Fill machine, into pub on opposite corner smartish, have a pint and mull over life on the dole,' he told himself, depression settling in like an old friend.

He closed the window and picked up the sack.

* * *

Giles emerged from King's Cross station, took a look at the traffic inching its way down the Euston Road, the pavements crowded with home-going commuters, the number of police hanging around, and broke into a sweat of panic.

Blind and hungry said the note around the neck of a tall black man rattling a yoghurt pot at passers-by. Giles caught his vacant eye and could have sworn that the man winked. He turned in the direction of the King's Cross Road and hurried across the traffic lights. Behind him, one of the police officers standing with his hands behind his back outside the mainline station said something to a colleague and both men laughed.

Outside a boarded-up shop window covered in stickers advertising adult sex aids and porno videos, he found what he was looking for, standing inside a doorway smoking a fag. Very young, she still had a childlike look, until you saw the eyes.

'Hi, big boy,' she said listlessly.

'I'm looking for someone,' he said.

'Try me.'

She sounded bored, dropped the cigarette and stamped it out, emerged from her doorway. In sunlight, she looked very pale, unhealthy, as though she was using something slowly killing her, or had AIDS.

'No, thank you,' he said politely, anxious not to lose her. 'That's very kind of you, but do you know someone called Angelina? She's known as Angelina Tutti Frutti, though that's not her real name.'

She couldn't be bothered to answer, turned away and wandered up the road towards the crowds, her thin red dress and thin pale legs standing out among all the grey people in grey suits, like a child at a grown-up party.

Garlick dumped his laundry on the pavement and read the notice in the launderette window. Closed for installation of new machines. Sorry for any inconvenience. Will give you better service when . . . blah, blah, blah.

'A pint of best,' he ordered in the pub two minutes later. He took his drink, wandered outside, sat on a bench on the pavement, breathing in passing fumes, the evening sun warm on the back of his jacket. Slowly, he worked his way through the beer, went inside for another. The bar was filling up with people, chatter and smoke. A group of students perched on the edge of the gutter, sitting on the paving stones, drinking German lager. Garlick watched them idly, nostalgically recalled his student days, relaxed, went inside for a refill, left the bulging laundry bag to guard his seat. The bar was three deep, service slow.

'Fuck,' said Garlick, looking under his bench, finding his laundry gone.

'They took it while you were getting your drink.'

The heavily accented English was otherwise perfect. The students had gone, and so had his laundry. A neat row of glasses was stacked all along the kerb, to show where they had been sitting.

'Why the . . . didn't you stop them, if you were watching?' he wailed. 'That bag had all my clothes in it.'

She shrugged, sipped at a glass of wine and went back to reading her magazine.

'You speak German,' he said a little later, reading *Der Stern* as she lifted it from her lap. 'I can read it, but only in scientific journals. Can't speak it very well.'

'I *am* German,' she said, not looking up, implying *idiot*.

She had chestnut-brown hair, hazel eyes, was maybe five foot nothing. He guessed she was not more than twenty-five.

'Not a Nordic, Aryan, blonde and blue-eyed six-foot-tall kind of German,' he observed.

'A Westphalian kind of German,' she retorted. 'You want Aryans, you can find stereotypes anywhere.'

Garlick studied his feet while she went back to *Der Stern*.

'Westphalia. Ham.'

'Pigs,' she said without raising her eyes. 'A lot of pigs. Animals. I don't mean people.'

She had a sense of humour.

'Pigs are extremely interesting creatures,' he agreed solemnly.

'And versatile,' she said. 'Bacon. Chops. Parma ham. Frankfurters. *Very* interesting, especially by the pound. Or the deutschmark. Pigs are *big* business and the bigger the pig, the bigger the business. That is what I do.'

The hazel eyes met his.

'We develop food for superpigs.' She grinned, showing wide, even white teeth. 'I am here to work with Fisons. Animal foods research.'

She went back to her magazine. Garlick stared at the top of her hand, his heart doing cartwheels in his chest.

'I'm sorry I suggested you should have looked after my washing. Not reasonable. Had a trying day. Would you let me buy you a drink and introduce myself. Amadeus Garlick, teacher of biology.' Soon to become ex-teacher of biology. He didn't care.

'*Amadeus?*' she demanded, as everyone did.

'My parents liked their little joke, and Mozart. I like him, too, but no connection.'

'Marta Spielberg,' she said, shaking his hand. 'I like his films, but no connection. I like chilled dry white German wine, never Liebfraumilch.'

A German biologist, who would know that Krebs cycle was not a kind of fancy motorbike, loved pork, with a black and mocking sense of humour, the humour of the underdog, like his own.

'Dry white German wine, coming up,' he cried.

She finally looked right up at him, as he got up to go to the bar. She was very pretty, if you liked short women with intense, dark, intelligent features. Ecstatic, Garlick went to see if he could find chilled dry white German wine in an English East End pub.

Chapter Thirty-Seven

It isn't easy to tell streetwalkers from office girls on their way home from work, Giles concluded, terror growing like a cancer in his chest as he realized he was taking a risk greater than he had been able to imagine; turn back, go home, forget all about Angelina. His heart pounded, his hands sweated, his head ached. As he passed the traffic lights, opposite King's Cross station, they changed to red. The traffic slowed and stopped.

Gripped by fear, he stared across four lanes of revving cars, across the Euston Road at the station. As the lights went to amber and green, he bolted, charged head down across the road. Cars leaped forward, brakes screamed, someone yelled abuse. Sidestepping an *Evening Standard* van on its way back to base, he scurried into the mainline station, headed across the concourse, feeling in his pocket for his Tube ticket.

'Oi,' a voice called. 'You.'

Over his shoulder, he saw a young policeman staring after him, shouting.

Caught.

Dodging under the huge arrival and departure boards, he raced past platform entrances crowded with commuters, ricocheted off a barrier, and shot out of the far side of the station, into the car park, back on to the street. He stopped in a deserted building yard, and tried to catch his breath.

'What was that all about?' the young policeman asked, frustrated at realizing just too late that he had failed to cop someone doing something they plainly thought they shouldn't. 'I only wanted to tell him off for jaywalking down the middle of the Euston Road.'

Standing in the rubbish-strewn yard, where pigeons pecked refuse from discarded McDonald's cartons, Giles could hear the announcer's voice echoing from the long platforms inside the station. Its bright lights spelled danger. They were on the lookout now, and would stop him if he went back in, question him. *Why did you run?* That was what they'd asked him, over and over, last time. *Why did you run?* He moved like a sleepwalker towards the warm evening pavement, and knew he had no choice but to search out Angelina, and along with her, his fate.

Crisscrossing the huge traffic junction outside the mainline station, Giles hurried along, keeping up with commuters hiding in thinning crowds, hugging shop fronts in the hope it made him inconspicuous, looking and looking, trying to spot Angelina, or someone who could tell him where she was.

The clock in the station stood at seven o'clock, the sun cast long shadows between buildings, rush hour began to wane. He turned, escaping emptying streets, into the Gray's Inn Road, marching along with his eyes on the pavement, hardly daring to look up, unable to look into the faces of women he passed, most going home to bedsits and flats in tall terraced houses, not the kind of woman he was looking for, his stomach churning.

They caught the Director of Public Prosecutions, Green, here, kerb crawling, he thought dismally, reading the destinations on a bus stop, trying to look purposeful and busy, then moving on.

Wanting, said the psychologists, to be caught. Green was asking for it.

Maybe *I* want to be caught. The thought snagged on his mind, made him trip. Hopping around the loose paving stone, his ankle wrenched, he gritted his teeth, hissing, until the pain passed, and there she was, out of the dusk, like a pale vampire up early, standing in a doorway, in an entrance half hidden by a pile of refuse bags ravaged by cats and an untidy stack of empty cardboard boxes. Her face floated in gloom, watching him hop up and down.

'Show you a good time, big boy.'

Standing on one foot, like a small boy caught with his trousers down, Giles gawped and realized his mistake. He had simply come out looking too early.

'I just want to ask you something,' he cried eagerly, skirting the rubbish, kicking the side of one of the boxes out of his way.

'Eh, you're trashing my home.'

The indignant voice was followed by a tousled head, thrust out of the end of a greasy sleeping bag, and the rolling clank of glass bottles, disturbed in their Tesco carrier. Grandma glared up at him, hair cropped after a recent stay in a hostel, more than ever like a human bottlebrush.

'Oh. It's you.'

'Me?' he yelped looking behind him.

''*Ere*,' she whispered conspiratorially, leering round the corner of her box, a knowing grin spreading over her face. 'What you doin' round 'ere, vicar?'

'Oh, *God*,' he yelped despairingly, and leaped into the doorway. Grandma cackled and withdrew indoors.

''E's back 'ome, where you oughta be,' came lugubriously from the depths of the cardboard shack, followed by the clink of glass.

'I'm looking for Angelina,' he said frantically.

'Call me Angelina, if you want.'

The phantom in the doorway looked no older than Alice, had skinny pale arms and legs so thin they bowed. Bleached yellow hair made the port wine stain across her face stand out like a mask. Giles swallowed hard.

'Do you know Angelina Tutti Frutti?'

Her eyes slid over him, expressionless.

'You police?'

He closed his eyes, shook his head.

'No.'

'Ange isn't always here. I haven't seen her tonight. Ask Jude. Tall one. Bald. Can't miss her.'

She pointed up towards the Euston Road, spat, and watched him walk away.

In the gathering dark they were everywhere and he cursed himself for his naivety. If he'd *thought*, of course they wouldn't be there in rush hour. Tall bald Judy, with broken-down stiletto heels and heroin-washed eyes, was easy to pick out, reminded him of Bertie. He could see her, smoking in the middle of the pavement, gossiping with another woman, as though they were in Sainsbury's, innocently leaning on each other's trolleys.

Hey Jude.

He waited for the lights to change, to cross the Euston Road once more. From the far side, he looked back, through the lines of cars and buses, saw the anorexic child with the port wine stain watching.

''E didn't take long, did 'e?' demanded Grandma, creeping up behind her, well refreshed by the contents of the Tesco bag.

'He didn't take nothing,' snapped the street child, marching away. 'He wanted someone else.'

'Here we go,' said Judy, spotting a customer.

But Giles's gaze went right past her. He hadn't recognized her, but the other woman, gone to the kerb to talk to a cruising motorist, was Angelina. Her curls cascaded round a painted face, a painted doll with round and rosy cheeks, a pretty dumpling, short and stout, in a button-through floral Laura Ashley frock whose tucks and gathers strained across her breasts. She lit a fag, jammed it between scarlet pouting lips, looked into the open grey Cabriolet, its driver as bald as Jude.

'Show you a good time, big boy,' she drawled.

'A night at bingo would be more exciting,' snarled the driver.

'Stay,' Giles called, distraught.

She looked round and saw him standing there.

'I'm not interested in being saved,' she yelled. 'If that's what you come for, you can bugger off.'

She marched off up the road, her hips full and wide under the flowered frock. A dark blue Granada slowed, cruised, slowed to walking pace, wound its electric window down. Angelina leaned in, got in, disappeared up the Euston Road.

'She won't be long,' said Jude.

'You still here?' she cried shrilly, climbing out of the Granada and not bothering to look as it pulled away. 'What d'you want?'

'You,' said Giles, standing close to her, in the gutter. 'I'll pay.'

She hesitated, then shook her head as if in disbelief.

'Me mum always had a feeling about you,' she said contemptuously. 'She said you always did look at me funny. Come with me.'

Contract Parking, said a sign, covered in sprayed graffiti. The concrete yard was full of cars, parked for the night behind iron posts and chains.

'I like BMWs,' she said, leaning on the bonnet of a big black car, reaching expertly for his flies. He pulled away.

'Not like that,' he muttered. 'Properly.'

She froze.

'I don't do it no other way.'

'Ian Paisley has straight brown hair,' he said in her ear, pressing her against the car, forcing her back, splayed on the bonnet, his face an inch from hers. His eyes gleamed in the light from the streetlamp. 'And the wrong-coloured eyes. You do it, Angelina.'

'Not with tricks,' she hissed, writhing, arching her back to get him off.

'With me.'

He lifted the flowered skirt, tore open the tucked and gathered top across the big black bonnet.

'Hundred quid, and you use a condom,' she gasped, her eyes clenched tight with fury.

'I said *properly*.'

She froze with rage and helplessness as he forced her legs apart and his mouth closed on her breast, sweet with milk from feeding Ian Paisley.

The unspeakable pleasure, like the high from crack, was over in moments.

'Get off me,' she said bitterly.

'Forgive me,' he mumbled, his face in her neck.

'Get *off*, before I scream,' she said stonily.

'Say you forgive me,' he begged.

'I'd rather see you in hell. A hundred quid,' Angelina snarled. 'And don't come back here blubbing again, you bastard. *What?*'

He was incoherent, tears on his face in the orange light.

'Like Christ, you see. The Last Temptation, Madonna and whore, you see.'

'All I see is a fuck in a car park,' snapped Angelina, looking at her torn buttons in outrage. 'I want my money, mister crazy, and I want it *now*, or I'll go to the police and say you raped me.'

She held her hand out.

'Gimme.'

Chapter Thirty-Eight

'We've got newts in our pond,' Bunny told her contented guests.

A small fountain splashed in a very small pond in one corner of Bunny and Hugo's patio garden. 'You don't expect newts in the middle of London in a tiny little garden, do you? I wonder how they got here.'

'Puddle,' said Hugo. 'You can't call what we've got a pond.'

'The newts like it,' she answered.

'They've got a bijou little number on the Crown estate,' Alastair said, driving her over. 'Nice, if you like modern houses with walls made of paper. Personally, I don't.'

They had had to wait in the staff room until seven o'clock, because Melanie couldn't go home, Giles believing that she was at the theatre.

'We had ducks and fish in Norfolk,' said Melanie.

'Do you miss the country?' Bunny asked.

Melanie, in Madame Lucie's ivory silk lingerie and her only good pair of linen slacks, with an ivory silk blouse that added wickedly to the total on her Visa card, was in want of an honest answer. Alastair's hand on the back of her chair, casually resting just close enough for her to sense it, was all she knew. It made her giddy. She simply smiled and shook her head.

No one else seemed to notice.

'Bunny, that was superb. You cook like a painter paints, or a writer writes,' Alastair said appreciatively. 'With passion.'

'Hah. She does everything with passion,' said Hugo. 'Cooks, eats, gardens, argues with me; never walks, only runs. I can tell you, passion's exhausting.'

'That's rich, coming from one who sleeps four hours a night, then has the nerve to complain I wear him out,' snorted Bunny. 'He's been waking me up with his insomnia for so many years, I'm an insomniac too. If I am silly enough to drift off and want to stay asleep, as like as not he'll wake me up. He was on the phone to David Absalom until one in the morning the other night. Opt-out, opt-out, opt-out. He comes marching in at half past to shake me out of a lovely sleep. I came to to hear him shouting, Bunny, Bunny, *wake up, wake up,* I want to talk to you.'

She laughed.

'What do you call behaviour like that?' she asked.

'Compatibility,' said the bearded psychologist lounging in the place opposite Melanie, in worn green cords and a jacket with patches on the sleeves. He had been at the same Oxford college as Hugo, was one of his oldest friends, despite an abrupt and abrasive manner.

'Don't start on marriage guidance,' pleaded his wife. 'Last time, we had to leave and the people haven't spoken to us since.'

'I haven't spoken to *them,*' he answered. 'Let's examine a proposition.'

He reached for the wine bottle, to fill up his glass.

'Must we?' she said plaintively.

'What's your proposition?' asked Bunny.

'That shared vices make happy marriages. What are your vices? Are you happily married?'

He leaned forward, planted his elbows on the table and stared challengingly at Melanie and Alastair, waiting for an answer, sat grinning when he didn't get one, finding himself very funny. His wife, beside him, kicked him under the table.

'Elizabeth disagrees with my table manners,' he told them blandly. 'She does not think I should ask you personal questions.'

'Too much wine,' said his wife sharply. 'You're addled. They're not married. They work for Hugo.'

She looked down the table at Melanie.

'I apologize for my husband. Al has had more than enough of that, Hugo,' she added sharply.

Melanie smiled back. Deaf, Hugo refilled their glasses as Al grinned through his beard and winked affectionately.

'You're driving, darling,' he said.

'I go along with you,' Hugo agreed, picking black grapes off a bunch with his hairy hands. 'We are happily married to a mutual addiction to wine, cream and eating Belgian truffles in bed. Have some of these.'

He pushed the fruit into the middle of the table. Bunny looked indignant.

'*Mutual*. Who ate all the truffles?' she accused. 'I looked in the box this morning and I thought, what a pig.'

'You fed them to me,' he protested. 'Anyway, what were you doing checking up, if not planning to eat them yourself?'

Bunny smiled radiantly, offered the bowl of grapes to Melanie.

'Has to be Belgian chocs,' she explained. 'Dairy Box are no good at all. To do anything interesting, it has to be real cream, or truffle, or liqueur, *really* squishy. Hugo eats them off my nipples and he likes putting cream . . .'

'*Don't* put ideas in my husband's head,' said Elizabeth sharply. 'I can't be bothered with the washing.'

'It's not washing you're worried about. That's what machines are for,' said Hugo, grinning.

Elizabeth picked at a bit of French cheese, half eaten in front of her, and ignored him.

'I adore sex, don't you? Can't get enough of it,' Bunny went on dreamily. 'When you can have nookie instead, who wants sleep?'

Melanie gulped, swallowed her grape whole, and choked so badly they were scared.

'You got some problem about foreplay?' demanded Al, when he had finished taking turns with Alastair to bang

Melanie on the back until she could breathe again.

'Alan,' hissed his wife.

Melanie's skin burned like fire.

'Stop it,' cried Elizabeth.

'Take no notice of them, Mels,' said Bunny kindly, getting up and bringing the conversation to a close. 'Let's go next door and have coffee.'

'Not everyone is as upfront as Bunny,' Alastair said. 'Take no notice.'

As the others left the table, Melanie stayed where she was, her cheeks brilliant with embarrassment. He got up, then sat down again.

'Look, Hugo never drinks in front of anyone from school, but Bunny doesn't care. She's a bit plastered, and when she is, she says what she thinks. Don't take any notice of the teasing.'

'It's not that,' she whispered.

'What, then?'

Melanie could hear Bunny rattling coffee cups in her tiny kitchen, voices and laughter from the other room.

'I'd love to *be* like Bunny,' she admitted. 'Don't laugh at me.'

'Bunny laughs at herself.'

She looked crestfallen.

'You mean, I don't.'

'I don't mean that. If you want to be like Bunny, you need to learn to ask for what you want without being ashamed of it,' he said, putting his face close to hers. 'It doesn't have to be Belgian truffles and cream on your fanny. What do you want out of life, Mels?'

'If I tell you, you won't tell me it's anything to be ashamed of?'

'The worst that happens is you don't get it.'

'Coffee,' Bunny called, her footsteps sounding in the small hall.

It was now or never, before she interrupted.

'I want you,' she said.

Chapter Thirty-Nine

They came at him like animals, kicking and twisting, silent except for the panting of their breath, stripping him of his possessions in a single moment, disappearing into the night like shadows.

He lay in the gutter of a narrow alleyway, where they had dragged him into the dark. After a while, he pulled himself up and felt his heart leap in terror as something touched him. A prowling cat came out of the dustbins lining the alley, bringing with it a strong smell of fried fish. It mewed and sat down beside him, licking its chops, cleaning its whiskers after its meal.

'I wish I could lick myself clean,' Giles told it mournfully, feeling his head cautiously. It was wet and sticky, throbbed like a pile-driver, left the salt taste of blood on his fingers. He tried to stand up, reeled and slid down again on the cobbles, lay with only his feet in a puddle of light from the street at the end of the alley.

'Don't go,' he pleaded, as the cat got up and stretched. 'Stay with me.'

Its eyes caught the light, gleamed like emeralds, then vanished.

'Don't leave me alone,' begged Giles, to the empty alley.

'What we got 'ere?' muttered Grandma, shuffling to a halt, doing a round of bins. She woke up with the munchies at two in the morning to find the bin men had already cleared the leavings from the station cafeteria. She knew where there were more.

The feet stuck out into the light, didn't move. Grandma

stared at the soles of their shoes for a while, her stomach rumbling, decided it wasn't worth the trouble if the police caught her rummaging round a body. She mumbled her gums and grumbled her way off up the street. People could be inconsiderate, dying, so she couldn't get at her second-best bins.

The warm night brought the punters out and Angelina had been busy. She took a break at half past midnight, stood smoking, leaning against the wall of St Pancras Town Hall, when she heard her name.

'There's that man what was looking for you, down the alley,' the girl with the port wine stain said. 'I took a trick in there, and he tripped over his feet and scarpered. He's hurt. You better get an ambulance.'

'Why me?' yelled Angelina after the skinny child's retreating back. 'What have I done?'

The thin shoulders shrugged, didn't turn round.

'He'll die, otherwise,' drifted back.

Exasperated beyond words, Angelina kicked St Pancras Town Hall wall.

'Rapes me. Ruins me dress. Then expects me to look after him,' she muttered incredulously. 'Bloody *men*.'

Thinking it over, the fucking law would be capable of accusing her of murder. Furious and resentful, Angelina stormed down the Euston Road and went to have a look.

'Is there someone we can call?' asked the nurse in casualty at University College Hospital, dabbing carefully at the blood on his face. 'They'll want to keep you in, with a head wound.'

Giles closed his eyes. It was the early hours of the morning.

'If I give you a telephone number, would you leave a message on someone's answerphone?' he asked weakly.

'Certainly,' she agreed, with brisk, professional kindness.

They admitted him on to the neurological ward and spent the morning doing tests.

'Not brain damaged, then?' he joked feebly, when they

said he seemed to be all right but would be in for a couple of days for care and further observation.

'You have to be brain damaged to wander round King's Cross after midnight, down back alleys. I suppose men do what they do,' Sister replied tartly. 'Frankly, I sometimes think you deserve what you get.'

He collapsed into secretive silence. No one had asked him *precisely* what he was doing, and no one had insisted on telling his wife. They left how he would deal with his embarrassment up to him.

Sister drew Giles's curtains, gave his nondescript visitor a sloping, uncomfortable armchair from the day room, brought them a cup of tea.

'I'll leave you to talk,' she said.

Giles's curtains closed.

The ward was busy around them, no one interested in Giles's tormented soul except his boss, who listened with a calm, noncommittal face to the wretched story.

'I think I have a thing about prostitutes,' Giles finished. 'I've been wanting to do it for a long time.'

'Do you think she'll report it?' asked the Bishop.

'No.'

Giles shook his bandaged head and winced.

Standing over him in the alley, she had looked down like some avenging angel, her mass of hair haloed on the light from the lamp behind her.

'I could just leave you here,' she suggested. 'Only then they'd blame *me* if you go 'n' die. I'm going to call an ambulance, not tell them any names, and then I'm going home, and you ever come sniffin' after me again, anywhere *near* me, I'll tell the police everything you done. *And* your wife.'

'I can't go back,' Giles said with absolute certainty in his voice. 'I can't go back to Melanie, or All Hallows, or stay in the Church.'

'You can stay in the Church, but the clergy I rather doubt,' agreed his boss. 'Have you any idea of the alternatives?'

'Enclosure,' Giles muttered. 'There's a place in Italy. I have been thinking about it for a very long time, but there was Melanie, and the kids . . . the contemplative life seemed quite out of reach.'

'There are still Melanie and the kids,' the Bishop pointed out acidly.

'We were already thinking about separating.'

'I see. You didn't by any chance *know* this prostitute, did you?' the Bishop asked shrewdly.

The heavy silence from the bandaged figure told the untold story.

'I have a small house in the Lake District,' he went on, when the silence stretched so far there was nothing more to be wrung from it on the matter of Giles's guilt. 'I will send you the key and directions tomorrow, and you must go there when they let you out of here. You can stay up there in solitude, give yourself time to sort this sad mess out.'

Giles began to thank him, but the spare little man in a sports jacket, no trace of the church about him, raised his hand.

'All Hallows was the wrong place to send you, and without very much support. I will make this clear to Italy. Meanwhile,' he said, with a slight smile, 'my house is a *very* long way from the nearest temptation, I promise you. It is on the mountainside, overlooking Lake Windermere and is so quiet, it eats at your soul. Wait and see how it suits you before you thank me.'

'I can never go home,' Giles muttered, trying to grasp that he had made himself an outcast.

The worldly look in the Bishop's grey eyes was knowing; much worse than knowing. *Withering*.

I know *that*, it said.

Chapter Forty

The coins clanked inside the telephone box as someone answered his call.

'Mels?'

'*Giles*. Where are you?' she cried. 'We've been sick with worry.'

'I'm standing in Euston station,' Giles said.

Now the moment came to tell her, his voice quivered at the irony that the mainline station for Lake Windermere was on the Euston Road, like Angelina.

'I am going to the Lake District.'

In the silence, he could hear her trying to make sense of that.

'If it isn't a silly question, what for?' she asked, knowing already what his answer would be.

'I got mugged,' he said. He had thought and thought about it, lying in the hard hospital bed, decided that the truth was his own problem, that telling them would only cause worse pain. 'I've been out cold for a bit, and when I came round they kept me in hospital. I've been lying here with a splitting headache and a couple of stitches, and it's given me time to think. I realized we can't go on. I don't want to any more.'

She caught her breath, and he closed his eyes in the telephone box. *Please don't cry or argue, Mels, let's do it right this time.*

'How can you go and stay in the Lake District? You don't know anyone,' she protested irritably.

'Dickie has a house there. He's lending it to me until we

get things sorted out. Would you be kind enough to pack as much as you can in a case and send it up? I'll let you know where.'

'A case? Dickie's in on this?'

He sensed her mind racing, coming to the right conclusions, on the wrong facts.

'My money's running out. They took my wallet. Dickie . . .'

The pips started.

'I'll write to you,' he shouted and the line buzzed. He put the receiver down carefully and pushed open the door; beyond it the station speakers echoed.

The train now standing at platform eighteen is the two fifteen for . . .

He picked up the small bag that Dickie had lent him, with its few essentials, and walked with the hurrying crowd through the last barrier, to face the future.

Chapter Forty-One

'Trust him to do it this sneaky, I'm-a-mugging-victim way, leaving me to do all the dirty work, like telling the kids,' Melanie cried angrily, looking out of the staff-room window at the crowds piling in below to Hugo's karaoke evening.

'How did they take it?' Alastair asked, standing behind her. 'Good grief, Hugo's packing 'em in.'

'First they said he'd come back, wouldn't he? Then when I said I didn't think so, they cried, then they both went off to Bertie's looking tragic, saying don't lock the door, and not to wait up, because they might or might not be back. I thought, blow it, I might as well go out too and have a nice evening over here.' She sounded half angry, half about to cry.

'Even when you want it to finish, like you do, it's sad, as if someone's died,' said Alastair, moving away as the staff-room door opened.

'You lot coming down?' cried Bunny, grabbing a bulging bag of music tapes out of Garlick's empty fish tank. 'We're about to start. State-of-the-art equipment organized by Ernie, not just your old ghetto blaster. They've been fixing up enormous speakers all afternoon. Just listen to that.'

Clunks and whistles vibrated beneath their feet, as little Garlick, in DJ and bow tie, bald spot flashing in the strobes, turned his sound system on, twiddled knobs and tried the microphones. It was deafening, had a bass like a blow between the ears.

'I nearly forgot,' Bunny yelled above the noise. She opened the staff fridge and took out a bottle of wine. 'Chilled, for Marta.'

'Garlick's a lost cause,' shouted Alastair. 'He's going native. Be eating sauerkraut and pumpernickel next.'

'Garlick's in love, it's lovely,' cried Bunny, whisking out again.

'Thank God *I'm* in love with an Englishwoman is all I can say,' Alastair said lightly, right in her ear so that she could hear above the music pounding from below. 'Who comes with good old English bacon and eggs, two very nice children and a bad case of the sniffles.'

He wiped two big tears from Melanie's cheeks with the tip of his finger.

'Let's go down,' she said.

The noise met them like a brick wall, solid, like the wall of people standing in front of the door. Garlick turned the volume up a tad and waved at Marta. The hall was absolutely packed.

'Where did you get all this?' Alastair shouted at Hugo, who was doing a good impersonation of John Cleese behind the bar, long arms windmilling dangerously among a staggering array of bottles and casks.

'Ernie,' mouthed Hugo, looking about to take caps off bottles with his teeth. 'Who's got the bottle opener?'

Ernie threw it to him.

'Didn't know you had an off licence, Ernie,' shouted Alastair, holding out a glass for red wine for Melanie. Behind him, a queue pressed forward, impatient for its drinks.

'Donations,' yelled Ernie proudly, lining up wine glasses with precision, unmoved by the crowd.

'Donations?' Hugo shouted back, overhearing. 'Who gives *us* freebies?'

Ernie looked at him, eerily jumping about in the strobe lights as though he were a side of pork that didn't live up to quality control.

'Have you been getting goods with menaces?' Hugo bellowed incredulously, waving the red wine menacingly.

'Who said I had to menace?' Ernie screamed back, into a sudden pause as Garlick changed tape.

Only the lonely . . .

''Ere comes the light of my life,' Ernie roared, dropping the matter of menaces.

The light of his life? Hugo looked round, startled, to see who qualified for that interesting position.

'Marta's wine,' Bunny shrieked, thrusting the cold bottle underneath his nose.

'My wife is the light of Ernie's life?' he mouthed to himself, confused, then caught sight of Winanda in the jumping lights, knocking back a pint of beer. Five minutes later she was on the stage with a microphone, skipping about in a dirndl skirt, an overblown parody of Julie Andrews, pretending to be Mary Poppins.

'Who'd ever have thought it?' Hugo bawled, leaning over the bar to yell in Alastair's ear, pointing at the stage. 'Look at them all.'

'We'll win yet,' Alastair yelled back, and took Melanie to join the other staff at a packed and excited table.

God help the sister who comes between me and my man.

Four grannies from the estate's old people's bungalows had fought to get on stage, dressed to kill in crimplene skirts and Marks and Spencer's short-sleeved knits, well away on schooners of Ernie's extorted sherry. They gripped each others' middles, launched into a raucous imitation of the Beverly Sisters, hopping and swaying, alternately singing and screaming, collapsing with laughter. Stuttering Stan skulked at the back of the hall, watching. On duty, he was banned by Hugo from so much as a single pint and it didn't improve his temper.

'Shouldn't be doin' that,' he threatened inaudibly. 'It's a no-smokin' do. Him what must be obeyed says so.'

'What?' bellowed Ernie, taking a break from the bar, yelling right in his ear in the voice he normally kept for haggling in the Smithfield meat market.

'Aw, I give up,' said Stan, banging the side of his head to stop the ringing.

No one cared. The hall was thick, a smog of smoke and sweat, despite the care he had taken behind the tightly closed curtains to make sure that all the windows were open.

Stuttering Stan retreated to his spot by the door and watched them slide their arms around each other in the semi dark, his narrowed eyes flashing like Dracula's in the brilliance of the blue and red strobes whirling around the walls. Thinking the dark darker than it was, Ernie inched his free hand underneath her T-shirt and grinned happily.

'An-n-n-n-nim-m-m-m-m-mals.' Stan shook his head enviously and looked away.

Giles got off his train into a wet and windy night, clouds hanging thick and chill over the fells. Sitting in the taxi, all his present possessions in one small bag, he listened to wind howl across the hills and headed into solitude.

'High Borrans isn't far from Windermere, but the cottage is isolated,' Dickie had said. 'There's a bicycle in the hall. '

Giles contemplated the idea of bicycling around the countryside in vile weather, felt more miserable than he had ever felt in his life, and wondered, against all his better judgement, what *exactly* his wife and Alastair Croke were doing.

Garlick parked Madonna on the CD turntable, watched a woman in lurex leggings and little black top singing 'Material Girl'. He dabbed at his bald spot, hot, thirsty, desperate for a beer. Marta was at the staff table below, taking no notice. He reached over, switched off the CD player, and produced a shocking, ear-ringing silence.

'The hired help is thirsty,' he yelled down the microphone. 'Will one of you remember the poor sod up here who is giving you all this wonderful time?'

As Material Girl got back into her stride, started strutting her lurex stuff, Marta climbed on to the stage with a glass of Director's in her hand.

'Hugo says you like this one,' she shouted, squeezing behind the table with all his gear on it, putting the beer down. 'Enjoy it.'

'I do,' cried Garlick, emboldened by noise and excitement, grabbing her. 'I enjoy it very much, and I'm helplessly in love with it, and I want to marry it.'

He lunged, grabbed her round the waist, lifted her, reeled, lurched against his sound system, and in thundering silence, kissed her. The sound carried clearly into every corner of the hall.

Whistles and cheers drowned it out, died away.

'Say you'll marry me,' bawled the speakers as Garlick, oblivious, sat on the control panel, on the *off/on* switch, with Marta in his lap, his microphone hooked round his neck.

'Oh . . .' cried Marta, picking it out of his collar. 'Look what you do.'

Marta, Marta, give me your answer, do, I'm half crazy, all for the love of you.

The staff table began it, the hall took it up, and Garlick looked earnestly into Marta's face by the light of the strobe, and begged.

''All right. *Ja*,' she said, putting the microphone to her lips. 'Amadeus, I will marry you.'

Bunny screamed with excitement and delight, and the whole hall went crazy.

Alastair put his hand casually on Melanie's neck and stroked it, feeling her shiver.

'I'm half crazy . . .' he whispered beneath the bedlam.

Madonna gave way to Dire Straits. The Stud keened 'Brothers in Arms' over the loudspeakers, and Melanie listened to Alastair laughing uncontrollably as his precise, pedantic, old-woman voice was magnified a thousandfold, microphone clutched to his heaving chest, picking up fragments of water biscuit. The Stud had enjoyed biscuits and cheese for his supper and what didn't stick to his shirt stuck to his false teeth, fluorescent in the lights.

'Will you look at that. Neon noshers,' Alastair cackled.

'He doesn't have the first idea he glows in the dark. Do you want to have a go?'

'I don't want to sing.' Melanie shook her head. She felt for his hand in the dark, and held it.

As the Stud stood down, and Absalom emerged from nowhere to sing Frank Sinatra's 'My Way' in a reedy cockroach voice, Alastair peered at her intently in the spinning light.

'I can tell you what I want. Now Giles isn't there, would you come home with me, Mels? I'll get you back. Early as you like, for the kids.'

I did it my way, squeaked Absalom, to an indifferent audience.

'You do it my way, and you'll never do it again,' muttered Garlick over his betrothed's shoulder as they snogged happily behind the turntables. He reached out one hand and slipped a *Hits of the Sixties* into the cassette player. 'That'll keep them busy for a bit.'

Down at the staff table, Bunny watched Alastair and Melanie, too intent on each other to care. Melanie's face danced like a manic kaleidoscope in the strobes. Her hand lay in his, and she didn't seem to answer.

'It doesn't matter if you don't want to,' he shouted in her ear, thinking furiously *what a time to choose, you nerd. What a monumental piece of tactlessness. You've lost her.*

Melanie had her head down, had taken his hand in both of hers, was having difficulty with something. It finally dawned upon him, as Bunny saw first, to her amusement, that in all the mayhem, Melanie was shyly trying to say yes.

Chapter Forty-Two

'I'm scared,' Melanie said. 'Nervous. Shy. I've been dreaming this for so long, and how romantic it would be, but I'm going to start giggling with nerves in a minute and annoy you to death. You'll think you've got a teenager on your hands.'

'I'm terrified. When Honor left me, I thought, I'll never want anyone again,' Alastair said, fingering the steering wheel as they sat in the car outside his house. 'I haven't, except for Bunny, until I met you.'

'I used to think you were in love with Bunny.'

'I was. She kept me going. Kept me alive. I never imagined for one minute that anything would come of it.' He gave a short laugh. 'I'd probably have run a mile if it had.'

'I haven't, either,' Melanie said quietly. 'Since Giles had the affair with Daffodil, he's been preoccupied with wanting other women, and what it was doing to his soul. There wasn't room in his life for me.'

They sat in darkness, the nearest streetlamp shrouded in the leaves of a lilac bush in the first green flush of spring, the hum of distant traffic through the open windows, each waiting for the other to lead the way.

'It is almost like living in the country, looking right over the park,' she said, to fill the silence.

'Yes. This all belongs to the Crown. The Benedicts and I share the privilege of having the Queen as our landlady. Very classy.'

'I once saw her, walking on the beach in Norfolk. She was small and dowdy and looked terribly lonely,' she said.

'I live up there, right at the top, and at this time of year all

I can see from my window are roofs and the tops of the chestnut trees. I warn you, I have no curtains and also that the Stud lives on the ground floor, with Barney.'

'Who is Barney?'

'Barney's the reason the Stud never went to Hong Kong to make his fortune. He could have done, he was good enough. But Barney's a retired jockey and he's so bent and twisted from breaking just about every bone in his body, he's needed endless treatment. The Stud couldn't have afforded it anywhere but on the NHS. They've been together for years and years.'

A cat ran across the quiet road into the bushes at the edge of the park, its eyes shining.

'I've got a kitten,' he said. 'She's Siamese, nearly grown. Makes a hell of a racket, yowling at night.'

Something gave a coughing scream, somewhere further away, in the dark park.

Melanie shivered.

'Foxes,' said Alastair. 'They come and root in the bins. There's a vixen with three legs who picks over my garbage. She's a down-and-out, very miserable-looking. Sometimes we bump into each other if I can't sleep and I get up very early. I call her Limping Lily. I'll introduce you in the morning.'

It was his invitation to climb out of the car, stand in the lighted hall by the Stud's front door, looking up.

'Lot of stairs,' he said, in the quiet, empty hall.

'If Bunny was here, she'd run up,' she said, shaking with nerves. 'Wouldn't she?'

'What about you?'

The hall was painted cream, its green carpet held in place by old-fashioned brass rods, polished like gold.

'How many are there?'

'I never counted,' he said. 'And I'm not about to. All I can think about is how much I love you, and how scared I am.'

'Then I'll beat you to it,' she cried, and ran towards the stairs.

* * *

They were curled, asleep, when the doorbell rang, after midnight. She half woke, to find the moon shining into the room through uncurtained windows, bright enough to see by. She hesitated, waited for him to wake. The bell rang again. She eased her arm from under his body, slipped out of bed, found a dressing gown on the floor and went to answer the door.

The Stud was looking into the inside of his jacket, where Alastair's little cat nestled, clucking tipsily at the tiny creature.

'You've lost your pussy,' he said fussily. 'I found her running all over the road.'

He lifted the kitten out and raised his eyes.

'Ah,' he said, nonplussed, the cat dangling and struggling in his hand. 'Er, thought you'd be Alastair, Melanie. Have you lost your pussy?'

'We lost our pussy an hour or more ago,' Melanie answered, looking him ingenuously in the eye, taking the kitten. 'Since you ask.'

She could hear him clearing his throat all the way down the stairs.

'Goodnight,' she called over the banisters.

She went back in, put the kitten on Alastair's bed, got in, and laughed so much she woke him up again.

Chapter Forty-Three

The chestnut trees darkened and began to turn in late September as Limping Lily's fur began to matt and thicken ready for winter. In July the Secretary of State had given East Stepney permission to opt out and the Department of Education agreed a large sum of money for capital expenditure. When the new school year started, Hugo went into overdrive, advertised for more staff. The governors made Alastair deputy head.

'Alice and Tom went to Italy,' Melanie told Bunny, swapping holiday stories in the staff room.

'Villa party?'

'They should be so lucky. No. Three days in Tuscany, saying goodbye to their father. The staff should know – Alice is upset, though she doesn't show it.'

'What do you mean? How, *goodbye*?' demanded Bunny.

'He spent the summer hiding in the Lake District, and now he's gone into an enclosed order, in Italy, and can never come out again or have visitors. Not even his parents. I thought they'd both have heart attacks when he told them he's as dead to the world as if they'd buried him.'

Bunny looked shocked.

'I mean it. Now we're divorcing, at least my father's talking to *me* again. The kids came home saying the main thing they'll remember will be how much he smelled. Giles was always fastidious, but they don't let the monks shave or use deodorant.'

'That's *bizarre*, in a hot climate,' cried Bunny. 'Phew!'

'No more than being made a widow while he's still alive,'

said Melanie shortly. 'Can you imagine?'

Bunny shook with laughter.

'They broke the mould when he was born,' she cried. 'Talk about perverse.'

'I'm talking about perverse all the way to the divorce court,' Melanie answered. 'And perverse it is. He hasn't left one *penny*.'

A *Sold* sign was tacked to the holly tree outside the house, the foundations of a new, small, modern rectory laid a quarter of a mile away, cheaper to run, to be paid for by the sale of the flats which the old house was to be converted to. The new house would be ready in five months, when the new man arrived.

'Mum's moving in with Mr Croke,' Alice and Tom announced to Bertie.

'D'you mind?'

'I'll be in Manchester and too far away to be embarrassed,' said Tom.

'Alastair's all right,' said Alice. 'Haven't got much choice, with Dad struck off the register, have we?'

Bertie cleared her throat and fished in her bag.

'Talking of being around and being embarrassed. I got this,' she said. 'Would your mum and Alastair have Baby Jane? Just for a few weeks?'

She held out a fat brown envelope.

'It sounds horrible,' cried Alice, reading the contents. 'You *really* want to do it?'

'I been going to that gender clinic for *years*, to get my operation,' Bertie retorted. 'Now I've got it, you try and stop me. I *absolutely* can't wait.'

Chapter Forty-Four

The golden October that followed Tom's leaving for Manchester, and Giles's farewell to the world, brought many changes. Along with autumn, yellow leaves, crisp, sunny days, it brought Melanie's decree nisi on grounds of unreasonable behaviour and a tiny, premature baby girl with a fuzz of red hair for Angelina. At the end of the month, it brought Garlick's German wedding in Westphalia.

'You will come, won't you?' he asked the staff room anxiously. 'I'm very short on relatives, and she has so many it's a nightmare. They're all German.'

'Well, they would be, wouldn't they?' observed the Stud.

'What I mean is, they don't speak English,' explained Garlick plaintively. 'Marta's trying to teach me, but I can only read scientific papers in German, which doesn't go far when it comes to holding down a real conversation.'

'You've managed all right so far in English without being able to hold down a real conversation. It's not the handicap it sounds, in biologists,' taunted Alastair.

Garlick was too preoccupied to take offence.

'Are the relatives all into pigs as much as Marta?' asked Bunny.

'Oink, oink,' Alastair suggested cruelly.

'Most,' answered Garlick, cheering up.

'You're trying to tease him, but perhaps you haven't noticed how the mere mention of pigs makes him happy,' Melanie said.

'If some marriages are made in heaven, this one is about to be made in a pigsty,' the Stud put in, stacking textbooks fussily. 'And what we all need to know, before replying to your kind invitation to come to your nuptials, is what's the air fare, Amy?'

'Garlick,' Garlick snarled. 'Marta's dad's done a charter deal with Eurowings and it's cheap. Very.'

The Stud paused in his packing, impressed.

'Really. My word, there must be serious money in ham and bacon,' he remarked. 'You're not so daft after all.'

'It was bring my family and friends over or Marta got married over here, and they wouldn't hear of that.'

'How are you going to marry her if you can't speak the lingo?' asked the Stud a few minutes later.

Garlick had a peculiar look on his face.

'Go on, spit it out, whatever it is,' said Alastair. 'Don't make us have to beat it out of you.'

Garlick looked shifty.

'Marta's Catholic. The village priest speaks no English. I speak no German. We racked our brains and Marta's dad came up with a brilliant idea.'

'Go on. You are hard enough work in your own language,' snapped Alastair.

Garlick sulked.

'He's sorry,' said Melanie. 'I promise.'

'Marta's dad walked home from Moscow to Westphalia when the Russians threw Hitler out,' Garlick said stoically. 'You had to be someone special to do that. Somewhere along the way he met up with an Indian, who was doing I know not what in the middle of it all, and who found walking from Moscow to Germany a religious experience. He became a priest.'

'I'm not sure I like this story,' muttered Melanie.

Garlick glared and threatened not to tell them the rest.

'Shut up, Mels,' ordered Alastair.

Mollified, Garlick continued.

'Marta's dad and the chap from Bombay were both going the same way, and to stay alive they shared their boots and just about everything else. Reverend Farahani is *thrilled* to come all the way from Bombay to marry Marta and me.'

There was a respectful silence.

'Indian?' demanded Alastair. '*Moscow*. Coming from Bombay! You're having us on. How old is Mr Gandhi?'

'Farahani. Eighty-odd, mostly deaf, but bilingual.'

'In *Bombay*?' said the Stud.

'Well. Equally bad at German and English,' Garlick admitted unwillingly. 'No one'll feel put down. You can manage, for goodness' sake. Sight-read. Improvise. Hum along with the hymns. So long as Marta and I know what we're promising each other, the rest doesn't matter. The only thing you mustn't do, is . . . *please* don't laugh.'

The staff room collapsed. Mohammed, taking lunchtime aerobics with fifth and sixth form fitness fanatics, heard howls of laughter all the way from the gym.

'Peter Sellers and pigs' trotters,' Alastair gasped. 'Garlick, old son, you're a dream. Put us down for two air tickets. This is going to be the farce of the year, and *nothing* is going to make me and Mels miss it.'

'Pigs, pigs, pigs. Marriages made in . . . many a true word . . . you have no idea what's coming, and if you did, you might not come, never mind cheap tickets,' muttered Garlick furiously under his breath. 'Put it in your archives, and have something *real* to look back on.' He scuttled off to his laboratory before anyone could ask him what he meant.

'Oooooooh,' moaned Garlick, throwing up into a bag on the Eurowings flight to Padderborn, to the annoyance of the Lufthansa stewardess. Afflicted by severe turbulence, the plane threw itself about and bucketed up and down like a yo-yo.

'Yuk,' said his beloved, unconcerned, not in the least green herself. She ignored the *fasten your seatbelt* signs and the captain's orders to stay in their seats, and went off to fix her make-up in the loo, leaving the furious stewardess to hold his head.

'Why isn't my future wife obsessive and law-abiding, like

the rest of you?' he groaned. 'Germans are supposed to be so controllable.'

'I expect that's what you love about her.' The blonde and elegant stewardess smiled thinly and pushed his head into his bag. The turbulence got worse, the plane tossed like a cork, and as he grabbed the seat in front of him, in terror, he and the stewardess both heard something snap.

'The elastic's gone,' Garlick hissed, waddling through Padderborn's small airport, dropping a trail of luggage. 'I can smell pigs already.'

He snuffed the air, put his hands in his trousers pockets and hitched his underwear up.

'Here,' said Marta, handing him a case.

'I can't,' he wailed. 'My knickers are round my knees.'

'You look like Charlie Chaplin,' Marta told him, neat as a pin in slacks and yellow Jaeger jumper, heaving luggage through swing doors. 'You look ridiculous. Can't you lend a hand?'

'No,' he snapped. 'I can't. My smalls are hobbling me.'

'You could lend *one* hand,' she snapped back with Teutonic pedantry. 'And push this while I go and find a cab.'

Reluctantly taking his left hand out of his trousers, he wheeled the trolley with difficulty out into the car park, manoeuvred his way through crowds, barked half a dozen shins, and found her nose to nose with a taxi driver, getting nowhere.

'He's thick as two short planks,' she hissed, frustrated, raised her voice and yelled, *'Do you speak German?'*

'Marta,' Garlick said placatingly, running the trolley one-handedly over the driver's toes. 'Darling.'

'What?'

The man yelped, leaped in the air with agony, and swore.

'He is German,' Garlick pointed out, running the trolley back for good measure.

The taxi driver hopped up and down, speechless, then put up his fists.

'They all speak German. We are in Germany,' Garlick cried, pitting the trolley hastily between him and the enraged driver.

'So we are. Put the cases in the boot while I tell him.'

Ignoring Garlick's protests that his boxer shorts were in a knot, and did she *want* a neutered husband, Marta dismissed the tears in the taxi driver's eyes, and told him where to go. In German.

Chapter Forty-Five

The following Friday evening, East Stepney staff room spilled out of a Lufthansa charter plane on to the tarmac of Padderborn airport, well oiled on free in-air refreshment and top-ups from the duty-free trolley.

They had their instructions. Marta's military father had drawn up a battle plan, made her translate it and send it out to each and every guest. Hugo held the master copy, standing before the overexcited horde at the front of the plane as though in charge of a fourth-form outing, which, in a way, he thought with amusement, he was.

'Right. This is the batting order. Taxis. Hotel. Check in, change into best bib and tucker. A coach comes at half past seven to take us to Marta's home,' Hugo read, lurching as the plane banked steeply and dipped its nose for the final approach to the runway.

'Sehtzen Sie Sich.'

The elegant stewardess raced from her landing seat near the galley and pushed him towards his seat.

'Hang on,' said Hugo, fighting back. 'I haven't finished.'

'He's a headmaster. It'll be, do you want to do wee wees and have some juice before you get out of the coach?' the Stud told the girl kindly, from the opposite seat. 'Just be firm.'

'Sit,' yelped the stewardess, wacking him in the solar plexus.

Bunny leaned down the aisle and tugged at her husband's jacket.

'We are *landing,'* said the hostess, baring her beautiful

white teeth in a forced and furious airline smile. '*Sit down.*'

The plane slid towards the runway and its engines howled.

'Go back to charm school,' mumbled Hugo, buckling his seat belt. 'I was only telling them what to do.'

'The German military mind is more than up to the job of getting a large group of tipsy Brits sorted out,' observed Alastair, as a sleek and shiny coach did a hundred and twenty miles an hour down the autobahn. 'What's the speed limit here?'

'There isn't one,' said Mohammed, relaxed and impossibly beautiful in kohl and an Armani suit.

'Where did you get that?' Alastair enquired.

'Cast-off from the creator of *Sticky Moments*,' said Mohammed proudly. 'I hadn't a thing to wear, and he said . . .'

'Ah, from *you-know-who*,' Alastair chuckled, watching pig farm after pig farm whizzing past. 'Now, *he'd* go down a treat around here.'

Mohammed looked out of the window and sulked.

'Good grief,' he squawked half an hour later, watching the coach drive away, hitching his Armani turn-ups out of the mud. They stood huddled on a stone path that seemed to go nowhere.

'You've got the marching orders,' said Alastair to Hugo. 'If this is a joke . . .'

'I'm *freezing*,' said Bunny, through chattering teeth.

'I think we have to walk down, because the coach wouldn't fit,' suggested the Stud.

'You *have* been hiding your little light under a bushel,' remarked Alastair. 'How many other foreign languages do you secretly understand?'

They marched in Indian file up the track in their party best, into the teeth of a gale sweeping across the vast flat Westphalian plain. Around the bend in the path stood a squat stone farmhouse, attached to a stone barn, enclosing an immense farmyard on three sides, a cobbled square crowded with people.

'Hugo,' shouted Garlick, hurrying towards them. 'They're here, everyone.'

'I smell pig, loud and clear, and here is the happy groom. We're here at last,' Alastair shouted back.

'Marta's brother works for the local brewery. They donated a bit of booze,' explained Garlick excitedly, showing them round.

'Good lord,' exclaimed Alastair, examining the booze wagon, the size of a regular oil tanker, awed. 'And they seem to like pork, too,' he added, looking at the barbecue next to it.

It was huge and hot, giving out a rich smell of cooking meat.

'Do you think it does awful things to the psyche of the rest of their pigs – gives them the feeling that they are about to follow all their aunties and uncles into the chops and frankfurter department?' Alastair asked. 'It is terribly unfortunate.'

'Never mind pigs, help yourselves to drinks,' cried Garlick, tugging at his arm. 'And come and say hello to Marta's family.'

'Oh, dear,' said the Stud, taking his beer out of the freezing wind into the barn freshly swept and laid with trestle tables and benches. He peered through a door into the other half of the building.

'What?' asked Melanie, coming up behind him.

'It's the maternity ward,' he said, moving aside for her to see.

The smell of roast meat billowed in it.

'All those little piglets,' she cried. 'Smelling their relatives drifting past. That's *horrible.*'

'This really *is* a wedding in a pigsty.'

Melanie began to giggle, but the Stud closed the door, sat down at one of the trestles and looked a little sick.

* * *

Garlick waved everyone inside.

'Go on in. It's warm. The tables are laid, and you can sit down.'

'Where?' asked Mohammed, eyeing up a blonde German youth twice his size.

'The pigsty,' hissed Garlick, and vanished smartly into the crowd of Marta's relatives, drinking steadily and determinedly in the freezing wind.

'That beer wagon's a challenge the like of which they can't have seen since the Second World War,' observed the Stud. 'I wonder if they'd open odds on finishing it.'

'They'd take you to the cleaners,' said Hugo scornfully. 'They've got no sense of humour, but the bastards can *drink*. That's not a bar, that's an intravenous alcoholic drip.'

Eyeing lager flowing down a clear plastic pipe from the tanker, straight into a continuous round of refills, the Stud regretfully nodded in agreement.

'And don't you mention the war,' Hugo added. 'We don't want any trouble.'

On the barbecue, pork chops roasted alongside pork ribs, marinaded and delicious. Pork sausages turned and blackened, pork schnitzel cooked more gently on the outer edges.

'Can I have the marinade recipe for this?' Bunny asked, filling a roll with a chop.

'No, you can't,' said Melanie, dragging her off. 'I am dying of hypothermia and I am not brave enough to go past all those Germans into a pigsty, by myself. We've lost Hugo and Alastair to the challenge of the tanker. We could have a national drinking contest brewing, if you'll pardon the pun. You are coming inside with me.'

'Did you see *Leon the Pig Farmer*?' Alastair asked, edging down the long barn with a tray of lagers and a pile of hot dogs.

'No,' Melanie said through a mouthful of bread and lardy

cheese with holes it. 'How can you eat those with five hundred piglets next door?'

'Easily,' he said, and did.

'I've had enough of this,' he announced, an hour later, full of sausage, pork ribs and lager, eyeing the Germans gathered at the entrance, studiously avoiding looking at the British huddled for warmth right inside the barn. 'Bring on John Cleese.'

'Don't you dare. No one's speaking to anyone else, because they can't,' said Hugo, sitting with Bunny, who was into schnapps and decidedly the worse for it. 'Don't start trouble, Alastair. I've got my hands full already.'

'We've got *plenty* of language in common, you Krauts,' shouted Alastair, jumping on to the trestle table, waving his glass at the Germans. 'Sauerkraut, pumpernickel, frankfurter, Deutschmark, Herr Kohl, interest rates, Bundesbank, Blitzkrieg, *achtung*, Ausch—' He caught Hugo's furious eye, could dimly see a row of gaping faces down at the far end of the pigsty. 'Ah, not down that path . . . poor taste . . . sorry, sorreee . . . mustn't mention ze var.'

The Westphalian farmers gazed awestruck at the capering figure dancing on its trestle, and swallowed beer in mystified silence.

'Come on, you miserable buggers,' Alastair yelled. '"Tannenbaum, O Tannenbaum", "The Future Belongs to Us", er . . . "Deutschland Über Alles". Come *on*, sing.'

'The dirty song contest was a stroke of pure genius, Alastair,' Hugo moaned the next day, watching Alka Seltzer dissolving in a beer mug in the hotel bar. 'I have never felt so ghastly in my life, and we have a wedding to go to.'

'Hair of the dog would do you better,' the Stud suggested.

Hugo groaned, looking past him, screwed up his face and muttered, 'God preserve us.'

Alastair turned to see.

Mohammed waddled down, looking desperately

uncomfortable, perched his bottom on a bar stool and waved for a beer.

'What are you all staring at?' he demanded.

'You,' groaned Hugo.

Mohammed preened.

'Dog's dinner,' muttered Hugo, swallowing the Alka Seltzer gloomily. 'I hate this stuff. How *can* you?'

Mohammed pouted, tricked out in *lederhosen* and a smart little hat with a feather. He hitched his bottom on to the stool more comfortably, took off the hunting hat and looked at it closely.

'When in Rome . . .' he said airily. 'My friend gave them to me. *Hans!* Where is he?'

To a gale of very English laughter, the enormous blond German followed him sheepishly into the bar and stood them all a round of drinks.

'Old Farahani did his stuff *splendidly,*' Garlick said later, tucking his wife's hand under his arm and posing in the freezing wind for pictures. 'No one understood a word, and they were so hung over, they didn't even notice.'

'You see why my father loves him,' said Marta, looking at her husband tenderly. '*And* he wants to come into the family business.'

'I see exactly why your father loves him, and here's to an *extremely* suitable marriage, which will be happy and give the world the kind of piglets it's been waiting for. Here's to both of you, and to both of us.'

Alastair put his arm round Melanie's shoulders, raised his glass and kissed her on the church steps, then knocked back a dose of good plum schnapps.

Chapter Forty-Six

The morning after the wedding was bright and clear, the wind died down. Melanie lay listening to Alastair's regular breathing, while around them the hotel stirred and came to life. Plumbing clunked, footsteps creaked overhead and a bread van with squeaky brakes opened its doors, sending the delicious smell of fresh rolls and caraway seeds through their open shutters. She nudged him gently.

'You're awake, really,' she said. 'We have to go at eleven o'clock and it's eight already.'

'Not asleep. Lying here thinking and telling myself I haven't really got a hangover. I haven't, compared to yesterday.'

'What else are you thinking?'

'About pigs, and Garlick and Marta being married by a clone of Peter Sellers, and schnapps coming out of everyone's ears. It was a brilliant wedding. I'd *never* have guessed it of Garlick. I'll miss him.'

'It was the wackiest wedding,' she said, turning to him.

'A pig maternity ward next to the barbecue. It takes a German to dream that up. Our Amy will fit in nicely.' He turned his face, dark with stubble, to hers, his long dark locks tangled with her fair hair on the pillow. 'Come here, I want to ask you something.'

She put her head on his chest and listened to the steady beat of his heart.

'Could we give us a year, then think about getting married? Would that be too soon, after Giles? And Tom and Alice need time. But if we are as happy then as we are now, we should get married, don't you think? Would you stay with me and see?'

Lying in the October sunlight spilling through the shutters, she could see Madame Lucie's yellow silk robe thrown across a chair.

'I used to dream a dream,' she answered. 'I dreamed about lying in a sunny room, one day, with the man I would live with, work with, make love with. I dreamed about a man who would make me feel strong and beautiful all over, like pure silk.'

'You are strong and beautiful all over,' he said.

She slid her hand down his chest and lifted her head to kiss him.

'And I want to stay.'

The bread delivery boy heard the woman's cry from behind the first-floor shutters and grinned knowingly as he closed his van doors and drove away.

More Compelling Fiction from Headline

CATHERINE ALLIOTT

THE OLD-GIRL NETWORK

A SPARKLING FRESH TALENT FOR ALL JILLY COOPER FANS

Why didn't anyone warn her that the path to true love would be filled with potholes?

Dreamy, scatty and impossibly romantic, Polly McLaren is a secretary in an advertising agency, but the day a stranger on a train catches her eye, her life changes for ever. This American Romeo, who's recognised her old school scarf, begs Polly to help him find his missing Juliet. Over an intoxicating dinner at the Savoy, Polly agrees to play Cupid – St Gertrude's girls must, after all, stick together – and her investigations begin. The last thing she needs now is trouble from the men in her life . . .

. . . like Harry Lloyd Roberts – Polly's madly attractive but infuriatingly elusive boyfriend. It's he who goads her into turning detective – on the grounds that it might give her something to do for a change. Not to mention distract her from his own lustful pursuits . . .

. . . and Nick Penhalligan – Polly's rude, arrogant and ridiculously demanding boss, who's not best pleased that her mind is everywhere but on her job. But even he gets entangled when the old-girl network turns into a spider's web of complications, deceit and finally, love.

More Enchanting Fiction from Headline

Pamela Evans

A Fashionable Address

The Potters of elegant Sycamore Square in Kensington take for granted all the comforts of their position in life, maintained by the large family drapery store. Then, one day, everything changes; Cyril Potter is a secret gambler whose debts have become so crippling that he resorts to suicide. Shocked, disgraced and left to clear the debts, his wife and daughters are forced to sell everything.

Young Kate Potter shoulders the responsibility for her pampered mother, Gertie, and frivolous sister, Esme, finding accommodation in the two dingy rooms of a dilapidated Hammersmith tenement house. Despite the dirt and poverty of their new lives, Kate is ever cheerful as she tries to rally her family to make the best of the situation, and she promises them she will move heaven and earth to make it possible for them to return to Sycamore Square.

As she labours long hours for low pay in Dexter's hat-making factory, Kate's dreams seem far away. The more so when she catches the lascivious eye of the factory owner Reggie Dexter and is left pregnant by him. Close to despair she is persuaded to have her son adopted so that he can enjoy a better life than she is able to offer. As she tries to come to terms with her guilt, Kate struggles to set up her own millinery business – and start on the slow road to achieve prosperity and a fashionable address.

FICTION / SAGA 0 7472 4313 1

A selection of bestsellers from Headline

BODY OF A CRIME	Michael C. Eberhardt	£5.99	☐
TESTIMONY	Craig A. Lewis	£5.99	☐
LIFE PENALTY	Joy Fielding	£5.99	☐
SLAYGROUND	Philip Caveney	£5.99	☐
BURN OUT	Alan Scholefield	£4.99	☐
SPECIAL VICTIMS	Nick Gaitano	£4.99	☐
DESPERATE MEASURES	David Morrell	£5.99	☐
JUDGMENT HOUR	Stephen Smoke	£5.99	☐
DEEP PURSUIT	Geoffrey Norman	£4.99	☐
THE CHIMNEY SWEEPER	John Peyton Cooke	£4.99	☐
TRAP DOOR	Deanie Francis Mills	£5.99	☐
VANISHING ACT	Thomas Perry	£4.99	☐

All Headline books are available at your local bookshop or newsagent, or can be ordered direct from the publisher. Just tick the titles you want and fill in the form below. Prices and availability subject to change without notice.

Headline Book Publishing, Cash Sales Department, Bookpoint, 39 Milton Park, Abingdon, OXON, OX14 4TD, UK. If you have a credit card you may order by telephone – 01235 400400.

Please enclose a cheque or postal order made payable to Bookpoint Ltd to the value of the cover price and allow the following for postage and packing:

UK & BFPO: £1.00 for the first book, 50p for the second book and 30p for each additional book ordered up to a maximum charge of £3.00.
OVERSEAS & EIRE: £2.00 for the first book, £1.00 for the second book and 50p for each additional book.

Name ..

Address ..

..

..

If you would prefer to pay by credit card, please complete:
Please debit my Visa/Access/Diner's Card/American Express (delete as applicable) card no:

Signature .. Expiry Date